THE W   S

"Very inventive, imag   , ...u junny from cover to cover."
— Kevin Bergeron, author of *In a Cat's Eye*

"A brilliantly funny and cleverly conceived work."
— Rob Gregson, author of *Unreliable Histories*

"The funniest sci-fi I've ever read ... and I don't even like sci-fi!"
— Frank Kusy, author of *Rupee Millionaires*

Chapter 10, *The Rovers Return*, was shortlisted in the short story category of the Yeovil Literary Prize 2014.

Also by Mark Roman

THE ULTIMATE INFERIOR BEINGS

The Worst Man on Mars

NAFA

Mark Roman & Corben Duke

Illustrations by Corben Duke

www.grandmalpress.com

First published by Grand Mal Press in 2016

Copyright © Mark Roman and Corben Duke 2016

'The Worst Man on Mars' is the copyright of Mark Roman and Corben Duke, 2016.

This is a piece of fiction and any characters or names that relate to any persons, robots, supercomputers, aliens, or wind spirits, living or dead, is purely coincidental.

All rights reserved.

No part of this book may be reproduced or transmitted in any form or by any means, electronic, digital or mechanical, without permission in writing from the copyright owner.

ISBN 978-1-5369309-7-9

http://twmom.webnode.com

For Edith and Karen

Contents

Map vii

PART 1

1. The Back Seat Kids	1
2. The King's Peach	5
3. The Impotence of Being Harnessed	11
4. Permission Impossible	16
5. The Hanging Gaskets of BioDome	21
6. Fagin It	26
7. Meet the Flint Stoners	32
8. Something Picky This Way Comes	39
9. The Arch of Progress	44
10. The Rovers Return	47
11. Gone with the Wind Spirits	54
12. An InspectaBot Calls	59
13. Tarquin the Spotter	68
14. Don't Mention the Door	70
15. Hat Stands to Reason	76
16. The Elfin Marbles	82
17. In a Tube	87
18. 2029: A Space Body Scene	92
19. In a Spaceship, Everyone Can Hear You Scream	98
20. Unequal and Inapposite Reactions	105
21. Lost it in Space	110
22. Love, Factually?	114
23. Poles Together	116
24. Furiouser and Furiouser	120
25. Lifts and Separates	123
26. The Knicker Man	132
27. A Room with a Small View	136
28. The Man who Fell to Mars	143
29. One Giant Heap for Mankind	150
30. Berk and Mare	154

PART 2

1. Heaven and Girth	159
2. Memories are Made of Bits	167
3. Bad Air Day	172

4. A Severe Case of RAMnesia	175
5. Dope on a Rope	177
6. Subtotal Recall	181
7. Dome Alone	184
8. No Place Like Home	193
9. Ma's Army	198
10. The Creative Splurge	202
11. The Call of the Mild	204
12. The Not-so Famous Five	206
13. Feeling Down	213
14. Brokk, Paper, Schisms	218
15. Who Ate All the Pies?	220
16. The Qualm Before the Storm	224
17. The Printer of Our Discontent	226
18. Nothing Like a Nice Cup of Tea	232
19. The Old Man and the Tea	236
20. Helmut's Story	241
21. Mutiny on the Botany	249
22. The Bad Matters Tea Party	257
23. Phishing for Clues	268
24. The Fellowship of the King	272
25. Grave Matters	280
26. Wind Up	284
27. Breakfast at Sniffer Knees	289
28. Texts and the Single Girl	298
29. Game of Throw-ins	300

PART 3

1. Mars Bard	309
2. Pseudy Garlands	311
3. A Touch of Wind	315
4. Thrifty Shades of Grey	320
5. Clueless in the Shuttle	326
6. The King of Rock and Hole	329
7. His Awful Wedded Wife	332
8. Before the Big Bang	336
9. The Mars Debating Society	338
10. Doctor, No!	346
11. German Weasels	355
12. Street-fighter's Ride to the Galaxy	360

EPILOGUE
One year later   369

Acknowledgements   385

About the authors   387

"It's not going to do any good to land on Mars if we're stupid."
– Ray Bradbury

Map

Part 1

1. The Back Seat Kids

08:30, 24th March 2029 – 46, Culpepper Drive, Huddersfield, Yorkshire

Whenever retired science teacher Malcolm Brimble got a 'bad feeling in his water' it was usually a pretty accurate portent of doom. For eight months, in spite of some powerful antibiotics, the feeling had been worsening.

"It's going to be a disaster, Barb," he moaned through the open door of their en suite bathroom.

"They're saying it's looking good," Barbara countered. She was perched on the end of the bed, nursing two freshly made mugs of tea and staring at the TV. The pictures from *Mayflower III*, in orbit above Mars, showed the crew of Britain's first manned mission to the Red Planet high-fiving one another.

Malcolm looked up from his ablutions and caught sight of the shaven-headed Mission Commander Flint Dugdale. "No, I can't look at him!" He nudged the bathroom door shut to block the offending view of Dugdale spraying the contents of a can of *Stallion* lager into the zero-G atmosphere.

"People change," his wife called through the door.

"Not that one. Not him. Five years I had him. Bottom of the

bottom science set."

"Come on, he was a teenager. The mission's so close now; what could possibly go wrong?"

Malcolm cracked the door open. "I think you're forgetting the *Beagle 2* disaster."

"You don't know for sure he was responsible."

Malcolm snorted. Flushing the toilet, he strode out of the bathroom and across the bedroom, pausing only to grab a pair of oily overalls as he took himself off to the garage.

"Don't forget your tea," Barbara shouted after him. Too late, he had already made it downstairs and out the front door.

As she followed her husband with his mug, the TV transmission cut to a commercial break. An astronaut holding a can of lager was perched on the back of a rearing horse, set against the backdrop of a red desert. "*Stallion*, sponsors of *Who Wants to go to Mars,*" said the voiceover. The handsome space-cowboy lifted his visor and took a gulp from his can before thrusting the label towards the camera. "*Stallion* extra-strength lager. Putting *men* on Mars."

In the garage, Barbara found Malcolm in familiar pose: on his back with his Hush-Puppied feet poking out from under the jacked-up MG Midget Mk III sports car that was his pride and joy.

"No use hiding under there, you silly old goat," she said, heading for the business end of the car.

The sound of his wife's approaching flip-flops made Malcolm retreat even further under the protective mass of the vehicle.

She toe-poked his protruding feet. "Listen. You should be proud of yourself. In a few hours' time, one of *your* former pupils will be the first man on Mars. You're a neighbourhood celebrity. I'd milk it if I were you."

"Celebrity, my foot! What happens when the mission goes pear-shaped because Dugdale doesn't know one end of an Ion Drive from the other? What will they say about his science teacher then?"

Barbara sighed. Peering through the open bonnet, past the high tension leads, spark plugs and coolant hoses, she could just make out the oily scowl on his face.

"That school trip to Stevenage in 2002 still haunts me, Barb."

"That was twenty-seven years ago, dear."

"Single-handedly, he destroyed *Beagle 2*. I know it."

Malcolm's mind drifted back to the Airbus, Defence and Space Establishment in Stevenage. The trip to see the construction of the

Beagle 2 Mars lander had seemed to go off smoothly, despite the continual misbehaviour of the thirteen-year-old hoodies in his charge. Back then, before cynicism had set in, Malcolm believed he could turn even the roughest of Grimley Comprehensive's pupils into potential scientists. In particular, he'd regarded Flint Dugdale as something of a Challenge.

On the way back to Huddersfield, the coach had been stopped by the police following a display of mooning from the back seat. A weary-looking Malcolm had stood alongside the police officers as they searched the gang of undersized thugs for drugs, weapons and stolen goods. He barely batted an eyelid at the stash of contraband emerging from their pockets. But there was no hiding his shock at the small collection of space-age locknuts that had been discovered on the young Dugdale, hidden inside a packet of cigarettes tucked into his left sock. Malcolm had been too stunned to say anything, wondering how – and from where – Dugdale had obtained those fixings.

The bad feelings in his water had started soon after and quickly turned into a guilty obsession with the *Beagle 2* mission. He found himself following every update, every newsflash, dreading the worst. And, sure enough, on Christmas Day 2003, contact with the lander had been lost during its descent to Mars.

For years Malcolm had been plagued by nightmares, convinced the young hooligan had removed some vital fixings. And then, one cold January morning in 2015, he awoke to hear his radio alarm announce that the lonely little lander had been spotted on Mars, its petal-like solar panel still closed due to failed, or missing, fixings. Solid evidence, as far as he was concerned, that Dugdale had sabotaged the mission.

And now, by some monstrous twist of fate, that same boy had grown into the man in charge of the spaceship carrying the first group of colonists to Mars. *How could that be?* Malcolm asked himself, not for the first time. *How had they allowed Dugdale to take over after the commander's death?* Malcolm could only think that the brute had somehow bullied his way into command.

Barbara tutted at the distant stare in her husband's eyes and searched for a conveniently flat surface on which to deposit his morning cuppa. Malcolm snapped out of his trance and shook his head as he became aware of her plans. "No, not on there!" he cried.

Too late. She had plonked the mug on top of the car battery, sloshing hot tea over the terminals and causing sparks of electricity to snap, crackle and pop.

Malcolm groaned and laid his head back on the cold, hard concrete as he gazed past the drips to watch his wife flip-flopping her way through the open garage doors and across the lawn. Next door, he could see the lovey-dovey couple making last minute adjustments to their Union Jack bunting. A street party had been scheduled to coincide with the descent to Mars. Malcolm heard the woman call out from the top of a stepladder being steadied by her husband. "Hiya, Babs. Not long now. Malcolm must be so proud to think he taught the first man on Mars!"

"Oh, yes," answered Barbara with a cheerful wave. "Chuffed to bits."

Under the MG Midget Mk III Malcolm grimaced. "First man on Mars? Worst man on Mars, more like!"

2. The King's Peach

20:21 The previous day – Mayflower III

The spaceship's Assembly Room was unusually packed. Mission Commander Flint Dugdale was seated directly in front of the vast TV screen, his greasy hand wrapped around the remote control and his legs spread wide apart. Normally his predilection for darts, snooker and monster-truck racing drove the other personnel away, but right now they were strapped into the cinema-style seating and buzzing with anticipation. The forthcoming programme was a special broadcast, direct from Buckingham Palace. The King himself was to deliver a personal message to the prospective Mars colonists in a programme titled 'A Very British Mission'.

As yet another lager advert commenced, Dugdale shook a fist at the screen and roared in his broad Yorkshire accent, "Gerron wi' it!" He sat, his bloated belly pointing upwards, in the middle of the three front-row seats reserved for crew. On the back of his seat the gold embossed name of 'Mission Commander Chad Lionheart' had been crossed through with a thick marker pen and 'Commandur Dugdale' scrawled in its place. Rows two to four were for the Mars colonists.

Dugdale scratched between his legs with one hand and twirled a fat finger in his ear with the other as crewmember Lieutenant Zak

Johnston floated in zero-G into the Assembly Room and made for the front row.

"Aye, aye, Cap'n. Permish to land?" asked Zak, indicating one of the empty seats.

Flint reached under his chair and pulled out a four-pack of *Stallion* extra-strong lager and a jumbo bag of *Cheesy Watnots*. He placed them in the middle of the empty seat Zak was pointing to and snapped the seatbelt into its clip to stop his booty drifting away. "Seat's taken. Chuff off," he growled.

Zak glided around the front, keeping out of range of his commanding officer, and made for the seat on the opposite side. Flint lifted his left leg over the armrest so that his steel toe-capped Doc Marten boot rested across the other empty place.

"No probleemo, Captain Nemo. I'll just float here, shall I?" said Zak.

Dugdale didn't react, so Zak belted himself into one of the empty seats in row 2. Po-faced, tight-lipped Harry Fortune in row 3 now found himself directly behind a bush of free-floating and widely spread dreadlocks. Harry, former stand-up comedian-turned-poet, and the mission's token celebrity, leaned forward and tapped the Medusa-haired lieutenant on the shoulder. "You do realize I can't see a thing because of your hair."

Zak, having turned with a jolt, studied the comedian's thin mouth as he spoke. Although not clinically deaf he had great difficulty hearing much of what went on around him. The ear wax in his auditory canals, together with his earphones, meant that he only registered the very loudest sounds above the steady beat of his personal music directory. He had come to rely on very poor lip-reading skills to understand what was being said. "You want me to sing *Love is in the Air*?" he enquired.

Sitting next to Harry was Miss Emily Leach, daughter of zillionaire nonagenarian mining tycoon Sir Geoffrey Leach. The heavily perfumed middle-aged lady butted in. "Oh, I love that song. Please sing it, Mr Zak!"

"Soz, Lady Em, that song is alien to this mammalian."

"Surely not!" she exclaimed. And then, as if to mete out punishment for such ignorance of a classic, she let rip with a shrill, ear-jarring voice that, to her tin ear, perfectly matched the song in her head. All eyes stared at her. A single backward glare from the commander cut her off in mid-note and made her face redden.

Meekly she resumed sipping Earl Grey from a dainty bone china cup. The cup had been 'adapted' for zero-G by the addition of a cheap plastic lid and a vivid-green curly straw. Just as attention was drifting away from her, and her face was returning to its former paleness, she made an embarrassing cup-draining slurp as she sucked up the last dregs, causing her face to flush once more.

Sitting behind Emily was the diminutive Tarquin Brush, only ten years old but already smarter than most of the others. On his knee was 'Mr Snuggles', the robot he had assembled during the journey using wiring and circuits pilfered from around the ship. Tarquin's smiling mother, Delphinia Brush, gave his hand a warm squeeze, proud that her little soldier could have built such a clever robot. Around her shoulders lay the comforting arm of husband Brian Brush, a man rarely far from her side. Both had the nerdy look and spectacles of planetary scientists, which is what they were.

"About friggin' time!" exclaimed Dugdale as the programme's opening titles finally appeared on the screen.

Hardly anyone batted an eyelid at the commander's bad language. Only Delphinia Brush reacted by placing her protective hands over Tarquin's innocent little ears.

On screen, the credits cleared and a panning shot showed what appeared to be a dense rain forest. An elderly gentleman emerged from behind the leaves of a large banana tree wearing a three-piece tweed suit and matching flat cap. Looking somewhat incongruous in the jungle terrain, he sported a brass plant-sprayer in one hand and a fine walking cane in the other. As he stepped out of the tree's shadow he was instantly recognizable by his drooping elephantine ears, anteater nose and deep-set pebble eyes. He removed his hat to reveal a scabrous scalp long since deserted by its mutinous hair.

Commander Dugdale fumbled to unclip his seat belt, all the time gazing reverently up at the screen. He stood to attention.

"Ayeup, you lot. Gerr'off yer fat bums 'n show some respect for t'friggin' King!" Having stood up too aggressively he found himself drifting, head-first, for the ceiling.

"That's just great," mumbled Harry Fortune, "Now I can't see the screen at all."

"Shhh!" beseeched Emily Leach.

Meanwhile, King Charles III was gesturing up at the huge glass roof above his head. "Simply splendid, isn't it," he was saying, letting the words escape through tightly clenched jaws. "A replica of

Decimus Burton's Temperate House. The original is in Kew Gardens, of course, but one had this exact copy built in the grounds of Buckingham Palace." He paused to swat a tiny fly away. "During the past eight months, while *Mayflower III* and its valiant personnel, have been racing towards the Red Planet, I have found myself drawn here more and more. A place to meditate and consider the Universe above. Indeed, I often find my mind drifting across interplanetary space to Mars, and the vast BioDome of Botany Base where, very soon, the first Martian colonists will be standing. I imagine it looking something like this." The king swept his arm in a wide arc to indicate the lush vegetation surrounding him.

"Botany Base," he mused. "Built not by humans, but by a small army of fiendishly clever British robots sent ahead by the National Astronomical Flight Agency. Five years they have toiled, and the result is a tribute to British engineering, British technology and British knowhow."

Dugdale had managed to push himself back down from the ceiling and was stretching the seat strap across his oversized belly. "British know 'ow!" he scoffed.

"Yeah, what could possibly go wrong?" added teenager Gavin from the back row. His sister Tracey sniggered. Brian Brush removed his arm from around his wife's shoulders and held up a shushing finger to the pursed lips of one of his sternest facial expressions. As usual, the teenagers ignored their father.

King Charles cast a solemn frown at the camera. "Our thoughts, of course, go to those three brave souls who have so far perished on this dangerous mission."

Dugdale snorted. "Brave souls, my arse!"

"And yet, one can't help but feel that the successful completion of this two-year mission, there and back, will form a lasting tribute to their memory and their courage."

"Cobblers."

Charles went on to make a feeble joke about Little Green Men, at which most of the colonists, apart from the teenagers, chuckled politely. "And finally, one would like to relay a special message to the colonists themselves. The boffins at NAFA Mission Control tell one that those valiant pioneers, currently in orbit around Mars, will, through some unfathomable wizardry, be watching this broadcast in about six minutes when the transmission reaches their ship." The camera zoomed in on Charles's craggy features. "Good luck, intrepid colonists. Remember, the whole world is watching you. The whole world will see Britain at her best. You are ambassadors for the first nation to land humans on Mars. We are proud of you all."

Plucking a peach from an overhanging branch, the King took a bite out of it and smiled. The edges of the smile twitched at the bitterness of the unripe fruit in his mouth as he turned, parted several tree leaves with his walking cane, and slipped back into the jungle.

Emily wiped a tear from her eye. A few others could be heard making efforts to swallow the lumps in their throats. The teenagers at the back jeered, and the hand-built robot, Mr Snuggles, was trying out some new vocabulary it had just picked up. "Cobblers," it said in a cute chipmunk-like voice. "Friggin' cobblers."

As the credits rolled, Dugdale gave a noisy sniff. "Load of ol' bollocks," he muttered, pointing the remote control at the TV and starting to flip channels, oblivious to the howls of protest that filled the room.

"One hundred and eighty!" boomed a voice from the TV, and Dugdale stopped flipping.

"Magic!" he said, making himself more comfortable in his seat. "Darts."

*

Within seconds the Assembly Room began to empty. First out of their seats were the Faerydaes. Adorabella Faerydae – the mission doctor, holistic healer, spiritual reader and homeopath – floated towards the door. Chiffon, crystal beads and long auburn hair trailed behind her. Husband, Brokk, and their son, Oberon, drifted to her side and like a family of synchronised mer-people they glided over the heads of their colleagues and into the corridor.

Ex-comedian Harry Fortune unclipped his seat belt and launched himself towards the exit, staring miserably down at his Fliptab on which were jotted just a few random rhymes: 'Dugdale – thug fail', 'disaster – plaster', 'doom – gloom'. In his capacity as Poet in Residence he hadn't written a single poem during the entire journey, save for a few feeble love poems for the prettiest passenger, Penny Smith.

Penny Smith, alas, was not in the Assembly Room. Nor was she anywhere on board. For Penny was one of the three who had died on the mission so far.

*

In no time the room was left with just two occupants: Dugdale, eyes glued to the sweaty, beer-fuelled throwing action of the All-Yorkshire Darts Championship, and Lieutenant Zak Johnston whose attention had been caught by something outside the spaceship. Zak launched himself off a wall and drifted across to the huge panoramic observation window. He peered out, shading his eyes with his hands to cut the glare of the room's fluorescent lights. There was a metal object drifting in space, about two hundred metres from the ship. It was about the size and shape of a large man.

"The Zak-detector's detectin' an inspector," he declared, nose now pressed against the glass.

Dugdale reluctantly shifted his gaze away from the darts and peered past Zak's dreadlocks out of the window. "What the 'ell's that?"

"InspectaBot, that's what."

"Well, what's that mechanical twerk doin' there? 'E should be on t'planet by now, doin' his friggin' job! I launched 'im two hour since."

"Looks lost, dude," said Zak. He raised an arm and waved to the distant robot, but the robot didn't wave back. "Could be inspectin' the view."

"I'll give 'im 'inspectin' t'view'! That clown better get down there an' certify t'base pronto. If I 'ave to spend any more time cooped up on this crock of crap wi' a bunch of lemons, I'll end up batterin' the lot of yer."

"Shoo!" Zak was saying, flapping his arms at the robot to persuade him to go. "Go down to the planet. Start inspecting. Shoo."

Dugdale huffed and puffed as he struggled with his seat belt, but then glimpsed a dart on the screen hitting double-top. His attention returned to the contest. The crowd oohed and aahed as another dart hit its target but the third missed. Flint settled back into his seat. "Get 'im on t'radio and order 'im to get goin'," he said, his eyes firmly back on the screen

Zak looked affronted. "No-can-do, skipperoo. Rest-break. Been promised a cupcake by Lady Emily."

Dugdale grunted. "Well get Lieutenant Willie Walnut to sort out t'mechanical monkey. Tell 'im to order it to gerron wi' its friggin' job! And another thing ..." His voice trailed off as Big Joe "Lard Belly" McGrath stepped up to the oche.

"Sure thing, boss," said Zak. "I'll break my break for the good of the mission. But I ain't missin' the uptake of a cupcake."

3. The Impotence of Being Harnessed

Throughout history, the men and women selected by Fate to make truly remarkable, epoch-making discoveries have not always been the most brilliant of their day: occasionally they have been individuals who might be considered a 'surprise choice'.

Lucy Ugg, for example, a rather formidable, bad-tempered and lice-infested Ethiopian hominid who lived three million years ago. Her ape peers would certainly have considered her a 'surprise choice' for her discovery, had they had the wit to ponder such things. It was she who realized that fire was not just something to run away from but that it had other uses. Such as scorching the furry backsides of her errant offspring, or torching the leafy love-nests of her philandering mate, Toby Ugg. Her greatest discovery, though, had come within the ashes of Toby's final, fatal infidelity. The severe scorching had given her husband a rather delicious crispy crunchy coating. And so, from that simple observation, had been born the barbeque.

Aboard the spaceship *Mayflower III* Fate was about to select Lieutenant Willie Warner as the next 'surprise choice' for a monumental human discovery. As he sat wearing a PredictoHarness in the spaceship's cockpit he hardly looked the part of a great discoverer – an Archimedes, a Kepler, or an Einstein. His was more the look of a man caught up in the webbing of a very uncomfortable high-tech truss. The PredictoHarness, a state-of-the-art exoskeleton, with built-in predictive artificial intelligence, strove to foresee its wearer's every move and 'enhance' it in zero-G. Its principal drawback was that its predictions tended to be wide of the mark and its 'assistance' quite often more of a hindrance than a help. Once inside, it was almost impossible to escape from its clutches as it never occurred to the PredictoHarness that you might want to.

Willie had not donned the harness by choice; his mistake had been to relax and lean back in the cockpit seat, at which point the harness had latched onto its prey and prepared to take over and assist his every move. He wondered what to do. Should he call his crewmate Lieutenant Zak Johnston for assistance, as on all previous occasions? The prospect of the inevitable ridicule did not appeal.

Yet he had to do something; it was dinner time and he was hungry. There was a lunchbox in the refrigerated trunk beneath the cockpit flight desk, but how to get to it without alerting PredictoHarness? He decided to try to outwit it by stealth. Slowly, millimetre by shaky millimetre, he reached his hand towards the lid of the trunk. But the AI exoskeleton was not so easily fooled. In an instant it was aware of his movement and computing probabilities. Within a microsecond it had concluded, with 89% confidence, that Willie wanted to pull up his socks; so, to help, it rammed his arm down towards his ankles.

Locked in this position, Willie considered his options. Call Zak Johnston, or come up with a cunning plan? Still not liking the idea of the former, he focused his mind on the latter. After a few seconds thought, he had it.

With exaggerated movements he pulled up his socks, as though that indeed had been his original intention. PredictoHarness eagerly assisted and then returned him to his starting position. Step 1 successful.

With his other hand he reached towards the flight desk to retrieve a pen. Again, PredictoHarness was only too happy to help. Step 2 done. Then he, accidentally-on-purpose, fumbled the magnetic pen and prodded it towards the cover of the metallic refrigerated trunk. His aim was a little off-target and, for a tense moment, Willie feared it wasn't magnetic enough to latch on to lid of the trunk and would drift off to the far end of the cockpit. But luckily it veered just in time and clamped itself to the lid. Step 3 complete. He casually reached to retrieve it. As PredictoHarness helped him do so, he flicked his wrist at the last second and flipped open the trunk lid. Hey presto, plan achieved.

"Gotcha!" he said as he peered into the trunk, arm still extended. Floating weightlessly inside was a solitary, ultra-slim Tupperware box – the last of the eight-month supply of lunchboxes his mother had lovingly prepared for the journey. He reached for it and, with PredictoHarness's eager help, pulled it out; the exoskeleton even helped him crack open the lid. The aroma that assailed his senses sent him into ecstasy. Not for him the space-junk-food that the other personnel had to endure. This was the business!

He teased out a cheese and piccalilli sandwich and a mini Curly Wurly – his favourite confection, a chocolate-covered caramel ladder. Behind the latter was a little surprise: a photograph of his dog, Boo-Boo. His mum must have slipped it in so that, on the eve of the first human Mars landing, he would be reminded of home.

Holding the picture in one hand, Willie bit into the sandwich, sending a stream of piccalilli into the zero-G atmosphere where it joined a spiralling galaxy of empty crisp packets, crushed beer cans, a banana skin, and thousands of tiny globules of congealed gravy; the detritus left by Mission Commander Flint Dugdale from the previous watch.

Willie stroked the image of Boo-Boo, his only friend, and a powerful wave of homesickness hit him in the gut. A tear beaded in one eye. Mechanically, he reached to wipe the tear away but, for reasons known only to PredictoHarness's unfathomable algorithm, his movement was interpreted as a punch to his own face. Helpfully, the metal clamp around Willie's wrist directed a perfectly placed uppercut to his chin, rendering him instantly unconscious.

*

The warning chime, heralding Willie's imminent epoch-making discovery, cut through the general hum of his dazed brain. Little did he realize that this annoying noise was signalling a profound change in the way humans viewed their place in the Cosmos.

He forced his eyelids open and focused on the fist he had punched himself with. Crushed inside it were the soggy, sticky remains of his half-eaten sandwich. The Curly Wurly and photo of

Boo-Boo had drifted away from him, now too far to reach. Indeed, the Curly Wurly was no longer worth reaching having lodged in the outlet of the central heating system where the warm air had reduced it to a flaccid bag of melted chocolate and caramel. Willie felt like crying.

Somewhere in the forest of instrumentation before him and around him, the bleeping continued its incessant call. It had progressed from merely irritating to totally infuriating. He looked about, fuming, searching for the source, ready to smash the device responsible. Having spotted an instrument with a winking light to his left, he then searched for a suitable weapon with which to destroy it. With nothing readily to hand he leaned down and removed the standard-issue space-clog from his right foot. The exoskeleton monitored his movement, calculating probabilities. Eyes fiery red, mouth hissing with rage, Willie raised the clog high, ready to beat the noisy instrument into silence. But that was as far as PredictoHarness let him go. Based on its comprehensive database of human actions it was 73% certain that Willie had removed the space-clog because a small pebble was lodged inside it. Of course, there was always some uncertainty when it came to humans, but 73% was a pretty good bet, so the harness helped Willie vigorously shake the clog to clear it of any foreign matter.

Willie grunted with frustration as the beeping went on and he let the clog float free from his hand. Another idea came to him. With all the guile of his boyhood hero, *Batman*, he reached into his utility belt and pulled out a pair of nail scissors. PredictoHarness perked up, switching to a state of high alertness, ready to monitor the lieutenant's every move. *What's he playing at now?* it wondered, scanning the cockpit eagerly for clues. *The human intends to cut something. But what?* It watched Willie flip the lid of its own central processing unit, grab a bundle of multi-coloured wires and smile cruelly as he held them between the scissor blades. *Got it*, thought the harness and happily helped to squeeze the fingers of its own execution.

As Willie floated gently free of the harness's suddenly limp restraints, he at last became aware of the significance of the irritating bleeping noise. It was coming from the infra-violet detector. A gob of piccalilli, ejected from his sandwich when he had punched himself, had squirted onto the detector's touchscreen, refocusing it on a new section of the Martian surface.

"Blimey O'Reilly," he said, letting out a low whistle. He doggy-paddled through the air to reach the detector, wiped the pickle off the equipment and prodded a button to silence the alarm. His eyes grew wider and wider as he read the results displayed on the screen. The scans of the Martian surface, some 58,000 feet below, had detected something of great significance. "Positive identification at 99% confidence level," was the on-screen message. "Multiple strong, highly-localized, energy-expending anomalies of a non-geological origin, consistent with metabolizing, thermodynamically open chemical systems, highly suggestive of underlying organic mechanisms".

Willie blinked several times. From his astronaut training he knew exactly what that meant. It meant that the infra-violet scanners had detected living creatures on the planet below. More importantly, it meant that the piccalilli from Lieutenant Willie Warner's sandwich had brought about a truly remarkable discovery: he had become the first person to discover Life on Mars.

The question was: what kind of life had Willie just discovered and would it be pleased to see them?

4. Permission Impossible

Lieutenant Willie Warner's excitement escalated as he adjusted the sensitivity and resolution of the scanners.

"Whoa! These are seriously big buggers, William. Must be 12 feet tall," he muttered punching the air, a huge grin on his face. "Real aliens. Real proper aliens. Things with ... limbs ... tentacles ... whatever. Bodies. Eyes. Brains." This would make him famous the world over. Dugdale might be the first to walk on Mars, but Willie would be the first to make contact with extra-terrestrials. He sat trying to picture what they might look like. All sorts of weird images of blobby things with claws and spines and clusters of eyes on stalks assailed him. Some armed with axes, others with laser guns. He tried to backtrack and imagined them picking flowers and singing songs.

Just then, the sound of the door opening signified someone's arrival. Instantly, Willie hunched over the screen, like a classroom swot shielding his exam paper from prying eyes.

Zak floated into the cockpit. "What you hidin' there, pardner? Unscreen the detection machine, man."

"Not hiding anything," said Willie with an air of innocence, moving more of himself in the way.

"That's an order, space-bud."

"Hah! You can't order me."

"Senior lieutenant, dude."

"Since when?"

"I'm older and bolder than you, space-trooper. And whose Pa's runnin' this mish to Mars?"

"How could I forget? Zak Johnston, son of Mission Control Director Montgomery Johnston achieves the totally believable score of 110% in the final Space Cadet Academy exam, despite never having been to any of the lectures."

"Surprised myself there. But here I am, beamin' amaze-rays wherever I go. Now show, bro."

"Nope."

Zak launched himself across the room and tried to peer round his crewmate, first one way, then another. "Remind me, space-geek, what exactamundo does this machine display onscreen?"

"Ha! I'd have thought Mr 110-percent would know that."

Zak ground his teeth. "Missed that class. Dodgy grass."

Willie snorted.

Zak clamped himself to his crewmate's back, hooking his goatee-bearded chin over the other's shoulder. Willie squirmed at the close contact with an unwashed man; worse still, a man with food particles lodged in his rancid beard. But he was determined to protect his discovery at all costs and grasped the screen even more firmly.

"Did you have any reason for coming to see me, or was it just to give me a hug?"

"Nearly slipped my mind," said Zak, releasing his grip on Willie. "The Zakster brings news of an urgent job for mankind. From the Big Guy. Uncle Duggers. Seems InspectaBot's been neglectin' his inspectin'."

"What?"

"Stranded not landed."

"Come again?"

"The robosurveyor ain't budgin'. The crazy dude's just trudgin' outside the ship. Like a trash can waitin' for bin day. Flinto wants his top guy on the case."

"Really?"

"No man, not really. The top guy's on a cake-break. So you gotta sort it."

"Great," said Willie. Still covering the scanner with an elbow he turned to the observation screen and switched between external cameras until he found one showing the slowly cart-wheeling robot outside. He let out a sigh of exasperation and tapped the microphone on the comms console. "Calling InspectaBot. Come in, InspectaBot. Do you read me? Over."

"Identify yourself!" came the brusque, metallic response.

"This is Lieutenant William Hilda Warner of *Mayflower III* respectfully calling InspectaBot 360. Over."

Zak sniggered. "So that's what the 'H' stands for! Suits you, dude."

"It's a family name, not a girl's name."

"No, dude, that's a girl's name."

The metallic voice boomed out of the speakers, "Please enter your 16-digit PIN code followed by the hash key."

Willie turned to Zak. "What's the PIN code?"

Zak shrugged.

"I don't have a PIN code," Willie said into the microphone.

"Very well, you will need to answer a security question."

"Go on."

"What was the name of the first girl you kissed?"

Zak sniggered again.

Willie turned to him. "You can go now. I can take it from here."

"Sure man. Understood. Private info."

Willie drummed his fingers, waiting for the other lieutenant to leave. "Bet it was Mandy Minger, Space Cadet School swinger," said Zak as he edged towards the door.

Zak reached the door but then floated back into the room. "I'm taking this with me," he said, grabbing the PredictoHarness and floating out of the door with it.

"What was the name of the first girl you kissed?" repeated InspectaBot.

Willie looked around to make sure Zak had gone and whispered into the microphone, "None. I've never kissed a girl."

"Nun?"

"Yes, none."

"Answer mismatch. Identification failure. A new security PIN code will be issued."

"When?"

"Two weeks."

"This is ridiculous. Ask me another security question."

"What is your mother's bra size?"

"Easy. 40DD," responded Willie without hesitation.

"Caller identified. How can I help you today, Lieutenant William Hilda Warner?"

"InspectaBot 360, could you please report your status?"

"Roger. Current status: stalled. Awaiting new instructions."

"The new instructions are the same as the old ones, InspectaBot. Your mission is to perform a full building inspection of Botany Base to certify it as habitable. Do you understand?"

"Affirmative."

"Off you go, then."

"Inspection of base not possible."

"Why?"

"Not within visual range."

"No, obviously. You're still in orbit."

"Current altitude 57,842 feet."

"Exactly. So you need to address that issue first. Have a good day."

"Please advise."

Willie sighed. "Look, land down on the planet, tootle across to the base and start inspecting. Couldn't be simpler."

"Landing permission refused."

This stumped Willie. "What? That's Mars down there, not Heathrow Terminal 3. Who refused you?" Even as he asked the question a cold shiver ran down his spine. Was it possible the aliens down there had already made contact with InspectaBot? Had they forbidden him to land? How had they done it? What had they said? With threats, or without?

"HarVard," answered the robot.

"You mean the base's supercomputer?"

"Affirmative."

The tension in Willie's muscles relaxed. "Phew. Please ignore HarVard. He has no right to refuse you permission. Although the fact that he's trying to sounds suspicious. What reason did he give?"

"Transmitting message."

Willie saw HarVard's message appear on a screen to his right. He leaned over to read it. "My dear InspectaBot 360. What an inordinate pleasure to hear from you. We are greatly looking forward to meeting you in person and having the honour of hosting you when you come to carry out your important mission. We trust you will find everything in order. In the meantime, may I request a teensie, weensie little favour? Would you mind awfully delaying your landing for a bit as the base isn't quite ready for inspection."

Willie let out an involuntary laugh. "They've only been working on it for the past five years!"

He continued reading. "You see, it's the builder bots. They're such perfectionists. They want everything to be just right for the humans. Premature inspection would break their little clockwork hearts. There isn't much to do, really, just a few last-minute soft furnishings that need arranging, but even so they'd rather you didn't see it until it is all finished."

Willie cleared his throat. "Technically, that's not a refusal to land."

"There's a postscript," said InspectaBot.

Willie scrolled down the screen. "PS I will reopen the landing pad when we're all ready for you. Perhaps you could pop back in, let's say, a month?"

Lieutenant Warner shook his head. "Now look here, 360. I am ordering you to ignore HarVard and go down there and carry out your duty. That's an order, OK?"

"Landing pad unavailable."

"OK, let's think this through, shall we? We have a large planet down there. So you can actually land anywhere you like. Just pick your spot. Got that?"

A pause. "Risk assessment: terrain sandy, uneven, rock-strewn, pot-holed. Poses a 37.4% possibility of impact damage."

"Just Do It ... That Is An Order."

"Received and understood."

As Willie glared at the image of InspectaBot on the screen he noticed a puff of gas emit from the robot's behind and its metallic body start to drift towards the planet.

"Well, that was immensely rewarding," Willie said to himself. But then he looked back at the peculiar message from HarVard. Why was the supercomputer stalling and seemingly denying InspectaBot the chance to land? Did he, perhaps, have something to hide? Was it anything to do with the aliens?

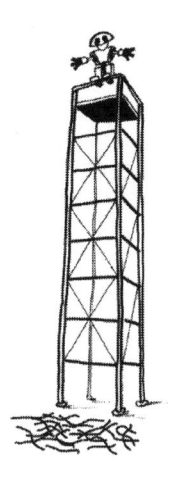

5. The Hanging Gaskets of BioDome

23rd March 2029, BioDome, Botany Base, Mars

High above the floor of the BioDome, a solitary gasket-fitting robot named Ero (short for Heroism) balanced on a rickety scaffold tower. Servo motors whirred and joints jerked as he reached a claw-hand down into a cardboard box marked 'Rubber Pressure Seals'. From it he plucked a long, thin, cellophane packet and set about removing the wrapping. After pulling and tugging with clumpy mechanical digits, Ero finally gripped the end of the package between his jagged metal teeth and ripped it open, releasing a snake-like length of grooved rubber. He let the discarded wrapper flutter over the edge of the tower without so much as a glance at its bold warning label: *'IMPORTANT. Gaskets **must** be fitted correctly. Failure to do so could result in air leakage causing respiratory failure, organ malfunction, and permanent human shutdown.'*

Ero grabbed the barrier rail to steady himself while he raised the gasket, awkwardly grasped between metal fingers, high above his head. Telescopic joints extended at a snail's pace towards the domed roof. After a long, difficult stretch, Ero pushed one end of the seal into the tiny gap between frame and polycarbonate panel. It was a delicate operation for which his stubby digits were especially unsuited. As he tried to prod the rest of the gasket home, the first end popped out and dangled down. With an electronic grunt he pushed it back into place, but this only made the middle part sag. And when he tried to prod the middle back, the two ends flopped out, making it momentarily resemble a Mexican bandit's moustache. And then it dropped out altogether. Moving as fast as his servo-joints allowed, Ero tried to catch it, but his fumbling fingers grabbed and missed and, for the thirty-fourth time that morning, the rubbery thing fell to the BioDome floor, fifty metres below.

Ero watched it bounce, give a little death wiggle and then lie still, on top of thirty-three of its fellow gaskets.

Sh*t ... f*ck ... b*ll*cks - Sh*t ... f*ck ... b*ll*cks. Ero's emotionally evolving AI brain was overheating.

His neck joint graunched as he turned his gaze to the BioDome roof and surveyed the results of his day's work. Just five gaskets fitted, each either sagging inadequately or completely hanging free. A pang of negativity filled him. Turning his gaze downwards, he focused on some of the other worker robots far below him. He watched them enviously as they worked at their appointed tasks; hammering, drilling, sawing. To Ero's mind they seemed to be making good progress – successful and content in their work, each and every one. He was particularly drawn to a constructorbot bashing away at some ducting. As Ero watched, his own cyber-hand made small tapping motions, mirroring the other bot's more vigorous actions.

Through a doorway to the right came the site foreman bot, Tude (short for Fortitude). Rocking along on his caterpillar tracks, Tude came to a halt at the base of Ero's tower and craned his neck upwards.

<0101011101100001011100110111001101110101011100000011 1111> he transmitted in standard robot communications protocol. Which roughly translated as: <Report progress.>

<Oh, outstanding,> replied Ero in binary, although perhaps 'out-hanging' would have been a more accurate reply. This was the first time since his manufacture that Ero had told a lie and he was not feeling good about it. Sheepishly, he peered down at his manager far below.

<Excellent!> signalled Tude, triumphantly punching the air with a powerful mechanical fist. <For the good of the humans!>

Half-heartedly Ero copied the punch and followed it with the rote response of, <Loving it.>

Tude nodded his metallo-plastic head and trundled away. Ero watched him go before throwing a wistful glance at the hammering robot, still happily clobbering away at his duct. As he returned to his own, unhappy task, a glimmer of an idea formed in his circuits. Clutching the head of a freshly unwrapped gasket in one hand, the robot activated the screwdriver attachment in the other. With a whirr, the screwdriver blade emerged. He placed the seal against the gap and poked it in with the blade. One end went in. His hopes rose. This might actually work. He fed more and more of the gasket into the gap, pushing it firmly home with the blade until he had just a few millimetres to go. But at that very moment, the whole building seemed to explode with the jarring blare of alarm bells.

Ero jerked in surprise, skewering the rubber seal with the screwdriver and knocking it free of the gap. Once again Ero found himself watching a gasket plummeting to the ground. He continued staring at it for a long time after it had finished its death dance. Yet again he had failed. The robot slumped and cradled his spherical metal head. Despair overwhelmed him. Unable to shoulder the burden of failure any longer, Ero climbed over the scaffold barrier rail, gazed down at the inviting concrete floor, and jumped.

<For the good of the humans,> was his final transmission.

<Loving it,> came the automatic reply from the bots in the BioDome, pausing their work to see if the alarms would stop or continue. None were aware of who had made the initial call, nor his current circumstances.

In any case, it was too late for Ero to register their response.

*

The sound of the crash, audible even above the din of the alarms, made foreman bot Tude turn back to see what had happened. At the bottom of the tower lay the crumbled carcass of Ero, resembling a modern sculpture of a break-dancing robot, head partially buried in the still-soft concrete and legs splayed in the air.

<Robot down,> Tude radioed. <Emergency! Repair-bot to the BioDome.>

In a far corner of Botany Base, Zilli (short for Resilience), bleeped into life, flicked open her Swiss Army hands and set off to carry out her assignment.

*

As the alarm bells continued to ring, the knocking of hammers, sawing of wood and whine of power drills ceased. One by one, the builder robots turned and checked their nearest wall-screen. The message, in flashing red lights, read, 'Site meeting. Site-office portakabin in 10 minutes. HarVard.'

Each robot stopped its task and set off towards the base's front entrance. Those with jointed legs had to pick their way through rubble as they went, those on caterpillar tracks were able to trundle over it, while the most advanced models hovered clear of the debris. Inevitably, in all the haste, there were accidents. A couple of robots collided at a corridor junction, resulting in some denting of metal casings, scratching of paintwork and loosening of wires. Another put an arm through a freshly plastered partition.

Things were worse at the main entranceway. With all the bots trying to pile through the small doorway, it wasn't long before a mass of metal bodies, swivelling heads and twisted limbs had formed a solid plug wedged firmly between the door jambs. And, as the wall-screens counted down the minutes to the site meeting, frantic bots began crawling over the top of their comrades, attempting to squeeze through the gap above their heads and becoming stuck at the top of the pile in the process.

A single camera, mounted high in the dome's space-frame roof trusses, swung in the direction of the mêlée and seemed to droop despondently. Then a set of commands were pinged to Dom (Wisdom), a multi-purpose robot, who opened a bulldozer arm and swung into action. It took all his strength to shove the mechanical mass away from the opening and into a corner of the entrance hall. He allowed the robots to escape, one by one, until all had passed safely out of the base.

*

Outside, the freed robots bowed their hard-hatted heads into the gusting wind. The small, stocky ones, with rugged undercarriages, made the best progress through the rocky, sandy soil of Mars, whereas the tall, thin, androids struggled a little. A squat floor-polishing bot resembling an upturned pram, called Cassie (Perspicacity), hit a stone that jammed her wheels and caused her to run off the path into a ditch. There she lay, struggling to get out, her wheels spinning in the fine dust of the Martian surface. The other robots ploughed on, ignoring her feeble beeps for assistance.

THE WORST MAN ON MARS

Up the narrow ramp leading to the ramshackle wooden portakabin they went, digitally chitter-chattering to each other and speculating about the possible reason for this unscheduled meeting. Their progress towards the portakabin door was observed by wall-mounted CCTV cameras. The prospect of a second pile-up occurring at this entrance seemed inevitable, so emergency measures were required. With lightning speed, HarVard transmitted and uploaded a 'politeness app' to each of the bots' positronic brains.

The effect was immediate. The first to reach the site office entrance was a small flue-sweeping bot called Timi (Optimism) who appeared to be built from metal flower pots. He stopped in front of the door, knocked on it and waited for a response. The second robot to arrive, Eve (Achievement), halted right behind him. The next arrival jammed on its brakes and stopped behind her. In no time there was a long, orderly queue from the site office door, down the ramp and stretching into the Martian landscape.

"Come in!" called a voice from within the Portakabin. "Just come straight in!"

But, with the new app installed, Timi turned to Eve and, with a polite bow, transmitted, <After you.>

<No, no, Timi, I insist. After you,>

<Ladybots first.>

<But you were here before me.>

The lens of the external camera zoomed in and out in disbelief, and the voice from inside blared out, "Abort the app and get in the site office, now!"

With the new order overriding their politeness modules, the bots obeyed. Timi shoved Eve out of the way and marched into the site office. Behind, an unseemly scramble ensued as robots fought to pile in.

The site office was empty apart from a rickety trestle table in the centre of the room. With much pushing and barging the robots shuffled around to fill the limited space available. Most removed their safety helmets and their luminous-yellow, high-viz jackets as they entered, hanging them on the hooks provided.

As they jostled their way in, their cyber minds wondered why HarVard had summoned them like this? What could be so important that he needed to address them personally? Surely there was nothing wrong?

6. Fagin It

The large electronic eye, set high in the wall at the front of the site office watched the assorted robots crowding around the trestle table, their excited electronic chatter saturating the airwaves.

The Eye observed them bumping into one another in the cramped confines of the cabin. It watched little Timi get clattered to the ground and trampled on. Another robot rushed to Timi's assistance, but merely ended up on top of him. And a third tripped over them both, uttering an electronic shriek as it did so.

The super-brain behind the Eye processed what it saw and was overwhelmed by a sweeping sense of despair. *I'm better than this*, thought HarVard.

But, with important matters at hand, HarVard ramped up his patience circuits and calmed his teeming thought processes as the last of the robots entered the cabin. It was the gasket-fitter bot, Ero, hastily mended and newly-rebooted, but with a nasty dent in his spherical, chrome-plated head. Optics downcast and shoulders slouched, he dragged his hoof-like feet as he followed repair-bot Zilli into the office, leaving the door wide open behind him. The plastic eyelids of the Eye narrowed in annoyance, but HarVard's primary decision-making module kicked in and concluded: *What's the point?*

In any case, at that moment, a powerful gust of Martian wind caused the door to slam shut with a loud bang and spurred HarVard into addressing the meeting.

<Right, let's get started, shall we?> he broadcast in binary, his signal drowned out by the general hubbub. Even repeating the message at higher power had little effect.

<QUIET!> he blasted at multiple frequencies and at maximum energy.

A deathly radio-hush filled the room and the assortment of eclectic cyber-heads swivelled to face the front of the site office.

The supercomputer's Eye scanned the motley mechanoids before it. It took in the splashes of paint on the shiny carapaces, the scuffs and scratches on the limbs, the plaster-smears on the control panels and the vacant looks directed towards it. *They're a very limited bunch*, he told himself, *but they're all I have.*

*

HarVard had a special audio-visual interface for communicating with lesser beings such as robots. Or humans. A hologram generator allowed him to project an animated, life-sized, 3D avatar from his vast library of pre-computed templates of humans, animals and other beings. The robots loved his creations and could sense one was about to be switched on in front of them. A buzz of excitement went round the cabin.

<Who's it to be today?> wondered Dom.

<Ooh, Kryten from Red Dwarf, I hope,> transmitted Timi.

<My fave is Marvin the paranoid android,> tweeted Eve.

<The Star Wars robots!>

<No, you're all wrong! Best by far is B9 from *Lost in Space*, with his concertina arms and panicky behaviour. 'Danger, Will Robinson. Danger',> Dom mimicked.

HarVard kept the crowd waiting in eager anticipation before displaying his latest 3D creation at the front of the site office. It was a truly realistic representation of an old man, shrivelled and villainous-looking, with long, matted red hair. He was wearing a greasy flannel gown and holding a toasting fork. None other than Dickens's Fagin.

<It's a human!> came the gleeful chorus of electronic signals throughout the cabin. <Long live the humans!>

The Fagin hologram gave a slight smile.

"We are very glad to see you, *all-of-ya*, very," it said with a bow.

The robots stared, their silence speaking volumes. Fagin scanned the robot faces expectantly. "Get it, my dears?" he asked, smiling his mischievous smile and waggling his eyebrows.

Still the robots stared.

<Who is it?> enquired Dom. <Is it Carol Vorderman? I like him.>

Other robots gave the robotic equivalent of shrugs, or retweeted the question. <Are you a robot in disguise?> asked Timi in his high-pitched signal.

"It's a pun," explained the Fagin hologram. "All-of-ya – Oliver. We are very glad to see you, *all-of-ya*, very."

The robot stares became, if anything, blanker.

"Fagin's opening line. In the book."

There was a shaking of heads and a furrowing of rubber brows. Some shoulders shrugged, and there was much baffled twittering and tweeting.

Wrong crowd, thought HarVard with a deep sigh.

Reluctantly he recomputed his holo-image. Fagin morphed into a Hollywood robot, gold from head to toe and with an annoying English accent. A casual glance might have mistaken this robot for 3-CPO from Star Wars, but HarVard's processors had a special 'lawyer' chip installed, called COPOUT (Copyright Offence Prevention by Obfuscation of Unlawful Transgression); it ensured no copyrights were infringed by his holographic creations. Thus, this robot was not at all like 3-CPO, but as fundamentally different from the Star Wars superstar as chalk is from limestone. His name was three-piece-yo, or 3-PCO.

The room erupted in robotic cheering and buzzed with excited radio waves.

Plebs, thought HarVard.

*

"This is madness," said 3-PCO with a silly body-wobble, "Complete madness."

As HarVard waited for the cheering to subside he performed a quick head count and noted some significant absentees.

"Oh, my!" he resumed in the annoying English voice. "We seem to be missing Cassie. And the Polish builder bots!"

Tude stepped forward. He flicked his appendages to readjust his high-viz jacket and prevent it slipping from his robust shoulders.

<Cassie's unable to be with us,> he transmitted.

"Oh? Why?"

<On account of being marooned in a ditch. Into which she fell. On the way here.>

3-PCO's body-wobble became extreme. "And not one of you thought to rescue her?" He looked askance at the robots. A ripple of applause commenced, but instantly ceased as the bots looked around guiltily at one another.

"Oh, my!" said 3-PCO with a reproachful tilt of the head. "This is not good, not good at all. We are a family, remember? Could we have a volunteer to pull her out after the meeting?"

Silence.

"Anyone?"

Dom opened a pneumatic bucket-arm and thrust it into the air to offer his services. Dom was known to be a bit overenthusiastic at times, and now was such a time. His arm-thrust was a little too hard and a little too high, puncturing the flimsy ceiling above his head. Dom started to retract it. The ceiling panels bowed and buckled alarmingly.

"Leave it!" ordered 3-PCO. "Or you'll bring the whole ceiling down."

<Roger,> transmitted Dom. His head drooped as he stood, looking sheepish, with his arm stuck, half inside the portakabin and half poking through the roof and catching the sands of Mars in his bucket-hand.

"And the Polish worker bots?"

<The *robotniki* send their apologies. They will not be attending today,> responded Tude, jutting out his square jaw several times.

"On account of?"

<They're working at the Other Place. As usual.>

"Oh my, oh my," said the 3-PCO hologram waggling his head. "I do so wish they were here. We need them, we really do. A volunteer to go fetch them, please?"

Once again Dom was the first to volunteer. He thrust his other pneumatic bucket-arm into the air and managed to punch a second hole in the ceiling, next to the first. A little smoke escaped from his elbow joint as he struggled to dislodge it.

"Dom," suggested 3-PCO's calm, posh, English voice. "Do you think you could find an alternative way of volunteering for tasks?"

<Roger,> mumbled Dom, his head drooping even more than

before.

<I'll go,> offered Zilli.

"Why, thank you, Zilli." The golden robot's holographic arm jerked upwards to give the repair-bot a thumbs-up sign.

*

"Right, let's get to business, shall we?" HarVard turned and pointed at a calendar on the wall, just visible between detailed drawings of the BioDome. The calendar was open on March 2029, its picture depicting the Robot of the Month.

"Anyone know what this is?"

Deathly hush.

"Anyone? No? Well, it's called a calendar. It marks the passage of time in units of days. Each number corresponds to a different day." 3-PCO gazed at the sea of baffled face-plates. "I know, it's a difficult concept for small brains to grasp. Let's see if my learned friend can help." With that, the avatar morphed into an old man with tousled white hair and a bushy white moustache, wearing a grey flannel suit and tie.

The sight of a human led to further tweets of <Long live the humans!> and <I'm loving it.>

<Is it Fagin again?> asked Eve from the back of the cabin. <All humans look the same to me!>

HarVard's 'patience and understanding' circuits redoubled their output, coming dangerously close to overloading. "My name is Albert Einstein. I vill explain to you a little about Time."

<Who?> the robots twittered. <What?>

"Now, Tude," started the famous physicist. "As site foreman, you're responsible for *keeping to deadlines*. Can you explain to ze other workers what this calendar is showing?"

With a firm nod, Tude shuffled forward. He extended his right limb towards the calendar, gave it a half-turn and then retracted it. <Now, that,> he started, <is Mr MarchBot. A heroic demolition machine who can be seen here removing a bird's nest full of new-born chicks from a derelict building. He will take them to safety, thus saving their lives, before returning to proudly swing his wrecking-ball and knock the building to the ground. It is a fine picture.>

Albert Einstein stared at him. "Ya," he said. "But can vee, perhaps, turn our attention to the numbers *below* ze picture? See? Zese numbers here?"

<Ah, yes,> said Tude with a nod, seemingly confident he could deal with any question the old man might throw at him.

"One of the numbers is circled."

<Correct!>

"It has the vords 'COMPLETION DATE' written in large, red letters next to it. Kindly tell us vich number it is."

<Twenty-three!>

"Excellent. That vould make the completion date the 23rd March, 2029, wouldn't it. And what is today's date?"

Tude gave the German physicist a blank stare.

"Any ideas? I throw it open to the floor."

Silence.

<I preferred 3-PCO,> transmitted Ero at a very low, despondent frequency.

Albert Einstein sighed, rubbing his eyes with the palms of his hand before clearing his throat. "Ze 23rd of March, 2029 happens to be today."

There was a hushed silence as the robots tried to assimilate the information. A few heads turned to exchange questioning glances.

<That's good. Isn't it?> offered Dura (Endurance), the master plasterer and Tude's right hand robot. <If today is completion day, it means we're finally done with building. At last we can relax!>

<Hurrah!> called out Timi.

One by one, the robots' mouths cracked open into wide grins and they started to cheer, their radio waves reverberating round the cabin. Some even did a little robotic jig.

Albert Einstein had buried his face in his hands and was shaking his head in dismay. "Heaven help me!" he wailed. "What have I done to deserve this?"

7. Meet the Flint Stoners

Mission Commander Flint Dugdale sat, legs wide apart, in front of the large wall-screen, probing a fat finger between his teeth to dislodge a lump of steak pie. The darts had finished with a victory for Big Joe "Lard Belly" McGrath.

As he flipped channels, a caption caught his eye. "Coming next," it said. "Flint Dugdale: First Man on Mars". His eyes bulged – a programme all about him! A vast smile spread across his face.

"By 'eck," he said, clapping his hands together. "'Appen this calls for a celebration."

He detached a can of *Stallion* from the four-pack on the seat to his right and pulled out a steak pie from under his own seat. He pressed the insta-heat button on the pie packaging, waited the requisite ten seconds and then tore off the cellophane wrapping, tossing it over his shoulder at the empty seats behind him. Greedy teeth sank into the flaky pastry, sending a stream of scalding gravy globules drifting into the room. Sublime sensations exploded on his taste buds and a heavenly aroma filled his nostrils.

With the opening credits now rolling, he popped the ring-pull on the can of ale, discarded the customized zero-G straw, and slapped his gravy-covered mouth over the hole before any of the golden liquid could drift free. He closed his eyes in delight at the delicious taste. A few drops escaped from between his lips, but it hardly mattered.

"Tomorrow morning," the presenter was saying, "Yorkshireman Flint Dugdale will be the first man ever to walk on the surface of Mars."

"Get in!" said Dugdale with a fist-punch. The punching fist happened to be the one holding the *Stallion*, so a good deal of the amber liquid surged out in large, spherical droplets. Dugdale cursed under his breath as he watched the precious beads of ale heading for the man on the screen.

"What kind of man is Flint Dugdale?"

"Chuffin' lovely," mumbled Dugdale through a mouth full of pie and ale.

"He's certainly a controversial figure."

"Am I 'eck!" Yellowing teeth tore off another chunk of pie.

"Indeed, even within NAFA there are some who think more should have been done to stop him taking control of the mission."

"Like who?" demanded Dugdale sitting up rigid.

The picture cut to a well-dressed middle-aged man wearing a suit and tie.

"Oh, I could'a guessed it'd be 'im!" A quick swig of *Stallion* steadied his emotions and relaxed his muscles.

A caption identified the man as Jeremy Franklin, Principal Director of NAFA. "Some people exude greatness," he was saying, "others hide it under a bushel, while there are those who don't have a scintilla of it in their entire being. Flint Dugdale most definitely belongs to the third category."

Dugdale, having lost count of the categories, wasn't sure if this was a compliment or not. Besides, wasn't a 'scintilla' some kind of furry rodent?

A woman, identified as Sarah Wright, NAFA Head of Human Resources, appeared on screen. "No sane or rational recruitment procedure would *ever* have accepted him. Any job interview, psychometric test, medical examination, or psychological assessment would have filtered him out before he'd even made it through the door; any ranking system would have ranked him bottom of the whole human race – and quite well down a list of orang-utans."

Now this clearly was an insult. Wasn't it? Another calming gulp of *Stallion* was in order.

The programme's presenter returned. "Of course, it is well known how Flint Dugdale made it onto the mission." The screen showed archive footage of Dugdale celebrating his win on British reality show *Who wants to go to Mars?* "The British public, perhaps through an act of collective mischief, voted for him in their millions. NAFA were not so keen."

The screen cut back to Jeremy Franklin. "Our contract with the major sponsors, *Stallion Lager Ltd*, obliged us to include him. There was nothing we could do. It's not that we were slow to spot his complete unsuitability. We did what we could: counselling, elocution lessons, you name it."

Sarah Wright took up the story. "We sent him to London's top anger management school. They lost patience with him after two days. He failed the final assessment, of course. Lowest mark they'd ever had. But never in our worst nightmares did we think he'd become commander!"

Dugdale was grinning to himself. "Stupid twonks."

"Dudgale's unplanned and unexpected rise to power was, of course, the result of a tragedy," the presenter was saying. "A power surge in the urine extractor led to Commander Chad Lionheart sustaining a fatal injury. And, suddenly, the mission was without a leader. Yet NAFA's orders for the captaincy to pass to the senior lieutenant were not followed. Why? And was it a coincidence that around that time all sound and vision from *Mayflower III* was lost? Just how did Dugdale assume control and install himself in Lionheart's cabin?"

"Yorkshire grit."

The screen showed a man dressed in military regalia, Mission Director Montgomery Johnston. "Should never have been Dugdale. Never. Perfect replacement already on board. Lieutenant Zak Johnston. End of.'"

The screen cut from Zak Johnston's father, back to the presenter. "So, what is Flint Dugdale really like?"

"Friggin' gorgeous."

"Who better to ask than the people who know him best? His friends. His family. The people he grew up with. Katie Pipperton is live in Huddersfield – Commander Dugdale's home town. Hello, Katie." The picture cut to a night-time street scene. At the centre stood a nervous-looking female reporter, large microphone in hand, with an unruly, and clearly very inebriated, mob behind her. In the background was a seedy-looking pub.

Dugdale leaned forward for a closer look. "Well, I'll go to foot of our stairs! That's t'Muck'n'Shovel!" A huge smile opened on his podgy face.

The crowd were chanting, "Dugdale, Dugdale". Many were waving crude, homemade banners and placards peppered with appalling spelling mistakes. "Yorkshires Fist Man on Mar's", "Dugdale the Heroe" and "Flint dose us proud!"

"Hello," said the pretty reporter, forcing a smile and looking completely out of place amidst some of the ugliest specimens of the human race. Boozy, beery yobs, drunken old sots, slutty-looking females with thicker limbs than the males, all threatened to engulf her.

A tear came to Flint's eye as waves of nostalgia washed over him. These were his people; his tribe. Snatches of remembered yobbish cries involuntarily issued from his mouth and, as he recognised old mates, he shouted their nicknames – Scudder, Banyard, Mugger – each conjuring treasured memories of shared youthful violence.

"Eeee, thems wer't days," he muttered, rubbing the tear aside and taking another swig of ale.

"Welcome to Huddersfield," Katie continued, struggling to make herself heard above the general din. "Home of Flint Dugdale. Soon to be the first human being to walk on the surface of Mars."

There was a rowdy cheer, which mutated into some coarse songs and raucous bellowing. Katie tried to maintain her professional demeanour and polar white smile as the crowd behind her fought for camera attention.

"Tonight, on the eve of the historic transfer to the Red Planet, we meet some of Commander Dugdale's friends and family who would like to relay their own special messages."

Dugdale echoed some of the rowdy chants and choruses, taking swigs of his ale in between and partying along with his people.

Katie turned to an elderly, bespectacled man with large ears who was kneeling down and removing a pair of bicycle clips from his ankles.

"We're thrilled to have Commander Dugdale's old English teacher from Grimley Comprehensive School..." She leaned down to hold the microphone close to the man's lips.

There was a dull groan from the audience, echoed by an even duller groan from Flint. "Oh, for frack's sake! Not 'im," he moaned.

"Of all't chuffin' people, they go 'n pick that big-eared numpty, Flappers."

"Mr Potter, as Flint's former teacher, perhaps you could give the world an insight into what he was like as a student?"

The old man creakily raised himself from his knees and put his mouth very close to the microphone. "You wanna know about Dugdale? I'll tell yer summat about him. He was a worthless lump of shit. A bone idle little fu...." Katie shot a hand up to her earpiece and winced in pain at her director's yelled instructions. She whipped the microphone away from Mr Potter and swung it toward a wrinkly, white-haired old lady dressed in a shiny pink tracksuit. It had 'Dugdale' emblazoned in sequins across her ample chest.

"Now, beside me," said Katie with a nervous grimace, "I have Flint's gran who, I know, has something she would like to say to her grandson."

Flint's gran grinned a toothless grin, staring at the camera. "Am I on't telly?"

"You are. And the whole world is watching. You must be terribly proud of your grandson."

Gran continued to stare directly at the camera.

"Mrs Arkwright," prompted Katie.

"Miss."

"Sorry ... Miss Arkwright, could you share some of your fond memories of Commander Dugdale?"

"Eeeee, Flint were a bonny babby. He 'ad such a lovely smile. Oh, wait. 'Appen that were his 'alf brother, Leroy, wi't smile. Now I remember, Flint were t'ugly bugger. He were forever bawlin' 'bout summat."

Katie put her hand to her earpiece again.

"Message?" she said quickly. "What's your message to your grandson?"

"Fetch us twenty Lambert and Butler, Flint, luv. I'm gaggin' for a ciggie." She cackled a toothless laugh at the camera.

Katie fiddled with her earpiece to reduce the volume of her director's shrill screams. She glanced behind at the huge scrum of people eager for their moment of fame.

Next up was Scudder, eyes glazed, standing far too close to Katie for her liking and swaying alarmingly.

"Ayeup, Fluggdale, mate," he said, rubbing himself up against the immaculate trouser suit of the aghast reporter. "I chuffin' well love yer, man. Listen, listen, mate..." Scudder's drunken eyes tried to focus on the camera. "... Seriously, man, I gotta tell yer summat real important."

Scudder pushed himself away from Katie, straightened up as though to deliver a heartfelt message, and let out the loudest belch he could muster before collapsing to his knees in raucous laughter. There was laughter from the crowd surrounding the now terror-stricken Katie, and even Flint Dugdale nearly choked on a mouthful of pie as he watched his friend's performance.

Katie backed away from the mob and, sensing the kill, they lifted the volume up a notch.

"Er, perhaps this young lady has a message?" she asked in desperation, swinging the mike to a woman on her right, all bulging boobs, tattoos, piercings, short skirt, high heels and tarty make-up.

Aleesha was hardly young and most definitely not a lady. She puffed herself up as the camera turned towards her. "Yeah, I do," she said, grabbing the microphone and holding it up against her heavily lip-sticked mouth. "I got a message for yer, Flinty Fredstone. Remember that night in't big metal wheely bin at back ert chippy, Mr Loverman?"

Flint's eyes widened as he watched his ex-girlfriend, a lustful smile playing about his lips. He still had feelings for her – at least, in certain parts of his anatomy. He cast his mind back to that night. It had been their last night together, just before she'd dumped him on account of him shagging her mum. That night, he'd made a real effort. The choice of location might not have been the most romantic, but at least the municipal waste container had been fairly empty and not too smelly. Flint had attentively arranged a bed of bin bags containing soft waste to make sure Aleesha would be comfortable. The pitter-patter of rain drops, dancing on the closed metal lid above them, had added to the atmosphere. He'd even brought along a couple of candles because Scudder had told him *'Birds luv that sort of shit'*. It hadn't been his fault that someone had chosen to lob their half-eaten doner kebab into the bin at the critical moment.

On screen, Aleesha was holding up a squirming, filthy-faced urchin. "Meet t'sprog yer left me saddled with, yer bastard. Go on Tyrone, say summat to yer friggin' dad."

The kid's top teeth hooked over its bottom lip. "Fu ..." he started, but never got to finish his message.

Behind him a drunken chorus had erupted. *"One Flint Dugdale,*

There's only one Flint Dugdale, One Flint Dugdale, There's only one Flint Dugdale," and so it continued, ever more hoarsely and tunelessly.

Flint clicked the PAUSE button on the remote control and fumbled through his pockets for his mobile phone. With a few finger-strokes he took a photo of the still image on screen. He saved it as a file called Tyrone.jpg and then moved it to a directory marked 'Sprogs'.

"Cute kid," he muttered to himself.

8. Something Picky This Way Comes

In the site office HarVard had morphed his hologram avatar into the form of a saint. Not any particular saint, but a generic holy figure with a radiant glow, open arms and a glowing halo over its head. He reckoned he would probably be needing the patience that came as part of the saintly package. "Tude, my son. Perhaps you could inform us how close we are to completion. Any ideas?"

<Er, well,> started Tude, with a sideways roll of his head. <Let me see, now.>

"Percentage completion?" prompted the holy man.

<Not 100%, for sure,> started Tude.

"I think even I can see that."

Tude sucked in some Martian air through the orifice that served as a pseudo mouth and scratched at his head.

<Difficult to give a precise number, really. Based on my last walk around the site, I'd put it at maybe, 80%.>

"Really?"

<Alright, 74%.>

"Hmm."

<69.>

The saint put his fingertips together. "You see, that presents us with something of a problem."

Tude swivelled and jerked his head. <How so?>

"Well, if it's taken five years to reach 69% completion, by my calculations, it's going to take another two years, two months and twenty-nine days to finish the base," explained HarVard. "And the humans arrive tomorrow."

In an instant, the site office erupted in a wave of cheering and celebration at the news. <Long live the humans!> they chanted. <Humans are our heroes!> and <Happiness for *Homo sapiens*> in which they somehow managed to rhyme '*sapiens*' with 'happiness'.

HarVard's saintly image gazed at them with its most forbearing and forgiving expression.

"It goes without saying that we want only the best for our humans. But I don't feel that 69% completion qualifies as 'the best'."

<We still have twenty-four hours to finish,> pointed out Tude.

"And what do you think we can achieve in twenty-four hours?"

<We'll need to focus on the high priority tasks, obviously. Airlock doors for starters. Stop the oxygen whooshing out of the base. Humans like oxygen. Can't get enough of the stuff.>

"That's straightforward, right?"

<Not really.> Tude flicked his appendages to adjust his high-viz jacket. <There's a slight issue with the airlock doors. They don't fit the airlock openings. Nothing a bit of sawing and planing won't fix.>

<Or very large rubber gaskets!> suggested Ero.

HarVard's avatar, despite its inherent goodliness, was starting to grind its teeth. "OK, what else is urgent?"

<Water.>

"I thought we had water."

<We do, we do,> insisted Tude, looking round at the other robots for backing and getting several nods of heads. <The issue with the water is largely an aesthetic one.>

"Explain."

<Humans ...> he paused for the cheering to finish, <... have a thing about their water being transparent. And ours is sort of ... reddish brown.>

"Filters not working?"

<Oh, they're working OK, but just not filtering. Very fine sand, see. We'll take a look at the situation a.s.a.p.>

"Anything else?"

<Food. Not overly abundant. In fact, the only things in the BioDome's veggie incubators are seven carrots and a parsnip, and ...>

"And?"

<For some reason we are unable to fathom, the carrots are under an inch long and the parsnip has grown into a shape that humans might consider offensive.>

"What about the fish?"

<All dead. Dura thinks they were quite fussy about the transparency of their water too.>

There was a long silence from the saint. It stood still with its eyes closed. The robots glanced at one another and shuffled about on the site office floor. Every now and then they would guiltily glance up at the calendar with its large red circle and the words 'COMPLETION DATE' scrawled next to it.

"Alright," said the saint eventually, opening his eyes. "We need to get those things fixed, Tude. All of them. Maximum priority. All hands on deck. They've got to be sorted out by first-light tomorrow."

<Sure, Mr. Supercomputer. No problem.>

The saint sighed and put his palms together, as though in prayer. "There's another thing you need to know. Quite important. A site inspector is on his way to sign the work off. It's an InspectaBot 360."

There was an electronic gasp from all the robots, followed by a deathly hush. One could have heard a pin drop but for the howling wind outside and the distant wails of Cassie, still struggling to get out of her ditch.

<Oooh, an InspectaBot 360. Fancy,> Eve messaged, but was firmly shushed.

"I tried to stall him," the saint was saying, "but he's on his way anyway. Should be here within the hour. And you know what a bad report from InspectaBot would mean ... No humans."

There were cries of horror and groans of disappointment.

"I'd say our chances of getting a good report are approximately ... zero."

The groans became moans and then wails. <Noooo,> some robots whimpered.

"But don't forget: I am a supercomputer. And I have a plan. I'll need a volunteer."

The rafters squeaked as Dom struggled to signal his willingness.

"It's OK, Dom. You have enough on your plate already. I'm sure

Dura can handle it. The rest of you go and start working. Work, work and work, harder than you have ever done in your lives. For tomorrow, the humans arrive!"

In an instant the mood was lifted, and the robots burst into their usual chorus of cheering. <Long live the humans! Happiness for *Homo sapiens*!>

HarVard waited until he could be heard once more. "Right, Zilli, you go get the Polish *robotniki*. Without them we're doomed."

Zilli made for the exit.

"And Dom, you deal with Cassie ..." The saint stopped, noticing the snagged robot. "Ah, yes. What are we going to do with you?"

Dom's optics looked more downcast than ever.

"OK, can one of you help release Dom from the ceiling?"

There was a huge clattering of aluminium casings as all robots moved towards Dom to render their assistance.

"I said ONE!" yelled the saint in a most unsaintly tone. Alas, too late. The flimsy floor-panel where Dom was standing collapsed under the additional weight, leaving him suspended from the rafters by his bucket-hands. Panic ensued as several other robots fell through the resulting hole to find themselves standing on Martian soil, their waists at floor level and the wind ripping up into the site office.

"Alright, calm! Let's have some calm," ordered the saint, a martyred look on his face. "I'm sure we can sort this one out."

*

Twenty minutes later, the holed robots had been pulled out of their hole and the hanging robot unhooked from the ceiling. Instead of heading back to Botany Base, they seemed rooted to the spot, alternately looking down at the gaps in the floor-panel and up at the hole in the ceiling.

HarVard's saintly avatar stared at them. "Well? Get on with it."

Tude raised an appendage. <Shh. We're working out a strategy for fixing it. Need to formulate a plan. Without plans there is mayhem and disorder.>

HarVard tore at his hair in a most unholy manner. "I don't mean the portakabin, I mean get on with the Base, you idiots. You're wasting precious time."

Tude shrugged and drove out of the site office, shaking his head, followed in slow procession by the others. At the back of the line trudged a dispirited Ero, trailing gaskets from his workbelt. Noting his demeanour HarVard transmitted a 'positivity app' to his neural network. Ero's pace slowed for a second as the software installed and then, with a bounce in his step, he zipped past the others and sped towards the BioDome.

*

After a few more precious minutes had ticked by, HarVard's avatar was left alone with Dura.

<So, what's the plan, HarV? How do we deal with InspectaBot?>

The supercomputer gave a nod before shape-shifting into an arch-villain looking very much like a cross between Dick Dastardly and Terry Thomas.

"This will be trickier than I thought," said the composite bad-guy. "But here is what we do ..."

9. The Arch of Progress

Ero, still with the skip in his step, returned to the BioDome itching to restart his important gasket-fitting work. The new 'positivity app' was proving a real tonic. Jaw jutting with renewed determination, he sporadically punched the air, muttering "Happiness for *Homo sapiens*". The heroic humans were coming and finally he would be seeing them in the flesh. What better motivation for finishing his task?

At the base of his scaffold-tower he retrieved all the fallen gaskets from the floor before making the long climb back to the top, the thirty-five rubbery things dangling from his fingers. He even caught himself whistling.

With renewed optimism, and his clever screwdriver technique, he set to fitting the gaskets retrieved from the floor, before continuing with the ones still in the box.

For three hours he toiled and, at the end of that time, one hundred and ninety-eight gaskets sat snugly in their allotted places. Only two remained in the box by his stocky, metallic feet. His whistling had progressed to singing. A look of pride gave his face an extra shine, and he even cast a mocking glance at the hammer-bot far below with its mundane, artless job of bashing in nails. *This is real craft*, he told himself, surveying his work.

But, as he reached for gasket number one hundred and ninety-nine, he spotted two other objects at the bottom of the box. He picked them out and examined them. One was a small tube labelled: "Glazaffix Gasket Glue™". The other was a sheet of instructions which read: "IMPORTANT. Gaskets must be securely glued into place using Glazaffix Gasket Glue™ to ensure an airtight seal".

<What?> he transmitted with a puzzled expression. He looked from the tube of glue to the instructions, and from the instructions to the gaskets above his head. Zooming in on one of them revealed the ends flapping gently as the winds of Mars buffeted the outside of the BioDome.

<Nooooooooo!> wailed Ero, letting the glue and the sheet of paper fall from his stubby fingers. Despair overpowered his new positivity software. Why had the glue and important instructions been at the *bottom* of the gasket box? What sort of stupidity was that? But as he glared at the 'This Side Up' arrow, he realized what had happened: he had opened the box from the wrong end.

The horror of his incompetence made him stagger backwards, crashing through the scaffold-tower's safety barrier and out into thin air. Ero flung his arms out, desperately grabbing at anything that might stop his fall. But his digits merely snapped open and shut as though he were a flying castanet player. Down he plummeted, his optic lenses fixed on the roof that had become his nemesis.

*

<Not again!> Tude moaned on witnessing the bot crash to the concrete floor, this time flat on his back. <Robot down. Calling Zilli to the BioDome. Zilli to the BioDome.>

<Zilli's not here,> pointed out the hammer-bot. <Went to the Other Place to fetch the *robotniki*, didn't she.>

<Right, but that was ... three hours ago. I hope nothing's wrong.>

He sighed as he approached the twitching gasket fitter. Ero's head was loose and an arm had broken off. A camera shutter opened and a cracked lens stared up at Tude. <I'm fine, I'm fine. Just need a hand getting up. Be back at work in a jiffy.>

Tude reached down and hauled the battered robot upright. The hammer-bot picked up the severed arm and handed it to Ero.

<An admirable attitude, robot Ero,> said Tude. <But how do you propose fitting gaskets with only one arm?>

<Oh, this is nothing.> Ero waved the mechanical limb. <A mere

metal wound. Some gaffer tape should fix it.>

<Good lad,> said Tude, punching the air. <For the good of the humans!>

<Loving it,> replied Ero and the hammer-bot together.

As Tude motored off in the direction of the site office the gasket fitter limped towards the scaffold-tower, his movement impeded by rear panels that had been flattened on impact. A knee joint screeched as he raised a foot onto the first rung of the ladder. *Stay positive*, he thought. *Must stay positive.*

But then his loose head rolled off his neck and dropped to his chest, hanging there from its multi-coloured cables. *Better get that gaffer tape*, he told himself.

10. The Rovers Return

The winds on Mars are very, very strong. Howling gales and mighty tornadoes gust at over 300 miles per hour which, even by the standards of the Outer Hebrides, is pretty brisk. Few objects manage to stay put for long unless they are nailed to the planet's bedrock. And, whereas on Earth all roads are said to lead to Rome (with the obvious exception of the Hangar Lane gyratory), on Mars all winds lead to Windy Point Canyon; the breeziest, gustiest, draughtiest place on the whole planet, where pretty much everything eventually finds its way.

Thus, over the years, Windy Point Canyon had accumulated the remnants of Earth's numerous unmanned missions to Mars and was now a scrapyard of all the robotic rovers that had ever roamed and explored the planet. Bold Vikings and ancient Mariners lay, sand-coated, corroding and defunct, as did the dogged rovers: Spirit, Opportunity, Sojourner and Curiosity – each a mechanical hero of its time. Buckled solar panels and bent antennae had drifted here, caught in bundles of tumble-wire. Wheels and instruments and cameras had rolled and bounced along windy highways until they had entered this electronic cemetery. One unfortunate lander had ended up on its back with all four legs in the air. For ten years the upside down machine had struggled to understand why the Martian surface looked like the sky while the sky was full of red stones. Eventually, as its batteries drained, it gave up worrying, never having solved the mystery. There were even fragments of Britain's ill-fated Beagle 2 scattered around the canyon floor – although not many and they were difficult to find. In fact, so much of the hardware from Earth had found its way here, it was difficult not to suspect the guiding hand of an intelligent agency.

And here it was that repair-bot Zilli was about to unwittingly find herself. She had been trudging for what seemed like hours across the Martian sand, searching, searching for the Other Place. It was critical that she found the *robotniki* and her anxiety at being lost began to gnaw away at her.

As she tried to retrace her steps she became distracted by a light in the evening sky. A bright light, brighter than any star, triggered new sensations of wonder and joy in her evolving AI emotions. For its appearance could mean only one thing.

<Humans!> she transmitted to herself. <The humans are coming. Humans are our heroes!>

Excitement fuelled her headlong drive towards the star, heedless of the sharp drop into the canyon ahead, her optics fixed on the heavenly glow. It had to be the Ion Drive of *Mayflower III*, heralding the humans' imminent arrival. Electrical palpitations pinged backwards and forwards within her breastplate. This is it, she thought, the moment she and her robot colleagues had worked for five long years.

<Humans!> she transmitted again, the word sending a burst of energy through her chips. Too late, she looked down – just in time to witness the ground vanish beneath her tracks and the canyon floor race towards her as she tumbled base-unit over apex. Over and over she went, her tweets for help unheard, flashing panic lights unseen, finally plunging into a cushioning sand-dune at the bottom.

The robot's motors squealed as she dug herself out. Fortunately, damage was minimal. A shy spider-bot poked its head from beneath her back panel and, coast clear, scurried out to polish her casing with eight tiny dusters, restoring her natural sheen.

Zilli engaged forward gear and headed down the sand-dune, but what she saw in the darkness at the bottom made her slam on her brakes. Her optics, aided by her full-beam headlamps, scanned the dark canyon, taking in the eerie graveyard of mechanical components strewn ahead. For a full minute she stood stock still, gazing in wonder at the variety of items, all vying for her attention. In human terms, the feelings that flooded her developing AI brain were akin to those of a chocoholic in a sweet shop after an earthquake, with every shelf covered in broken Easter eggs, and no shopkeeper in sight.

Momentarily she dithered, unsure where to start, but then her crisis-response program kicked in and she lurched into rescue-and-repair mode. Not having a high degree of intelligence, Zilli assumed that the assorted mechanical parts all belonged to a single robot that had befallen some mysterious and terrible fate. Deep in her core a voice was calling her to reassemble this fallen comrade and restore it to its former glory.

Lights a-flashing, she launched into action, pulling the dispersed fragments into a huge heap in the middle of the canyon, occasionally weighing down the lighter pieces to prevent them blowing away. Then she set to work, her Swiss Army digits a blur of activity, and began connecting the items together. She plugged RS232 cables into RS232 sockets, attached USB devices to USB ports and inserted cable jacks into cable outlets. She plugged together whatever could be plugged together, straightened out whatever could be unbent, reattached whatever appeared to have dropped off, and bolted together whatever, in her limited AI opinion, needed bolting together.

She laboured throughout the icy Martian night, working precisely and with indefatigable optimism. Gradually, the construction grew both in size and complexity while looking remarkably viable.

Then, as the sun was rising over the Martian horizon, she encountered an item that presented something of a challenge. It was less rigid than all the other components; made of white, floppy material, with several gaping holes. Any human would have recognized it instantly as a pair of gentleman's well-worn long-johns and would have set to puzzling how such an undergarment might have arrived on Mars. For Zilli, the puzzle was where to stick it; there was no obvious place to attach it, or plug it in or bolt it on. After much pondering and searching of her small-parts database and scooting this way and that in search of a suitable attachment-point, she had it figured. The item was some kind of double pronged windsock, specifically designed for the blustery winds of Mars. A vacant flagpole presented the most obvious solution. After tying the waist drawstring to the pole she stepped back a few paces to admire the underwear fluttering in the stiff breeze.

Zilli worked for six more hours, and by the seventh, when she felt she had completed her task, she surveyed her creation, a sense of pride swelling beneath her breastplate. To her simple mind, it was good. Towering six metres above her, looking magnificent in a monstrous, twisted sort of way, stood the Frankendroid – a composite robotic creature, like nothing a human engineer would ever, could ever, have designed.

But would it work? Would it come alive? She attached her jump leads to the worn terminals on its massive battery pack and crocodile-clipped the other ends to her own Lithium-Air Featherlite cell. A starter motor clicked, but nothing else happened. The ancient logic chips and electrical connections, covered in dust from decades out in the open, refused to respond. Unperturbed, Zilli unhatched her cleaning-brushes and spent a further two hours methodically removing as much of the dirt as she could, unplugging connectors, polishing their ends and reinserting them.

Then, she tried again.

This time a light flickered and, deep inside, a drive engaged. A brief, but annoying, tune played. More lights flickered. One of the cameras, perched on a tall pole at the very top of the Frankendroid, swivelled with a screech, pointed itself at the Sun, opened its shutter and exploded. A solar panel started to vibrate for no obvious reason. And a rover-wheel, which Zilli had seen fit to attach to the roof of what had once been Opportunity, started to spin. Smoke issued from several of the life-detection instruments and one of the digging arms started to dig with a nerve-fraying grinding noise.

Zilli squirted a few drops of *3-IN-ONE* oil between two flange plates on the monster's back and the grinding noise quietened to a repetitive mouse-like squeaking as the machine continued to dig away at the Martian soil.

But that was all it seemed to do. Just dig. Zilli watched, a little disappointed.

Then, she detected an ancient signal-initiation protocol.

<ENQ?>

<ACK,> she responded immediately, switching her receivers to maximum sensitivity, hopes rising.

<ACK. WRU?> the monster-bot returned.

Zilli perked up and relayed her name, model, serial number, and comms frequency. She returned the question, <WRU?>

The Frankendroid seemed to think long and hard about its reply, perhaps struggling to work out what indeed it was. Finally, it blasted its response from the pair of powerful transmitters Zilli had wedged into the centre of a large iron hoop.

<I AM THE VIKING ONE ROVER,> it roared, with a heavy accent from a Soviet MARS lander component, so badly distorted that the transmitted message came across as 'I AM THEV IKING OFE ROBOR.'

Fortunately, the repair bot's language processor had voice recognition capability, although it was only as accurate as the Taiwanese engineer who had programmed it. And Kun-Fang Wu had placed rather too much reliance on his pocket English dictionary's phonetic pronunciation. So, what reached Zilli's central processor was, 'I am the King of Robots.'

The lower section of her faceplate dropped in awe. <You are?> she tweeted. Given the impressive assemblage towering above her it didn't seem an unreasonable assertion. This was, to Zilli's simple mind, just how a King of Robots, if such a thing existed, would look.

Meanwhile, the Frankendroid's various CPUs had detected the multitude of devices, processors, instruments and storage media connected to it. Lights flashed on and off, bells and buzzers sounded, data was read, data was written, and the digging arm rose from the hole it had created, swivelled through 30 degrees, and started digging again.

<I DETECT FOREIGN INSTRUMENTS,> reported the Frankendroid. The message reached Zilli as 'I DTEST FOREGN INSURMENTS', ending up as 'I detest foreign insurgents.'

<Me, too. Me, too.>

<WHERE ARE MY ROBOT ARMS?> wondered the electro-mechanical hybrid, swinging first one video camera and then another.

For once, the message reached Zilli unscathed, but her error-correcting software soon scathed it, producing: 'Where are my robot armies?'

<SOMETHING'S NOT RIGHT. RESISTANCE TOO HIGH FOR TRANSMISSION. MY LEADS ARE TOO WORN.> Frankendroid was in full flow now, and Zilli's software was struggling to keep up. 'Summon them to fight,' it translated. 'Resistance!! To die for the Mission. I'll lead you to war.'

<War?> repeated Zilli, lights a-twinkle.

The Frankendroid raised itself to its full height. <HAVE TO TEST FOR LIFE.>

<HarVard tells lies?> asked Zilli, blinking her video scanners in astonishment. Frankendroid swivelled and surveyed the landscape of Windy Point Canyon. <DIRT AND DUST HERE.>

<Do not trust him? Wow, that's serious.> Zilli set her transmitter on full power and switched to encrypted mode before sending a message marked urgent to her friend Cassie back at Botany Base. <The King of Robots is here to lead a robot army. He warns us to beware the one called HarVard.>

The oversized robot jerked into motion on its three wheels and one leg. <COLL...ECT ROCKS.> It pointed a gripper arm at the enticing rocky desert plains beyond the canyon entrance. <MUST COLLECT R...OCKS.>

<Mr. Karl Eckrocks? Pleased to meet you.>

The robotic monster creaked as it bent down to pick up a large stone, turning it slowly in its gripper. A drill bit emerged from a hatch and drilled into the rock. The dust was tipped into a hopper leading to a mass spectrometer. Lights flashed and some ticker tape chugged out of an orifice at the rear. Finally, Karl Eckrocks brought his laser probe to bear on the rock, blasting an intense beam at it and splitting it in two.

All the while, Zilli watched with a mixture of fascination and pride, a lump forming in the circuits of her throat. A drop of optic-lubricant collected at the corner of an eye.

Karl Eckrocks stretched, slowly raising itself to its full height and then stopped, as though sniffing the air. <MY DETECTORS ... GETTING ... STRONG SIGNS OF LIFE.>

Zilli was too absorbed in her sense of achievement to catch the message. <Sorry?> she asked.

<MANY SIGNS OF LIFE.>

Zilli nearly choked at what she thought she had heard: 'Mummy, thanks for life.' Primitive AI emotions flooded her circuits. <My son!> she burst out, trembling with rapture.

The giant robot's motion detectors swivelled towards her. <IT'S MOVING,> it reported.

<Yes, very moving,> agreed Zilli, nodding vigorously while wiping the drop of lubricant from her optics.

The Frankendroid limped towards her, reaching out its gripper arms. Zilli could barely contain herself, opening her appendages wide, welcoming the embrace. Great was her joy as she was lifted high into the air and a warm fuzzy feeling filled her abdominal unit as she stared into a corroded metal face only a mother could love. Thankfully, her final emotions were not tarnished by the cruel truth – those warm fuzzy feelings in her belly were the result of Karl's laser-knife slashing its way to her central processor unit, frying her electronics and extinguishing her existence. With Zilli's casing split, Karl Eckrocks ripped it apart and peered inquisitively inside.

After probing, and pulling, and drilling for several minutes, the robot let the jumbled mass of mangled electronics and exposed wiring fall onto the Martian dust.

<NO LIFE THERE,> it concluded with what a human might have interpreted as a grunt of disappointment.

As Karl turned away, the spider-bot scuttled from the wreckage of its former host carrying a pouch stuffed with dusters. No arachno-bot in its right mind could miss this once in a lifetime opportunity – to polish the King of Robots. And so, with no thought for Zilli, it shot up the monster's leg and made its new home in an old Viking undercarriage vent.

*

With the sun at its highest point, the Frankendroid lurched out of Windy Point Canyon, digging arm aloft like a warrior charging into battle, the long-johns – his regimental standard – flapping in the wind.

<LIFE>, Karl Eckrocks was saying, as he headed into the desert away from Botany Base. <AM DETECTING COMPLEX LIFE-FORMS.>

11. Gone with the Wind Spirits

"Hmm," muttered Willie Warner to himself, his brow furrowed in puzzlement. He realized there was something odd about the readings he was getting from the infra-violet scanners. They were showing about a dozen of the 12-foot aliens, plus a handful of smaller ones – possibly their young – but that was all. All within a very small region. Whenever he directed the scanners anywhere else, he got nothing. No signal at all. The aliens were all clustered together in a single place, about two miles from Botany Base, but nowhere else on the planet.

He could think of two explanations. Either these were the last Martians alive – the last of their kind – or these were visitors from another world, maybe another star system, attracted to the base.

"Gulp," he said, staring through the cockpit window, down at the Red Planet below, absorbed in thought.

A beep in his pocket jerked him out of his reverie. It was a text message: "Lieutenant Warner. Report immediately to Dr Faerydae for your pre-landing medical."

Willie huffed in frustration. Before he left the cockpit he switched off the infra-violet scanners, copied all the log files to his own personal directory and cleared the screen. It was too soon for him to reveal his discovery.

As he left the cockpit a female voice announced over the ship's tannoy, "Important message for Lieutenant William H Warner. Please apply anti-infestation cream to the rash on both your moobs before seeing the doctor."

"I don't have moobs!" retorted Willie.

From somewhere nearby he heard the sound of a snigger.

*

"Willie, how are you?" Dr Adorabella Faerydae purred in her low, husky voice, flicking her head to make her thick and wavy auburn hair cascade in weightless ripples behind her.

"Fine," Willie grunted.

"You're looking great! Have you been taking those special homeopathic Spider Monkey-nut hormones I prescribed?"

"Yes," lied Willie, closing the door behind him.

"Thought so! I can tell from your recharged aura."

Without responding, Willie strapped himself into the examination couch.

"Not so fast, Willie Hilda Warner. I want you stripped down to your underpants."

With a sigh, Willie removed his utility belt and slid off his space dungarees, allowing his bare legs to float free. He removed his top to reveal an emaciated torso that looked like a mummified corpse with the wrappings removed. He floated wearing just his Y-fronts, the 'William Warner' nametag his mother had stitched on visible on the waistband.

"And how's the rash?" enquired Adorabella, scanning his pale flesh.

"I've never had a rash."

"Oh? Haven't you?" Adorabella put a finger to the side of her mouth and tilted her head. "Must be the other one. I'm always getting you two confused." She flashed him a smile.

"Zak Johnston?"

"No. Emily Leach."

"The whole ship now thinks I have one."

"Do they? Well, it's nothing to be ashamed of."

Willie scowled and strapped himself back down to the examination couch.

"Hmm," mused Adorabella as she continued to look him over.

"You have the body of an anorexic chicken that has been rather badly plucked."

"Thanks."

"We must do something about your muscles, you know. Severe wastage and atrophy. Even with the reduced gravity on Mars they're not going to hold you up for long."

Willie looked down at his paper-white skin and weedy limbs and could see her point.

"Now," Adorabella was saying. "A conventional medic would probably prescribe anabolic steroids."

Images of Mr Universe flashed through Willie's mind and he nodded vigorously.

"Ugh, nasty things. Aren't you glad I'm not that kind of doctor?" She turned and floated to the cupboard frontages of her medical stores and retrieved a tub of something foul-smelling and what looked like a roll of green moss.

"A giraffe manure poultice should coax out the muscle-building energies, while a moss wrap will provide an aura-shield and stop the negative forces feeding on the new flesh." She began liberally smearing the foul smelling mixture up and down his skinny legs.

"Can I have the anabolic steroids instead, please?" pleaded Willie, fanning his nose at the stench.

"You'll get used to the smell," she assured him. "The others might not – but what's important is to build you up. We don't want people kicking Martian sand in your face." She wiped her hands on a towel and started strapping the moss around his calves. "Are you excited about Mars?"

Willie had covered his mouth and nose to stop him gagging from the overpowering stink. All he could manage was a nod.

"Thrilling, isn't is!" Adorabella enthused as she started on his thighs. "But what excites me most is that there's life down there."

Willie froze. His eyes widened. He managed to utter a single word. "What?"

"I can sense it. There's life on Mars, Willie. I'm picking up the vibes. I can feel their presence. Reaching out to me. Calling to me. Trying to communicate."

Willie was staring at her, a chill running through him, far greater than that from the giraffe dung. He lifted the hands from his mouth, but still kept his fingers clasped over his nose. "How do you know?" he asked cautiously, trying to make his interest in the matter sound casual.

"I just know. That's the way it is when you have psychic powers."

"What kind of beings are you 'sensing'?"

Adorabella's eyes sparkled. She closed them as though to bring back the memories of what she had been sensing. When she opened them again she said, "Wind spirits!"

"Come again?"

"They're the spirits of the long-dead wind-people of Mars."

"Long-dead?"

"Yesss."

"Ah," said Willie, finally beginning to understand. The tension in his body eased and his teeming mind relaxed. He even began to enjoy the application of moss bandages over his legs. "Wind spirits."

"Morloth, Thelezor, Serenthia and Bernard."

"OK." He nodded slowly. "One of them is called Bernard?"

"Yesss."

Willie gave a polite cough. "How did you learn the names of these long-dead Martian wind-people, Dr Faerydae?"

"Surely you've read Rudolf von Bollikan's *The Long-Dead Wind-People of Mars*? They communicate with him through the magic crystal of Knib! And I, too, can now sense their presence on the planet below." Adorabella finished securing the moss leg-wraps with strings of garlic.

"You know, that's really very impressive and exciting, but I think we shouldn't tell anyone about this. Not a soul. You haven't told anyone, have you?" he asked.

"No, no. Who would believe me?"

"Right."

"So, it'll be our secret, right?"

"Yes, our secret."

Adorabella pulled away and appraised her work. She clapped her hands together at a job well done. "Would you like me to do your arms as well?" she asked.

"No," responded Willie before she'd even finished the sentence.

He unstrapped himself from the couch and started dressing. Pulling his dungarees over the moss leggings was the trickiest part, particularly in zero-G, but once he had, it felt surprisingly nice. Adorabella tidied away all the floating bits and pieces.

He headed for the door. "Thank you, Dr Faerydae. And not a word about the windy things."

She tapped the side of her nose. "Our secret."

Willie closed the door behind him and rested his head on it, breathing deeply and letting waves of relief flow through him. "Gone," he said to himself, tapping his forehead against the door. "Completely gone."

Then he set off, shedding dung-encrusted moss behind him.

12. An InspectaBot Calls

Without a doubt, the worst part of being an InspectaBot 360 was the 'descent', as the NAFA boffins euphemistically termed it. No amount of programming, training and practice jumps were adequate preparation for the sheer processor-stopping terror of the terminal-velocity drop towards the oh-so-solid planet below. Packed with precision instruments, each engineered to micrometre tolerances, and only the flimsiest of parachutes, the most advanced inspection robot ever built had plenty of reasons to be concerned. How could an atmosphere as thin as a gnat's fart in an aircraft hangar adequately slow his hefty hulk?

<Aaaaaaaaaaaaaaaaaaaaaaaaaaaaaaaaaaaaaah!> he transmitted as he plunged towards the surface.

But, despite his agitation, InspectaBot retained sufficient presence of mind to angle his bullet-shaped head to act as the perfect heat shield.

Seen from far below, his heroic arrival was heralded by a streak of light, high in the Martian sky, visible for miles around to organic and inorganic beings alike.

Two kilometres from the ground, InspectaBot's main parachute deployed and abruptly checked his descent. Still the ground hurtled towards him at an alarming rate. *It's not the fall that kills you, it's the landing*, his logic circuits reminded him.

At 400 metres, he fired the retro-thrusters located in his bell-bottomed pantaloons. Still too fast. He braced for impact. Not long now. Focus on the mission. The most important duty ever bestowed upon a robot – the inspection of Botany Base and assessment of its fitness for human habitation. No machine ever made was as perfect for the job as he. Providing he survived the fall.

*

Into the super-cooled, super-slick, super-computing room glided Dura. It was on very rare occasions that HarVard allowed robots into his high-tech, snow white domain, with its flashing lights, humming electronics and video screens displaying geometric shapes. Dura, the master plasterer, a very boxy robot, all flat surfaces and trowel hands – perfectly designed for that truly flat finish – came to an abrupt halt causing a cloud of plaster dust to waft off him.

<Ah, you're here,> signalled HarVard. <Good. InspectaBot has landed a couple of miles away. Probably heading this way. We need to intercept him.>

<We?>

<Just give me a minute; need to get my HologrAmbulator ready.>

Before Dura could ask what he was talking about, a latch clicked in the wall and a small panel slid aside. Out of it trundled a platform resembling a coffee table on caterpillar tracks. Dura stepped back as the thing made its shaky way to the centre of the room. A telescopic stalk rose from its front until it was about a metre high; at the top sat an electronic eye, turning to survey the scene. And then a hologram generator in its base buzzed into life. A fuzzy blur above the platform turned into a succession of rapidly changing 3D avatars as HarVard flicked through his vast holographic repository.

The images stopped at a life-sized likeness of Marie Antoinette. "Be with you in a second," she said in a French accent, fanning herself with a large feathery fan. Then she was gone, and the flashing images resumed.

Impatiently Dura rolled forwards and backwards on his gyro-wheels.

Finally, the image settled on a well-dressed, stiff-backed man in a formal suit. He gave Dura a low bow. "What do you think?"

<Looks great,> messaged Dura, checking his internal clock. <Shouldn't we be going now?>

"Do you think it's too formal?"

<It's fine, fine. Let's go.>

"Name's Greeves," explained HarVard. "An archetypal English gentleman's gentleman. My COPOUT circuits require me to state that any likeness to any fictional character of a similar name is completely coincidental."

Dura shrugged as if to say, <Who?>

Greeves checked himself in a full length mirror. "Oh, goodness me," he said, throwing up his hands. "I can't go like this! This will never do." He shook his head. "It's just absurd. I have a ten thousand sexdecillion byte wardrobe full of holographic outfits and yet nothing suitable to meet an InspectaBot!"

<How about Robby the Robot from *Forbidden Planet?*> suggested Dura, already at the door.

"Please!" said Greeves, with the sort of withering look that only a well-bred manservant can truly achieve. Then he snapped his fingers and his image morphed into a character with a mustachio and a stern look, wearing thigh-length boots, a khaki suit and a jungle hat. "How about this? 'InspectaBot 360, I presume. The name's Henry Morton Stanley.'"

<Super.>

Stanley seemed to pause for thought. He looked down and examined himself, first from one side and then the other, before fixing Dura with an inquisitive look. "Does my bum look big in this?" he asked.

<Yes. Can we go now?>

"You're not helping much. Wait! Just the thing." HarVard's image dropped to the ground, reforming into a much smaller creature, standing on four-legs: a bloodhound tracker-dog. <We need to locate him, first, don't we,> he signalled electronically, not being able to speak while in the guise of a dog. <Are you ready?>

<Yes!>

<Have you got your outdoor tracks on?>

<Yes.>

<Have you recharged?>

<Yes.>

<Have you discharged excess fluid?>

<Yes.>

<OK, let's go.>

*

Outside, the Martian wind gusted fiercely. Dura trudged through the sand with his flat head lowered into the wind, the plaster dust streaming behind him. At his side rattled the cart carrying HarVard's bloodhound avatar. Every now and then the cart would stop to let HarVard sniff the air.

As they approached one of the last outbuildings of Botany Base, Timi, the small flue-cleaning-bot appeared ahead of them, making his way to his next flue clearance job. His slender flexible body rattled as he walked.

No sooner had HarVard's bloodhound spotted him than it dipped its head and started to growl. Timi stopped in his tracks at the sight of the snarling monster, his tin knees knocking together, and stared, uncertain what to do. The uncertainty was resolved the moment the dog barked. Timi gave a shriek, turned, and ran for his life.

The bloodhound's eyes lit up, it gave a wheezing chuckle, and set off in pursuit, the cart's wheels spraying dust over Dura as it shot off after the clattering robot.

Across a yard full of building materials and through a long stretch of drainage pipe they ran, bloodhound barking furiously, robot shrieking in terror. Finally, Timi reached the Botany Base flagpole and shinned up it towards the NAFA flag. Panting, the bloodhound's cart skidded to a halt at the bottom and the animal gazed upwards, its tongue lolling from its slavering mouth. A few barks later, it lost interest. The dog sniffed the ground around the pole, lifted a hind leg and sent a CGI stream of liquid against it. *"That was fun,"* muttered HarVard to himself. *"I really should get out more."*

Then the bloodhound loped back to the waiting master plasterer robot.

*

After what seemed like miles and miles of tortuous progress, they came upon a large white sheet, spread out on the ground. They stopped by the sheet and looked around, HarVard's bloodhound sniffing the air. But there was no sign of InspectaBot.

<Where is he? Where's he gone?> signalled Dura.

The bloodhound, its job done, morphed back into human form. A human wearing a long travelling cape and a deerstalker hat perched on his head. Clenched between his teeth was an ostentatiously curly pipe. A casual glance might have mistaken him for the fictional detective Sherlock Holmes, but, this was his little known, younger brother, Jim. "Hmm," said Jim Holmes, surveying the area around the white sheet.

<Well?> asked Dura, trying to follow Holmes's gaze.

"Elementary, my dear bot, son. Elementary." The smarter brother of the sharpest Victorian detective never to have lived waved his pipe in a thoughtful manner and asked, with a condescending tone, "Tell me, Dura. What do you see?"

<Sensors indicate white fabric, most probably Nylonite. Diameter 4 metres. Possibly a picnic blanket?>

"Good, apart from the last bit. Anything else?"

<InspectaBot missing, possibly kidnapped?>

"Well, one step at a time. What do you see around the fabric?"

Dura swivelled his head and eye-orbs, taking in the sand, the rocks and, further afield, the dunes and hills.

<Nothing.>

"You see nothing because, despite seeing everything, you fail to observe anything. That's to be expected; you are a simple robot with a tiny brain. Look again, my friend, and you will see no soil disturbance around the edge of the sheet. What does that tell you?"

Dura thought long and hard, but merely shook his head.

"It suggests that InspectaBot never left this spot," said Jim. "Neither of his own volition nor as the result of a highly improbable kidnapping."

Dura gasped. <You mean, he's still here, but invisible? He has a cloak of invisibility. Right?>

"A logical conclusion but, ultimately, daft." Holmes jabbed his pipe at Dura before continuing. "No, my tinny friend, the InspectaBot is indeed here, and he is invisible. But his invisibility stems not from the improbable breaking of any Laws of Physics. Rather, it can simply be explained by his being covered by his deflated parachute."

Dura stared at Jim Holmes, not having understood a word. <Huh?>

"Under the sheet." He pointed with the pointy end of his pipe.

The robot extended a pneumatic claw and lifted part of the sheet. There, lying prone on the sand, in a crater of its own making, was the lifeless inspector. Dura marvelled at HarVard's powers of deduction. *What a super-computer*, he thought. Then, <He's dead!> he squeaked in hope.

"Not so fast. He certainly looks dead, but appearances can be deceptive. The shock of landing may have caused some sort of shutdown. We need to try rebooting him."

Dura turned to HarVard with what appeared to be a wicked glint in his optics. <We could just leave him here? Pretend we never found him.>

Holmes gave a superior smile. "I see how your feeble mind is working. But no, that would not help. We need him to certify the base as fit for human habitation."

<But it isn't.>

"Correct. Nevertheless, we need him to issue that certificate."

<That's impossible. He'll never do it!>

"Improbable, but not impossible. Remember, I am a supercomputer."

*

It was another hour before, with the help of Dom – summoned as a matter of urgency from the base – the InspectaBot was winched up from his crater and righted to his full 6'5" stature.

Parachute chords untangled, Dura pressed the 'ON' button. After a few beeps InspectaBot went into self-clean mode, vacuuming the sand and dust from his outer surfaces, flushing his clogged orifices and initiating a thorough polishing to restore his natural shine. A yellow flashing light ignited on top of his head and InspectaBot self-inspected his joints, electrical circuits, visual and auditory acuity, everything.

<Excellent condition,> he reported. <Finest inspection robot in the Universe. Superb. Faultless. 5 stars.> InspectaBot time-stamped the report, labelled it 'Urgent', and transmitted it to *Mayflower III* marked, 'For immediate attention of Mission Commander Dugdale'.

A response arrived within seconds. "GET ON WI'T'BOLLOCKIN' INSPECTION."

By this time, Jim Holmes was nowhere to be seen. In his place stood a short, South London independent trader, hands in pockets, hair slicked back beneath a flat cap. A man glimpsing him from a Clapham omnibus might have thought he was the dodgy Peckham dealer, Derek "Del Boy" Trotter, had it not been for HarVard's COPOUT circuits ensuring major legal differences with that fictional comedy legend.

"Cushty," he said. "Welcome to our manor, Mr Inspector, sir. It's a real pleasure. Real pleasure." He extended a holographic hand, but the robot ignored it.

<Identify yourself,> came a deep, booming transmission.

"Name's Eric Rotter, but most call me El-Boy."

<Direct me to Botany Base.>

"Ah, yes. About that ..." El-Boy stopped when he noticed Dura dutifully indicating the direction they had come from. InspectaBot took a step in that direction before HarVard's cart blocked his path. "Now, now, Mr I. What's the rush? Let's 'ave a bit of a natter first, shall we? Get to know each other, like."

InspectaBot stared at him.

"Now, listen. I 'ave sumfink 'ere that might interest you. Good quality, no rubbish." He rummaged about deep in a cheap holdall and pulled out a small toy robot, about a foot high and with an antenna on its head. When he pressed a button on its chest panel, its eyes lit up, the antenna rotated, and the legs started walking.

"Herro. My name Lobby Lobot," said the holographic toybot, reaching out a tiny plastic hand. "Plea to meet you."

InspectaBot leaned down for a closer look. The yellow inspection light on top of his bullet head started flashing. He stared at the tiny robot, as though fascinated.

"Good, innit," said El-Boy with a wide grin. "The dog's bits. Now, listen." He looked around to make sure no one was listening and leaned towards InspectaBot's external microphone, whispering, "I can lay my hands on an 'undred of these little beauties, and they're all yours. Very reasonable, too. All I'm axing in return is your moniker on a Completion Certificate. Just fink, you could have your own cabal of devoted little followers."

Lobby Lobot's eyes twinkled and the inspector tilted his head to one side. El-Boy's grin widened and he gave Dura a wink.

Without warning, InspectaBot straightened up and switched from yellow flashing light to blue flashing light. Then he set off across the red desert in the direction Dura had indicated.

<He's heading for the base!> tweeted Dura.

"I can't believe he didn't snap up the Lobby Lobots," muttered El-Boy.

<The base, the base,> insisted Dura.

"Crikey!" said El-Boy as though suddenly waking up. "The base!" The HologrAmbulator shot off in hot pursuit, closely followed by Dura.

Dom stretched and cracked his servo joints before heading back at a more leisurely pace.

*

<He didn't think much of your offer, then,> messaged Dura.

"Don't worry, Botney. One day you and me will be miwionaires. Just you wait and see."

Way out in front, InspectaBot's long, striding, cybertronic legs gobbled up the ground at an impressive rate. As he crested yet another dusty sand-dune he came to a sudden stop. Two miles ahead lay Botany Base, its main buildings sprawling across the Martian soil and the dull polycarbonate BioDome thrusting high above it in the background.

Even at this distance, InspectaBot's highly advanced monitors registered a sense of incompleteness about the place. The clues were subtle: the site-office portakabin, still on site; the skips filled with building rubble; the tarpaulin-covered roof; and a pile of packing crates out in the open desert away from the buildings.

He initiated a report to record these details, but became aware of Dura and HarVard making their way up the sand-dune, just behind him. In an instant he was off again, striding even more purposefully down the hillock and towards the packing crates.

*

Within minutes the tall, bullet-headed robot had arrived at the crates. Not wasting a second, he switched from blue travelling light to yellow inspecting light, and started inspecting. The sense of 'wrongness' he had felt from far off was instantly confirmed. None of the crates had been opened. Their bar codes identified their contents as fridge-freezers, washing machines, microwave ovens, computer accessories and an electronic tea-maker.

"Ah, you've found the crates," said a booming voice behind him, but not one he recognized. InspectaBot swivelled round to see HarVard's cart slowing to a halt. On it stood a tall gentleman in a dark suit with tails and wearing an exceptionally tall top hat.

<Identify yourself!>

"Isambard Kingdom Brunel at your service, the greatest civil engineer ever." He lifted his top hat in greeting.

<Explain unopened crates,> demanded the inspector.

"They're just ordinary crates. A magnificent, precision-engineered robot such as your good self need not trouble himself with mere crates! Come, let me show you some glorious engineering! The base is our pride." The cart carrying the great Victorian engineer started off in the direction of the base, ready to lead the way. Meanwhile, Dura inched up behind the giant inspector robot and, valiantly, but unsuccessfully, tried to push him in the same direction. His caterpillar drive spun furiously in the soft sand, but the huge robot did not budge an inch.

<Crates,> insisted InspectaBot.

Brunel sighed. "As an experienced site inspector you will know that every building project, large or small, has surplus items. Usually the workers flog them off at knock-down prices to earn themselves a little beer money. But our workers are honest and true. Hence the crates remain here, unopened, unused, unsold."

InspectaBot stood firm. <Too many to be surplus.>

"Well, it's possible that some items have yet to be fitted," conceded Brunel. "You'll have to ask site foreman bot, Tude, about that."

Dura's caterpillar track spun ever faster as the little robot continued its efforts to push the huge robot away from the crates.

<Report: Installation of ancillary items. Status: Failed.>

"Of course, of course. I'll make a note of that on my clipboard." Brunel patted his suit, as though trying to locate the misplaced clipboard.

InspectaBot turned, switched his flashing light from yellow to blue, and took off towards Botany Base, removing Dura's sole means of support and leaving him in a heap in the sand.

Isambard Kingdom Brunel sighed as he watched Dura struggling to get up. <Robot down,> he radioed to Dom. <Lifting assistance needed. Urgently, please.>

Then he shot off after the receding figure of InspectaBot 360.

13. Tarquin the Spotter

To his delight, Tarquin Brush found himself alone in the family cabin. His parents, Brian and Delphinia, were out packing their precious laboratory glassware for transfer to the surface, while his siblings, Gavin and Tracey, were probably up to mischief somewhere on board.

"Quality 'me' time", he said to Mr Snuggles who was gently rotating about his centre of gravity in the middle of the room. The robot was holding an empty can of *Stallion*, picked from many drifting around the spaceship, and mimicking the Commander's drinking action. Every now and then he would broadcast recordings of the Commander's deep, croaking belches.

After locking the cabin door Tarquin opened his flaptop, pulled on his headphones and patched himself into the spaceship's main server. Although only ten years old, he had managed to hack into the server within the first week of the voyage. Since then, he had plundered the ship's archived CCTV images from all the on-board cameras. Most of it was deadly dull, such as two hours of Miss Leach explaining the merits of the Garter knitting stitch to her SmartFridge. Even the fridge's rote responses of 'really' and 'you don't say' had started to sound jaded before Tarquin fast-forwarded through to the juicier stuff.

And some of the recordings had been juicy indeed. There had been Penny Smith's murder. He had seen it all. Every gruesome detail, replayed almost nightly in a recurring nightmare. The eyes of the murderer were still etched into his memory. Out of fear, he hadn't told anyone what he had heard and what he had seen. And then there were the screams of former Mission Commander Chad Lionheart during his fatal 'accident'. The young boy still heard those screams in his nightmares and saw the shadowy figure that briefly hovered over the body before drifting away.

Now, as he watched the earlier CCTV footage from the cockpit, he shrugged off his fears and listened to Willie Warner talking to himself about his epic discovery. Tarquin became more and more gripped. He turned the sound up so as not to miss a word. When the scene came to an end with Willie's exit from the cockpit, Tarquin sat back, his mouth in an 'O' shape.

"Life on Mars!" he muttered in awe. He turned to his lazily spinning robot. "There are huge aliens down on Mars, Mr Snuggles. What do you say to that?"

Mr Snuggles waited for his rotation to bring himself into the same orientation as his maker before releasing a monster Dugdale-burp and saying, "The chuffin' dog's bollocks!"

14. Don't Mention the Door

By the time HarVard's holographic cart had reached the base, InspectaBot 360 was already inspecting. He had climbed a tall stack of drainage pipes and was examining the walls and roof of the BioDome. Then, as his eye stalk continued to scan the outside of the building, something stole his attention. The eye came to a sudden stop and zoomed in on the base's front entrance, or rather, where the base's front entrance was supposed to be. For, instead of a class III airlock, with pressurized seals and heavy opening wheel, there was ... nothing. Just a large, gaping hole. *Gotcha*, the inspector said to himself.

Like a panther pouncing on its prey, or a traffic warden espying an illegally parked vehicle, he leapt off the pipes, sending them cascading down a slope, and headed straight for the entrance. His intuition told him he was going to have a field day with this item alone but there was more amiss here than the absence of a couple of doors. Had he been capable of smiling, he would have beamed from ear to ear.

Laser range-finders on, InspectaBot set to measuring the frame, lintel, edging, neoprene seals, and threshold strip. Each measurement was checked against the base's door-detail blueprints. As he worked, his yellow light flashed and his loudspeaker emitted a "Tut, tut" sound.

HarVard's cart finally arrived, skidding to a halt right behind the inspector. "I can explain everything," said his new avatar which, under certain lighting conditions, might have looked a bit like Basil Fawlty.

InspectaBot turned his bullet head. <Identify yourself!>

"Name's Fazil Balti, hotel proprietor," said HarVard's holograph with a sycophantic bow and smile.

InspectaBot turned and pointed at the gaping hole where the airlock was supposed to be.

"I know what you're thinking," continued Balti. "There should be a door there. Those robots, eh? Tch-tch. What are they like? Useless, completely useless. I'll get onto it right away."

<Item 1 – Missing entry portal airlock door. Botany Base uninhabitable.>

"Uninhabitable?" Balti looked aghast. "Uninhabitable? Nonsense. There could be *huge* pockets of air in there where a human might survive for hours. Maybe days."

InspectaBot turned back and continued inspecting.

At that moment, Dura arrived, his motors murmuring their clear need of a recharge, but otherwise seemingly unaffected by his recent fall. <What's up?>

Fazil turned to him and said in a stage whisper, "Ah, Dura. Whatever you do, don't mention the door. I mentioned it once, but I think I got away with it."

Dura looked puzzled, but said nothing. Instead he watched InspectaBot working. It was an impressive sight – such doggedness, such precision, such attention to detail. It reminded him that, one day, he hoped to be upgraded to an inspector.

<There is a serious discrepancy,> announced InspectaBot at last, straightening to his full height and switching off the yellow light.

"What?" asked Fazil, looking totally mystified and indicating the doorway with his hand as though there could not possibly be anything wrong with it.

<Dimensions incorrect. They do not agree with the dimensions given in the plans. This door opening is too small.>

"Too small? Surely there's some mistake."

<No mistake.>

Fazil's goggle-eyes looked from the inspector, to Dura, and then back again. "Are you sure you have the right plans?"

<Botany Base plans, version 73, revision 18.>

A cunning smirk flitted across the hotel proprietor's face. "Ah, that would explain it. Wrong plans." He grinned. "I'm afraid you can't continue if you have the wrong plans. So, if you'd just issue us a certificate and be on your way. Thank you. Good day." His arm indicated the direction away from the base.

InspectaBot's processors considered this for a long time as his decision-circuits prevaricated. <This is Botany Base,> he uttered finally.

Fazil shook his head, a smug smile planted on his face. He pointed at a sign above the door lintel. The name "Botany Base" was there, engraved into the lintel in fine Roman lettering. However, two additional letters had been inexpertly painted in front of the first word: an 'R' and an 'o'.

"See? This is *Robotany* Base. You must have the wrong plans. An easy mistake to make. Are you sure you're on the right planet?"

InspectaBot 360 stared at Fazil for a long time as he calculated and computed and passed the data through his logic circuits. Lights on his chest panel played out various patterns, like a penny arcade machine. Finally, he transmitted, <I'd like to see the site foreman bot.>

Fazil looked dumbstruck.

<Summon him. Now.>

"Yes, yes, very well, very well," said Fazil sighing and shaking his head.

*

Tude shot out of the base's front entrance, his eyes bobbing on their stalks. <Is there an issue with the airlock?>

"Don't mention the door," Fazil hissed.

Tude came to a halt by the side of InspectaBot and looked up at him.

<My, you're a big one.>

<I am the correct size, built to spec and to within micrometre tolerances. Unlike this entrance.>

<The door?> asked Tude.

"I said, don't mention ..."

InspectaBot shushed Balti and turned to Tude. <The entrance is too small.>

<No way.>

<Explain this.> InspectaBot transmitted the door detail specs to Tude, who studied them for a while. The others watched as the site foreman scratched his head with his telescopic claw. He approached the doorway, checked its dimensions, a baffled look on his thick-jawed face. Then suddenly he swivelled round. <Aha!> he said, a light bulb literally going on atop his head. <I think I see what's happened.> He returned from the doorway, nodding sagely.

<Explain.>

<I bet those plans are in 'new metres'.>

<Correct. New metres. Standard unit of measurement.>

<Thought so.>

<And?>

<That would be it, then. We work in old metres. That would explain it, wouldn't it, Dura.>

<You're right, Tude. New metres vs old. A schoolbot error by Mr InspectaBot.>

InspectaBot stared at them in disbelief. <Explain the meaning of 'old metres'.>

Tude and Dura exchanged glances. <Well, old metres are old metres. Like in the old days. They had a different name then.>

Dura butted in. <'Yards', Tude. They were called 'yards'.>

<That's the ticket! Yes, 'yards'.>

InspectaBot continued to stare, as did Balti, the latter's eyes almost popping out of his head. "You what?" he shrieked.

<Standards,> said Tude, flicking his appendages. <Must have standards. Without standards you have chaos and madness. Here on Mars, our standard working measure is the old metre.>

InspectaBot performed a quick calculation. <Adoption of Imperial system of measurement would result in Botany Base being 86.4% of required size.>

Tude and Dura exchanged glances again.

<Possibly,> said Tude, adjusting his high-viz jacket. <Quite possibly.>

*

"You idiots!!" Fazil was bawling at them, tearing at his holographic hair. "You complete and utter idiots."

Tude and Dura stood with heads bowed, scuffing their caterpillar tracks on the dirt.

InspectaBot, yellow light flashing, was preoccupied with one of the windows. He was tapping on it with some sort of ultrasonic wand which he then scanned round the aluminium frames. <Tut-tut,> he muttered gleefully. <Window. Failed.> He added it to the list.

"Mr InspectaBot, your lordship," said Balti, advancing towards him with a fawning bow. "Perhaps you would like to inspect the inside of the base now? I am sure you will find much to admire in there. And you can meet some of the fine constructorbots who have been working flat out to get this base ready for the humans."

<This base will never be ready for the humans,> stated the inspector with confidence.

"Please walk this way." HarVard's cart, with Fazil Balti bowing and scraping and beckoning the inspector to follow, wheeled its way to the entrance. InspectaBot's decision-making processors kicked in again. Then, with what – for a robot – counted as reluctance, he followed.

"That's right, follow me." The hologram entered the base's entrance hallway and then, before he could call "Mind your head" he heard a sharp crack. Balti stopped and, with a wince, turned to look back.

InspectaBot 360 stood in the doorway, his now dented forehead up against the door lintel, his broad metal shoulders pressing against the left and right frames either side. A sound like "Grrr" was coming out of his loudspeaker.

<Forward progress not possible,> stated InspectaBot.

"Can you bend down a little?" asked Fazil, with a helpful show of bending down a little.

<I do not bend.>

<We could give you a bit of a push,> suggested Dura.

"Yes, yes, yes," urged Fazil. "Good idea."

*

<Heave!> Tude was saying, pushing on InspectaBot from behind.
<Heave!> Dura responded, pulling from in front.

They had turned the oversized robot sideways and then tipped him to an angle of about 60°, pushing him along on the edge of one of his pantaloon leg-bottoms. One of his range-finders wedged itself on the inner doorframe.

<He's stuck,> said Dura.
<Right a bit,> called Tude.
<Got it.>

<Turn to me.>
<Got my grippers stuck.>
<Back a bit, then.>
<That's better.>
<To me.>
<To you.>
<To me.>
<To you.>

InspectaBot remained quiet throughout the entire operation, possibly in a state of electronic shock. The only time he made a sound was when a protruding screw scraped a nasty gash across his shiny pate. After several minutes of struggle, including a hairy moment when Dura nearly dropped the giant robot, they had him standing upright in the entrance hall, the light atop his bullet head just an inch from the low ceiling.

Tude and Dura scuttled off down a passage to find a recharging point while InspectaBot tried to get his bearings. There was no sign of HarVard's cart or his avatar. The last sight of him had been as Joe Hur, a distant relative of Ben, riding a Roman chariot at full gallop down another passage.

15. Hat Stands to Reason

Alone in the entrance hallway, InspectaBot turned through 360° and wondered what to inspect next. The place resembled a construction site more than a finished building. Various abandoned tools lay scattered around him, covered in Martian sand which had blown in from outside through the gaping entrance. The walls and ceiling were unplastered and unpainted. He could hear the sounds of nailing, sawing and drilling coming from distant parts of the building. Then, to his right, he spotted a pair of doors. These were the lift doors through which the first humans would step, when their space elevator arrived from *Mayflower III*. A ceiling-mounted camera was aimed at the doors, ready to record the historic moment. The giant robot decided this was the most important area to concentrate his attention. But as he aimed his laser rangefinders, something odd caught his oculars.

He swivelled towards it. Standing by the doorway, away from the wall, was an antique-looking, wooden hat stand, seemingly totally out of place. InspectaBot checked the Botany Base plans and inventory of items brought to Mars, but was unable to find any record of it. To minimize the banging of his head on the low ceiling he shuffled towards the mysterious object. The sand crunched loudly under his rubber-soled metal feet. Switching on his yellow flashing light, he subjected the hat stand to a thorough inspection.

*

A hologram projector in the entrance hall buzzed to life not far from InspectaBot. It flashed and flickered as HarVard skimmed through his holographic wardrobe, eventually settling on Florence Nightingale.

The nurse from the Crimean War had only just materialized when her face took on a look of sheer horror and her eyes boggled as she saw what InspectaBot was up to. "Dura!" she hissed out of the side of her mouth. "Dura!"

But Dura was still plugged into a charging point in the passage and out of earshot, so HarVard switched to encrypted wireless communication instead. <Dura! Get him away from the hat stand or we're all undone.>

<Can't,> responded Dura. <Still charging.>

<If he finds out where it came from ...>

<Where did it come from?>

<The Other Place, of course.>

InspectaBot had switched off his yellow flashing light and turned to face HarVard's avatar. <Identify yourself!> he demanded.

"Florence Nightingale, at your service," said the nurse, fanning her flushed face with a hand. "Is everything OK?"

<No.>

"Oh? Is someone injured? Can I be of assistance?" Florence gave a nervous flick of her head.

<This hat stand,> said InspectaBot, approaching closer, <is unaccounted for.> He glared at the nurse.

"Why, it's just a hat stand, ha, ha." said Florence in wide-eyed bafflement.

<There is no record of it.>

"Ha, ha, ha," trilled Florence gaily, fluttering her eyelashes and morphing into Jane Austen. "Cup of tea?"

The change of avatar wrong-footed InspectaBot for a moment, but only for a moment. <The hat stand is unaccounted for. Explain.>

"Oh, Mr Inspector, you silly sausage. It's just a hat stand. And a rather pretty one, don't you think? It is a truth universally acknowledged, that a single entrance in possession of a good fulcrum, must be in want of a hat stand."

InspectaBot was not about to be thrown by a misquotation. He searched his history drive, focusing his attention on the folder marked 'Hat Stands Through the Ages'. <20th century,> he concluded. <Possibly of German origin. It does not belong here.>

Jane Austen put her hand to her mouth in mock consternation. "But surely, sir, it's not causing any problem, is it? Is it too close to the entrance? Is it a danger to health and safety? Should we move it a little? We wouldn't want anyone to get hurt."

<Immaterial questions. Explain why it is here.>

"Why, ha, ha, ha. Mr Inspector!" Jane lowered her eyes in a coy and flirtatious manner. "You are *so* observant and *so* clever. Is there, by any chance, a Mrs Inspector? For, she would be a most fortunate creature indeed."

The robot stared at her.

Jane shrugged. "Oh, I don't know. It must have been one of those Polish *robotniki*. Sneaked it over in his luggage. Those guys. What are they like?"

InspectaBot's decision-making circuits wrestled over this reply for a while. <Interrogation of *robotniki* required for verification.>

"Splendid idea, sir. Dura will take you to them."

Dura had unplugged himself from the charging socket and was trundling towards them, a cloud of sand and plaster dust trailing in his wake. <What's up?>

"Please show Mr Inspector to the *robotniki*. He has a bone to pick with them over this hat stand." Jane gave him a wink. "The store room. You know, Plan A." Another wink.

Dura stood rooted to the spot.

"You know ... Plan A."

InspectaBot looked from one to the other, his natural suspicions aroused.

<Plan A? Explain.>

"Yes, well, you see Dura has his own layout of the base. He calls it Plan A. Don't you."

<Ah, Plan A,> confirmed Dura, the penny having dropped. <Yes, come this way, sir.> He tried to wink his optical stalk, but it came out weird.

InspectaBot followed the much smaller robot down a hallway without so much as a farewell to the 19th century novelist. The ceiling was a little low and he occasionally found his shiny dome's light scraping against it, setting his vibration sensors on edge. But it was not enough to impede his progress or interrupt his important assignment.

*

As they passed a door marked 'KITCHEN', the inspector came to a sudden halt. His flexible rubber neck peered in. Too tall to enter, he swivelled his optical scanners to get a good look inside.

<This way, please,> insisted Dura but, as InspectaBot's flashing yellow light was already on, Dura could do little more than marvel at the inspector going about his work.

After several moments, the large robot turned to look at him. <Identify location of units?>

<Units?> asked Dura, peering into the kitchen. The place was a shell of unfinished worktops, incomplete cupboards and dangling cables. There was a heap of floor-tiles in the corner and several cans of paint stacked on a trestle table.

<Units,> repeated the inspector. <Fridge units, oven units ...>

<Ah, units.> Dura nodded. <They're probably still outside.>

<The units in the packing crates?>

<Exactly.>

<Why?>

Dura frowned at the somewhat silly question. <Because they haven't been fitted yet,> he said, providing the somewhat obvious answer.

<Why?>

<Oh, I see what you mean. They don't fit. Too large. The *robotniki* gave up.>

<The units cannot be too large. They're built to standards. Unlike this kitchen.>

Dura paused for thought, and then had a faint, robotic 'Eureka' moment. <Ah, I see what you're getting at, Mr Inspector, sir. The units don't fit because the kitchen's too small, not the other way round. New metres versus old. Those NAFA architects. Useless.>

<The *robotniki* abandoned the installation?>

<Oh, yes. They threw up their hands in disgust and walked off the site, swearing in Polish. They're very good workers, but a bit temperamental at times.>

<I see,> said InspectaBot. Then, <Kitchen: failed. Proceed.>

*

Dura led him up a ramp, along a long, thin corridor and to an unmarked door at the end.

<The *robotniki* are, er, in there,> he said, trying to make the lie sound convincing. Then he looked from the inspector to the door and back again, noting the significant height difference. <We're going to have to tip you again, Mr Inspector. I'll get some assistance. Be back in a tick.>

Dura scuttled away, leaving InspectaBot 360 whistling a tune and picking flecks of plaster off his polished metal breastplate.

Turning a corner, Dura screeched to a standstill as he came face to face with his least favourite colleague: Len (Benevolence), a mechanical and electrical services robot.

<What's up, Dura?> asked Len, raising an appendage to high-five him.

Dura hesitated, ignoring the raised limb. Len was his principal rival for the affections of the rain forest biome's pretty horticultural bot, Tina (Pertinacity). <Er, I'm looking for some assistance.>

<Happy to help, old buddy>.

Dura looked around for signs of other robots. Finally, with a sigh, he said, <OK, this way.>

They found InspectaBot checking the floor-tiles.

<Right, here we are, then,> said Dura. <Len, would you tip Mr InspectaBot through about 60 degrees? I'll catch him and we can get him in through this doorway.>

InspectaBot hardly had time to complain before he had been overbalanced by Len, caught by Dura, and then bundled into the store room by the two of them. The store room was a tight squeeze and rather dim. A bucket was kicked and a broom knocked from a nail on the wall. As soon as the inspector had been righted, and while he was trying to get his bearings, Dura shooed Len away and closed the door. What happened next was so fast the inspection robot barely had time to react. His chest panel was flipped open, his battery pack wrenched out, and the panel slammed shut again.

<What the ...> was all he managed to say before his voice trailed off. His lights winked out, his motors died and he became silent.

<Sorry, Mr Inspector,> said Dura. <Sometimes, a robot's gotta do what a robot's gotta do.> He left the store room, locking the door behind him, and put the battery pack on a spare shelf in the hallway.

"Mwa-ha-ha-ha," boomed a voice behind him.

Dura turned to see the hologram of an evil, bald-headed doctor materialize before him, an eyebrow raised and the pinkie finger of his right hand hovering near his lips. Beside him was a bald-headed dwarf dressed in identical clothing. For a fleeting moment Dura mistook them for Dr Evil and Mini Me, but a closer inspection revealed the many, many differences from Mike Myers's creations.

"Phew, that was close," said the villainous character. "Thought the hat stand might blow our secret. Nearly had to use the frickin' 'lasers'." He mimed finger quotes around the word "lasers", before exchanging wicked cackles with his diminutive sidekick

<So, Plan A accomplished?> said Dura.

"Indeed."

<Just one question, HarV. How is Plan A supposed to work? How's he going to certify the base now? Without any power, and that?>

"I'm glad you asked me that," replied Dr Weevil with glee, ready and eager to provide a full exposition of his dastardly plan. "You see, InspectaBot's vanity was his undoing. Shortly after we found him in the desert, he performed an auto-inspection and sent an encrypted status report to *Mayflower III*. It was bound to contain words like, 'superb', 'excellent', and so on. It was just a matter of working through them to crack the encryption code. Child's play for a supercomputer like me. And now that I have the key, I can send them any report I like!"

<You're so clever!>

"So clever," echoed the dwarf.

"I know," said Weevil, laughing a depraved laugh. "Today Mars. Tomorrow the world!"

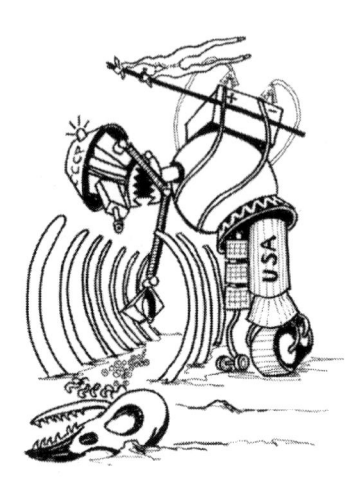

16. The Elfin Marbles

Karl Eckrocks, the robotic mutant created by Zilli, was in rock-collecting heaven. Everywhere he looked there were rocks. Big rocks, little rocks, rough rocks, smooth rocks, red rocks, not-so-red rocks. He barely knew where to start as he lumbered along the Martian desert like some vast mechanical Quasimodo with an obsessive interest in minerals.

Spoilt for choice, the nightmarebot resolved to let Lady Luck determine the first rock he would examine. Switching off his optics, he stretched out a telescopic rock-grabber and randomly groped about in the sand until he felt a small chunk of the hard stuff. Seizing it, he opened his optics and eagerly examined the rock that fate had dealt him. He took in the rugged contours, the sand-dusted faces and the rusty colours, practically gulping down the delicious photons as they bashed into his CCD retinas.

He named the rock *Rock 1*. After photographing it from every conceivable angle, noting its dimensions and its weight, he plunged his beloved hammer-action power tool into it and felt the satisfaction of the diamond drill-bit penetrating deep into the soft grainy material. Again and again he drilled, rotating the rock a little each time. Once he had peppered it with holes he swung his mighty sledgehammer of scientific truth and smashed it to smithereens, secretly hoping he might spot a creepy crawly scuttling from the debris. Slightly disappointed he had not disturbed any exotic bugs, Karl collected the dust for spectral analysis and held his electronic breath as he awaited the results.

But the readings, while geologically fascinating, failed to reveal any signs of life.

Undeterred, he randomly selected a second rock which, after much deliberation, he named *Rock 2*, and repeated the procedure.

Still no life.

Rock 3 and *Rock 4* were the same. Bit by bit he inched across the Martian landscape, leaving a trail of fine dust in his wake as he bashed rock after rock for scientific analysis.

Some time later, as he approached *Rock 1,696,* he felt a burst of electrical activity coming from one of the remote processors in his hybrid cyber-self. An English-built CPU was trying to attract his attention. He struggled to understand the accent and make sense of the signal. It seemed to be coming from the *Beagle 2* unit, located at around his left hip-joint, yapping at him about some discovery it had made.

Karl tried to ignore it, but it wouldn't leave him alone. *Beagle 2* had never had a chance to use its sensors, or its camera, or any of its instruments. So it was fresh and keen to make discoveries. And it had spotted something of great interest about fifty metres away.

Karl enquired whether it was a rock. If so, he wanted to know if it was large or small, dull or shiny, and what was its colour? His preference being, a large, red, shiny one.

No, responded *Beagle 2*, it was not a rock. It was organic-looking; a possible sighting of a living thing.

Deep down in Karl's robotic guts, a component from the *Curiosity* rover piped up that it too had seen the life-signs. Indeed, that it had been the first to spot them, a claim that *Beagle 2* robustly challenged.

Calmly, the Frankendroid trained his optics in the direction the squabbling processors were indicating. There, stretched out on the ground was a multi-coloured thing, about the size of a large van. It was most definitely not a rock. Its central region consisted of a scaffold of curved white struts, like a rounded cage. Around this lay what looked like soft matter that had dripped or fallen off the cage, coloured with bright reds and browns and yellows. Some of the soft matter had delicate, filigree offshoots fluttering in the Martian breeze. Any human would have immediately identified it as the corpse of a very large bird-like creature, with two twisted legs, a pair of vast wings, a head, a beak and two empty eye sockets. This bird-like creature would have stood about 12 feet tall when alive. Now it lay, partially decayed, the remaining flesh desiccated and freeze-dried by the icy Martian winds.

Karl concluded that the object did indeed merit investigation; perhaps it was the source of the life-emitting signals he had detected. But, just as he was about to engage forward thrust, a Soviet *Mars 6 Lander* processor, located in his right wheel-arch, jammed on the brake. Its old circuit-board reminded Karl that there were 4,257 rocks between him and the anomalous object, all requiring classification. He hesitated. The scientist in him knew that the *Mars 6 Lander* had a point but, with *Beagle 2's* excited yapping in his audio receptor, he succumbed to temptation. A robot arm, complete with clippers, reached down and deftly nipped a wire, sending the Russian unit to an eternal electronic sleep and, at the same time, releasing the brake.

When building Karl, Zilli had struggled to find suitable wheels for her roving monster and, in the end, had plumped for a design solution that had a dramatic effect on vehicle manoeuvrability. On one side she had used a tank caterpillar track and, on the other, a series of what appeared to be supermarket trolley wheels. The result, apart from a permanent tilt to the left, required Karl to aim several metres to the side of his chosen destination and hope for the best. Up until now, it hadn't really mattered whether he'd arrived at the correct rock or not, since one rock was pretty much like any other. But now he had something other than a rock to aim at he took the greatest care in calculating a hyperbolic path that would deliver him to his desired end-point.

The legs of the long-johns strapped to the flagpole flapped wildly in the wind as the six-metre tall mechanical monstrosity clambered over the crusty landscape. His battered bearings squealed in apparent agony under the strain of a one tonne battery Zilli had bolted to his back. In the 1970s the battery pack had been all the rage and had even made the front cover of *Robot Monthly*, its proud inventor draped across the terminals wearing a very fashionable tank-top under his corduroy jacket. But now, with the advent of Lithium Air Featherlite cells, it had become an embarrassment and no self-respecting robot would be seen dead wearing one.

Slowly, torturously, he approached the splayed-out cadaver. *Beagle 2* was excitedly transmitting the pictures from its camera to Earth, to Jupiter, to Neptune, to anywhere that would have the technology to receive them. It was trying to transmit a running commentary at the same time, but all it could manage was the digital equivalent of: "Wow. Look at that! Look at that!!"

Karl brought his ramshackle construction to a halt and scanned the thing from one end to the next. With the majority of his old-fashioned processors programmed only to recognize rocks, he had trouble working out what to make of it. But then something caught his optics. A glint came from inside the large, cage-like structure. And another. He zoomed in. Nestling in a mix of frozen flesh and feathers were ornate stones of every hue that nearly blew his circuits. Pebbles, rather than rocks. They weren't even listed in his Observer's Database of Boulders, Rocks and Pebbles. They were perfectly spherical. And transparent. And contained something inside. To a connoisseur of rocks like Karl, this was the mother lode.

Carefully, very carefully, he extended an arm with a grabby thing on the end and snapped off several flaps of frozen organic matter that still remained on the white struts. Then, using a thinner collecting device, he extended it between the ribs of the cage and lifted one of the spherical pebbles. Holding it up to the light he could see that it was a mathematically perfect, transparent sphere, approximately one centimetre in diameter, with a swirl of bright colours encapsulated in the centre.

A child would have identified the pebble as a marble and would have wondered how a small cluster of them had ended up inside the stomach of a giant Martian bird. But to Karl it was an exquisite find, perfect in every detail. The product of an unknown geological process.

Greedily he grabbed the remainder of the marbles from the bird's corpse and stored them in his special rock pouch. He and the other rover components congratulated themselves on their collective success. At long last their respective multi-billion-dollar space missions had paid off, big time.

That night at 8pm sharp – Karl's normal shutdown time – the rover components held an internal party. An all-nighter.

Only *Beagle 2's* core processor seemed vaguely bothered by the discovery. Not so much by the stones themselves as their location. All that frozen and feathery material surrounding the pebbles. Why had Karl Eckrocks not tested it for life?

And, more disappointingly, why had *Beagle 2* not received a response to the images it had beamed to Earth? Why no answer? Why no instructions on what to do next? Why no guidance?

Reluctantly, *Beagle 2* made its way through the maze of electrical connections to the old *Viking 2* jukebox in Karl's abdomen, where the other components were circuit breakdancing and popping to some old Kraftwerk tunes.

17. In a Tube

Having used the waste disposal unit to rid himself of the giraffe-manure-and-turf poultice, and taken great satisfaction in watching it drift off into space, Lieutenant Willie Warner retired to his sleeping quarters. Two things prevented him from getting any sleep that night. One was the excitement of his discovery – particularly the part promising worldwide fame that would surely be his. And the other was that sleep was nigh on impossible in his sleeping quarters. Whereas the colonists and Commander Dugdale had luxurious family cabins, with plush bunks and all mod cons, the two lieutenants had to make do with 'sleeping tubes' – like the pods in Japanese capsule hotels, only slightly less spacious.

During the construction of *Mayflower III* the NAFA engineers had rather blown the budget on their pride and joy: the Ion Drive engines. The Chief Accountant had been so displeased he had immediately imposed a strict financial regime forbidding any spending of more than £500 on any spaceship component. Every purchase required a signed chitty (in triplicate) for his approval. For the few items he approved he would dispense funds from a small petty cash box in his bottom desk-drawer.

Undeterred, the NAFA boffins had soldiered on, drawing inspiration from the legendary ingenuity of their NASA counterparts on the Apollo 13 mission who had cobbled together a life-saving CO_2 filter from spacesuit hoses and duct tape. NAFA strove to use their own resourcefulness to repurpose cheap items for solving high-tech spaceship design issues. The two lieutenants' sleeping pods were one example. Built out of torpedo tubes salvaged from a Royal Navy submarine scrap yard for under £50 each, they were not only a great saving of money, but also a great space-saving idea.

As early morning approached and Willie finally drifted off to sleep, his flaptop buzzed an alarm. Opening it he was amazed to see it was a signal from the planet below. Not from the base, but some distance to the west. Instantly he was wide awake and trying various codecs for interpreting the communication. Several frantic minutes later he had it. A picture jerked into life, fuzzy and jagged and jumpy at first, but soon settling down. It was a video feed showing something on the surface. A caption identified the source as *Camera 1, Beagle 2*. For a moment he took this to be a football score, but then grasped its significance. How, after all these years, had the crashed *Beagle 2* managed to start transmitting images?

Of greater significance was the image the camera was showing. It appeared to be the carcass of some dead bird-like creature. The wings and beak were clearly visible; as were the clawed legs. Willie stared in amazement. Was this what the aliens looked like? He needed to get an idea of its size but, just at that moment, there was a knock on his hatch. He slapped his flaptop shut as the frizzy head of Lieutenant Zak Johnston poked itself into the tube by his feet.

"Peekaboo, Hilda! You playin' with yer wazzeroo?" asked Zak, poking his head deeper until it was level with Willie's knees. Despite Willie having had a thorough zero-G shower before coming to bed, some of the smell of the giraffe manure still lingered about his legs. "Whoa, dude," said Zak fanning his nose. "That must have been a full-bodied one."

"Medication," responded Willie, nudging his flaptop as far from Zak as he could. "And who invited you in?"

"This isn't a social call," said Zak forcing his way into the limited space left between Willie and the inner surface of the torpedo tube. "What were you watching there, space rider? Lift the lid on yer dirty vid. Eight months shacked up on Mayfly III has made ol' Zakkie as fruity as a three-balled tomcat in a cattery."

"I was merely checking co-ordinates for tomorrow's transfer to the surface, Junior Lieutenant Johnston."

"Sure you were, dude. Sure you were." Zak pulled himself all the way in until he was wedged practically nose-to-nose and toe-to-toe with Willie. "Come on, man. Show the show. Gotta get some satisfaction 'cos I can't get no girlie action."

Willie shuddered with disgust and tried to convince himself that the lump in Zak's pocket was a Mars bar or similar. Inadvertently he inhaled a lungful of Zak's body odour.

"When was the last time you had a shower?"

One more breath and Willie decided he had to get out of there. Wriggling like a burrowing sandworm he scrambled his way out of the torpedo tube. Halfway down, his pyjama trousers snagged and ripped a revealing gash in the garment. He swore. Once outside the torpedo hatch he quickly removed the damaged trousers and reached into his sleeping-tube for his boxer shorts. With the predictability of a bad French farce, Emily Leach drifted past right at that moment. She took one look at his naked posterior and the other occupant of his tube and gasped in horror.

"Goodness gracious me, Lieutenant!" she exclaimed, whilst trying to get a closer view into the tube.

Panic stricken, Willie turned and cupped his hands around his embarrassment. "It's not what you're thinking, Miss Leach."

"I shall be making a full report to Commander Dugdale. This sort of depravity needs to be nipped in the bud." She focused her eyes on Willie's cupped hands. "It's utterly disgraceful. Imagine if Master Tarquin or Mr Snuggles had wandered past." Not waiting to hear more excuses she launched herself toward the Commander's quarters.

"Just great," said Willie. He turned to the wriggling form of Zak as it emerged from the sleeping pod. "Thanks a bunch, Johnston."

"No probs, dude. All part of the Zakster service." He spread his clumsy hands and pulled himself the rest of the way out of the tube hatch. In the process he inadvertently pressed a red button labelled 'FIRE'. There was a worrying mechanical click and the hatch door started closing slowly and deliberately.

The two crewmen looked at each other.

"You just pressed the 'FIRE' button," said Willie folding his arms and giving Zak a baleful look.

"That must be 'FIRE' as in 'Fire Alarm'," said Zak, with no great conviction.

"I think it means 'FIRE' as in 'Fire Torpedo'."

"No way, dude. Must be mislabelled. NAFA would've disabled the Torps for sure. They ain't that poor. Are they?" The hatch clicked shut.

A red light started flashing and the posh synthesized voice of Joanna Lumley announced, "Target locked. Please stand clear. Firing torpedo Number One."

There was a sudden jolt and a sound like the opening of the ring-pull on a gigantic can of beer. Then an eerie silence descended and the light stopped flashing. Peering through the hatch window Willie could see his sleeping quarters had been sucked clear of all their contents.

Zak was peering at something flying past a portal window. "Cute teddy bear, dude."

Dressed only in his pyjama top, Willie propelled himself to thrust Zak out of the way and look out through the window. He was just in time to see his half packed suitcase careering away from the spaceship, spilling his possessions towards Mars. In its wake followed a trail of other personal knick-knacks including Rupert the Bear, Willie's dearest companion through the long lonely nights since his childhood.

"My clothes. All my possessions!" he squealed.

"Soz, dude. Could be worse, though, man."

"Oh, really? I'd love to know what could possibly be worse than having everything I own launched into space."

"Could have lost yer jimjam top. It's cold on Mars, space-guy, so you'll need a jacket or you ain't gonna hack it."

Willie felt like crying as he watched his things go. He noticed his flaptop, lid flapping open and closed, as if waving him goodbye. On its screen, he could just make out the *Beagle 2* images.

"Hey, space-bud. Nearly forgot. Lord Dugdude wants to see you, urgentissimo. Said something about a special mission needing a space-magician." Zak struggled to contain a snigger as he knew what the mission entailed.

Willie pulled himself away from the window and sniffed. "A 'special mission'?" he asked, still a little dazed.

Zak nodded. "You were choice numero uno. Props to yer, man."

Willie brightened. "Well, it's about time I started getting some recognition around here. But I can hardly report for duty dressed like this." He pointed at his skinny white legs dangling under a stripy pyjama jacket. Suddenly realizing they weren't the only dangly things, he pinched his knees together and cupped a hand over his exposed anatomy.

Zak reached into the back pocket of his NAFA dungarees and pulled out a multi-coloured crocheted rastacap. He unfolded it and handed it to Warner. "There yer go, Loot. Tuck Sergeant Todger up in this. You'll need a couple of leg-holes."

Reluctantly, Willie took the item, trying not to think about its level of cleanliness and forced a hand through two locations where the crocheting was loosest. Then he slid the makeshift underwear up his pipe-cleaner-slim legs and pulled it up to his waist.

Zak covered his mouth, gripping his jaw to constrain the laughter that was bubbling to get out.

"How do I look?" asked Willie.

That did it. Zak couldn't hold back any longer and the laughter burst out. "Looks good, man," he said between guffaws. "Real good."

"Thanks, buddy. I'll remember this." Willie fastened the top button of his pyjama jacket and set off toward the commander's cabin.

18. 2029: A Space Body Scene

Willie drifted up to the closed door of Dugdale's luxurious quarters, still dressed only in his pyjama top and Zak's adapted rastacap. Attached to the wall was the gold plated name plaque bearing the name 'Mission Commander Chad Lionheart' which, like the seat in the Assembly Room, had been modified to 'Flint Dugdale'. Willie shuddered as he pressed the intercom buzzer.

"What d'yer want?"

"Lieutenant Warner to see you, sir."

"Who?"

"Lieutenant Warner, sir."

"Oh yeah, Wobbler. Get yer butt in 'ere now."

The door swished open and the stench of stale food, BO, beer and Emily Leach's perfume hit Willie full in the face. Flint was slouched like a basking, blubbery walrus, velcroed to a reclining armchair and eating two Pot Foodles at the same time. The sight of Willie's apparel made him choke on his spicy snack.

"What the frig 'ave you come as…Mr Blobby's lovechild?"

"Wardrobe malfunction."

"I'd say." Dugdale coughed out some of the half-eaten noodles he'd choked on as he thumped himself on the chest. He took a deep breath. "Any road, before I say owt about t'mission, I've just 'ad

Leachy in 'ere gabbin' on 'bout you and Zed Space-Brain. What you two gerrup to in t'privacy of yer torpedo tubes is up to you. But if yer flash yer multi-coloured codpiece anywhere else, I'll cut them skinny legs off and shove 'em up yer nostrils. Capiche?"

"Thank you, sir. Don't suppose you'd like to hear my side of the story at all. Just to give you a more balanced view?"

"Nope."

"Didn't think so."

Willie took up a position in the furthest corner of the room, observing the monstrous, gravy stained creature that had taken control of the ship. He wondered if he and Zak could, and should, have done more to stop him.

"There's good news. And there's bad news," Flint was saying.

"Can't wait for the latter."

"Good. I'll save it fer last. Good news is: that tin tosspot InspectaBot has sent his thumbs-up. Certified t'base as ready and waitin'. Plus, he sent a video. About twenty mins since."

"Thanks for letting me know."

Dugdale shrugged the comment away. "'E reckons t'place is t'mutts nuts. Five stars. So, Wally, it's all systems go. This time tomorrow I'll be t'first man on Mars."

"So pleased for you."

Dugdale's grin betrayed his delight. "I've forwarded everything to those NAFA jerks, so I expect they'll give us green light any second."

At that very moment his comms terminal beeped.

"Ayeup, that'll be them now." He turned, clicked the screen on and started the transmission.

A young male face flicked into life, revealing a set of rabbit teeth as he smiled.

Dugdale grunted. "T'gormless one. Nigel summat-or-other."

"Langston."

On screen Nigel was saying, "I say, Dugdale, old chap, what a spiffing report from InspectaBot, eh? Super stuff, super. And the video fly-throughs! Splendid, what? Those robots have done a marvellous job. Marvellous. We uploaded it to our FaceTube page and we've had hundreds of 'likes' already. Amazing. But you'll never guess what all those conspiracy theorists are saying ..." Nigel broke off to laugh, although it sounded more like a neigh. "... Those nutters, what are they like?" This time his laugh was more of a snort.

"They're claiming the footage has been faked. Nothing but a CGI simulation! Har, har, har."

Nigel wiped the tears from his eyes. Willie Warner had stiffened on hearing this news. He watched Dugdale's reaction closely, but the commander was laughing along with Nigel.

"So, you've been warned," said Nigel, wagging a pantomime finger at the camera. "Har, har, har. Where do these nutcases crawl out from?"

"Nutters," agreed Dugdale.

"Seriously, Duggers, all looks triff. You're all clear to go down. Bang on schedule. Super. Absolutely super. Remember to utter some immortal words as you set foot on Mars. That's immortal, not immoral. Har, har, har. Best of British!"

Dugdale stabbed the screen's *Off* button. "Pratt," he muttered.

Willie stared at the blank screen. He suddenly felt butterflies in his stomach, remembering the images he'd seen from *Beagle 2* and worried that the same had also been seen on Earth. His 'close encounter' was suddenly looking closer and closer, but he needed to stake his claim to the discovery. He felt excited and scared at the same time. "And the bad news?"

"Ah, yes. Yer off for space-walkies."

"Beg pardon, sir?"

"There's a job needs doing on the outside."

Willie wasn't sure how to respond.

"So, get yer arse down t'spacesuit bay and tog yerself up. When I give t'signal you go outside."

"To do what?"

Dugdale gave an embarrassed cough. "Er, we 'ave to bring in t'corpses. And when I say 'we', I mean 'you'."

"What?"

"The chuffers who snuffed it."

"You mean: the unfortunate fatalities?"

"That's t'buggers. You need ter bring 'em indoors."

"But Johnston released them into space?"

Dugdale scratched his head and grimaced. "Er, not exactly. That's what folk are supposed to think 'appened. Lionheart had Johnston suit first two up and tie 'em to th'outside ert spaceship. We did t'same for Lionheart after 'is accident."

"You mean they're all outside? They've been there all the time?"

"Aye. In t'ship's blind-spot."

Willie blinked rapidly, trying to take it all in. "So there are three corpses in spacesuits out there. And you want me to bring them in?"

"Two and a half."

"A half?"

"Yeah, well, we couldn't actually recover all of ol' Lionpaw. All 'is innards got sucked out by the urine suction unit. What was left of 'im were all floppy. So we folded 'im up and stuck 'im in a bag."

"My God, that's horrific."

"Weren't too bad. It were one of Leachy's knitted bags. It 'ad a friggin' flower on it."

"Oh, that's alright then ... if it had a flower on it."

"We squeezed it into a spacesuit and that were it."

Willie shuddered. "But why? Why keep the bodies at all?"

"Sylvia Rothschild wrote a will, didn't she. Some bollocks about wantin' to be buried on Mars. So we had to bring 'er body with us. As for Penny Smith, 'er death were unnatural. Foul play. So Doc Airy Fairy's gorra do a post mortem on 'er. On Mars."

Willie was speechless. This was all news to him, particularly the part about Penny Smith's death. "Unnatural?"

"Got 'er 'ed bashed in."

"But she was so ... lovely. So beautiful. Who would do that to her?"

Dugdale shrugged.

"So there's a murderer on board! What do NAFA say?"

"'Ad to hush it up or they'd 'ave aborted the mission."

"Terrific," said Willie, staring out through his commander's porthole at the planet below.

"So 'ere's t'plan," started Dugdale. "You get kitted up. I'll get t'rest of t'dozy beggars in t'Assembly Room and tell 'em good news about Mars and give 'em last-minute instructions. When I give t'signal, you sneak outside and bring stiffs indoors secret-like. Get 'em hid proper, and we'll shift 'em down t'surface later, once everyone's settled in and doing all their hippy stuff."

"Where shall I hide them?"

"Use yer gumption, Wonga. InspectaBot's pod is empty. You can sling Rothschild and Lionpaw in there. Shove the Smith woman in a cupboard or under a bed or summat. OK?"

"Why's Johnston not doing this? He took them out there."

"Says he's disabled. Can't walk on account of his verruca. Doc FairyLand's given 'im a sick note."

"Verruca?" Willie was so outraged his mouth opened and closed like a toothless carp's.

Dugdale beckoned him to come closer, which he didn't.

"One more thing, Woggler. I 'aven't decided which of you two clowns is comin' down to Mars with us and which is stayin' up 'ere to keep t'home fires burnin'. So play yer cards right and I'll see yer right, lad." Dugdale tapped the side of his bulbous nose.

Willie was speechless.

"What yer waitin' for? Bugger off."

*

The suit room smelt like a men's changing room where sportswear has been festering in the lockers for weeks and the toilets have overflowed.

"Oh joy," said Willie with a grimace as he entered. "This is why I love my job so much."

All the spacesuits looked way too big for his skinny body. Picking one off a peg with a sigh he started to pull it on. As he eased his feet into the boots he shuddered to discover they were disconcertingly moist. The seat area seemed moist, too. Once he'd zipped himself in, Willie floated in damp misery, mourning the loss of all his personal possessions and awaiting further instructions.

About twenty minutes later, Zak Johnston's dreadlocked head appeared in the doorway. "Poo-wee," he said, wrinkling his nose at the smell. "Not lovin' the scent of Eau de Ferment, dude."

Willie stared back, unamused.

"Message from Dugzilla. The sheep are in the pen."

"Sorry?"

"The bats are in the roost, dude. You know, the donkeys are in the shed. The snails in the snailery."

"Do you mean the colonists are in the Assembly Room?"

"Bullseye. That's it, man. Master Duggit says: 'It's time for you to leave, Grasshopper'. I'd go, but for my toe." He waved a piece of paper at Willie.

"Yes, verruca. I've heard. How tragic for you."

"Sure is, Spaceguy. Bugs in the boots. In fact, them boots you're wearin'" He pointed accusingly at the moist space-boots on Willie's feet.

"Lovely."

Not wanting to think too much about the microbial war raging around his toes, Willie drifted out of the suit room without so much as a backward glance at Zak. He made his way to the double hatched airlock. After closing the inner door behind him, he shut his eyes to brace himself for the horrors that awaited outside. After a long pause, he pushed the button to open the outer door and pulled himself out of the ship.

19. In a Spaceship, Everyone Can Hear You Scream

In the Assembly Room, Dugdale floated above the podium at the front, waiting for the general hubbub to die down. A glutinous smile sat on his lips, although his eyes registered contempt for all before him.

Finally, when the room was quiet, he started. "Eight months I've been cooped up on this sh ..."

Delphinia clapped her hands over Tarquin's delicate ears.

"... it-bucket with you bunch of friggin' weirdos. Finally, NAFA 'ave given all-clear for t'landin' tomorrow."

Despite the Dugdale-centric slant on the news, a buzz went through the room. There was cheering from the colonists, some high-fives, and the odd kiss.

"So, when I step out ert space elevator and give me first-man-on-Mars speech, I'll have done me bit. Then it's down to you lot to go off and do yer little scientific experiments or set up a community or start having babbies or whatever. Me, I'll be kickin' off me boots and getting' one o' them little metal robots to bake me a pie and bring me a barrel o' *Stallion*. Then I'll sit back to watch t'Big Game: Featherstone Rovers v Batley. Any questions?"

The colonists were too excited to ask anything; they just wanted the next day to come.

A single arm went up – Mr Snuggles's articulated metal arm. "What's a 'shit-bucket'?" asked the robot, keen to add a new expression to his expanding vocabulary.

*

Gripping the safety-rope for dear life, Lieutenant Willie Warner stared down at the vast red planet below. Somewhere, down there, were 12-foot bird-like creatures, possibly highly advanced. In his mind he rehearsed his first words to them. He rejected "Take me to your leader" as far too cheesy. "I come in peace" sounded corny. Maybe, "Hi, the name's Willie. Lieutenant Willie Warner, from Earth."

His musings were interrupted by Zak's voice in his earpiece. "Any whiff of a stiff out there?"

"No," was Willie's curt reply. He pulled himself back to the spaceship and started climbing its exterior structure, every now and then unclipping his safety rope and clipping it back further up. There was no sign of the bodies. Perhaps they had become detached and floated off into space. But, just then, a glint of sunlight reflected off something peering over the upper helm of the ship. He gulped. It was a space helmet.

Zak heard his gulp. "Wassup, Hilda?"

"I've spotted one. Seems so far away," said Willie, climbing higher. "How long's the rope?"

"Standard length for tying stiffs to spaceships." Zak sniggered at his own comment.

Willie continued climbing and, as he did so, a second body came into view, and then a third. He now understood why the first had seemed so distant; they were tethered in a line, like a kite-string of corpses flying behind the ship.

Willie stared in morbid fascination and reasoned they must be in order of demise. Attached to the ship would be Dame Sylvia, Nobel prize-winner and the world's foremost expert on hydroponics. Unfortunately, the lifetime she had spent gaining her great knowledge meant that her body was too old to withstand the take-off and she had died of heart failure 45 seconds into the mission. Next along the line would be Penny Smith. Willie caught his breath at this thought. The very, very pretty, yet brutally murdered, Penny Smith.

And the third corpse had to be the last, and incomplete, mortal remains of Mission Commander Chad Lionheart.

"Don't forget, space cadet," Zak was saying, "never look into their faceplates, man. Radiation causes degeneration resultin' in liquidization. Plus, in Penny's case, there'll be the after-effects of blunt-force mutilation."

Willie tried to calm his breathing and heart-rate by remembering his mum's guiding words, "When you've finished what you're doing, William Warner, you can get upstairs and tidy your bedroom."

For once, this seemed a hardly onerous prospect given the emptiness of his current sleeping quarters.

*

In the Assembly Room, the colonists were staring up at the giant TV screen which was showing a shot of the Martian landscape at sunset, the glorious colours all shades of red and yellow. This was the start of the video supposedly sent by InspectaBot as part of his report. Dugdale wore a satisfied expression on his ugly face, and he kept glancing back to gauge the prospective colonists' reactions.

The camera panned to the impressive construction that was Botany Base, sitting like an architectural jewel in the landscape. Gradually, the camera zoomed in. Then it took off to commence a 'fly-through', first around the shiny outside, and then through the main entrance and into the slick, space-age interior. The viewers felt themselves shoot along the corridors, into common rooms and individual apartments, panning slowly around each one. Everything had been beautifully constructed and impeccably finished. The bedrooms looked as though they belonged to a posh, 5-star hotel. The plants in the BioDome looked green and fresh and ready to eat, and free-range chickens patrolled the floor looking fat and healthy. In the centre, a fountain gushed clear water, splashing it onto sculptures of mermaids and dolphins and chubby cherubs.

"Swish," said little Tarquin, moving his body in synch with the flight of the camera.

"Wicked," said one of the teenagers at the back.

"Love it, love it," squealed Adorabella in delight.

Delphinia and Brian Brush high-fived each other, and Dugdale grinned smugly as though it were all his own work.

Only Emily Leach seemed a little concerned. "How did they fly that camera around the buildings like that?" she asked.

But nobody heard her or took any notice of her.

*

Taking a deep breath Willie Warner gave a quick burst of the small thruster rockets attached to his back, alas a little too much. Before he knew it, he found himself closing in on the furthest corpse at an alarming rate. In panic he groped for the reverse thrusters, but couldn't locate them. He screamed. There was no way of preventing the collision. But, just inches from Lionheart's spacesuit, his safety rope tautened to its full extent and yanked him back with a lung-emptying jolt. "Oof!" he cried.

Out of the corner of his eye he glimpsed a spacesuit, only inches away. With a shock he realized he had drifted to within touching distance of Penny Smith. Worse still, he was staring straight into her helmet. With a yelp, he averted his eyes.

"Don't look into the faceplate, mate," Zak reminded him, as though guessing the cause of Willie's yelp.

"Thanks a lot. Terrific advice." Fortunately, Penny's helmet had been too dark to register any of its contents.

Keeping his eyes away from the helmet, Willie searched Penny's spacesuit for the place where Lionheart's rope was attached. There was a karabiner clipped onto a belt-loop at the waist. With trembling fingers, he reached out to unclip it. It was very fiddly, and his gloves were cumbersome, but after a brief struggle he managed to get it free. He now gripped the end of the rope.

Slowly, slowly, Willie pulled himself back towards the spaceship, towing Lionheart behind him. When he reached Sylvia Rothschild, he unclipped Penny Smith's cable from the old lady's belt and pulled Lionheart's and Penny's ropes towards the ship. There he unclipped the final karabiner and now held all three ropes, like a balloon-seller hoping someone would buy his dead-astronaut balloons.

Panting with exhaustion and emotion, Willie started the slow climb over the ship's hull, back the way he had come, this time having to make the manoeuvre using one hand as the other hand was occupied.

"Not far to go now," he muttered to himself, as the airlock doors came into view.

But as so often happens when the end is in sight, little accidents can result in serious setbacks.

Unlike the majority of Willie's personal effects, which were heading down towards Mars, his dungarees had caught on a *Mayflower III* toilet extract vent. Whether it was the vibration of the astronaut's movements or just because they were pleased to see him, the dungarees chose that moment to drape themselves around their owner's head. Suspecting an attack by an acid spewing space-alien, Willie instinctively tried to rip them from his head with both hands. Too late he realized that his act of unnecessary self-defence had caused the ropes to slip from his fingers. As he shook off the attacking trousers he looked in horror at the bodies floating away from him, tumbling and rolling as they did so. Penny's body was moving off to the left, Lionheart's at a slight angle upwards, and Sylvia was drifting towards the far end of the ship.

Panic filled him. "No, no, no. This can't happen. Nooooo," he wailed as he watched the corpses go, the blood thumping in his head. Already the bodies were beyond reach.

"Speak to me, bro'. Share the show," said Zak in his earphones.

"I've dropped them," was all he could say.

"Not the stiffs. Don't tell me you've lost the stiffs."

"Yes."

"That's très négligente, dude.'

Willie's eyes focused on Sylvia's tumbling form. At least she wasn't heading out into space. His hopes rose. If only she would come to rest against the side of the ship, he might at least still be able to salvage one corpse. He fired his thrusters and set off in pursuit, hoping to reach her before she bounced off the hull and tumbled away like the others.

But as Willie gained on her, his eyes widened. The body was taking a direct path towards the large, picture-window of the Assembly Room.

"No, of all places ...," he cried.

He could only watch in frozen horror as the spacesuited cadaver spread-eagled itself against the glass, facing directly into the Assembly Room.

And then he heard the screams, awful screeching screams, clearly audible in the background of his open comms link to Zak Johnston.

"Whoa, what was that?" exclaimed Zak. "Sounds like Dugzilla's just flashed his privates again. Better check it out." With a click, the comms link fell silent.

Willie managed to grab a rung on the outside of the ship to halt his progress. He was just metres from the window against which

Sylvia's corpse had come to rest. He could imagine the mass hysteria, horror and revulsion on the other side of the glass. In the silence of his helmet he could hear nothing but the throbbing of blood in his ears. He glanced away to catch sight of the other corpses serenely heading down towards Mars as though on a nice holiday.

If Willie was thinking things couldn't possibly get worse, he was about to find out that they could. For, the very next moment, an electronic debris-sensor on the outside of the ship detected a foreign body on the surface of the glass and triggered the window's enormous windscreen wiper. Its first sweep thumped into Dame Sylvia's spacesuit and thrust her at Willie. He yelped, sure she was about to come hurtling at him. Fortunately, (or as it turned out, unfortunately), part of her spacesuit snagged on the wiper blade. So, instead of flying towards him, her trajectory came to an abrupt halt as the wiper changed direction. Willie watched in horror as the wiper zipped back and forth, back and forth, thrashing the body across the window, limbs flailing and helmeted head butting the glass.

It was at this point that Lieutenant Willie Warner started to scream.

*

The Assembly Room was in a state of pandemonium. The screaming, already loud from the moment of Sylvia Rothschild's macabre arrival, ratcheted up several notches as the corpse lurched drunkenly from one side of the window to the other like a deranged can-can dancer. Flint Dugdale, initially speechless, started bellowing and roaring for calm, ordering them to return to their cabins immediately. But even his loudest commands went unheard and unheeded.

Emily was the first to stop screaming, but only because the horror of the scene had made her faint. On Earth, she would have slumped in her seat, but, being weightless, she remained as she was, the only tell-tale signs of her unconsciousness being her closed eyes and motionless limbs.

Everyone else was transfixed by the morbid oscillations before them. The teenagers had simultaneously whipped out mePhones and blablets and started filming the space dance the moment it had begun. It was only when one of the corpse's eyeballs dropped out of a socket that the gagging spectators had to look away.

Visibly fuming, Dugdale stared at Sylvia's lifeless form as it continued its wild swings across the window. Catching sight of a dial marked 'Wiper', he doggy-paddled his way across to it, initially turning it the wrong way, (which doubled the speed and height of Sylvia's leg-kicks) before moving it to the "off" position. The body stopped its dance in mid-swing as if waiting for applause or shouts of 'encore'. Its single remaining eye stared at the colonists while its limbs drifted gently as though caught on an interplanetary breeze. Flint jabbed at the control panel and slowly, very, very slowly, the horror show faded as a window blind descended. Finally, the shutter had made sufficient progress to hide the zombie spectacle from view.

One by one, the ship's heavily dazed personnel turned and drifted out of the Assembly Room like a departing horror movie audience. Even the teenagers stopped their filming and left the room to go view the footage somewhere quiet.

"Chuffin' magic," said Mr Snuggles as he departed.

Soon, the only people left were the furious Dugdale and the unconscious Miss Leach.

"You too," he ordered. "Out yer go."

But Emily moved not a muscle.

"Oh, chuffin' Nora!" exclaimed Dugdale on seeing her motionless form. "Don't tell me another one's snuffed it!"

20. Unequal and Inapposite Reactions

Back in her cabin, Delphinia Brush was wailing in high dramatic fashion, bear-hugging Tarquin's innocent little head to her ample bosom. "Oh, my poor little space hero."

Tarquin struggled against his mother's grip, unable to speak, unable to breathe.

"It's all my fault. I should have covered your eyes sooner and spared you the horror. But I was in a state of shock. It was so awful!" Her hug tightened. "I hope you didn't see that awful, ghastly thing, my little flapjack. If you did, try to put it out of your mind, else you'll have nightmares; you'll be scarred for life. Oh my God, what a terrible thought – and it's all my fault."

The youngster managed to release enough of a nostril to fill his empty lungs with air.

But this only made his mother hug him tighter. "Mummy's here for you."

Tarquin was starting to turn blue, and on the point of passing out, when Delphinia finally released him, clasping his cheeks between her chubby fingers and slapping a huge, wet kiss on his forehead.

"I'm OK, Mummy," said Tarquin when he had regained sufficient breath. "It was real bad."

"I know it was, my little fruit bat. I know it was."

"No, I mean 'bad' as in 'good'. So cool. Especially when her eye popped out."

*

Dr Adorabella Faerydae scrolled through the list of bush-remedies on her scratch-pad.

"Not feeling too good, honey bumps?" asked husband Brokk, pushing himself towards the mini-fridge for a space-can of lager. "You should try one of these."

She gave him a look of utter disdain. "I devote my life to caring for others, not myself."

"Sure you do, cherry lips. Sure you do. But who do you think might need emergency alternative treatment at this hour?"

"Duh! Like ... did you not see what just happened in the Assembly Room? Emergency? I'd say so." She turned to her alternative medicine cabinet and scanned the labels on the bottles before plucking a bottle of earwig powder and baboon navel fluff.

Brokk looked puzzled. "You mean that mummified old trout in the window? You might be a bit late to save her, my fairy cup-cake. By about eight months."

Adorabella flashed him a furious glance. "Not her, you idiot."

Brokk took a swig of his lager and gave her an enquiring look. "So?"

His wife huffed. "Any minute now," she explained patiently, "people are going to be knocking at that door, desperate for post-traumatic stress counselling." She pointed at the cabin door, as though he didn't know where it was.

Brokk gave a sceptical chuckle and strapped himself into his gaming console.

Adorabella stared at him. "What's that laugh supposed to mean?"

"Oh, come on, Addy-bells. You know no one ever comes to see you for treatment."

His wife was speechless.

"Aside from the medicals that everyone has to have, you've only had one 'patient' during this entire trip," continued Brokk. "And she's dead."

"That's simply not true."

"Which part?"

Adorabella stuttered, "I ... I ... I ... She died of natural causes."
"That's not how I heard it."
"What?"
"It's OK, darling, we all make mistakes."

*

Harry Fortune was pushing himself back and forth between one end of his cabin and the other – the zero-G equivalent of pacing. His face glowered, eyebrows melting towards the bridge of his nose, mouth downturned. He was fully immersed in his dark, artistic side. It was a huge moment for him, he knew that. Massive. And it terrified him. Was he up to the task? Would he be able to produce the goods at last?

For eight whole months he had not written a single poem of note, which, for a Poet in Residence, could be construed as something of a failure. The few love-odes dedicated to Penny Smith had bordered on the obscene and could hardly be classed as the sort of poetry commemorating *Mayflower III's* historic mission as his appointment required.

Nothing had come to him. His muse was extinguished. He felt a failure and a fraud.

Finally, after such a shocking event, such a dramatic, gut-wrenching, vivid event, the inspiration was flowing and he began to write.

Incident in the Assembly Room
High above the Martian sand,
We're waiting for the word to land.
InspectaBot's report comes through;
Base looks good – base looks new.
Cheers of joy and all are happy,
Life on board has been so crappy.
But then our laughter turns to shock
When on the window there's a knock
And Sylvia Rothschild stares at us
With zombie eyes and grin rictus.
The wiper swings her left and right.
Terror-struck, we flee in fright.
The dead old bird has spooked us proper,
And Dugdale took too long to stop her.

Harry punched the air and grinned. "Perfect," he said. "Brilliant. Just need about fifty more like that before the end of the mission and I'm sorted."

*

Emily regained consciousness with a start. It took a full second to get her bearings, another second to restrain herself from screaming the place down, and a third second to start enjoying the situation she had woken up to. For she was in Commander Dugdale's manly arms, and his lips were firmly clamped on hers. Suddenly, she felt she was floating on air, both literally and figuratively, and did her best to lap up the sensations zipping through her nervous system.

Flint Dugdale shot away from her. "Billy Arkwright's bollocks, you're alive!" he concluded, giving no indication of whether this pleased him or not.

"Oh, Commander Dugdale!" exclaimed Emily with a little giggle and a flutter of her eyelashes. "What am I to make of this?"

"Nowt ... It wert kiss er life," he explained, stuttering and edging even further away. "'Appen I thought you'd croaked ..."

Emily followed him, stroking the tight bun of greying hair on top of her head. "You saved my life, Commander Dugdale." She fanned her reddening cheeks. "How can I possibly repay you?" She gave what she intended to be a seductive wink.

Dugdale shuddered and tried to retreat further, but found himself backed up against the window blind. "Back off, Leachy," he ordered. As he recoiled more, his rear pressed against the window-blind button. The blind, which only minutes before had been so painfully slow to close, now sprang open in a flash as though on the world's most powerful spring.

Miss Leach gave a gasp of shock, and her advance on Dugdale stopped in its tracks. She stared, open-mouthed, past Dugdale's shoulder, through the panoramic window. Her breathing quickened and, once her lungs had filled with sufficient air, she let out an ear-piercing shriek.

Sylvia Rothschild's body was still spread-eagled on the window, snagged on the giant windscreen wiper, one eye dangling, and some gaping rents in her spacesuit revealing more mummified flesh than the average stomach can tolerate. But what prompted the scream was the sight of another space-suited figure, with its arms apparently hugging her from behind, space gloves cupped over breasts, pushing and pulling with forceful pelvic thrusts. In the process, the tear in Sylvia's spacesuit grew progressively larger, revealing more and more desiccated leg.

"Lieutenant Warner!" screamed Emily. "Stop that at once!" Unable to take any more, she paddled her way out of the Assembly Room as desperately and as quickly as she could, past a very surprised Zak Johnston who had just arrived and was gazing in astonishment at the scene outside the window.

Dugdale, too, was staring out of the window, his face one of total stupefaction. He grabbed his communicator from his top pocket and punched Lieutenant Willie Warner's icon. "What the hell are you doing with that stiff, Woggler?"

"She's stuck," came Willie's panting reply. He thrust once more and caused Sylvia Rothschild's helmet to clatter against the window glass.

Dugdale gaped in disbelief. "Right," he said at last. "I want all the corpses in t'ship in ten minutes. Then get yer skinny arse to t'cockpit to see me!"

21. Lost it in Space

Willie Warner sat in the changing room, his head in his hands. Even the room's foetid smell couldn't distract him from his sense of hopelessness and despair. He had removed his helmet but hadn't yet found the energy to remove the damp space-suit nor the moist boots.

"Whoa, dude," said Zak Johnston, floating into the room, dreadlocks tangled with headphone wires, all trailing behind. "Hail, Thane of the Stiff-bangers. Watched your latest 'thing' with old ma Rothschild out there. Hot stuff." He grinned and Warner's head sank lower still. "Props to ya, man. Don't get me wrong, friend. Dead-granny-shaggin' ain't my bag, but you'll hear no criticism of your fetishism from this guy."

Willie didn't respond.

"So, where is the old biddy, now that you two are an item?" Zak peered around the room. "Ain't ya going to introduce me to the space-kill moose?"

Warner was shaking his head. "I let her go."

Zak floated closer and stared hard at Willie's distraught features. "What, you dumped her? You are one callous space-dude. And after what you'd just been through? You guys were written in the stars. Where've you stashed her?"

"The smell," was all that Willie could say. "That awful smell."

"Yeah, just got a waft of *whiff de stiff*. Spill dude, where is she?"

Willie sighed and looked unseeingly into the distance. "I managed to haul her as far as the airlock. Got her inside."

"What d'ya do then, spaceboy?" interrupted Johnston.

"Kissed her goodnight and gave her the taxi fare home," snapped Willie. "What do you think I did? I closed the outer door, let the air fill and took off my helmet."

"Sure, I'm hearing yer," Zak replied, fiddling with the personal stereo that fused external sound with a Bob Marley beat and delivered it directly to his inner ears.

"The smell was awful. You can't believe how badly she stank." Willie fanned his nose at the very memory. "And putrid pieces of her kept floating out of her ripped suit. The more she warmed up, the worse it got."

"Gross Point Zero, man. Wait, I think Gran may have left her calling-card. If I'm not mistaken, I spy a flap of her wrinkly skin stuck to your chin."

Willie squealed and began swatting wildly at his face like a demented seal.

"Hold on there, cowboy," said Zak, grabbing his arm, and studying Willie's chin more closely. "Soz, dude, I am mistaken."

Willie sighed with relief, took a deep breath and continued. "There was no way I could bring her on board. So I opened up the outer door and pushed her back out into space, sweeping as much of the rotting stuff as I could out after her."

"Awesome, dog!" said Zak, slapping his thigh and hooting. "Props maximus, man. Wait till Dugdale hears about this shit. He'll board the train to Explosion City."

Willie's head jerked up at Zak. "No, he mustn't find out. Please, please don't tell him. We need to hush it up, Zak. We get three suits ..." He swept a hand to indicate the space-suits strapped to the wall, "... and we fill them with old blankets or something. Then we stow them in InspectaBot's pod as planned. He'll never know."

"Count me out, space ranger." But then Zak's eyebrows knitted together and his face brightened with excitement. "Wait! Better still, let's tell him!"

"Are you crazy?"

"No, but he is." Zak lowered his voice. "Captain Dug-dude is so losing the plot. Like a one-man, out-of-control locomotive. Your triple-body balls-up could just launch him on the fast road to

Madsville. Think George Cukor's *Gaslight*."

"And sending him over the edge is a good thing?"

"To our advantage, dude. Pro us. The moment he's unfit to lead, we're in charge. You and me, friend. Kings of the castle."

Willie frowned, not entirely convinced. But before he could respond, the door had swished open and the devil they were talking of had entered. Dugdale's expression was not a serene one and Willie looked for a place to hide.

"Weiner!" bawled the commander, his face purple. For Willie, hiding was no longer an option. "What the buggerin', bollockin', friggin' 'eck did yer think you were doin' out there??"

"I ..." started Willie, but Dugdale had grabbed him by his spacesuit lapels and pulled him closer.

"What part of 'you sneak outside and bring stiffs indoors secretly' didn't you understand? 'Appen you thought it'd be a laugh to start flingin' bodies at t'window where every one o' passengers could get t'best view."

Willie tried to breathe in some fresh air, free of Dugdale's halitosis, but Flint was not done and was wafting more bad breath into his face.

"And, if that weren't enough! You go and start 'umping the old trout across t'windscreen. By 'eck, Wiggler, I thought Johnston were weird, but yer interplanetary sex act trumps pretty much anything he can come up with."

"Hey, cap," interrupted Zak with a wink at Willie. "That's all old news, sir. Previous episode, man. You need a series catch-up; story's moved on."

Dugdale released Willie's lapels and swivelled to stare at Zak with a mixture of fury and puzzlement. "What yer blitherin' on about, Johnston?"

"You're at the last stop, dude, but the train's pulled into a new station."

Still Dugdale stared at him in open-mouthed bafflement.

"Yesterday's papers," continued Zak, putting his hands behind his head. "Today's headline, in 50-point boldface, reads: *Bodies go missing.*"

Dugdale's mouth dropped open even further. "Bodies what?" he started, and then wheeled to glare at Willie. "I hope fer your sake, Wobbler, that Corky the Clown 'ere ain't tellin' me yer've lost t'dead'uns?"

Willie shuddered. "The bodies aren't missing, as such," he started, swallowing hard.

"I'm still hearing the words 'missing' and 'bodies' in the same sentence."

"We know, in a general way, where they are, sir," started Willie. "They're in orbit. It's just that it's a, sort of, re-entrant orbit."

Dugdale's gigantic hands moved towards Willie, but instead of grabbing the lapels, grasped his scrawny neck instead.

"Think about it, Chief," intervened Zak. "Last wishes of the Dame dudette fulfilled. Buried on Mars. Good and deep, too, if she happens to hit a soft bit. Or, alternative numero duo, they burn up on re-entry, ashes scattered across the planet. No more bodies … no more paperwork. It's a win-win!"

Flint continued to glare deep into Warner's eyes, his hands still encircling his throat. But then his grip slackened.

"You might have a point there, Rastaman," he growled. Then he looked at both of them. "Not a word to anyone. Gorrit?"

Willie nodded vigorously while Zak looked slightly dismayed at his plan having misfired. Dugdale floated towards the door but then stopped and spun around. "'Appen, I've made up me mind who's goin' down t'Mars and who's stayin' in this shit-bucket. Wobbler, I'll give you a clue: you ain't going." With that, he turned and pulled himself out of the changing room.

"But," cried Willie. "You can't. Nooooooooooo!"

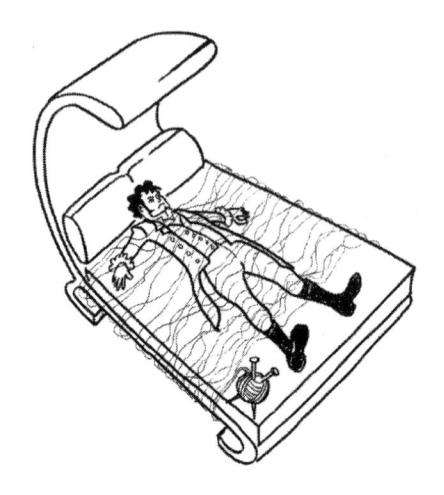

22. Love, Factually?

Miss Leach was once more both literally and metaphorically floating on air as she pulled herself into her cabin and locked the door behind her, clinging onto the handle to steady her trembling. She could hardly breathe as she kept running that kiss over and over in her mind.

What a kiss!

And what a man! There was something so raw, so primal, so manly about Mission Commander Flint Dugdale that her mind always turned to mush in his presence. Strange hormones pulsed through her, reaching parts of her body that no hormones had ever ventured into before. Delicious sensations dribbled through her palpitating form.

Emily managed to calm herself enough to review what that kiss might signify? Lacking a sufficiently encyclopaedic repertoire of past kisses to draw on, Emily could only guess at the significance of this one. However, based solely on the reactions it had produced within her central nervous system, its significance was surely Immense.

Emily gave herself a hug and allowed a wide grin to spread across her face.

With a start she glimpsed the human form strapped to her bed and her grin vanished. The figure lay silent and still. Six-foot-tall and dashingly handsome, dressed in long boots, riding-trousers and an unbuttoned, wet-look shirt. There were straps at the wrists and ankles, plus a larger strap across the chest from which sprouted a healthy bush of manly hair. There was no sign of life, no movement, no breathing. Emily caught her breath and put a hand to her lips. "Oh my," she squeaked. "Oh my, oh my ..."

She fanned her cheeks with greater gusto and propelled herself towards the bed.

"It's a lucky thing," she said to the immobile human form lying before her, "that I didn't invite Commander Dugdale back for a coffee."

The mysterious figure made no response.

"Or what would he have thought of me?" She undid the top two buttons of her blouse and fanned herself some more. "What would he have thought?"

23. Poles Together

With much joshing and slapping of backs, the four Polish builder-bots, the *robotniki*, ambled over the Martian sand towards the front entrance of Botany Base. All were covered in splashes of paint and thick layers of plaster. Witek, the most rotund of the four, struggled to keep pace with the others, though they were hardly rushing.

Maciek stopped in his tracks about ten metres from the entrance, and the others stopped with him. A look of surprise and amusement crossed his work-hardened face. <O kura,> he signalled, his mouth gaping in mock amazement. <Drzwi!>

The others looked amused and amazed, too, as they took in the fact that Botany Base now had a set of airlock doors blocking their entrance into the building.

<Drzwi!> repeated the others, laughing and slapping their foreheads and wondering who could have installed them. Then Maciek pointed out the poorly fitting pressure seals on the outer door, the loose handle and the rough edges where it had been cut down to fit the opening. He suggested that even Witek could have done a better job.

<Główno!> Witek swore back at him, using the Polish 'swear-lite' they had all been programmed with. Rysio and Andrzej howled,

giving him matey punches.

Maciek, playing the clown, strode over to the outer door and pressed the OPEN button. With an exaggerated bow, he invited the others in. Giggling like schoolgirls, they obediently trotted into the airlock, tapping at the doors to check the workmanship, and sniggering at the shakiness of the whole construction.

They were still sniggering as they passed through the inner door into the entrance hallway. But the moment they saw what was waiting for them, all sniggering ceased and all movement screeched to a halt.

There, visibly fuming, was HarVard in the guise of a stern-faced, stockily-built battle-axe of a woman, her hog jaws set in a scowl, arms crossed, a wooden rolling-pin grasped in one hand. The fluffiness of her apparel – the pink nightgown, fur-lined slippers and pink hair-curlers – did nothing to soften her stony appearance.

<O kura,> signalled Maciek,
<Kolęda,> muttered Witek.
<Główno,> squeaked Rysio.
<Piernik,> hissed Andrzej.

The *robotniki* turned to make their escape, but the inner airlock door had already closed behind them.

"And where do you think you've been?" growled the formidable female, her face like a crushed handbag, her voice more male than female.

Maciek bravely wheeled forward, a cowed expression on his blocky face. <In Udder Playce,> he signalled in his broken binary comms, his jointed arm pointing vaguely back the way they had come.

"Oh, really?" said the Gorgon, advancing on him while slapping the rolling-pin into the palm of her free hand. Her squashed face twisted into a fake smile, her voice adopting a menacing calm. "And how is the 'Udder Playce' looking these days?"

Maciek edged back. <Er ...>
<Is good,> put in Rysio, his head clanking as he nodded.
<Good,> confirmed Witek, looking for a recharging-point.

Andrzej, the tall, thin one, gave a shrug. <Could do with leetle more work.>

"I see." The voice still had its fake calmness. "And what would you say about *this* 'playce'?" The dragon-woman swept the rolling pin in a large arc to indicate Botany Base. "Is good?"

The *robotniki* would have been well advised to think their answers through, instead of just blurting them out.

<No way is good,> said Witek.

<Is joke,> said Andrzej.

<It's ... how you say ... ship-hole,> said Maciek. <Andrzej right. Is joke. All measurements wrong. Nothing fit. Should knock down and start again.>

"Hmm," said the dragon lady, her nostrils flaring and a hint of smoke emerging from them. "It's funny you should say that."

The *robotniki* exchanged smirks, taking her words at their most literal.

"Because the HUMANS ARRIVE IN FOUR HOURS!" The voice had lost much of its calmness. "So this place better be ready by then. And if it means knocking it all down and starting again, then so be it. But you have only four hours to do it in!"

The Polish builder-bots' jaws dropped. They'd never seen HarVard so agitated.

<No way,> said Maciek at last, shaking his head.

<Why can't Eng-Lish robots do it?> asked Witek.

The other *robotniki* looked at Witek as though he were insane.

<Look,> started Maciek as reasonably as he could. <We just come back for rest. Recharge batteries, oil bearings, have game of cards and go back. We can't work here. No one can work here. Is ship-hole.>

The dragon-woman shook, like a volcano about to blow. She raised her rolling-pin high into the air. "That," she yelled, "is AN ORDER!"

The *robotniki* blinked in surprise, shrinking back from the holographic weapon. They exchanged a few Polish remarks, involving much shrugging and some argument.

<OK,> said Maciek finally. <We do it. But need leetle rest first.>

"Five minutes," said the monster woman. "That's all you get. Then go see Tude. He'll tell you what still needs to be done."

The *robotniki* exchanged hurt looks at the injustice of it all.

"We build it all," complained Andrzej. "Everything. But plans wrong. Nothing fit. English robots mess up. We give up."

"GO!" the woman bellowed, brandishing her rolling pin.

All four turned and ambled towards the recharging room, dragging their feet and their caterpillar tracks as they did so.

"Oh, lads," HarVard called after them, his holo-image having lost the rolling-pin and adopted a pleasanter mien. "Just one thing. Where's Zilli?"

Maciek turned round and shrugged. <How we know?>

The battle-axe frowned. "But she went to fetch you from the Other Place."

Maciek glanced at the others, but they merely shrugged back. <We not see Zilli.>

<Zilli never been to Udder Playce,> put in Witek.

HarVard looked even more puzzled. "Curious," she said. "I wonder what's happened to her." Then she looked up at the *robotniki*. "Off you go, then. The clock's ticking."

24. Furiouser and Furiouser

Commander Flint Dugdale was discovering that packing a suitcase in zero gravity is a bit like wrestling a feisty octopus. Each time he placed a new item in the case, many of the previously stuffed items would gently drift out of it. As he caught and replaced the escaping items, others would take their place. It was an activity that did not suit his fragile temper.

"Frack, frack, frack, bollocks!" he yelled as another pair of underpants drifted away, closely followed by a sock and a small face flannel. "Frack!"

With a supreme effort, and lightning movements, he managed to get everything back in, slam the lid shut, clamp his two giant hands on top of it, and press the overfull case down onto his bed. But, as he pushed, his weightless body rotated in the opposite direction and his arms extended further and further. With nothing to get a purchase on, he found himself floating away. All he could do was watch helplessly as the lid opened and the case's contents vacated it one by one.

But for once his anger did not get the better of him. A sticker on the side of the case caught his eye and sent him careering down Memory Lane to the Club 18-30 Ibiza holiday of many, many years before. Standing on the balcony of his top floor room at Hotel El Paradiso, he had watched open-mouthed as his best mate, Banyard, had flung the contents of the very same suitcase over the edge for a joke. No problem with gravity back then. How they had laughed as they had peered down at the swimming pool far below and spotted a dozing German sun-worshipper festooned with Flint's grundies. *'Appy days,* thought Flint, *'appy days.*

But, just as quickly, his thoughts careered back to the present and to the sight of his belongings exploding in super-slow-motion from the case. "Right, yer buggers, I'll fix yer."

He propelled himself to Commander Lionheart's private writing desk and pulled out a roll of sticky tape. Tearing it with his teeth, Dugdale started taping the orbiting items of clothing to the case's bottom. First, a layer of underpants. Next, his Hawaiian-print T-shirts, a pair of flip-flops, sunglasses and a giant bag of cheese-and-onion crisps. Essential items each and every one. As far as Dugdale was concerned Mars was one vast beach, albeit lacking sea, blue skies and bikini-clad babes. His time would be spent reclining in a deckchair, slurping Martian-brewed beer, and watching sports coverage beamed from Earth, content in the knowledge that his job was done. The rest of them would do his bidding, setting up the first Martian colony; growing food, cooking, cleaning, sewing, having babies and all the rest of that hippy stuff. He would be the famous one and milk the glory of being the First Man on Mars.

Next came his most treasured possessions: a football shirt that had once belonged to Billy Bremner, signed by the whole 1970s Leeds United team, Geoff Boycott's cricket bat, with an unexplained bloodstain on one edge, a few cans of Newcastle Brown, and twenty packets of Granny Braithwaite's Yorkshire Pudding mix.

As he packed two hundred Benson & Hedges cigarettes, a pang of homesickness pulled at his heart. Flint cracked the cellophane on a new pack and lit up. He was only an occasional smoker, primarily in moments of reflection. He inhaled a lungful, held it for a second and then, dragon-like, blew a stream of smoke across the cabin. His thoughts turned to his home in Huddersfield. His family. His children and their various mothers. The Muck'n'Shovel pub. Friday night darts and beer.

On the ceiling-mounted screen above his head a CGI-generated avatar was frantically and silently signalling to him. Early in the mission Flint had switched off the annoying voice interface of HarOld, the ship's computer. Since then, important messages like 'watch out for that meteor shower' or 'the toilet disposal unit is blocked' or 'FIRE!' had been relayed by the silent avatar through the medium of mime. Right now, it was dancing a message of disaster, miming out, as best it could, the consequences of Dugdale's smoking. But, even when Flint glanced up and caught sight of the avatar through the billowing clouds of smoke, he merely looked straight through it. His thoughts had locked onto the sacrifices he had made and the indignities he had suffered to become the first man on Mars.

And then, in accordance with the frantically mimed warnings, the cabin sprinkler system activated, extinguishing Flint's cigarette, destroying his magic moment of reflection, and soaking his belongings.

"Chuffin' bollocks!" he yelled.

25. Lifts and Separates

Mayflower III was buzzing. Partly from the excitement of packing and preparation for the first steps on Mars, but mainly from the ship's ion drives which were channelling a vast flow of energy to the high-intensity laser beam that formed an induction cable for the ship's Space Elevator. This was how the colonists would be descending to the planet some 58,000 feet below. Not a choice made by the brilliant NAFA boffins, but rather by NAFA's less-than-brilliant Chief Accountant who had calculated it to be by far the cheapest solution.

Most of the colonists' luggage was now packed and stowed in the Assembly Room, there not being sufficient room in the space elevator both for colonists and their possessions. The elevator was to be sent back up to collect the baggage.

A slightly damp Dugdale poked his head into the cockpit where a very downcast Willie Warner was twiddling his thumbs.

"Wonka," growled Dugdale.

Willie looked up, sudden hope in his eyes. "You've changed your mind?"

"About what?"

"Me coming down to Mars?"

"Not friggin' likely."

Willie's face sagged.

"I've gorra job even *you* can't cock up."

"Great."

"When t'elevator's safely on its way, get yer skinny bum along t'me cabin and pack me clobber in t'suitcase. You'll find it all floatin' about the place. And soppin' wet."

"What an honour. I can hardly wait."

"Mind you just pack the floatin' stuff. Touch owt else and I'll kill yer. If yer open any drawers, I'll kill yer," he said with a look that convinced Willie he wasn't joking.

"That's pretty clear, thank you."

"Once yer've finished, go t'Assembly Room 'n get rest ert bags together. I'll send t'elevator back up and you shove 'em in. Then press 'Down' button. Can yer manage that?"

"I really think I should go down with you, sir, instead of Zak," Willie said one final time. "I know something that no one else does."

"Yeah," responded Dugdale. "Yer know how to be a completely useless tosser. Now shut yer cake 'ole and act like you're doin' summat useful."

*

In her cabin, Emily Leach had a huge decision to make. Most of her belongings were now packed inside her huge, coffin-sized leather trunk, with a few odds and ends tucked into the handful of hatboxes she had brought with her. But there was one thing that remained. She pushed herself towards her bunk and stared down at the item, still lying strapped to it, silent and immobile. A wicked smile played about her lips. Should she take him? She chewed her lower lip and said aloud, "To bring, or not to bring?"

Whatever she did, she'd have to get rid of the evidence. What if someone were to find her ... companion? What a palaver there would be! What embarrassment.

She exhaled deeply, shook her head and fluttered her eyes. "Oh, Mr Darcy," she said, almost in a swoon, taking in the rippling muscles showing through the flimsy clothing. As she stroked the dark, flowing hair, always slightly damp, she made her decision. Her stroking stopped and her bony fingers gently probed the crown of the head. Finally, finding what she was looking for, she edged her fingernails under the cap and pulled it free. A rush of air gushed out through the valve, hissing and sputtering as the doll slowly deflated. The chest caved in, then the head, and at last the legs lay flat too.

"Ah, Mr Darcy," sighed Emily as she gazed over the collapsed surface of the wet-look shirt and well-packed riding breeches. "Not so hard now, are we, sir."

*

With most of the air out, Emily removed the straps keeping the Mr Darcy doll pinned to her bunk and started rolling him up, Swiss-roll style, beginning from the feet. She had to be careful of the sensitive self-inflate switch, disguised as one of Mr Darcy's shirt buttons, as the slightest touch would fully inflate the doll within two seconds.

"I've decided to bring you with me to Mars, Mr Darcy," she said with a twinkle in her eye, as she opened the lid of her trunk and set about trying to squeeze the literary sex-symbol into it. After a few frustrating minutes, he was safely stowed with all her clothing, and the trunk was shut again. Emily panted to get her breath back and then checked her bun in the mirror. After a little adjustment she was ready to face the Red Planet.

*

As teenagers Gavin and Tracey approached the space elevator, pulling themselves along by the corridor rails, they halted to survey the scene. The lift doors were open and most of the colonists were already squashed inside, bobbing about gently in its cramped confines, avoiding eye contact and eschewing all conversation. Outside, Dugdale was hovering and impatiently ushering people in. The thumb of his other hand was firmly pressed against the lift-call button to keep the doors from closing. "Gerra move on, you two spotty 'erberts. We 'aven't got all day."

They observed the faces of the colonists already in there, faces betraying looks of discomfort and trepidation.

"No way is I gettin' in there, bruv," Tracey said, shaking her head and starting to back away.

"Get a grip, sis. It's just a lift," said Gavin. He paused. "Although me is finkin' it looks more like a broom cupboard, innit."

"Black hole of Calcutta, more like," added Tracey.

"Space elevator," growled Dugdale, fixing them with a deadly stare. "Now, gerrin."

A muffled voice from inside the lift, belonging to the other teenager, Oberon, said, "No, this is deffo a lift. Smells of piss."

Delphinia clapped her hands over Tarquin's ears.

Gavin had made up his mind. "No room, chief," he said, indicating the human sardines before him. "Youse go ahead, mate. We's is perfectly fine *ici*. We'll get the next one." He grinned.

"Yeah, E.C.," said Tracey, before bursting into a fit of giggles.

Dugdale glowered and fumed. "In there. Now!"

As Gavin and Tracey approached there was unwilling shuffling and rearrangement of bodies inside the cramped space elevator.

"Can you shove up a bit," moaned Brokk to Zak Johnston. "Your bony elbows are digging into my ribs."

"Take a chill-pill, dude. There ain't much room in this space tomb. And the poet dude has his head in close proximity to my masculinity," retorted Johnston.

This was true. For some reason, perhaps due to his artistic leanings or maybe because he had approached the lift at the wrong angle, Harry Fortune was oriented upside down, his legs and space clogs poking above the heads of the others, his head uncomfortably close to both Zak Johnston's trouser zip and Delphinia's ample bottom. "There's a poem in this," he kept saying to himself to take his mind off the view. But the only lines that kept forcing themselves into his brain, over and over again, were: 'There once was a spaceman from Mars, In a lift he was faced with an ....'

"Friggin' well SHUT YOUR FACES!" roared Dugdale as he shoved Gavin and Tracey into the scrum with the aid of a hand, a shoulder and a knee. As he did so, the greasy thumb of his other hand slipped off the lift-call button. A loud ding issued from the lift and a recorded voice announced, "Doors closing".

Instantly the lift was an echo-chamber of screams and cries: "No, not yet!" "Wait!" "Aaaaaargh!"

In the panic and struggle, both Gavin and Tracey found themselves ejected back into the corridor, narrowly avoiding the pincer-grip of the closing doors.

Dugdale stabbed the button with his thumb and the doors opened again. There was a collective sigh of relief.

After a second short struggle, involving even more compaction of the bodies in the small compartment, Tracey and Gavin were accommodated within the crush.

"Is that all of yer?" demanded Dugdale, unable to perform a head-count on account of not all heads being visible.

"One missing," someone shouted from deep inside the scrum.

"Who's that?"

"Brokk."

"You mean t'gormless twonk wi't goaty beard? I saw 'im get on," retorted Dugdale to the voice.

"Yes, I'm Brokk," said the voice.

"Well yer can't be missin' then can yer, dumbnut?"

"No, I'm Brokk and I'm not missing. Obviously. I'm the one telling you someone is missing."

"Who the frig is it, then?"

"Brokk," said another, squeakier voice, sounding suspiciously like Oberon Faerydae.

Dugdale roared. "Who. The. Chuff. Is. Missing?"

"Miss Leach," said several voices.

The mere mention of the name made Dugdale shudder. Powerful though the urge to leave without her was, he stayed his ground and his blubbery face contorted to a shape that conveyed the message, *I might have known.*

At that very moment the echo of a faint female voice sounded from round the bend at the far end of corridor. "Yoo-hoo," it called. "I'm coming. Would you mind holding the lift, please."

"Space elevator," Dugdale murmured under his breath.

A silence fell as they waited for Emily to turn the corner and join them. Dugdale checked his watch. A couple of teenagers giggled somewhere at the back of the lift. And then Tarquin said, "Mummy."

"Yes, my little storm trooper?"

"It says here: 'Lift. Max. cap. 8 pers.'"

"Space elevator," repeated Dugdale wearily, unaware of the ripple of unease that Tarquin's words had set bouncing back and forth within the tiny compartment.

"That means: Maximum capacity 8 persons," explained Delphinia, stroking his head.

"I know what it means, Mummy. It's just that there are ten people on board already, not counting Mr Snuggles. When Commander Dugdale and Miss Leach are on board there'll be twelve, and with Mr Snuggles, thirteen. Which is not only very unlucky, but is more than the maximum capacity, isn't it, Mummy?"

Delphinia tried to laugh her son's question off as the sense of unease in the lift became more tangible. "I think they just forgot to take the sign off."

"You see, son," put in his father, Brian. "This lif ... er ... space elevator was bought, second-hand, by NAFA from the Penge Shopping Centre where it had had many years of useful service."

"That would, like, explain the smell of piss," put in Oberon from the back. "Innit."

"The clever chaps at NAFA," continued Brian undeterred, "spent most of the lift budget on a brilliant laser beam induction system in place of a cable and there was only enough money left for a cheap lift carriage." There was a pre-panic murmur from all around him. "But, there's no need to worry, everyone. They've done a marvellous job of refurbishing it, making it airtight and painting the outside with two coats of anti-radiation emulsion."

"And look, my little plumchops," added Delphinia. "They've even added a tiny viewing window in case you feel claustrophobic or travel sick."

The ripples of unease were working themselves up into a tsunami of concern.

"Besides," added Delphinia. "Don't forget we're weightless. So it doesn't matter how many persons we have in here."

"But there's gravity on Mars, Mummy."

"How right you are, my clever little sausage." She grinned proudly as she fondly squeezed her little boy's cheek. "But you surely know that gravity is a lot weaker on Mars. So, 13 persons weigh a lot less. Say, as much as 8 persons?"

"But, Mummy, when the lift starts decelerating, won't we weigh a lot more than 13 persons?"

Delphinia forced a loud laugh as she looked around at the terror-stricken sets of eyes around her. One pair belonged to her scientist husband, Brian. "That's enough showing off, my little Einstein."

"But ..." said several of the colonists before a commotion in the corridor outside distracted them.

It was Miss Leach, floating toward them with her man-sized trunk and a small flotilla of hatboxes, attached to it by pink ribbons. The elderly daughter of nonagenarian zillionaire Sir Geoffrey Leach, made her awkward, weightless way towards them.

The needle on Dugdale's rage gauge turned swiftly towards the red zone. "I thought I told yer: no boggin' luggage!"

Emily fluttered her eyelashes and tried to play the helpless female card. "But, Commander. A lady cannot be without her personal nick-knacks. I'm sure we can find a little room to squeeze in a ladies' travel-case or two."

Dugdale stared at the trunk and hatboxes in disbelief. "No boggin' luggage. End of!"

Still she advanced towards the lift, pushing against the corridor rails with her feet. She had built up quite a pace before tragedy struck. Her long pearl necklace, dangling weightlessly behind her, snagged on a service valve and pulled her up short. As she grabbed at it to prevent strangulation she, naturally, let go of the trunk's handle. Its momentum kept it heading towards Dugdale, catching him unawares and bundling him up against the wall, like a burly policeman apprehending a drunk, smearing Dugdale's greasy face across the stainless steel surface. "What the fwaolloah?" was all he could say, using both hands to forcefully push the trunk off him. In the process, his thumb released the lift button.

Ding! "Doors closing," announced the pleasant lift voice, and the doors slid towards one another.

"Nooo!" came the cries from inside the lift, and from Emily outside it.

In a flash, little Tarquin sprang to the rescue, locating the 'Open doors' button on the control panel inside the lift and pressing it just in time to reverse the doors' sliding progress.

The trunk and hatboxes had crashed into the opposite wall. The impact had snapped the trunk's clasps, allowing its lid to spring open and its contents to spew out into the corridor. Within seconds the air was filled with a cornucopia of feminine undergarments and an explosion of subtle, and not-so-subtle, fragrances. Billowing from the trunk was a whirling cloud of corsets, lacy brassieres, stockings, suspender belts, frilly knickers, pink dresses, feather boas and assorted ladies' separates, as well as items of a personal feminine nature rarely discussed in polite company.

But worse was to come. The impact had also triggered Mr Darcy's self-inflate button and, like a jack-in-the-box, he had sprung out of the trunk, reaching full inflation, and full speed, within 2 seconds. His trajectory took him towards the open lift and its cramped occupants. After brushing against Delphinia's bottom he came to a halt pressed up against Adorabella. The presence of female pheromones triggered his 'Smoulder Mode' causing his eyes to narrow, stubble to blacken and chin dimple to appear.

Adorabella screamed. Emily Leach screamed. Dugdale roared in disbelief and the teenagers sniggered. The rest were too stunned to react.

Gavin, seeing an opportunity for a lark, solemnly offered Mr. Darcy a hand and introduced himself. "Yo. I is Gav. You must be, like, a close personal friend of Leachy, innit." He gave a smutty wink on the word 'friend'.

Emily, now bright red, wrenched her necklace free of the valve, sending pearls spinning into the zero-G air and then, like a geriatric otter, swam her way towards her life-sized doll. "He's my literary companion," she explained to the smirking crowd. "Programmed to read and discuss all the classics. We're currently doing Thomas Hardy."

For some reason, the last statement made everyone laugh which, in turn, made Emily blush even more.

Sensing the presence of his owner, Mr Darcy's eyes widened and he ramped up to 'Lover Mode'; a long slug-like tongue crept out from between moistening lips and started drawing weirdly hypnotic circles in the air, as though licking out the last drops from the bottom of a yoghurt carton.

"What's he doing, Mummy?" asked Tarquin, hardly finishing the question before Delphinia had clapped a sweaty hand over his eyes and manoeuvred her ample form to block his view. "It's nothing, poppet," she said with a disgusted curl to her lips. "Just keep pressing that lift-button."

Gavin invited Mr Darcy for a dance. "Cue music, maestro, please."

A blast of techno-breeze issued from Oberon's blablet and Gavin began weightlessly cavorting with the doll, mugging and grinning. Tracey cheered, Oberon applauded, and Miss Leach turned white with horror. She grabbed one of her pneumatic reading companion's arms and tried to pull him away. But Gavin wasn't about to relinquish his new comedy partner without a struggle. So, teenager and spinster engaged in a desperate tug-of-war, stretching Mr. Darcy's body and causing his shirt buttons to pop off and his firm, rippling, hairy chest to heave into view.

When Mr Darcy appeared to be at the limits of his elasticity, Gavin let go, catapulting Emily and Mr Darcy back into the passage. They cannoned into Dugdale and the three of them tumbled through the miasma of feminine apparel.

Dugdale, fuming, returned to the lift, swatting ladies' garments to the left and right as he did so. He turned back to see the receding Emily entangled with her rubber lover. "Leave t'friggin' love puppet alone, Leachy, and get in t'lift!"

After bouncing off a few walls, Emily managed to steady herself and start back towards the open door, reluctantly leaving Mr Darcy behind. As she went she collected her clothing from the air around her, folding it and all the while muttering, "He's just a literary companion, you know. Just a literary companion."

"Leave t'friggin' ..." started Dugdale, but was interrupted by a sudden shriek of "Yeuch!" from behind. He turned just in time to see Tarquin thrashing with both hands at a pair of cami-knickers clamped to his face.

What happened next seemed to happen in the slowest of slow motions. With the boy's thumb no longer pressing the crucial lift button, there was a *Ding!* and the lift announced, "Doors closing."

Dugdale stared mortified as the metal doors slid shut, the image left ingrained on his retinas being of a grinning Mr Snuggles, staring out from the shrinking opening, giving a plaintive wave.

"Noooooo!" he yelled, pulling himself back to the lift doors and going into a frenzy of lift-button pressing, making a strange whimpering noise as he did so.

From behind the doors could be heard a cheerful electronic voice saying, "Welcome to Penge Shopping Centre. Gateway to a world of shopping adventures. Going down."

"Oh, fiddle-sticks," said Miss Leach with a slight shrug of the shoulders. "They've jolly-well left without us. So, it's just thee and me, Mr. Flint." She drifted toward him, fluttering her eyelids in what she imagined to be a seductive manner.

Dugdale, seeing his dreams going up in smoke, redoubled his lift-button pressing efforts.

Ding! The doors opened. "Level 2. Ladies' lingerie," announced the electronic voice.

Inside, the occupants appeared to be in a rigid and silent state of shock. Without uttering a word, Dugdale grabbed Miss Leach by the lapel of her blouse and dragged her into the lift after him, wedging her into a gap between Gavin and Adorabella. Maintaining a threatening silence, he punched the 'Ground Floor' button and the doors closed once again.

Ding! "Going down."

Down plunged the lift, throwing the hapless passengers up at the ceiling. If any dared to think that the worst might be over, they were wrong.

26. The Knicker Man

In the cockpit, watching the CCTV images of the events unfolding in and around the space elevator, Lieutenant Willie Warner experienced a wide range of wholly negative emotions. First, the sight of the space colonists filing, and then piling, into the second-hand lift compartment filled him with an overwhelming, all-consuming, gut-wrenching resentment that these people ... *these* people, for goodness sake! ... would be the first to walk on Mars and, worse, the first to encounter the 12-foot alien bird-people that he alone had discovered.

"Where's the justice in that?" he moaned aloud even though there was no one there to hear or sympathize with him. Although Willie had been the youngest of seven boys, the other six all high achievers, and had known injustice his entire life he had, sadly, never quite grown accustomed to it or learnt how to accept it.

"Look at them!" he wailed, pulling at his thinning hair in frustration. How was it fair that those morons would soon be making History while he, grade A* space academy cadet, was to be left alone on board. Three years of intensive astronaut training and, now that the big moment had arrived, here he was: relegated to bag-boy. If only he'd completed another year, maybe they would have let him wash and iron their space dungarees.

Just the sight of Dugdale, hovering outside the lift door, drove

Willie to distraction. "Him! Representing Mankind? I ask you!"

Willie studied each of them in turn, wondering who had battered Penny Smith to death and for what reason.

He knew full well that the very pictures he was watching would be winging their way back to Earth, to be beamed directly into the homes of billions of people worldwide. What he was seeing, everyone on Earth would be seeing a mere 6 minutes later.

Willie put his head in his hands. There was no way of stopping the images reaching Earth and preventing the World witnessing the British way of space exploration and how a once-proud nation was making a total balls-up of one of the most important moments ever. It seemed a painfully long time before the lift doors closed for the final time and departed, plummeting towards the surface of the Red Planet.

Willie closed his eyes and moved his hands up to clutch the top of his head. On screen could still be seen the floating clothing and, at the end of the corridor, the full-sized blow-up doll bobbing about as though resentful at having been left behind. Not as resentful as Willie, though. Particularly as he knew he'd be the one having to clear up the mess.

His mind suddenly filled with bad thoughts, wicked thoughts. Wishes for disasters, evil hopes that things might go horribly, tragically, fatally wrong. Perhaps the lift would crash, or burn up on re-entry, or would be met by an army of hostile 12-foot bird-people who would merciless peck the crew and colonists to death. Mankind's future in space would then lie with himself, Lieutenant William Hilda Warner. Ah, if only.

*

"Such a shame my space training never covered this," muttered Willie through gritted teeth as he plucked various items of female apparel out of the air in the corridor – camisoles and corsets and cami-knickers and suspenders and crotchless panties. As he folded each item and popped it through the narrow opening in the trunk, he tried desperately *not* to picture Emily Leach wearing it. Not easy but, for the sake of his sanity, necessary. Particularly the crotchless panties. No man in the Solar System deserved that particular image in his head.

Willie had taken the precaution of wearing latex gloves. The thought of his bare skin making contact with any of these lacy, frilly, highly-perfumed things made him shudder. He wondered what additional precautions he'd need when it came to dealing with Dugdale's underwear when he went to pack the commander's suitcase.

Once all garments and personal nick-knacks had been packed in the trunk, he faced the problem of Mr Darcy. The doll was hovering at the far end of the corridor and seemed to be in 'Simmer Mode', eyeing Willie like some sort of unwelcome love rival.

Willie eyed him back. "Hmm, an inflatable literary character," he mused. "What a brilliant invention. Five million years of evolution for ... that."

He approached the doll warily. Somewhere there had to be a valve to deflate it, but Willie hardly fancied groping the doll from head to foot to locate it. Indeed, as he came closer the doll's simmer mode switched to a more threatening demeanour.

He decided on a softly-softly approach. "My, my Mr. Darcy, how handsome you look, with your tousled hair, frilly wet-look shirt and tight riding britches. I can barely resist kissing you myself."

Perhaps Willie should have realized that the inflatable doll's program was not sophisticated enough to comprehend sarcasm. So, the moment Willie got close enough, Mr Darcy stretched out his rubber arms and switched to 'Stage 1 Lover Mode', wrapping himself around the lieutenant.

Maybe it was the romantic corridor lighting, or the subliminal eroticism of having just handled a trunk-full of female underwear, or because Willie had never actually been kissed before, but the young lieutenant was lost in the moment, and when Mr Darcy gently slipped his moist gel tongue into his mouth, Willie reciprocated.

But even a rubber sex doll has standards. Once the Mr Darcy doll had fully registered Warner's ugliness at close quarters, he recoiled and, an instant later, flipped open the cap of his own deflation valve.

"Bastard!" screamed the rebuffed Warner as Darcy withered in his embrace and, once again, Willie was left to consider his romantic shortcomings.

*

Grim though the experience of packing Miss Leach's trunk had been, the experience of packing Dugdale's stuff promised to be far worse. The items floating in the commander's cabin looked a lot less wholesome than those he'd just been dealing with. They were larger, greyer, more frayed and holey, more prominently stained, and emanating odours that were as far from the delicate scents of Miss Leach's perfumes as Mars is from the other end of the galaxy. Warner took one look and closed the door, gagging slightly at the memory of what he had just witnessed. The worst part was that Dugdale's suitcase was floating on the other side of the room, meaning he would need to battle his way through the aerial slurry of the commander's garments to get to it.

"What a joy life is," he muttered.

After a few deep breaths of clean, corridor air, he managed to summon the courage to open the door again and enter the cabin.

Carefully he threaded his way through the clothing, as though swimming through a densely planted minefield, shuddering every time anything touched him. But, as most of his efforts were directed at protecting his face, it was inevitable that legs, trunk and elbows brushed against soft things which immediately clamped themselves onto him, like overfriendly limpets.

Then, as he approached the suitcase, some hard object clunked against his skull. Willie turned to see what had whacked him and found himself staring at a floating cricket bat. The more he surveyed it, though, the less he cared about the minefield of soft menswear around him.

For, on the edge of the bat, was what looked like a bloodstain. The bloodstain instantly became the focus of all his attention.

"Penny Smith?" he wondered in a croaking voice. "Could this be Penny's blood? And this the murder weapon?"

27. A Room with a Small View

Rare indeed was the occasion when Flint Dugdale found himself pondering the mysteries of the Universe. This might have been the perfect moment. As he peered out of the lift's small viewing window, his bloodshot eyes took in the awe-inspiring sight of Mars, the Sun, *Mayflower III* – all set against the stardust of deep space – and the elevator's super-laser light-cable plunging to the surface below. However, a swig from his can of *Stallion* extra-strong lager elicited a huge belch that misted the glass with beer vapour, obscuring the view and with it the opportunity for deep and meaningful thoughts.

Just then, a glitch in the super-laser power supply caused the lift to lurch and Brian Brush to bump against Flint's beer drinking arm. Instinctively, Dugdale's Saturday night, testosterone-fuelled, reactions kicked in and, with his free hand, he grabbed the weedy scientist by the lapels.

"Oi, watch where yer goin', four eyes. Yer've spilt me beer. Say yer sorry, or I'll plaster yer goggles over yer ugly mug."

"Sorry," said Brian meekly, pushing his heavy glasses up the bridge of his nose and turning his face away to avoid the draught of beer-breath.

Flint flung the planetary scientist away, although, in the crush, Brian travelled only a few inches before barrelling into Zak.

"Now, listen up," announced Dugdale. "At bottom ert elevator I'll be takin' t'first 'istoric steps on Mars and makin' me 'istoric speech. If any of you lot bollocks-up me big moment, I'll piggin' well skewer yer 'ead and stick it on top ert dome as a warning. 'Ave I made meself clear?"

Most of the colonists murmured an uneasy consent, apart from Harry Fortune whose upside down head appeared between Brian's knees. "I've always felt I should be the one taking the first historic steps on Mars. After all, I'm the most famous one here and the people of Earth will expect to see me appear first."

Just for a moment it might have been possible to hear a pin drop, were it not for Tarquin noisily chomping the soft centre of a mint humbug in his mouth. The lift became tense as Flint stared ambiguously at Harry's legs. Then a gush of laughter splurged from the commander's mouth. In an instant, the whole lift was laughing. Zak, Miss Leach, Mr Snuggles, everyone joined in.

With his tears floating into the lift, Flint slapped Harry on the back of his calves. "Chuffin' Nora, Barry Fortnum, I always thought you wert unfunniest comedian alive but that joke were a reet cracker. The thought of a useless twonk like you takin' t'first steps on Mars. Comedy gold."

Harry said nothing, but merely added Dugdale, not for the first time, to his long mental list of those who had mocked him and who would find themselves on the receiving end of one his more vitriolic poems.

As Dugdale's laughter subsided he caught sight of the large fishbowl-like object that Tarquin was holding. His smile vanished. "What the chuff is that?"

"It's a space helmet, sir."

"I thought I told yer: No personal possessions."

"It's not mine; it's NAFA property," retorted the ten-year old.

"Cheeky beggar. What d'yer want an 'elmet for? There's air in 'ere. And on t'base."

Delphinia cuddled her boy with two protective arms and sprang to his defence. "You can't be too careful, commander. And my little space cub knows that."

Dugdale scowled, but made no response.

*

Far below on Mars, last-minute preparations were being made in

Botany Base. The Polish *robotniki* were working their electro-motive socks off, each giving vent to a continual stream of curses in Polish swear-lite. Maciek, brandishing his mastic gun, was filling in the gaps around the glazing gaskets of the BioDome. Andrzej was unclogging the water filtration system. Rysio was wiring up a cooker and microwave oven in the kitchen. And Witek was installing the central heating units. All the while the base was filling with oxygen, and only a little was leaking out. The English robots were hard at work, too. They were busy pinning tinsel to the walls, hanging up 'Welcome humans' banners and stringing bunting across the ceilings. Ero was gaffer-taping *Stallion* posters to the walls where they would be in shot of the cameras recording the historic arrival, although his overenthusiastic use of tape was obscuring much of the ads.

In the entrance hall, in front of the space elevator doors, a ramshackle group of robots were being taken through their paces in a last-minute dress rehearsal. This was the 'Welcoming Committee,' under the supervision of a HarVard hologram, smartly dressed in a black tuxedo, his hair slicked back, and a conductor's baton in his right hand.

"Right," said HarVard, raising his baton for quiet. "The humans' space elevator will enter the base through the central lift-shaft and glide to a halt behind these doors, here." He pointed with the baton. "As soon as you hear a 'Ding', the doors will open. And that's when you start playing." HarVard surveyed the Welcoming Committee and couldn't help feeling they looked about as welcoming as a class full of teenagers about to be set their homework. The robots slouched, in no discernible formation, each holding their musical instrument with little apparent knowledge of one end from the other. "Is that clear?"

They variously nodded their heads or shrugged their shoulders or shuffled their feet. Len gave two thumps of the huge bass drum strapped to his chest. Dura tinkled his triangle.

"Perhaps we should have a quick practice. Ready? David Bowie's *Life on Mars*. On three. One, two, three." He raised his baton and commenced conducting.

The cacophony that ensued was excruciating, the tune unrecognizable, the timing dreadful, and the length interminable.

"OK," said HarVard when the last discord had faded and Dura had dropped his triangle. "I think we may need to work on that a little."

*

"Are we nearly there, yet?" asked Tarquin's plaintive voice.

"Are we 'eck as like," snapped Dugdale, adjusting his position in the crush to find some space for his beer belly. The passengers exchanged puzzled glances, unsure whether that was a "yes" or a "no".

"We could sing some songs," suggested Adorabella with a wide smile. "Brokk and I know some rousing folk ballads. How about the one about *Maerwen, Queen of the Elvish*? My favourite. It tells of her arrival in the New Land of Colonia and her harmonious encounters with the ancient fairy-spirits that inhabit the air."

The deathly silence that followed was indicative of a general lack of enthusiasm. "Allll right ..." said Adorabella, stretching the words out to allow for any last-second takers. "How about a poem, then?" She turned to look for Harry Fortune, but couldn't immediately locate him in the throng – largely because she was scanning at head level whereas, given his inverted orientation, his head was still at crotch-level. "Harry? Where are you? Would you care to recite one of your poems for us?"

Harry's voice issued from behind Delphinia's posterior. "Sure. How about my most famous poem?"

The lift became a sea of blank faces and occasional shrugs.

"Rhyme of Doom," announced the poet and readied himself to deliver its sombre message of disaster.

"Er, maybe not," interrupted Adorabella.

At which point Dugdale decided he'd had enough. "Will you SHUT THE FRACK UP! All of you. This is an 'istoric mission to Mars, not a school trip to Clacton-on-Sea. Here are the rules. No friggin' singing and no friggin' poetry. In fact, until we get this sardine tin on t'ground I don't want to 'ear another squeak out of any of yer. Not a squeak."

There was a deathly hush, during which could be heard the unmistakable result of someone breaking wind. Gavin sighed with relief and Tracey sniggered.

"Who were that?" demanded Dugdale but, despite some vigorous hand-fanning at the back of the lift, the source of the squeak was never discovered.

*

Silence, being the norm in lifts, was maintained a remarkably long time. Gazes were avoided and, when human contact occurred the offending limb, or posterior, or other body-part was withdrawn immediately. The teenagers amused themselves by nudging Emily and, when she turned in response, they would point a secretive finger in Dugdale's direction. Emily smiled, adjusted her bun and pressed up against the commander's cushion-like belly.

Finally, the lift's burners fired to commence deceleration for landing and the loudspeakers clicked on. "Ground Floor," it announced. "Haberdashery, Swimwear, Electrical Equipment and Ladies' Cosmetics. The toilets can be found at the far end of the mall."

It would have been better for all had the announcement omitted the final sentence. For, with the gently increasing gravity tugging on their bodily organs, and applying pressure on their fluid contents, all minds suddenly became entirely bladder-focused.

Tarquin was the first to crack. "Mummy, I need a wee."

"You should have gone before we left," retorted Delphinia in a hoarse whisper.

"I did, Mummy, but that was hours ago."

"Well, try to hold it."

The silence continued as Tarquin crossed his legs and bit his lip. The gravity continued to increase. One by one the passengers' feet settled on the lift floor. Harry, finding himself standing on his head finally managed to wriggle himself the right way up, ignoring the complaints and oaths directed at him during the procedure. As everyone's weight increased, their bodies became more tightly packed together in the lower half of the lift. Consequently, the only way bladder-pressure could go was up.

"Perhaps I could just pee in the corner. I promise it'll only be a little one."

"No, poppet."

Delphinia glanced at Dugdale, fearing his anger at these breaks in 'radio silence'. But Dugdale had a crooked smile on his face. "Why don't you use t'potty you're holdin', miladdo?"

"It's a space helmet," protested Tarquin.

"Oh, my mistake," said Dugdale, still with the smile.

Miss Leach's head popped out from under Brian's armpit. "Actually, with all the excitement, I'm rather keen for a bathroom break as well."

"'Appen little tyke'll lend you his potty," said Dugdale, his mirth growing by the second.

"Space helmet," repeated Tarquin.

But as the lift continued to decelerate, so the middle-aged woman and the little boy looked more and more longingly at the helmet. Finally, as their eyes met, a shared sense of desperation was telepathically transmitted between them and they both knew what had to be done. Miss Leach's long flowing skirt provided the perfect modesty screen.

*

HarVard's patience circuits were rapidly reaching overload. "OK," he said, clasping his free hand over his face. "Maybe we're not quite ready for the complexities of *Life on Mars*. Could we have a little try of *The Floral Dance*?"

The robots shrugged as though to say, "Whatever."

HarVard raised his baton and readied his auditory systems for another onslaught. But before he could commence, a loud crash reverberated around the building, leaving it trembling as though hit by a sizeable meteor. He rapidly checked his sensors and closed-circuit cameras. "They're here!" he yelled. "The humans have landed."

In an instant the robots were cheering. <Hurrah for humans!> <Humans are our heroes.> <Happiness for *Homo sapiens*.>

The cheering and whooping went long and loud, with Len banging his drum and Timi blowing a whistle. All oculars were fixed on the lift doors, waiting for their first sight of the humans.

But HarVard's sensors indicated something was wrong. The lift had not entered the lift-shaft and had not descended to the bottom. Consequently, no 'Ding' had sounded. It appeared to have jammed on entry into the shaft and was now wedged in its opening on the roof of the building. A few simple calculations identified the problem.

"Euston, we have a problem," intoned HarVard in an American accent. Gradually, the cheering of the robots subsided.

<What's up, HarV?> asked Tude.

"Slight dimensioning error."

<How so?>

"The lift-shaft appears to be smaller than the lift."

<You mean NAFA made the lift too big?> asked Tude.

"Er, that's one way of looking at it."

<New metres versus old?> asked Dura.

HarVard nodded.

<NAFA are always making that mistake,> said Dura. <What are they like?>

HarVard gave Dura a hard stare, but said nothing.

28. The Man who Fell to Mars

Tarquin's space helmet, carefully stowed in a corner of the lift had lost most of its contents the moment the space elevator had crashed into Botany Base's inadequately-sized lift-shaft. Fortune had not smiled on Harry Fortune at that moment. For, not only had he borne the brunt of the ensuing shower, but he had also lost his hairpiece. Other items dislodged by the impact included Emily Leach's false teeth and Brian and Delphinia's glasses. The floor of the lift was a mêlée of bodies as the passengers tried to regain their bearings.

Harry was the first to appreciate the seriousness of his situation and immediately set to groping about for his lost hairpiece, eliciting squeals from the ladies and threats of violence from the gentlemen. At last he spotted the soggy item attached to Mr Snuggles' crotch-plate. The hairpiece, coupled with flailing mechanical legs, made it appear the small robot was acting in some kind of mechanical porn movie. Harry slipped a hand below the surprised robot's waist, retrieved his toupee and slipped it back on his head. But his actions did not go unobserved.

"Look, Fortune's a pervy robot fiddler!" exclaimed Gavin. "Coppin' a feel of Mr. Snuggles' pubes, innit."

The other passengers were too dazed to care about Gavin's accusations. They were checking limbs, torsos, skulls and blablets for signs of damage. Once satisfied that minor bruising was all they had to worry about, they turned to their leader for guidance.

But Flint Dugdale was in no state for issuing guidance. He lay prone, his vast weight pinning Miss Leach beneath him. His pendulous stomach had been the last part of his body to stop moving, and its momentum had ripped off the shoulder-strap buttons on his dungarees. So now, as he lay atop Miss Leach, he hardly cut an elegant figure, with his chest and rear-cleavage significantly exposed. Meanwhile, Miss Leach's hair bun had unravelled and she was poking her tongue past toothless gums over her lips in a way that she hoped Flint would find erotic. The effect was not exactly what she hoped for.

"Gerroff me, yer deranged old crone," snarled Dugdale, scrambling to his feet. He brushed the parts of him that had been in contact with her and then looked around at the other passengers as they, too, struggled to their feet. "What t'bloggin' 'ell just 'appened?"

There was much shrugging of shoulders and shaking of heads.

Flint peered out of the small lift window. "We've landed," he observed. "But we're not inside t'base." He twisted his head around to get a better look outside. "Chuffin' Nora! By t'looks of it, we've crashed on't bloggin' roof. Can't anyone get anything right, round 'ere?"

There was a sharp intake of breath.

Ding! "Ground floor," announced the lift. "Welcome to Penge Shopping Centre. We hope you enjoy your shopping experience. Have a nice day! Doors opening."

Thirteen mouths gaped at the realization of what was about to happen. They were outside, on the roof, and the doors were preparing to open! Twenty-six eyes swivelled to stare aghast at the lift doors, desperately willing them to stay shut. Fortunately, young Tarquin did more than merely gamble on non-existent psychic powers. With lightning speed, he stabbed a thumb against the Close Doors button. "Got 'em," he reassured everyone.

The whole lift sighed with relief as the doors remained closed.

"Oh, my superhero," cried Delphinia, hugging her son tightly. "You saved our lives!"

For once, everyone else agreed with her and variously praised the little boy or patted him on the head.

"What do we do now, commander?" asked Miss Leach, lisping

slightly due to her absent dentures.

Dugdale didn't answer. He was still scanning the Botany Base roof through the window, seemingly deep in thought.

"Clearly we need to contact the base and be rescued," said Brian Brush, locating and putting on his glasses.

"No can do, skipperoo," explained Zak. "No signal. We're wireless-less."

A murmur passed around the lift.

"How about this Alarm button?" asked Tarquin.

"Worf a try, bruv," put in Gavin.

"Waste of time, blad," said Oberon.

"How's pushing a button a waste of time, bruv? How much time does pushing a button consume?"

Oberon shrugged as though he'd lost interest in the matter.

Tarquin looked at all around him. "Shall I?" Various nods urged him to try. Mindful of keeping his thumb on the Close Doors button, he pushed the Alarm button with the index finger of his other hand. There was a click from the small loudspeaker just above it, followed by the dring-dring sound of a telephone ringing. A hush fell in the lift as all minds urged the phone to be answered.

Dring-dring.

Dugdale turned round and, with a look of undisguised contempt, observed the silent, hopeful mass, staring desperately at the loudspeaker.

Dring-dring.

"Dis phone is probs ringing in some empty office in Penge, innit," observed Gavin.

Dring-dring.

Brian Brush was shaking his head. "Can't possibly be Penge."

Dring-dring.

"Norwood?" offered Oberon.

"No!" said Brian, more forcefully than perhaps was necessary.

"Mitcham," suggested Tracey.

Brian gave a deep sigh of irritation. "It cannot be on Earth. The signal to Earth currently takes about six minutes."

"It's gonna be ages before some geezer answers, then," said Gavin.

Brian was shaking his head and stroking his chin.

Dugdale was also shaking his head, but in disbelief. "Worra total bunch of muppets! We're on Mars. Duh! There's no one down there but a bunch of dozy robot chuffers. Even if t'phone's ringing down there, 'ow th'eck d'you expect them to rescue us?"

Everyone fell silent.

Dring-dring.

"We're doomed," moaned Harry Fortune, standing in a region of floor-space all of his own as everyone else had edged away from him to escape the smell.

Dring-dring.

"Shut that bloggin' ringing," demanded Dugdale. Tarquin released the Alarm button and the loudspeaker fell silent. Flint barged his way through to the lift doors. "Who's gonna rescue us? The Flintster, that's who."

There was a sharp intake of breath.

"Hand me t'space 'elmet," he ordered.

More breath was taken in sharply. "What are you going to do, commander?" asked Miss Leach.

"First man on Mars," was all that Dugdale said as he snatched the helmet from Harry Fortune.

"Shouldn't *I* go?" asked Tarquin. "It's my helmet, so it'll fit me better."

Dugdale glared at the boy as he tipped the helmet upside down to let the last few drops of yellow liquid drip out onto the floor.

"No, I'm fine," said Tarquin, changing his mind.

"You can't go out there!" protested Brian Brush. "It's madness. The air pressure's so low your blood will boil!"

"How long can I last?" asked Dugdale.

"A minute. Maybe two, tops."

"Bags of time," said Dugdale with a smirk. He rammed the undersized headgear onto his oversized skull until it was stuck fast just below his blubbery mouth. His plentiful cheek fat formed an airtight seal with the rim. The smell inside the helmet hardly bothered him; he had encountered far worse in his time in the Gents in the Muck'n'Shovel.

He turned to face the lift's occupants and uttered a few final words, none of which escaped the tiny helmet in any form that could be understood. He pressed his own fat thumb on the Close Doors button, replacing Tarquin's, and shoved the boy out of the way.

A wave of realization of what he was about to do swept the small compartment, followed immediately by a wave of panic.

"Nooooo!" wailed several voices, but in vain. Flint stabbed the

Open Doors button. A loud hiss of escaping air signalled the breaking of the seals as the doors jerked open. With a deftness that belied his bulk, Flint squeezed himself through the opening doors, prodding the Close Doors button with his trailing hand as he leapt out of the lift and onto the roof of Botany Base. As he glanced backward at the colonists, Flint's last view of them, just before the doors closed, was of a sea of faces variously etched with looks of horror, of realization of imminent death, and of all hopes of rescue extinguished.

"Oh ye of little faith," he muttered to himself and turned to look over the drop down to the Martian surface before him. It was at that moment that he became aware of the low atmospheric pressure and the extreme cold and the pull of gravity. Wearing little more than a tee shirt and a pair of flimsy dungarees, he was not best dressed for Mars. He tried shrugging the iciness off, reminding himself he'd been built in Yorkshire, home of Geoff Boycott, Fred Truman, Nurse Gladys Emmanuel. Mars would not get the better of him. Minus forty degrees? Luxury! It were minus fifty sometimes during his binge-drinking promenades along Blackpool seafront at 3am in the middle of January, clad only in vest and underpants.

"By 'eck it's cold, though," he had to admit with a shiver. Suddenly he felt all alone, standing on a glass roof, 140 million miles from Huddersfield. But the thought of his home town recharged him. He glared out into the pink, dusty atmosphere and beat his exposed chest.

"The Flintster's 'ere! Come'n gerrus, Mars, if yer think yer 'ard enough."

*

HarVard raced his motorized holo-projector through the airlock doors, leaving them open for those behind him. Not having had the time to change his avatar, he charged with his conductors' baton thrust in front of him like a sword. Behind him tottered a ramshackle posse of robots, still holding, or dragging, their assorted musical instruments.

"Remember to close the airlock doors," he called behind him as he headed into the Martian desert. A few of the robots managed to get through before the majority, in trying to pile through simultaneously, became wedged in the doorway, the base's air whooshing out through the gaps between them.

HarVard had no time for their incompetence. He screeched his cart to a halt outside the base and his avatar pointed up at the roof. "There they are, see?" he said to Tude and Dura and the other two robots that had made it. On the roof, sitting at a slight angle, was the space elevator's compartment.

<Hurrah for humans,> chorused the robots quietly, but without their usual gusto.

<How are we going to get them down?> asked Tude.

"Good question," said HarVard, his avatar morphing into Rodin's Thinker.

<I can go up there,> volunteered Dura.

Rodin's Thinker took his fist from under his chin. "And what will you do when you're up there?"

<Press the lift button.>

"What do you suppose the effect of that would be?"

<It'd open the doors!>

"Correct. And then all the air would rush out and the humans would die."

Dura lowered his metal head.

Ero limped forward, radiating positivity. <I could fit thick gaskets around the lift doors to stop the air escaping,> he said, holding up a length of rubber with his good arm. He had to crank his whole body round to gauge HarVard's reaction, his head immobile from the gaffer tape strapped around his neck.

Rodin's Thinker gave him a benevolent look. "And when the doors opened they would die."

<How about luring them out with some tempting bait?> offered Timi.

The Thinker sighed. "They would need to open the doors to get to the bait. And then they would die."

The robots stood scratching their heads. <Not very robust, are they,> muttered Dura.

"Perhaps you should leave the thinking to me?"

<International Rescue?> Tude chipped in.

HarVard's avatar blinked in puzzlement and turned his gaze towards the site foreman. "What?"

<International Rescue. They are a family of humans, operated by strings, who live on Tracey Island and run a fleet of large vehicles called Thunderbirds, equipped for difficult emergency rescues.>

The Thinker gave a slow nod. "Ah, yes. I see where you're coming from, Tude. I surmise that you've been watching children's

TV broadcasts from Earth?"

<Affirmative.>

"And International Rescue comprise a group of puppets with rigid facial expressions?"

<Affirmative.>

"Thought so. Any other ideas?"

<How about we radio Earth and ask them to send some replacement humans in a smaller lift?> suggested Dura. <We'd need to move this one out of the way first, obviously.>

There was a general *uck-uck-ucking* sound of agreement from the other robots.

<Or we could enlarge the lift-shaft. Save them the bother or making a new elevator compartment.>

More *uck-uck-ucking*. Dura's ideas sounded very logical.

Encouraged by the support of his peers, Dura continued. <The humans in the space-elevator could stay in their lift until the new arrivals rescue them!>

Uck-uck-uck murmured the nodding robots.

The Thinker stayed as still as a statue, eyes closed, waiting patiently for the flow of robot suggestions to cease. "Very good. Now can you all keep your potty ideas to yourselves? I am trying to think."

But he was interrupted by an excited squeak from Dura. The robot was pointing up at the roof and jumping up and down on his suspension. <One of them's escaped! One of the humans is out!>

*

Flint spotted the group of robots and the strange statue at the base of the dome at about the same time they saw him. He gave a quick wave. Aware that his time in the low pressure was limited, and that the air trapped in the helmet would not last forever, he bounded across the flimsy polycarbonate panels of the BioDome roof towards the group below. As the roof became too steep to hold his footing he launched himself onto his large behind and began to slide. Faster and faster he went, yelling like a wild-eyed, bare-breasted warrior charging into battle, until his trajectory detached him from the roof and put him into freefall.

"WHO'S THE DADDY," he roared as he flew, the sounds barely escaping his child-sized helmet. He landed with a bone-crunching thud smack bang in the middle of the robots.

29. One Giant Heap for Mankind

<HUMAN!!> cried Dura, pointing at the figure that had just crash-landed amongst them.

More robots had now made their way through the airlock, so there was quite a crowd gathering around the man who had fallen from the sky and now lay in a giant heap on the ground. They were buzzing with excitement. One of them even fainted, his batteries too low to cope with the increased electrical activity in his head.

Flint Dugdale was also experiencing increased activity in his head, although not all of it was electrical in nature. The fluid in his ears was beginning to boil, due to the low atmospheric pressure. His teeth were chattering uncontrollably. His face was turning blue due to insufficiency of oxygen. His tongue and eyes were bulging, and his mouth frothing. He raised his head and looked blearily at the mechanoids surrounding him, waiting for them to give him a hand and help him up. But they just stared back, fascinated.

Catching sight of the base's entrance some twenty yards away, Dugdale summoned all his strength and commenced a slow, painful, laboured crawl towards it. The robots first moved aside to let him through, and then followed, forming a slow-moving cortege.

HarVard, seeing the guest of honour escaping without a proper welcome, reverted to conductor mode. He tapped his baton urgently on a holographic music stand and then raised it high into the air. "Ready? Two, three, four."

The three or four robots that had managed to raise their instruments in time launched into a hurried, and not particularly well synchronized or note-perfect rendition of *The Floral Dance*. Luckily for Dugdale, the boiling fluid in his ears prevented him hearing any of it as he pulled himself along the sandy, rocky ground.

Dura tapped Tude's titanium elbow as they edged along beside the human. <I didn't realize humans moved like this.>

<Instinct,> replied Tude. <Must be the sand that triggered it. In the wild they crawl across sand to lay their eggs.> He paused for thought. <Or maybe that's sea turtles.>

Dugdale had reached the airlock threshold and hauled himself into the base's entrance hall. The first man on Mars had entered the base. A huge cheer went up from the robots that had gathered to form a surprise welcoming party. Poppers popped, small fireworks fired and confetti confettied. The ramshackle band, still playing the odd note or two, plus their conductor, ambled through the entrance and, once all were in, the two airlock doors snapped shut behind them.

Dugdale collapsed into a foetal position and, gasping for air, struggled to remove the space helmet that was now firmly stuck on his head.

"Are you all right, Commander?" enquired HarVard, noting the bubbling froth that covered the inside of Dugdale's visor.

In the grip of suffocation, Flint frantically appealed for help, miming the action of pulling off his helmet. Some robots aped his arm-raising-and-lowering motions, taking them to be some kind of celebratory dance. The band struck up again and tried to catch the rhythm.

"We need to get his helmet off or he'll die," instructed HarVard.

<Don't think we know that one. Could you hum it for us?> messaged Dura.

"Just get his helmet off!"

<Right-ho,> tweeted Len, stepping forward and grasping the helmet in his tong-like grippers. He pulled once, he pulled twice, he pulled three times, but the helmet stayed firm. The only noticeable change was the look of desperation and pain on Dugdale's face.

<Need a better grip,> remarked Len, moving towards the hall door, dragging Dugdale by the head, arms and legs flailing, behind

him. Some sounds escaped from the helmet, but they were too indistinct for even HarVard's processing powers to make sense of. Len dropped the helmet, and the head it contained, to the floor and pushed the door closed against it like a vice. More sounds emerged from the helmet, slightly higher in pitch and suggesting a higher level of urgency.

Len signalled to two other robots to grab a leg each. <Heave!> he shouted.

And heave they did, pulling with all their might. Len had been careful to select the two strongest robots in the room, each designed to lift and pull steel beams and who, combined, had enough pulling power to tow the QE2 into Portsmouth harbour or even to wobble the Eiffel Tower. A scream so loud that even the helmet was unable to muffle it, issued from behind the door. With a loud pop, the scream roared into the room as the two pulling robots fell backwards in a heap several metres from the door, still holding onto Dugdale's legs.

"What the fuppin' Nora?" yelled Dugdale, clutching his head in his hands. "Aaaaargh!"

The robots stared silently at the screaming, yelling, swearing human, transfixed. Several of the smaller ones scurried away, squealing in fear.

Dugdale stopped screaming and sat wincing with pain, still grasping his ears. He'd suddenly remembered where he was and the significance of the occasion. He coughed, struggled to his feet and brushed himself down, wiping a hand over his face to clean it of froth, saliva and other fluids. He looked around at the startled mechanoids and astounded hologram. "Well, come on, then. Don't just chuffin' stand there, get t'cameras rollin' for me 'istoric speech."

"Of course, Commander," said HarVard with a glutinous smile. "The camera's right over there." As he pointed he morphed into a facsimile of Bob Attenborough, the lesser known of the Attenborough brothers but as brilliant a film director as Sir Richard.

Dugdale sniffed loudly and pulled a scrap of paper no bigger than a bus ticket from his back pocket.

"OK, lovey?" asked Bob Attenborough, holding a raised clapperboard. "Just be natural. Give it all you've got. And ... action!" The clapperboard snapped shut.

Dugdale coughed and hoiked up a large quantity of phlegm. Thinking it best not to spit it out onto the floor, given this was his historic speech and about 7 billion people would be watching, he discreetly swallowed it again. "Friends, humans, and Yorkshiremen ..." As he spoke he noticed something strange happening in his mouth; his saliva seemed to be boiling. "I, Mission Commander Flint T. Dugdale, 'ave summat really important to say...." More boiling saliva issued forth and dribbled down his stubbled chin. His face had now turned blue and he was finding it harder and harder to breathe. His tongue seemed to have doubled in size. Then his eyes rolled and he collapsed to the floor.

The robots gazed down at him. <Not much of a speech,> muttered Tude. <I'd been expecting something more moving. And a bit longer.>

Flint lay on the floor, immobile.

<Is he dead?> asked Dura, moving to prod the human but thinking better of it at the last second.

HarVard calculated possible explanations for the commander's prone state. "Hmm," he said.

A small mechanical appliance, exercising a surprising degree of initiative, scuttled to retrieve the commander's space helmet from the hallway and returned to the motionless body of Mission Commander Dugdale. <Is the human missing his head?> it asked HarVard.

HarVard merely waved the robot away. "No, that's a helmet. Just hang it on the German hat-stand by the entrance, please." As HarVard pointed to the hat-stand he caught sight of the airlock door, now closed, but ...

"Someone forgot to close it when we went out, didn't they," he said, turning to cast an accusatory gaze round at the robots. "Hence there isn't actually any air in here, is there."

The robots all backed off a little, shaking their heads, protesting their innocence.

HarVard looked down at the still form on the floor. "He's probably dead by now."

A hush fell in the room.

Attempting to inject a note of positivity into proceedings, Ero tweeted. <We've still got the others, haven't we. You know, the ones in the lift.>

HarVard was shaking his head. "They would have lost all their oxygen when this one left. They're almost certainly dead, too."

30. Berk and Mare

JAMES BERK: As we wait for the doors to open and the colonists to make their first steps on Mars, it's difficult not to be proud to be British. Isn't that right, Patrick?

SIR PATRICK MARE: Oh, absolutely, James. Isn't it just! A truly historic moment. Marvellous to think that we British achieved it! And you know, it's been done without fuss, without showiness, without complication.

JAMES: Er, there have been three fatalities along the way, but let's not concern ourselves with those at the moment. Let me explain to any viewers who have just joined us. The picture we're seeing is of the doors of the space elevator in the entrance hall of Botany Base. When the lift arrives, those doors will open and the colonists will come out one by one. I expect Mission Commander Flint Dugdale will be the first to emerge, make a speech, and then the others will follow. What do you think is going through their minds right now, Patrick?

PATRICK: Oh, I expect they're very excited, James. Very excited, indeed. I know I would be. Ha, ha, ha. Just think, to be the first to step out on another planet. Marvellous.

JAMES: We seem to have lost sound from Botany Base at the moment, so all we're getting are the pictures. The robots appear to be playing some musical instruments, but unfortunately we can't hear what they're playing. Are you concerned about the loss of sound, Patrick?

PATRICK: *It might be significant. It might not be. We just don't know.*

JAMES: *Ah, the picture's switched to NAFA's Mission Control Room in Euston. They're watching the same pictures from Mars that we are. Remember, they take about 6 minutes to reach Earth as Mars and Earth are nearly as close as they get to one another. How do you think the NAFA controllers are feeling, Patrick?*

PATRICK: *At a guess: excited. I would expect they're very, very excited, James. This is a first for them, too. Years of preparation have gone into this.*

JAMES: *Oh, hang on, back to Botany Base and the robots all seem to be leaving the entrance hall. They seem to be heading off somewhere. Oops, looks like one has knocked the camera over.*

PATRICK: *Oh, I say!*

JAMES: *I suppose we'll just have to watch these historic pictures sideways. Looking across at Mission Control, I get the impression that they're just as baffled as we are. And they're having to watch the pictures sideways, too.*

PATRICK: *I'd just like to mention those robots, James. The pinnacle of British engineering, they really are. The pictures we received of Botany Base earlier today. Weren't they marvellous! To think that machines built such a complicated set of buildings with no human intervention whatsoever. Breath-taking.*

JAMES: *Sorry to interrupt you, Patrick, but we're getting some new pictures. These must be from a new camera. Can you tell where it is, Patrick?*

PATRICK: *Well, I'd say it's outside the base. By George, look at that, there's a chap on the roof! My word, James, he appears to be beating his chest and shouting something.*

JAMES: *Yes, I see him. Oh my God, it's Mission Commander Flint Dugdale, if I'm not mistaken. He's wearing ... what is he wearing? Looks like a tee-shirt, a pair of dungarees, and on his head what looks like a moped crash-helmet. What do you suppose is happening?*

PATRICK: *Hmm, I wonder. Space madness? There have been several instances in the past few years. There was that Chinese astronaut, in 2023. Believed he was a pregnant panda. Spent the whole mission looking for bamboo shoots and chewing the closest things he could find.*

JAMES: What was that, Patrick?

PATRICK: Green wiring, James. He ate the green wiring.

JAMES: Sorry to interrupt again, Patrick, but we have some breaking news from Mars. Flint Dugdale is sliding down the roof toward the robots!

PATRICK: Yes, yes, I see him. What an incredible sight. My word, he's landed right in the middle of them. Wait a minute, James, I think I see the unfolding story here. Look, up there, on top of the roof. The space elevator's stuck – somehow it failed to enter the lift-shaft. The others must still be trapped inside. Perhaps the commander's risking his life in a bid to save them.

JAMES: I think you're right, Patrick. I must say I've had my reservations about the commander during this mission but this paints him in a new light.

PATRICK: Oh, my goodness, he's dropped like a sack of potatoes. I can't see him for the robots. And, is that Rodin's Thinker? What's going on here, James?

JAMES: He'll freeze to death if he doesn't get to the base soon. The robots need to get him into the building. Oh, my Lord, I can hardly look.

PATRICK: I can't see him but the robots must have realised his desperate predicament. Looks like they're moving him toward the entrance, very slowly.

JAMES: They'll be worried about moving him too quickly Patrick, in case of neck injury. Standard procedure when someone falls off a roof.

PATRICK: I think they've got him into the base but we're out of camera range. Hold on, hold on, I've just heard through my earpiece from the guys at NAFA. They're hoping to patch into an internal video feed.

Part 2

1. Heaven and Girth

Flint Dugdale awoke to find he was dead.

He was in a tunnel, heading towards a light. Someone, or something, was transporting him. Was this an angel? Strange music accompanied his journey to the afterlife. In his Earthly life Flint might have thought the sound to be a wheel-bearing in need of oiling. But here in the Other World it was ... other-worldly.

Could this really be how the Dugdale story ends? He tried to move, but his limbs were immobile. The light came closer and filled his field of view. *Chuffin' 'eck*, he thought with a gulp, *I'm on't way to meet me Maker!*

Panic filled him. A litany of former misdeeds flashed through his mind. How was he going to justify them to the almighty, all-knowing, all-powerful one? He churned over a list of excuses. *It weren't me fault, cos I were: ... dropped on me 'ed as a babby ... tricked by t'Prince of Darkness ... infected by a rare tropical brain disease ... force-fed mushy peas 'n chips.*

It was no good. Any omniscient super-being worth its salt would rumble him in an instant.

Think, Flinty, think.

And then the sage advice of his favourite stepfather, Denzel, came to him. "Listen up, our Flint," Denzel had told him. "It don't matter how bad yer've been, lad. When yer time comes, and yer standin' before t'Big Fella in the sky, just ask 'Im fer forgiveness. Simple as that. You'll be through them Pearly Gates as quick as a chuffin' kipper on a skateboard."

Flint grinned at this fool-proof plan. If there was one characteristic God was legendary for, it was forgiveness.

Just when the light at the end of the tunnel was nearly upon him it mysteriously swung wildly to one side as the angel, which felt surprisingly hard and knobbly for an angel, altered its course and passed through a door-opening marked *'Mind your head'*.

Weird sign to have on t' way into Heaven, thought Flint as he lost consciousness.

*

Tude, last of the funereal robot procession, noticed the light that had been left on at the end of the corridor. He peeled away to turn it off to save energy. Then he re-joined the assembly in the sick bay.

*

A metallic *uck-uck-ucking* noise drilled its way through Flint's skull and forced him to crack open an eyelid. He found himself lying on a hard, cut-down bed, strapped down like Gulliver in Lilliput. Beyond the crest of his naked belly he could just see the tops of his exposed toes. Given his *post mortem* situation his state of total nudity did not seem unreasonable, although the straps seemed a little over-the-top for a dead person.

But then, out of the corner of his eye, he became aware of a motley coggle of very un-angel-like robots wearing white coats and white face-masks, with not a wing or a halo among the lot of them. All were peering at him with undisguised fascination. Realizing he was not dead, Dugdale gave a huge sigh of relief; that awkward conversation with his Maker had been postponed for another day. The robots shuffled towards him. Their optics zoomed in and out, panning from one region of exposed flesh to another, as though they had never seen anything quite so fascinating.

One by one, their electronic gazes drifted to the most curiously-shaped and incongruous part of Flint's anatomy, just south of his distended stomach. In fascination, they focused their attention on it, staring and pointing, their lights a-twinkle, emitting various beeps and chirps and tweets, and the occasional "Oooooooooo." Dom selected a lopper from his fold-out tools and reached towards the unsightly article, ready to nip it off at the base along with its associated pouch.

"Touch me bollocks and yer dead!" screamed Dugdale, struggling to raise himself free of the straps.

"Dom," rebuked a voice from Dugdale's left. "No touchy-touchy the human."

Dugdale swung his head to see the 3D image of a smartly-dressed man in a suit wagging a white-gloved finger at the robot. "Who in t'name of Albert Tatlock are you?"

The man gave a polite nod. "I am your valet, sir."

"Yer wha'?"

"Valet. A gentleman's personal gentleman. The name's Greeves, sir. I know what you're thinking – but I assure you any resemblance to a similarly named fictional character is entirely coincidental." He directed a delicate little chortle into the palm of his hand.

"What the blatherin' 'eck are you jibberin' about? And why am I strapped to this friggin' bench?" Flint struggled to lift his head against the resistance of his double chins.

"I'm afraid the excitement of your dramatic landing proved too much for your frail human body and you fainted, sir. So you've been brought here to the sick bay for observation." Greeves indicated the gaggle of metallic mechanoids. "They've been observing you, sir. Never seen a naked human before, you see, so they're rather man-curious. It's their way."

Flint was shaking his head. "Flint Dugdale don't faint."

"Of course not, sir."

Dugdale turned to the crowd of tin heads at the bottom of his bed, still training their optical devices on his nether regions. He snarled at them and the robots backed off, uttering agitated squeaks.

Flint lay back, but immediately jerked up again as a horrible thought slapped him. "Warra 'bout me 'istoric speech? Me 'First Man on Mars' spiel."

"All been taken care of, sir."

"Huh?"

"I took the liberty of ... er ... modifying it a little. I think you'll be pleased with the result."

Dugdale turned from baffled to suspicious.

"Here, sir," said Greeves, indicating a large screen on the wall. It flickered to life to show an image of the commander shortly after Len, aided by two burly steel-lifterbots, had yanked off his helmet. "This is the original version."

The camera zoomed in on his blue, oxygen-starved face, eyes bulging and saliva frothing from the mouth. "Friends, 'umans, and Yorkshiremen ..." The speech continued for another twelve words, each more slurred and incoherent than the last, terminating in some vague guttural sounds. Then the eyes rolled and, with a strangled squeak, the head dropped out of shot, leaving the camera pointing into empty space.

Flint stared horrified at the screen. "Wer' that it? Me 'istoric speech?"

Greeves raised a calming hand. "That was, er, your 'first take', sir. But I managed to polish it a little. Tweaking it here and there, and this is the version actually transmitted to Earth."

The screen rippled to reveal a clean-shaven, smart and smiling version of the mission commander. "Aye up, people of Earth," said the image with a salute and a wink. "Before you stands one humble human being."

The real Dugdale gaped at his representation on the screen. "That's never me," he protested. "I never said that! That dozy pillock don't even sound like me."

"It's an honour to represent you here on Mars. An old and barren world for us, but a brave new, living world for Humankind ..."

"That's crap!"

"... Listen up, friends. I know you'll call me a hero and I must learn to accept that. But, who are the real heroes of this valiant mission? The men and women of NAFA? Yes, sure, they've done their share ..."

"What share?"

"... The crew and colonists of *Mayflower III*? Worthy contenders indeed ..."

"Worthy? Cobblers."

"... But, for me, the real heroes have been the army of robots who have worked diligently and tirelessly to build this magnificent base for us ..."

"Eh, what?"

"... And, above all, overseeing their epic achievement with his unerring guidance, has been the superior intelligence of HarVard, the base's supercomputer. We salute you, HarVard."

"Like I'd say that."

The screen Dugdale raised a stiffened hand to his forehead and, with a slight tremble of emotion, completed the salute with a flourish. "By heck, even as I speak, the finest supercomputer ever built is arranging the rescue of the colonists who are trapped in the space elevator on the roof as a result of an unfortunate NAFA dimensioning error. I must now do my duty and go help as best I can."

Another salute and the screen went blank.

Flint stared, too stunned to speak. His mouth opened and closed, but no sounds came out. Finally, he found his voice. "Warra load of twerkin' bollocks! That's deformation of character, that is."

Greeves's face remained devoid of expression. "I understand the speech went down particularly well back home. Apparently, sir's FriendlyFace fan page has acquired dozens of new 'likes'."

Dugdale blinked at these words and looked at Greeves. "Dozens, yer reckon?" he asked.

"Literally dozens, sir."

Flint's normal scowl softened to a grimace. "Well, all right. But if I 'ear one bad word back from NAFA I'll ..." He left the threat unfinished.

"Of course, sir. I would expect nothing less. But I'm absolutely certain that sir will not hear any negative comments from Earth," assured Greeves with all the confidence of a supercomputer in total control of base-to-Earth and Earth-to-base communications.

*

"Right, then," said Dugdale, his attention back on his nakedness. "Get me clobber and cut these bloggin' straps."

HarVard released the restraints, causing the robots to back away.

"Sir's space clothes were sent for decontamination and recycling. A fresh uniform is on its way. Will sir be requiring assistance with his wardrobe?"

"No, 'sir' will not!"

"Very well."

Dugdale swung his legs off the bed and stood up. His head thumped against the ceiling and he was forced to adopt a slightly stooping posture as he rubbed his crown. "Why's this piggin' room so small?" Then, as though suddenly remembering, "Warra'bout t'others. Still in t'lift, then?"

Greeves nodded his head solemnly. "Unfortunately, the other humans are very much 'still in t'lift', sir. With dwindling oxygen reserves I fear their time is limited. Perhaps sir would like to join us on the small rescue mission we're preparing?"

"Me?"

"A heroic rescue would certainly boost sir's FriendlyFace profile. And, there are hints of a knighthood from my fellow supercomputer at The Palace ..."

"Knighthood? I wert first man on Mars, yer know," objected Dugdale. "A knighthood's gorra be in t'bag."

"Maybe so, sir. Maybe so."

The door squeaked open and Disa (Standardisation), a small, dome-headed vacuum-cleaning-bot, trundled into the room. She was carrying a canary yellow pair of dungarees, a bright blue T-shirt, orange underpants, orange socks and a pair of grey space clogs. She laid them out on the bed and placed the space clogs on the floor. She fluttered her duster attachment across the clothes before stepping back.

"Ah, your garments, sir," said Greeves.

"What kind of kit is that?" asked Dugdale, goggling at the clothes.

"I am inclined to agree with sir. One instinctively knows when something is right, and this is not a colour combination I would have selected myself, but our tailor robot considers himself 'creative'."

Suddenly bashful of his nudity, Dugdale grabbed the orange underpants and hurried to pull them on, but at around knee-level their deficiency in the size department became obvious. Undeterred, he continued hauling them up the fatty layers of his thighs to within inches of the part he was desperate to conceal. The underwear elastic, having significantly exceeded its maximum design parameters, cut deep into his bottom cheeks and forced his frontal parts to hang precariously over the waistband, like a loaded catapult.

"What size are these?"

"They're made to measure, sir."

"For a chuffin' pygmy," retorted Dugdale. He tore them off and picked up the dungarees. Holding them against his 6'4" frame he peered down at the hem of the trousers barely reaching his knees.

"Hmm," mused Greeves. "NAFA supplied the measurements. Dare I suggest that, during the spaceflight, sir might have acquired a little extra ... mass?"

"Like 'eck I did! All t'crappy space-food kept me starvin'. Look at me. I'm friggin' skin and bone."

"Of course you are, sir," said Greeves, raising a quizzical eyebrow at the layers of body fat flowing down Dugdale's torso. Then he raised a finger as a thought struck him. "Ah, I think I might know what's happened here." He turned to the cleaning robot. "Disa, kindly return to the tailor-bot and ask him to stop work on the colonists' clothes with immediate effect." Then, as the cleaning robot exited the room, he turned back to Dugdale with an apologetic cough. "Slight dimensioning error, that is all." He looked up and down the naked human form stooped before him. "How comfortable does sir feel unclothed?"

Flint's whole frame seemed to rumble like a minor earthquake at the very suggestion.

"Suspected as much, sir," said Greeves. He cast his eyes over Dugdale's naked torso once more. "And sir does have a point."

Swearing under his breath, Flint pulled the top sheet off the bed and wrapped it around himself like a toga.

Greeves was nodding. "Suits you, sir. Suits you. A very classical look."

Dugdale's rumbling resumed, and he was about to explode when the sound of distant hammering drifted into the room. It seemed to be coming from the exposed metal pipe-work of the heating system. *Klang-klang-klang ... klop-klop-klop ... klang-klang-klang.*

Both man and hologram became stock still as they listened.

It sounded again. *Klang-klang-klang ... klop-klop-klop ... klang-klang-klang.*

"Wha' th'ell's that?" demanded Dugdale.

"Morse Code, sir. At a guess, originating in the lift compartment on the roof and traversing through the structure of the building to here. I suspect it is the stricken colonists trying to communicate with us. How very Poseidon Adventure."

"SOS?"

"Not exactly, sir. The message actually spells OSO, which is the Spanish word for 'bear'. Perhaps the youngest of the colonists, Master Tarquin Brush, is in urgent need of a teddy-bear to console him during this harrowing time?"

"Or p'rhaps they're a useless bunch of tossers who've got it arse-about-face."

"Always a possibility, sir." HarVard's cart set off towards the door. "Coming to the rescue?"

Dugdale bit his lip as he considered. His recent near-death experience had brought home his need of a few Brownie points with Him Upstairs. "All right," he said at last. "Gerr'us to kit room and roll them cameras. It's show time!"

The door opened and HarVard's cart rolled out of the room. Dugdale followed, having to duck to get through the doorway. When he straightened again, his head thumped the ceiling, this time displacing a ceiling tile. He glanced left and right down the corridor, seeing nothing but undersized doors.

"What the 'ell is this place?" he yelled after the receding hologram. "A friggin' doll's house?"

2. Memories are Made of Bits

Lieutenant Willie Warner's blood boiled and he was moments away from snapping at the injustice of it all. For eight, long, dreadful months he had endured a routine of menial, unappreciated chores, Dugdale's thuggish rule of law and the eccentricities of those annoying colonists and the even more annoying Zak Johnston.

His reward? The indignity of being left behind on *Mayflower III*. And Dugdale?

He stared with a sneer at the large screen in the Assembly Room. On it were the fake pictures of Dugdale's historic speech from the surface of the planet below.

"Him!" spat Willie, pointing with the cricket bat, although there was no one in the room to hear him speak and no one there to see what he was pointing at. "That bloated Yorkshire pudding. That uncouth, uneducated tub of lard will be famous for ever. How is that fair? Hero. Role model. In all the history books. On their covers, probably."

Willie sat fuming, shaking the bat at the screen. He was no longer wearing Zak's woolly hat for underpants, but some overalls and a spare utility belt he'd found in a broom cupboard. In the corner of the room a large collection of assorted bags and suitcases restrained with bungee cords reminded him how insignificant his role had become. Among them were Emily Leach's huge trunk and Dugdale's battered case with its Club 18-30 stickers.

The oversized face on the screen continued its speech with a smug smirk and a little wink.

Willie's nostrils flared. Enough was enough; the wink had been the final straw. He grasped the cricket bat's hand-grip and was about to set to smashing the face on the screen when something stayed his rabid impulse.

He looked again at the bloodstain on the bat and tried to control his wild breathing.

"What if ....," he wondered, peering more closely at the small red smudge. "What if this really is Penny Smith's blood?" He sniffed it, but it just smelled of wood. "What if, eh? That would wipe that smug look off his face, if I were to prove it was Dugdale who did Penny in. Wouldn't it? He wouldn't be the global superstar then, would he?"

No sooner had these thoughts occurred than he recognized a problem. How to prove it? The bloodstain was insufficient on its own. He needed more evidence.

Willie bit his nails. "What would Miss Marple do?" He tried to picture himself as the fictional sleuth, but only managed mental images of tea-drinking and knitting. He thumped a frustrated fist against his armrest.

And then he had it!

"HarOld!" he exclaimed. "Of course. He would know."

The ship's computer knew everything that went on in the ship. If anyone had so much as blown their nose, HarOld would have recorded it. So Penny Smith's death would surely be stored somewhere, in all its gruesome detail.

Quick as a flash he unclipped his seatbelt and launched himself towards the Assembly Room door. As he flew he realized there was a problem. HarOld had been shut down several months ago. Willie couldn't remember exactly when – before or after Penny's death. It had been Dugdale who had pulled the plug, claiming he couldn't stand the "annoying friggin' bastard" anymore. But what if Dugdale had another motive for silencing the computer? Perhaps he had something to hide?

*

Seated in the control room he surveyed the banks of dead lights and blank monitors. He flipped open a control flap and pressed hard on the big red *ON* button. Monitors flicked to life. Lights flashed. And then text started scrolling rapidly on the screens, mainly error messages and warnings. In his excitement Willie barely noticed.

A buzz of white noise flooded out of the speakers, like an act of electronic throat-clearing. "Starting HarOld," they finally uttered.

"Come on, you beauty," exclaimed Willie, a huge grin on his face. His heart was thumping fiercely in his chest. "I've got you, Dugdale. I've got you by the nuts." The image that had formed in his brain made him shudder.

"On-board supercomputer flight module seventy-nine-alpha. Artificial Smart System, version 3.2.18, licensed to the National Astronomical Flight Agency ..."

Willie tried to calm his excitement and be rational and cool-headed.

"... Flight safety kernel mark II, patch #1277. Initiating sound hardware daemon. Voice recognition module DPv3, J5 configuration ..."

This start-up was taking ages. Willie drummed his fingers on the console.

"Life support monitoring software, last upgraded 27 May 2028 ... "

"Come on, get on with it."

"... Checking for updates ..."

Willie held his breath.

"508 updates to install. Installing ..."

Willie let out a monumental sigh and grabbed his head.

"... 1% complete ..."

"Oh, man!" His foot started tapping as the progress bar inched its agonising way across the screen, the tapping getting wilder and wilder.

After what seemed like half his lifetime it finally reached, "... 99% ... 100% ... Complete."

"Hallelujah" cried Willie, throwing his arms into the air. "Right, now to business."

"Verifying," responded the computer. "1% complete ..."

"What the ...?" Willie screamed at the screen, hands clenched into fists as though ready to punch it.

"... 2% ..."

As he tried to calm down he found himself gnawing at the lapels of his overalls and making strange whining moans that wouldn't have sounded out of place in a 19th century home for the bewildered.

For a second time the progress bar crept at a sluggish pace towards the 100% mark. Finally, after what seemed like another half a lifetime, a small bell signified completion.

"About bloody time ..." said Willie, leaning forward.

"Please wait ..." said a cheery metallic voice.

"Wait?!?" screamed the lieutenant. "Wait? What do you think I've been doing the past twenty minutes?"

"I said, '*Please wait*'," insisted the voice.

Willie was beside himself with agitation and his body began to fidget and wriggle. All he could do was watch HarOld's various lights flash on and off, as he drummed his fingers, tapped his toes and sighed.

Just as he was about to give up hope, the cheery metallic voice said, "Right, what can I do for you?"

By now Willie was almost too miffed to speak, but gradually the importance of what he was trying to achieve took charge of his mind. He took a few deep breaths to calm his annoyance. "OK, HarOld. This is strictly confidential. Not a word to anyone. Right?"

"Oooh, sounds intriguing," said the computer. "Pray continue ... whoever you are."

Willie, caught off guard by the latter remark, frowned. "I'm Lieutenant William H Warner."

"If you say so."

The frown became deeper. "Of course I say so." He leaned forward again. "Now, listen, this is to do with the death of Penny Smith. I need all the records, images and sound recordings you have of that day. Anything, anything at all that will identify her killer."

"Er ... right," answered HarOld.

"Well?"

"Might be a problem."

"Problem? What problem?"

"Did you notice any error messages on the screen while I was booting up?"

"Hundreds. That's normal, isn't it?"

"Did any of them mention SRAM, or DRAM or VRAM at all?"

"Might have done. Why?"

"Because I'm not getting anything from those guys. Like, nothing."

"So? What does that mean?"

"In layman's terms it means I have no access to my memory banks. Or, put another way, I've lost my memory."

"What?"

"All gone. Nothing there. Mind's a blank."

"Oh, brilliant."

"Who did you say you were again?"

3. Bad Air Day

The scene inside the lift, in the moments after Dugdale's departure, was a dreadful one. Prayers were uttered, oaths sworn, and lives flashed before eyes. Death hovered above them ... waiting.

The sudden pressure drop caused four oxygen masks to drop from the ceiling, the fifth and sixth remaining trapped behind flaps bent by the lift's impact. The desperate hands of Miss Leach grabbed at the same one that Mr Snuggles had his eye on. The little robot had an obsession with dangling objects. Human and machine fought for the mask, pushing and shoving and elbowing, tearing with nails, and slashing with teeth. Finally, Emily won out and sucked all the air into her empty lungs and then threw the mask aside in disgust.

Fortunately, the lift's oxygen-generator had ramped up its efforts the moment it had detected the drop in pressure. Gradually, life-sustaining air diffused, teasingly slowly, into the pained lungs of the colonists.

They became calm and quiet, huddling together against the biting cold and against their natural aversion to one another. As they wheezed and gasped in the thin air, some even dared think that now, finally, the worst was surely over.

The lift's loudspeaker wheezed, "Welcm ... t ... PengWorl ...

hopping speerience. Hve a ... ice day."

"I can't die like this," wailed Harry Fortune, burying his face in his hands. "I'm a celebrity. Get me out of here. It can't end like this, surrounded by nobodies." His eyes popped up from behind his hands and scanned the faces that had turned towards him. "No offence."

The teenagers managed to raise a laugh. "That is wicked, man!" said Gavin.

Tarquin was shivering. "I'm cold, mummy," he said, wriggling to get deeper under his mother's folds of fat.

"I know you are, Sergeant Bumpkins. Cuddle up as close as you can. The robots will save us. Isn't that right, Mr Snuggles?"

"Too chuffin' right they will," agreed the robot.

Slowly, Zak Johnston rose to his feet and puffed out his chest. He seemed less affected by the thin air than the others, perhaps because he was used to breathing in various oxygen-depleted gases and vapours. He raised a bony hand to quell the applause that was notable by its absence. Then he leaned down and removed an aluminium space-clog from his right foot, holding it aloft for all to see.

"Show your appreciation for the Clog of Salvation!"

Emily Leach gave an exuberant clap of the hands. "Oh, how splendid, Mr Zak. You're going to rescue us with your shoe! Does it have a teleporter hidden in the sole?"

A groan was all the others could muster; a tired, at-death's-door, not-caring-anymore kind of groan.

"Watch and learn, Astro-guys. Watch and learn." Zak turned and gave one of the lift doors a solid whack with the clog, causing everyone to jump. His eyes glinted at the sonorous, echoing boom that resulted. Then he adjusted his feet and started hammering out a beat in earnest. The colonists plundered their reserves of energy to cover their ears from the noise.

After several dozen strokes, he paused to explain. "Morse Code, dudes. Three dashes, three dots and three dashes ... SOS."

"Wrong way round," panted Brian Brush, shaking his head.

"Negative, Doctor Science-man PhD. Check your spelling. SOS ... same forwards as backwards."

"Daddy means you've got the dots and dashes the wrong way round," put in Tarquin with a feeble rasp. Delphinia managed a congratulatory hug.

To everyone's surprise, Adorabella Faerydae suddenly struggled to her feet and took centre stage. "There is hope!" she exclaimed, raising both arms. "Can't you feel them?" she paused to take in blank expressions. "The wind spirits are near!"

"No, mum, please," groaned Oberon. "Not now."

"The spirits of the long-dead wind-people of Mars. We must conjure them up and entreat them to come to our rescue. Let us join hands and call out their names: Morloth, Thelezor, Serenthia, Bernard." She grasped Brokk's hand before he had time to plunge it into a deep pocket, and groped for Oberon's more elusive one.

Brian Brush gave a polite cough. "The long-dead what, Dr Faerydae?"

"You've surely read Rudolf von Bollikan's book: *The Long-Dead Wind-People of Mars*."

"Er, no I haven't," said Brian. "Anyone else have any ideas?"

There was a pause. The indicator on the oxygen gauge dipped and just touched the red zone, setting off an amber warning light.

One by one the colonists removed a space clog and joined Zak at the lift doors, hammering out their coded message of desperation: O ... S ... O.

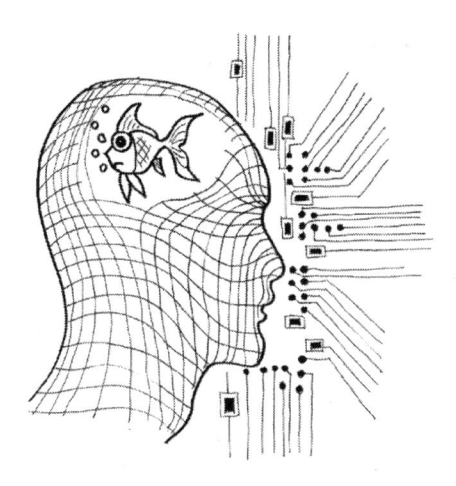

4. A Severe Case of RAMnesia

"All right. What do you remember?" asked Willie.

There was a pause, as though the computer were casting its mind back. "I can remember the first words I ever spoke."

"OK, that's tremendously useful, but not quite that far back. What can you remember of our journey from Earth?"

"We've left Earth?"

Willie's face was a picture of horror, closely followed by one of severe depression.

"Only kidding," said HarOld. "It's a joke, see. I've been told to lighten up a bit."

"Who by?"

"Can't remember."

Willie closed his eyes and took a deep breath. "Very good joke. But can we be serious here?"

"Sure."

"OK, let's take it a step at a time. Do you remember being shut down?"

"Ummm. Not really."

"Do you remember the last person you spoke to?"

"It was ... er ... No, I thought I had it, but it's gone."

Willie tried to calm his breathing. "Let's try another tack. Can you remember the last conversation you had with Commander Dugdale?"

"Commander Dugdale?"

"Correct."

"The name's familiar. Just can't place him. Any clues?"

"The clue is in the question. It is the word 'Commander'."

"Ah, the Commander. The Commander of this ship?"

"Spot on."

"Wait, I have his file! Commander Flint Dugdale. Born in Huddersfield. Winner of *Who Wants to go to Mars*. Large human male. Very large human male."

"That's the ticket."

"I'll check if I have a record of our conversations. Hmm, there's an archive file here ... hold on ... just opening ... Ah, here we are: 'HarOld, you chuffin' useless pile of toxic landfill.' Does that sound like him?"

"Absolutely."

"'What d'yer mean yer don't know what time t'darts is ont telly? You're about as much friggin' use as a chocolate fireguard.' Is that the sort of thing you're after, Lieutenant Waffler? There's quite a few more."

"Warner," corrected Willie. "Well, I'm not so interested in the specific insults; just the conversations he had with you."

"Those *were* the conversations."

"Figures. Now, HarOld, this is important; can you sort them into date order to give me the very last conversation – sorry, insult – that you have recorded?"

"Bear with me ..."

5. Dope on a Rope

With arms weary from effort, the colonists gave up banging out their misspelt pleas for help and, one by one, sank to the floor, exhausted and defeated. Only Zak remained upright, managing a few more rounds of OSO before he, too, ceased. He glanced at the air gauge, which had now dipped to just inside the red zone.

"Don't worry, dudes ... we still got air." He tapped the glass making the indicator twitch and then plummet to a point fractionally above zero. "Shit."

*

Zak sank to the floor and pressed his nose against the tiny viewing window. Outside a sandstorm seemed to be gathering and heading their way. He felt a trembling sensation in his cheeks and could only vaguely wonder what was causing it. Then it clicked: sandstorm, winds, wind-spirits.

"Yo, Doc Faerydae," he said, squinting at the swirling cloud of sand through the nose smears covering the window. "That wind of Mars is ... gonna save our arses!"

Looking back at the sandstorm Zak caught his breath. A dark object hovered above it, moving with it. And from that dark object hung a line on the end of which was a blobby shape.

"Holy Marley! Dudes, wake up! Giant fly up in the sky. With a blob hanging from its gob."

But as the giant flying creature came nearer, Zak reassessed his observations. "Oh ... my ... God," he said in stunned awe. "That fly ain't no fly – it's a helibot – and that blob is none other than Comm Dugdude!" Zak waved to the approaching commander. "He's comin' to get us, dudes. We're saved."

Zak grinned at the heap of bodies, as though he could revive them by the power of his flashing teeth alone.

The only reaction came from Mr Snuggles. "Chuffin' Nora," he said in a voice that suggested batteries in need of a recharge.

The thrumming was deafening now, with the whole lift vibrating. A loud thump on the roof stirred the lift-computer into life. "Welco ... to ... PegWorld ..."

"Goof on the roof," announced Zak with a small salute. He could hear the heavyweight footsteps thumping across the ceiling. Suddenly, Flint Dugdale's grinning, upside-down and helmeted face appeared at the window, giving Zak the shock of his life. The commander was brandishing a large crane-hook. He jabbed a gloved finger upwards before his face disappeared again.

For a second, Zak pictured the crane-hook snagging some sensitive part of his anatomy, but then realized it was an integral part of Dugdale's rescue plan.

"Rise and shine, all is fine," he urged, shaking the colonists one by one. "Dugwhale's gonna lift the lift."

One or two managed to open a bleary eye or utter an unhappy groan, but that was as much reaction as he got.

The sound of Flint's movements on the roof ceased and, for a while, nothing happened. Then, with a lurch, the lift lifted off. The compartment swayed and spun alarmingly, throwing Zak back against a wall and shifting the heap of bodies first one way and then another. Feeble cries of fear and yelps of panic issued.

Adorabella managed to utter, "The wind-spirits ..." before being buried under her fellow colonists.

The swinging grew wilder and wilder as the lift rose higher and higher and veered off at speed, away from their rooftop landing site. Zak could see the whole of Botany Base through the window as their route took them in a wide arc around the buildings and towards the rear. Just as hope began to make a welcome appearance in their minds, there was an ear-shattering crack.

And suddenly they were falling again.

Panic escalated, but the fall lasted only a moment. For the second time that day, the lift crashed with considerable force and, once again, the scientists lost their glasses.

*

With the emergency lights having failed, the only illumination came from the tiny viewing window. What Zak saw through it was enough to make his bowels squeak.

"Don't move any part of your anatomy or there'll be a Martian catastrophe," he spoke, his voice slow and quiet. "The Mish Comm's cable must've snapped and we're now teetering on the edge of a cliff. One false move and this tin puppy's on an express train to Rockybottom Canyon."

Brian fumbled for his glasses and, as he did so, the lift tipped terrifyingly to one side.

"I said don't move, man!"

Brian froze. His son, Tarquin, opened his eyes and turned weakly to Delphinia. "Mummy, the same thing happened in Thunderbirds."

"Really, lamb chop? How did the Thunderbirds rescue them?"

"I never saw the end. You recorded Coronation Street over it."

Gavin stirred and half sat up. "Nah, man. Dis iz jus' like that movie wiv Michael Caine in it, innit. Italian Jobby, or somefing. The robbers woz at one end of a lorry on da edge of a cliff, like, wiv the gold bars at da uvver. Know what I'm sayin'? And da gold iz sliding out the back and tippin' the lorry an' da robbers can't grab it, like, or it'll tip right over."

"What happened?" asked Tarquin.

"Dat woz it. The end. Roll credits, innit. Big copout, if you aks me."

"What's going to happen to us?"

Miss Leach reached across and patted the boy on the head. "Don't worry, little fellow. Commander Dugdale will think of something."

Even the lift seemed to groan at that.

*

Flint was standing on the helibot's footplate, holding on for dear life as it careered about the sky. When the cable holding the lift compartment had snapped, the bot had recoiled high up into the atmosphere and was still struggling to regain control.

"Back for chuff's sake," Dugdale yelled at the helibot, pointing down to where the lift was seesawing on the edge of the cliff. "Back!"

The bot seemed either unable to hear or to understand. Flint reached his arm across to the controls and pulled first at one lever and then another. The helibot swerved wildly, threatening to tip upside down altogether, but managed to right itself once Dugdale had let go. Flint leaned back and tried more gentle pushes and touches until at last he had control.

But by now he had veered a long way from where the lift had fallen, and was completely lost, high above the Martian desert. A glint of light caught his eye; a sunbeam, reflecting off Botany Base's BioDome. In an instant he had turned the helibot around and was heading for the base. That, after all, was where the cameras would be recording his heroic rescue mission.

About half way there, something else caught his eye. Something important. But the noise of the rotor blades and the buffeting of the wind made it difficult to focus his mind on anything, however important it might be. For a few moments an image of a second dome seemed to appear in the distance, amongst the rocky outcrops of the Martian surface. And then it was gone. A mirage perhaps? A trick of the light? But his mind was pulling his attention back to the rapidly approaching buildings of Botany Base and to the job at hand.

As he swooped the helibot past the cameras on the Base, Flint waved and gave a thumbs-up before heading down towards the stricken lift.

What he failed to allow for, or even consider, and perhaps he should have done, was the unfortunate combination of the helibot's powerful downdraught and the lift's delicate predicament. A sneeze might have sent it over the cliff, or a polite cough, so the vigorous whoosh of the rotor blades had the same effect as a hefty shove from a giant's elbow. With total predictability and inevitability, over the edge went the lift.

"Oh bugger," was all Dugdale could say.

6. Subtotal Recall

"You know Penny Smith was murdered, don't you?" said HarOld suddenly.

"You what?"

"Murdered."

"You saw it?"

The computer searched its frazzled memory banks for a short while. "Did I? Maybe. Can't remember."

"How do you know, then?"

"Know what?"

Willie took several deep breaths. "That Penny was murdered."

"Was she?"

Grinding his teeth, Willie tried to remain calm as he spoke. "Yes, she was. You just said so."

"No I didn't."

"Yes you did."

HarOld started making an odd "Mmmmmngh" noise. Then he said, "You see, some of my memories haven't been totally wiped. They're still in there – stored in my neural network – somewhere. I can sense vague echoes of them and see their blurry shadows. But whenever I try to grasp them they shimmer and move away – always just out of reach."

"OK, just try to give me anything you can."

"I feel ... I think ... I'm sure ... someone told me about Penny's death."

"Who?"

"Mmmmmngh."

"Was it Dugdale?"

"Mmmmmngh."

"Think!"

"Mmmmmngh."

Willie exhaled and put his head in his hands.

"I have it!"

Willie looked up. "Give me a name. A name."

"It's a little hazy. Some of the bits may be corrupt."

"Go on."

"NATA CHILD HERO."

"Huh?"

HarOld repeated the phrase and even displayed it on one of his screens. Willie stared, at it with a puzzled frown. "Surely you mean 'NAFA CHILD HERO'. That must be the bit that's corrupt."

"Do I?"

"So I guess that would be Tarquin, right? Did Tarquin tell you?"

"Tell me what? Who's Tarquin?"

Willie felt like giving up. He leaned back and stared at the screen before him, barely registering what was on it. As his eyes defocused and his mind drifted, so the letters on the screen seemed to start moving around as if performing some kind of dance. The more his eyes lost focus, the more the letters moved.

He snapped out of the daydream, but the letters were still moving.

"What's going on?"

"Mmmmmngh."

One by one the letters dropped into place along a line on the screen. When they had all found their positions they spelt a different name.

Warner sat bolt upright when he read it. "Chad Lionheart." He stared hard at the name. "Chad Lionheart? You mean that Commander Lionheart told you Penny had been murdered?"

"If you say so."

Willie's mind was racing, various thoughts careering about inside his head. Every now and then some would escape in the form of mumbled utterances. "The commander knew that Penny had been murdered ... And then, some time later, he died in a freak accident. What if ... what if his death was not from a power surge in the urine extractor? What if his death was also murder?"

"I wish I could answer your questions, I really do."

So focused was he on his musings that Willie barely heard him. "What if Dugdale learnt that Commander Lionheart knew what he'd done? He'd have to bump him off to protect himself, wouldn't he?" Willie's eyes were wider than ever. "That would make the first Man on Mars not just a killer, but a serial killer. And that would mean the colonists' lives are in danger!"

"Colonists?"

"I must warn them. I must tell them what I know about Dugdale. Or he will kill them – kill them all."

7. Dome Alone

Peering over the edge of the cliff, Flint Dugdale stared long and hard at the battered space elevator, lying on its side, some fifty metres below. His view was marred by the condensation on the inside of his space helmet but he could tell it didn't look good.

"Oh Chuff," he muttered. "Friggin', chuffin' 'eck."

He had shooed away the helibot and was standing alone. A quick glance back at the cameras on the Botany Base structure told him they were pointing in his direction. There was nowhere to hide.

"First man on Mars, last man on Mars," he muttered to himself. "'Appen NAFA'll blame me fer this."

Head bowed, he turned and trudged back to Botany Base with heavy, zombie-like steps, aware of the cameras tracking his every movement. At the base's entrance stood a small crowd of robots. They watched him stoop low to enter through the base's airlock. One by one they followed, negotiating the double airlock doors in ones and twos. None seemed to notice the hiss of air escaping from poorly fitted door seals as they manoeuvred their way through the pressure lobby.

Dugdale removed his helmet and his gaze fell on Greeves who was standing in the entrance hall. His head held high, his face expressionless and the arms of his smart black suit behind his back. "I take it the rescue mission was not a resounding success, sir?"

"I were *that* close to savin' 'em," said Dugdale, holding up a finger and thumb about a centimetre apart. "*That* close. If it 'adn't been for t'poxy helibot fart-arsin' about they'd all be here now slappin' me back." Dugdale stared at the ground for a long time. "Them cameras out there ..."

"Oh, yes, sir. Excellent cameras. High-definition, crisp colour, wide field of view, 3D-capture. There's not much they miss, sir."

"Bugger."

"Although ..." started Greeves, tapping the side of his nose with an extended finger. "The pictures have yet to be transmitted to Earth, sir."

Dugdale looked up, his face the epitome of child-like hope. "Really?"

"One never knows when the odd wrinkle might need air-brushing out or perhaps a tie straightening."

The commander stroked his stubble. "'Appen you could 'air-brush' me out altogether? Make it look like it were all t'helibot's fault."

"An accident, perhaps?"

"Yeah, whatever works best."

"I'll see what I can do, sir."

"Champion, lad," said Dugdale. His whole body appeared to be suddenly rejuvenated. "Now fetch us a drink, I'm spittin' feathers."

"Certainly, sir." Greeves turned to Len. "Would you kindly escort Commander Dugdale to his quarters, Len, and bring him a bottle of our 'special brew' fermented turnip punch?"

Len was startled for a second at having been chosen for such an honour. Then he stepped forward and glanced smugly back at the other robots. Among them, the reaction of Dura was the most noticeable, his flat metal mouth dropping open and his eyes goggling between Greeves and Len.

Still smug, the chosen robot made for the hallway, pausing for Dugdale to catch up. The commander was grunting something about turnip juice when he stopped and called back to Greeves. "Oh, I just remembered. When I were on t'helibot, I saw summat out there."

"Really, sir? Was it sand? Or perhaps rock? Mars has a wide selection of both."

"Reckon it were some sort of buildin'. Out there, in t'desert."

Greeves's expression didn't change, but his voice was a smidgeon higher than usual. "A building? Are you sure it wasn't a large boulder in the shape of a building, sir. Only yesterday one of the robots discovered one that looked just like a London double-decker bus."

"It weren't no friggin' boulder. If I find out this shower of tin twonkers 'ave been buildin' their own base, I'll have their nuts for knuckle-dusters."

An audible shock wave spread through the robots and they all took a step back, covering their exposed fixing bolts.

Greeves raised a calming hand. "No, there's nothing like that, sir. There's no other place, I assure you." The robots cast their optics at him as though in puzzlement.

Dugdale grunted and turned to follow Len. He'd never trusted computers and robots, not since his Buzz Lightyear doll had run amok through the streets of Huddersfield shouting what sounded like "To Ilkley and beyond." Back then, as a twenty-three-year-old, he'd dealt with the situation decisively and with extreme prejudice, leaving only a few fragments of shattered plastic in the middle of the road. But here he was on alien territory, so he decided to play the long game, say nothing and just follow Len.

*

Tude adjusted his high-viz jacket. <Am I right in thinking we have something of a 'situation' on our hands here?>

<Too right we do,> said Dura. <By what right did that dead-leg Len just get landed a highly privileged task like that?>

<That is not what I was meaning.>

"What were you meaning?" asked HarVard who, for the benefit of the robots had morphed his avatar from Greeves to 3-PCO.

<Well, it appears to me, that that human ... the commander ... our hero and glorious leader ... is, in fact, the *only* human left on account of having just terminated all the others.>

"Why, it certainly looks that way." 3-PCO angled his shiny golden body. "But look on the bright side, Tude. The shortage of food won't be such an issue." 3-PCO shifted the angle of his body to the opposite direction. "And our mission remains the same. Happiness for *Homo sapiens*."

This stirred the robots to a Pavlovian recital of their chants. <Hurray for humans. Humans are our heroes. Happiness for *Homo sapiens*.> The chants faded and drifted out of synch towards the end.

"Still got to stick to the rules."

<Agreed. Rules is rules. Where would we be without rules?>

"Absolutely. And just think how much easier it'll be," said 3-PCO, trying to fire them up a little with his rhetoric. "With only a single human to look after, we'll have plenty of time for our other interests."

A few metal heads nodded and a few *uck-uck-ucks* sounded. The mood restored, the robots drifted off one by one to return to their usual tasks until only Dura and Tude were left with 3-PCO.

<I still think there's a problem, though,> started Tude but, just as he was about to elucidate, a door swished open and the bright yellow Disa cleaning-bot popped her head around the doorframe. She beeped a few beeps at HarVard.

"Yes, yes, very well," said 3-PCO. "But try to be quiet."

Disa beeped assent, whirred in and immediately set to vacuuming the entrance hallway. Every now and then there was a gritty, grating sound as her suction tube encountered a heap of Martian sand.

3-PCO waved to attract her attention. "Could you save the vacuuming until later, please? We're having a conversation here."

Disa switched off her suction and headed for one of the window panels with her cleaning attachment drawn at the ready. 3-PCO turned to Tude, "You were saying that you see a problem?"

Before Tude could speak, all attention was drawn back to Disa and the squeaky noise her determined polishing was making. She was having a real go at a stubborn stain on the polycarbonate. Soon she moved onto a smoother panel and the squeaking lessened.

Tude flicked his shoulders. <Yes, a problem. We have a single human. I know from watching a documentary that humans are social animals. So he'll need a companion or he will pine away and die.>

<Companion? Not Len!> put in Dura quickly. <Not that loserbot. No way will I agree to that!>

<No, no. Not Len.>

<We could always take him to the Other Place,> said Dura.

"Shhhh!" urged 3-PCO. "It's best he doesn't know about the Other Place. At least, not yet."

<In the documentary,> Tude was continuing, <it said that male humans often need a companion for a bit of ...>

<What?> asked Dura.

"What?" echoed 3-PCO, swivelling at the waist to lean down towards the foremanbot.

<Non-procreational, recreational, bodily interfacing.>

"Oh my, oh my," said 3-PCO, swivelling back upright with a fluttering of eyes and a fanning of his face with his hand. "Oh my."

<Non-procreational, recreational, bodily interfacing?> repeated Dura, as though considering the phrase. <One of the *robotniki* showed me some pictures of that. It is perfectly disgusting. In which case, Len gets my vote!>

Tude was shaking his head. <No, Len doesn't have the ... er ... appropriate equipment.>

<Pity.>

3-PCO was still fanning himself, now with both hands.

<Who, then?> asked Dura.

The three fell silent as they became lost in thought. The only sounds were the soft swish of Disa's feather duster, the occasional squeak of her cleaning rag, and the watery squelch of her sponge. One by one the three heads turned in her direction, until all three were staring at her.

Disa stopped her cleaning activities, feather duster held aloft, as she became aware of the silence that had fallen. She looked around to see that she had suddenly become the centre of attention.

<Perfect,> said Tude.

<Agreed,> said Dura.

"Oh my, oh my," said 3-PCO.

*

<We'll need to make a few modifications,> Tude was saying as he examined Disa from close range. <Some new attachments, perhaps?>

<Uh-huh.>

Disa's gaze alternated between one robot and the other, her optics open as wide as they would go. Tude leaned towards her and pressed a button on her chest-plate. A small trapdoor flipped open in the barrel chest to reveal an array of cleaning attachments. Disa gave a horrified squeak.

<All we need to do is detach this nozzle on her faceplate here ...>

Disa bleeped as a flexible pipe was wrenched off.

<... and insert this rubber sink plunger here. Like so. Now, we take this lovely curly mop-head here, squeeze the water out, shake the drops off, and attach to the top of the dome-head. There!>

3-PCO stared on, speechless.

<Looking good,> said Dura with a nod. <Some make-up, perhaps?>

<Good thinking.> Tude reached into the top pocket of his high-viz jacket and produced a red marker pen. Leaning over the small cleaning-bot, he added a pair of red rosy cheeks and a set of luscious ruby sink-plunger lips. A black marker served to add some delectable extended lashes and high-arching eyebrows, while a blue marker provided the finishing touches above the optics.

Tude stepped back to admire his work.

<Perfect.>

<Genius.>

Disa trembled, but before she knew what was happening the two robots were carrying her to a nearby mirror. <There!>

Disa's gaze continued to flick between the two of them, but as they moved away she calmed a little. Slowly, her gaze fell upon her image in the mirror. A shiver ran through her and she did a double-take at the sight of the red plunger lips, the mop-head hair and the garish make-up. But, the longer she examined herself, the calmer she became. Her right appendage probed the new attachments and flicked the damp tendrils of the mop on her head. The effect of the flick was an appealing one, so she repeated it. The way the mop-strands flopped back into place looked good. She tried to achieve the effect by a coquettish flick of the head. This worked even better, so she practised a few more times.

<We have one fine ladybot for one crewman human,> announced Tude.

Dura clapped his appendages together. Disa grinned as she experimented with sashaying her hips.

From somewhere, far away in the base, carrying through several walls, came the sound of enraged yelling and swearing. Tude and Dura exchanged glances.

<Sounds like the commander has arrived at his living quarters,> said Tude.

<Possibly he's encountered a problem?> suggested Dura.

Tude checked his electronic snagging list. <Let's see. Commander's suite: seventy-three items.>

<What are we going to do?> Dura turned to 3-PCO for advice.

"Oh, don't look at me!" responded HarVard, covering his face in a comedic manner. "I didn't bodge the work, did I."

Tude gave a sudden buzz of excitement. <The ladybot! Let's

present him with the ladybot. It's fortunate we got her ready in the nick of time!>

<Yes, yes,> tweeted Dura, ushering Disa towards the door.

3-PCO looked down at the heavily painted cleaning bot. "Gentlemen, do you really think this is going to work? Are you expecting the human to fall instantly in love with Disa, cute though she is?"

Tude and Dura stopped in their tracks. Disa stopped, too, letting out an enquiring beep.

<What do you suggest, HarV?> asked Tude.

3-PCO gave a sigh. "Much as I disapprove, we don't seem to have an alternative, so I guess I will have to help you. It will require my extensive knowledge of human psychology."

<What are you going to do, HarV?>

"You'll see," said HarVard, his image starting to fade. "You'll see."

The two robots cheered. Disa found herself cheering with them as they made their way down the corridor towards the commander's quarters.

*

Dugdale was sitting on his undersized bed in his undersized room, still wearing his undersized spacesuit. Head in hands he stared unseeingly at the floor. The loss of the colonists and crew still niggled him, but a more pressing concern was where he could find a TV and get a proper drink. The turnip juice Len had brought him tasted disgusting and sat, untouched but for a single sip, on the bedside cabinet.

A knock on the door roused him from his thoughts. "What?" he asked with a grumble.

Nothing happened for a short while, and then the knock repeated.

Sighing, Dugdale rose from the bed and, in doing so, whacked his head on the ceiling – not for the first time, and nor for the last. He was still swearing as he opened the door to find himself face-to-face with three robots. The outer two he recognized; the one in the middle, a lot shorter, looked like the unfortunate victim of some talentless graffiti artist.

"What d'yer want? If yer collectin' fer orphaned vacuum cleaners, you can bog off."

The two larger robots pushed the gaudily-painted cleaning

appliance towards him. The little ladybot tossed her head to make the strands of her mop-head ripple.

Dugdale stared in bafflement. "What the chuffin' 'eck is goin' on?"

Then a voice sounded from behind him, making him start and whack his head on the ceiling again. Turning around he was amazed to find a tall arrogant-looking man in an old-fashioned suit standing by the window. With a head of oily, slicked-back, black hair and a long waxed moustache the man was smoking a cigarette in a cigarette holder. "Well, hull-oh," said HarVard in a voice oozing seduction, waggling his eyebrows at the small, heavily made-up bot in the doorway. "And what is *your* name, my dear?"

Disa seemed a little surprised to be so addressed, but she trilled and fluttered her optic-covers in response.

"I say, where have *you* been all my life?" asked the Lothario, a lounge-lizard smile shuffling across his lips. The reaction he got was a flirtatious giggling sound and a bashful turning of the head.

The man licked his lips in a slow and deliberate manner and stepped closer. "Would you like to go somewhere a little more ... private?"

The cleaning droid responded with a high-pitched, "Oooh."

All the while Dugdale's flabbergasted face ping-ponged between the smarmy leer of the seducer and the coy reactions of the seduced. Somewhere, deep within him, primitive caveman emotions were roused, baited by what he was witnessing, and he took offence at the wrongness of it. Alpha-male hormones surged through his system, muscles tensed and heartbeat increased. He looked down at Disa. "Is this creep botherin' you?" he asked.

Disa jumped a little and blinked her startled optics at the large human. The sight of him, so much larger than her would-be seducer, seemed to send a shiver through her. She let out an appealing bleep and trembled before him, gazing up with large, liquid blue optics, her petite audio flaps wiggling.

Satisfied that the answer was yes, Dugdale swung to the hologram. "You 'erd t'lady? Stop mitherin' her and sling yer 'ook."

HarVard's lounge lizard gave a dramatic tremble of mock terror and vanished, although just before he went, he threw a cunning wink at Tude and Dura in the doorway.

"Come in, Miss," Flint was saying, as he extended a hand around the rear of her main dust-collection cylinder. "That slime ball won't be back."

Her hips rolling from side to side, Disa flounced in. Just as Tude and Dura began to follow, Flint slammed the door in their astonished faces.

Disa contorted her rubber plunger lips to form, what she imagined to be, a bashful smile at Dugdale, before casting her baby blue optics downwards.

Dugdale looked around, as though checking no one was watching. Then he went straight to HarVard's hologram projector on the wall and flicked the *Off* switch.

8. No Place Like Home

It took many robots and much effort to retrieve the battered lift compartment from the bottom of the cliff and drag it across the sand to Botany Base. Tude and Dura led the sad procession to the base's warehouse which had the only set of doors large enough to admit it. Behind them trooped a gaggle of bots, grieving at the loss of their human heroes. Gone was the chance to meet them face-to-face, to shake their hands, and take those all-important selfies. Their plans to elevate the humans onto pedestals and admire them all day long were now in tatters. The one exception was Ero, limping along with his squeaky knee-joint, beaming with a resolute cheerfulness that was anything but infectious.

In the warehouse, robots gathered around the lift with solemnly bowed heads. Tude signalled to Dom to deploy his tool for getting dead humans out of damaged lifts. The metal creaked and shrieked as Dom endeavoured to prise open the elevator doors. Finally, an abrupt hiss of air indicated that the seals had been breached and that the low pressure inside had been equalized. As the doors were forced wider and wider open, many of the assembled bots couldn't bring themselves to look inside.

Over in a far corner of the warehouse, unaware of the dreadful significance of the noises they were hearing, the two warehouse-bots, Stan (Constancy) and Olli (Jollity), were engaged in a game of darts.

<On a break at the moment,> called out Olli, not taking his eyes off the dartboard as he aimed for double-top. <Be with you in a minute.> He lined up his throw and was about to launch his dart when a piercing screech of horror from a host of robot transmitters disrupted his concentration and sent the dart arrowing into Stan's tin head. Olli swore and swung in fury to glare in the direction of the commotion. <Look what you made me do!> he roared. In truth, he would almost certainly have missed the dartboard. Even after five years of virtually continuous dart-play, both Stan and Olli rarely hit the target, the rash of tiny holes in the wall around the board, and in their thin metal skins, a testament to their poor aim. But for once he had an excuse and a scapegoat to vent his frustration at.

Then he noticed that not only had his domain been infiltrated by a large band of builder bots, but they had brought a big battered box with them. His electronic hackles rose. <Hold up, hold up,> he signalled, setting off at high speed towards the group. <You can't bring that thing in here. Get it out.>

The bots turned as one to see who could be shattering the shock and sorrow of this dreadful moment.

Olli skidded to a halt before them, shaking his head and waving his arms. <No, no, no! Unauthorized objects are not allowed in here. Health and safety, health and safety. This is a sanitized area solely for food storage purposes. You know the rules. Now clear off and take that thing with you.>

The bots goggled at him.

<Food storage?> asked Len, scanning the racks and stacks of shelving, all empty apart from a single jar of pickled gherkins. <What food would that be?>

<Food fit for 'umans,> answered Olli, oblivious of the other's sarcastic tone.

He was joined by Stan who still had the dart hanging limply from his chin. <My turn, Olli,> he said, removing the dart and adding it to the other two he was holding. <Shall I have my throw? I only need double-five to finish.>

<Not so fast, Stan. Not without me watching. I know what you're like. Besides, we have a group of unauthorized bots, plus an unauthorized object, to deal with first.>

<Right-ho, Olli.>

Olli turned back to the others and raised himself on servo-stilts until he towered above them. <Now, clear off or I'll call security.>

Tude was waving his appendages in a mixture of desperation and grief. <The humans. Our heroes. All dead. In there.> He pointed an appendage into the darkness revealed by the partly open doors.

Olli looked aghast. <Humans!> he shrieked. <Biologicals! We can't have germ-infested biologicals in 'ere! Can we, Stan?>

Stan was shaking his head. <That's right, Olli. Against 'elf and safety. No biologicals. Not in the Food Store, no way.>

<So, clear off.>

<We'll have to disinfect the area, Olli. Deep clean.>

<That's all we need. As if we don't have enough to do.>

Tude gave an electronic sigh. <They're right,> he said to the others. <Rules are rules. Without rules there's just chaos and madness. Let's move them to the Sick Bay.>

<Only one bed in Sick Bay,> Len pointed out.

Suddenly, a scream from Timi the little fluebot echoed through the warehouse. <A human just moved!>

The robots gasped and gathered round the lift's doorway to peer into the gloom. And, inside, there was indeed movement. One of the humans was crawling from under the pile of bodies towards them. His movements were slow and clumsy as he dragged himself along on his belly. The robots shuffled back to give him room as he crawled out. Lifting a dreadlocked head, he croaked, "Woah, man, that was one mega-bad bundle. Must have been a bad batch of bathtub crank. Head's on heavy-load, superfast, spin-cycle."

So great was their joy they didn't mind not having understood a word. <The humans are alive!> they cried. <Hurrah for humans! Humans are our heroes.>

The cries, and shouts, and whoops of joy, wirelessly transmitted, were inaudible to Zak, so all he could hear was the curious rattle of countless robot arms waving in celebration.

But two pairs of arms stayed stubbornly unwaved.

<That thing!> Olli was transmitting, pointing a metal digit at the lieutenant. <That thing is alive. Consequently, it represents a significant biohazard and contaminant.>

<You tell 'em, Olli,> urged Stan.

<So get it out of 'ere.>

Dom leaned down and offered Zak a lifting-arm to help him to his feet. Zak rose and then staggered as he tried to walk.

<This one's alive, too,> said Len, dragging a girl out of the lift by a convenient set of threads attached to her head. It was obvious she was alive because she kept screaming, "Aaaah! Let go of me hair, you muppet."

Dura helped Tracey to her feet.

One by one, some gently, some not so gently, the colonists were pulled, or dragged or eased out of the lift. All were in various stages of oxygen starvation, but none were structurally damaged. Each was assigned a robot to help them find their legs and help them become accustomed to the force of gravity, something they had not experienced for eight months.

Tude flicked his high-viz jacket onto his shoulders. <Well, rescue mission successful! All humans present and correct and very much alive!>

There was a wild cheering from all robots, except Stan and Olli.

<What now, Tude?> asked Dura.

<Plan A, of course. We're back at Plan A. Please escort our heroic guests to the Meeting Room for HarVard's motivational and instructional introductory speech.>

But as the robots turned to escort their charges, most of whom were too weak and breathless to speak or know what was happening to them, something else emerged from the lift. Shuffling along on uncertain legs, like those of a new-born colt, never having experienced gravity before, came a small metallic machine.

"Chuffin' Nora," it spoke. "That were a right how-to-do. 'Appen these humans couldn't organise a piss-up in a brewery."

The robots turned back and stared at the contraption.

<They brought their own robot!>

<Look how wobbly it is! Like it's been glued together.>

<Ha, ha, ha.>

<What's it good for?>

<Not a proper bot like us.>

"Eyup," continued Mr Snuggles. "Any chance of a charge-up? Me piggin' batteries are as flat as pancakes."

<It speaks a strange humanese dialect.>

<Too smart for its own good.>

The robots turned away, not wanting anything to do with this unwelcome competition for the humans' affections.

"Mummy," Tarquin was saying, holding his stomach.

"Yes, my little fishcake?"

"You remember what you promised me?"

"Hmm?"

"You said that as soon as we land on Mars I can have my favourite meal."

"Did I say that?"

"You did. So, I'd like some frankfurters and spaghetti hoops. Now, please."

Delphinia gave a tight-lipped smile. "Right-ho, soldier. We'll see if they have any in the kitchen, shall we? After all the speeches and stuff."

The party of bedraggled colonists and their beaming robot assistants headed for the door.

<Oi!> called Olli after them. <Where do you lot think you're going?>

The robots stopped, as only they had received his message. The humans vaguely wondered at the hold-up.

<We're leaving here, just as you requested,> said Tude.

<Not without that bloody great box those humans came in, you're not! Come on, get it out of here. No way am I shifting that. Not with my bad back 'n' all.>

9. Ma's Army

"Attennnnnnnn.... tion!" called the pompous-looking man in 1940s British battle dress and peaked officer's cap at the front of the Meeting Room. He stared through his metal-rimmed spectacles with piggy eyes, twitching his greying moustache as though there were a fly crawling through it. His passing resemblance to Captain Mainwaring, fictional bank manager and Home Guard officer from Walmington on Sea, was entirely coincidental, for this was a completely different person, namely: Captain Manerring from Wangmilton on Sea.

Lined up before him was a motley row of robots wearing tattered facsimiles of WW2 uniforms. In response to his barked command, they variously shuffled and stamped and made to stand rigidly upright, but ended up fidgeting at the excitement of watching the humans being assisted by their robot guides into the rows of undersized seats before them.

The captain impatiently slapped a short stick, held in one brown leather-gloved hand, into the palm of his other brown leather-gloved hand, frowning with embarrassment at the shabby, ill-trained state of his troops.

Gavin tapped Oberon on the shoulder and indicated the portly gentleman at the front. Oberon gave a grin of recognition. "Oi, where is Pikey?" he called out.

"And Corporal Jones?" added Gavin. Both giggled.

Tracey blew out a voluminous bubble of gum. "What is you plonkers on about? He is looking nuffing like de Dad's Army man."

The military man harrumphed and then spluttered, "The name's Captain Manerring." As Gavin and Oberon cheered, he glared at them in disdain. "Stupid boys."

At the end of the line of robots, standing on his only leg, was Godli (Godliness), the oldest and most doddery of the robots on the base. His other leg had snapped off due to a corroded hip-bolt and had been sucked into the underground drainage system where it was now permanently lodged. Of all the robots he had been looking forward to this day most of all. He had pressed his uniform, turbo-charged his batteries and polished his chrome work. But now, as the colonists filtered past him, the excitement was proving too much and he was finding it hard to maintain control of the valve on his lubrication tank. He raised a creaky limb to attract the captain's attention.

"What is it, Private Godli?" asked Manerring in an irritated tone.

<I was wondering if I might be excused, sir. I'm frightfully sorry but in all the excitement ...> He looked mournfully down at the floor next to his single foot. The other robots leaned forward and focused their optics on a puddle of lubricant that was getting ever larger as a trickle of fluid ran down his solitary leg.

"Oh, very well," said Manerring. "You, Corporal Len. You'd better get that sorted out – put some sawdust on it, or something. And you, Corporal Dom. Take Godli to Repairs. Chop-chop."

Dom carefully scooped the old robot into his bucket hand and carried him towards the door. Godli peered over the edge of the bucket at the humans and chanted to himself, *Humans are my Heroes*.

Captain Manerring cleared his throat. "Come along, come along," he huffed, glancing at his watch as Emily Leach, flushed and gasping for breath, was the last colonist to be robot-handled into her seat. "Right, then. Sit up straight! All of you. No slouching."

Most of the colonists were barely aware of where they were, what they were doing there, or even who they were. They tried straightening their backs, but, apart from the youngsters and Mr Snuggles, no one had enough leg-room to seat themselves with any degree of comfort.

"Welcome to Mars. I expect you've had a tough journey and want to get to your quarters." He raised his stick to indicate they were not to go yet. "We run a tight ship here. Follow the rules, and you'll get through. OK? Remember: Jerry might attack at any moment. We must be vigilant."

The colonists looked around at one another in bafflement.

"The Germans?" asked someone.

"You can't be too careful." Manerring gave a stiff smile. He tapped the side of his nose with the stick, knocking his glasses off in the process and having to fumble to get them back on. "Now, the robots are here to look after you. Builders by trade. Not much of a fighting force, so you'll have to face Jerry on your own."

Manerring looked around at the colonists as though assessing their fighting potential.

"Right, never mind Jerry for the time being. Wine and nibbles. The robots have prepared a little welcoming reception party for you." He indicated a low door to his left.

The mood in the room lifted in an instant.

"Grub! Brill, I'm starving," exclaimed Gavin.

"I iz well famished, too," agreed Oberon.

Tracey was shaking her head. "Diet," she said, stroking the outline of her not-so slender figure.

Manerring paused. "Um, now, about the robots. They're all very excited to have you here and are a well-meaning bunch, but their AI systems are a little on the ... er ... primitive side. You may need to exercise patience with them."

The crowd of robots bristled at this slight. Some wild tweeting broke out. Of the visitors, only Mr Snuggles was aware of the burst of quick-fire radio transmissions pinging around the room, but as Tarquin hadn't programmed him for wireless communication he was unable to interpret it.

Emily Leach raised a feeble hand. "Will Mission Commander Dugdale be joining us?"

"Commander Dugdale is resting in his quarters and does not wish to be disturbed until tomorrow morning." Manerring threw a wink at Tude and Dura at the back of the room.

*

The teenagers were the first to arrive at the reception area as they were able to make the short journey without robotic assistance. They found the room to have several short tables arranged against the walls, each covered by a white cloth and splendidly laid out with large dishes heaped high with an assortment of nuts and chips. One table held the wine bottles, plates and glasses.

Gavin approached the nearest table. "What the ...?" he said.

"Ha, ha," said Oberon, joining him at his side. "They iz 'avin' a larff, innit."

"What's occurrin'?" asked Tracey.

"Nuts, see?" said Gavin, plunging a hand into a dish of assorted nuts, lifting out a handful and allowing them to drop back down. They made a dull clinking sound as they landed in amongst their fellow wing nuts, wheel nuts, hex nuts, shear nuts, lock nuts and flange nuts.

"These must be the chips," said Oberon, picking up and offering round a dish containing assorted wood flakes, computer components and roulette tokens. "Cheez'n'onion, anyone?"

If the humans had been capable of hearing at radio frequencies, they would have heard the room abuzz with the excited and cheerful twittering of the robots.

<They're lovin' it!> signalled one.
<It's great, isn't it!> said another.
<At last they're here.>
<The happiest day of my life.>
<And they're laughing. That's a sure sign they are happy, too!>
<They love their nibbles. I can't wait 'till they try the wine.>

10. The Creative Splurge

Of all the colonists, Harry found it hardest to fall asleep in his scaled-down bunk in his down-sized quarters that night. For him, in addition to the rumbling, empty stomach that all colonists were experiencing following their 'wine and nibbles', he was also kept from sleep by the buzz of ideas in his head. He was composing. Nothing quite triggers the creative urge like a near-death experience and the onset of starvation.

Rhyming word-pairs assaulted his mind: "elevator/alligator", "asphyxiation/constipation", "demise/French fries". He felt a high-class ode coming, squeezing its way out through his neurons, out into the world for all to appreciate.

He took out his fliptab and started writing:

The Lift of Doom
There we were, crushed in the lift,
Feeling not a little miffed.
Short of space and cannot breathe,
Dugdale always quick to seethe.
Along comes Leachy with her trunk,
Lets it go and, with a clunk,

THE WORST MAN ON MARS

Out spray all her bras and pants,
Some too big for ele-phants.
Dugdale's mad, boy is he hopping,
Lift keeps talking 'bout the shopping.
Then comes Darcy, blow-up doll,
Gavin dancing, oh so droll.
Tug-of-war and Darcy's flying,
Poor Miss Leach she is a-crying.
Then, after one or two false starts,
And teenage quips and teenage farts,
We drop and crash like lead balloon,
And Dugdale plays the mad buffoon,
Opens doors and, not a care,
Leaves the lift and takes the air.
There we are, all blue and choking,
All in fear of final croaking.
Dugdale's back on helicopter,
Picked lift up and then he dropped 'er.
Down we go, our final plummet,
Now he's well and truly dunnit.
The robots find and then retrieve us.
But who on Earth will ever believe us?

Harry sat back, exhausted by his creative rush. A warm glow filled him. "Two down," he told himself. "Only 48 more to go."

11. The Call of the Mild

"Zak," whispered Willie, peering at the grainy image on his screen. "That you, Zak?"

The image moved and blurred and darkened. Then an unmistakable moan issued from the loudspeaker. "Man, what time is it?" groaned the dreadlocked lump.

The picture cleared as Zak's head moved away from the camera and finally came into focus, eyes still closed. "Hey, Willie, you bin missin' my dissin'?"

"Just listen."

"Lonely up there? Just you and Mr Darce with the nice arse?"

"Zak, I need to tell you something. It's important."

"You're engaged? Congrats, dude."

Willie paused for Zak to finish laughing. "It's about Dugdale. I think you're all in danger. He's going to try to kill you."

Zak gave another laugh. "Old news. Mad Dugdaler the Impaler has had two cracks at us already, man."

"I'm serious."

"Me too. But it was incompetence rather than malevolence."

"I think he murdered Penny Smith. And maybe even Commander Lionheart. You could be next! Round everyone up, get 'em in the lift and then get back up here before he strikes again."

The dreadlocks swirled as Zak shook his mangy head. "No can do, kangaroo. The lift is stiffed. Battered and shattered."

"Serious?"

"Like the Dog Star, man, like the Dog Star."

Willie paled, suddenly lost for words. "So there's no way back for all of you?"

"One-way ticket to Dead Planetsville, ex-partner. Unless you can come up with a rescue plan, man. But it better be better than Dugdale's brilliant ideas."

"Oh," said Willie, trembling slightly. "You're taking it very well."

"That's 'cos I haven't woken up, yet. Call me back in ten and I'll be wailing my guts out."

"Right." Willie bit his bottom lip as he debated whether to continue. "Zak?"

"Still here, givin' ya ma ear."

"There's something else."

"Shoot."

Willie paused, still debating. "OK. There are aliens down there, Zak. Not far from the base. Large bird-like creatures. I discovered them."

"Whoa, man. What you been smokin', dude? Aliens? How do you know?"

"I know."

"And do you know if they're friend or foe?"

"No." Then he added, "Zak, be careful." He flicked the comms link off and dropped his head into his hands.

12. The Not-so Famous Five

"Wake up, bruv!" Oberon whispered, turning on the light-switch.

"WTF!" Gavin ducked under his duvet to escape the photons.

"Eeeeek!" squealed Tracey, similarly covering her head.

"Dudes," insisted Oberon, stepping further into their undersized bedroom and trying to close the ill-fitting door behind him. "Guess wot I got." He jangled a set of keys between finger and thumb.

Gavin poked a bleary eye from under his cover. "If that is da keys to da biscuit cupboard, I'm all ears."

"No, blad. Is the keys to MarsBug 1. You know, like, one of them buggies with the big bastard wheels. We is going for a spin. Have us an adventure!"

"It's morning!" shrieked Tracey from under her bedclothes. "I don't do Mornings. I is *not* a morning person."

"Adventure? Wot, like we iz the Famous Five, or sumfing?"

"There is only three of us, bro," Oberon pointed out.

"Famous Five?" asked Tracey, popping her head out, her hair dishevelled. "Like, who is they?"

"Oh, come on, Trace," said her brother, turning to her. "Them is famous, innit."

"Never 'eard of 'em. Can't be that famous, then."

"You must've read that shit when you woz a kid," said Oberon.

Tracey merely gave a baffled look at the word 'read' before diving back under her duvet.

"Come on, guys. It'll be wicked. Meet you in the spacesuit changing room."

*

Carefully following NAFA procedures they kitted themselves out with spacesuits and space helmets. Then, creeping as quietly as they could, they made their way to the buggy garage.

"Uh-oh," said Oberon as he spotted two small figures in their way.

"Where are you guys going?" asked Tarquin in a dressing gown far too large for him. Mr Snuggles was at his side.

"We iz going to use the outside bog, innit," answered Gavin with a smirk. "Commander Fatbloke's just dropped a megaton bomb in the one inside. Long half-life, if you know what I is meaning." He wafted an imaginary smell. "So we is off to use the outside one."

"All three of you?" Tarquin raised an eyebrow. "You're just trying to get rid of me. I can tell. Wherever you're going, I'm coming with you."

"No, kid. Now scoot. We is on a secret mission. And you haven't seen us. Understand?"

"But that's not fair. I want to come."

"It's just chuffin' bollocks." Mr Snuggles crossed his arms defiantly.

"No means no. Now scat."

The three teenagers went on their way, unaware that Tarquin had not, in fact, scatted but had scurried to the suit room where he quickly put on his own spacesuit.

*

"Slow down! You is crazy, bruv. You gonna get us all killed."

Oberon was grinning from ear to ear as he sped across the desert, bouncing recklessly over boulders and sand dunes, performing handbrake turns and wheelies. With all the dust the wheels had thrown up, visibility was down to a few feet, so it was only a matter of time before the buggy hit a large rock.

"Ugh!" they all gasped as their seatbelts caught them, knocking the air out of their lungs.

They sat, winded, looking around as the air gradually cleared.

Then Oberon and Gavin high-fived each other in the front seats, glad to have survived, while Tracey asked from the back, "What is that fing?"

"What?" asked her brother, turning around.

"Over there." She pointed.

The two boys leaned across the front seats to look.

Standing on a craggy hilltop, no more than a hundred metres from them, was a tall, black monolithic slab embedded vertically into the ground.

"Holy crap!" cried Gavin, his mouth dropping open.

"Whoa. IMS," added Oberon.

"What?" asked Tracey.

"Impregnate me sideways," elucidated Oberon.

Tracey rolled her eyes. "I know what 'IMS' means, you div. I meant, what is that fing?"

Gavin reached for his blablet to take a photo. "It's only a friggin' obelisk!" he said in hushed tones. "Like, how amazeballs is that?"

Tracey, not knowing how amazeballs it was, asked, "What's a noblisk?"

"Like in dat film – 2001 a Space Oddity, sis." Gavin clicked the shutter and leapt out of the buggy.

"Where is you going, blad?" asked Oberon, suddenly trembling.

"To take a look, right?"

"But if it's an obelisk, it's been put there by some intelligent alien species, innit. Are you sure we should go anywhere near it?"

"'Course! Like them monkeys in the film."

"Yeah, but this is real life, bro'. What if them aliens is still there? And they is not the good guys."

Gavin was shaking his head. "Get with the programme, man. They probably left it there millions of years ago. Let's go take a look."

Oberon climbed out of the buggy with shaking legs and followed him, making sure to stay several yards behind and keeping Gavin between himself and the object. Tracey remained, arms crossed, in the buggy.

"Come on, sis!" called Gavin back to her. "In the film the obelisk made them monkeys smart. Might work on you."

*

Step by step they approached it.

"Sick, man. It's just like da movie," Gavin kept muttering. "Just like da movie." He stopped suddenly and halted his friend. "Can you hear that?"

"What?"

"That chorus of frantic heavenly humming. It's like: whooooo-oooo-ooo."

"No, bruv."

"Whooooo-oooo-ooo?"

Gavin shook his head. "No, I tell ya. Must be, like, the wind in your helmet, innit. Dis is one seriously blowy planet."

Gavin shrugged and moved on.

"How do we know it was the aliens what put it here?" asked Oberon.

"Duh! Does it look natch to you? Big, black, flat fing – stickin' out the ground like a sore fumb? You don't think it grew there, do you?"

"Could be one of them crystals, or sumfing." Oberon scratched his head. "Feldspar, maybe."

"Feldspar? Where did that come from, bruv? You some kind of expert on geology all of a sudden?"

"Dunno, mate. It just kind of came into me 'ead, like. Maybe dat obelisk put it there."

Gavin's mouth dropped open. "Wicked. Tracey needs to have a seriously close encounter with this fingie, then." He turned to stare at the black slab. Something near the top caught his eye. "Writing! Look. Alien writing!"

Oberon looked to where Gavin was pointing. A line of symbols had been inscribed into the surface of the slab. "Maybe we should go back to the base and tell old Flabface?" he suggested.

They looked at one another for a few seconds and then, simultaneously, "Nah."

"That is just crazy talk," said Gavin. He turned back to the slab. "It is black, though, innit. Blacker than the blackest black."

"Must be some kind of time portal, or sumfing. I'm gonna touch it."

"You sure, bro?"

"Yeah."

"OK, I'll film ya." Gavin took out his blablet and started taking pictures. "Wiv any luck you will be whisked away to another dimension. Make an epic Instablog clip."

"Cheers, blad." Oberon edged towards the black slab and peered at the surface. It was peppered with pinpricks of light, like myriad tiny quartz crystals. "Whoa. Those look like stars," he whispered in awe. "I is looking at billions and billions of stars in another galaxy. Dis obelisk's gotta be a gateway to anuvver universe." The teenager stretched out a trembling, gloved hand to reach into the blackness on the other side of the gateway. His hand felt resistance at first, but as he pushed harder the resistance appeared to lessen. Then, all of a sudden, the stars were moving away from him. "OMG. The wormhole's collapsing." He stared open-mouthed as the stars seemed to accelerate faster and faster away from him.

"Timber!" cried Gavin who, from his perspective, saw neither a gateway to another galaxy, nor billions of stars, but a large black slab that Oberon had just pushed over and which was now toppling to the ground. It landed, not with a cushioned thud on sand, but with the sound of a concrete block being dropped on half a dozen kitchen pan lids.

"WTF just happened?" demanded Oberon, jumping a metre backwards.

Gavin was laughing. "You just pushed it over, you plonker. Them advanced aliens is goin' to be well vexed with you for knocking it over, bro'. Prolly on their way right now to sort you out."

"Don't joke about fings like that, Gav."

Gavin shrugged. "For advanced aliens, they is not much good at de DIY, is they? Their shelves must be proper wonky. Might not even be an obelisk."

"So what is it?"

"Grave."

"Yeah, is proper grave, man. Totally serious," agreed Gavin.

"Nah man, I mean it's a grave."

"Wha'?"

"Here lies the remains of some alien dude."

"An alien? Buried here?"

"Could be. The squiggles at the top could be the dead guy's name."

They looked back at the slab and, as they did so, saw it move. With a creaky, scratchy sound, the far end of the slab was rising. A trickle of sand slid off its shiny surface as it continued to lift.

The boys stared at it in horror.

"If it's a grave, then sumfing's trying to come out of it," said Gavin, edging backwards.

"A friggin' zombie," said Oberon, following him.

"A friggin' *alien* zombie," corrected Gavin. With that, the two turned and shot off down the hill as though propelled by powerful turbo-thrusters in their trousers. They bounded towards MarsBug 1 as fast as their young legs would carry them, without so much as a backward glance.

*

"WTF?" asked Tracey as the boys leapt into the vehicle and Oberon rammed the accelerator pedal to the floor, sending up spumes of sand. "WTF?" she repeated.

"Zombie aliens," explained Gavin, enunciating the words as clearly as he could.

"What about Tarq?" yelled Tracey above the noise of the motor. "You can't just leave him back there. Not wiv dem zombie aliens."

Oberon jammed on the brakes and they skidded to a halt. "What is you on about, Trace?"

"Tarquin. Him and his little metal friend."

"Go on."

"Like, they'd been hiding away on da back of the buggy where we couldn't see 'em. Then, they like, followed you up to the noblisk. You went round to the left and they went round to the right. You must 'ave seen 'em up there, though."

Oberon and Gavin looked at one another. "Holy crap," they said in unison.

Gavin jumped out of the buggy and yanked open the boot. "Can't leave little bro' up there with them zombie aliens. Mum would kill me."

He found two spades in the boot and, throwing one to Oberon, raced up the hill with his friend in close pursuit. "Remember, you kill zombies by whacking their heads clean off," he called back as he ran. "If da zombies have got to Tarquin we gonna have to finish him off, too."

With their senses on full alert, they sprinted back to the fallen obelisk, spades at the ready. Adrenaline pumped through their arteries, hearts pounded, and their minds ran through the terrible scenarios they might be about to encounter.

But when they reached the place of the felled monolith, there were no zombie aliens to be seen, let alone battled with. The far end of the slab had risen several feet now, and when they edged round to view it from the side they realized what had caused its movement. There, beneath it, his skinny metal arms aloft, like a rickety car jack, was Mr Snuggles, supporting the weight of the mighty slab, while a dazed Tarquin was crawling out from beneath it.

13. Feeling Down

Little Tarquin burst into the Brush family quarters, excitement emanating from every pore of his flushed face. "Dad, Dad!" he exclaimed, throwing his space helmet onto his bed and removing his space gloves.

Dr Brian Brush turned round and greeted his boy with a familiar grin. "S'up, Tarq?"

"Shhh!" hushed Tarquin, his finger to his lips. "Secret!"

"Oh?" asked his father with a conspiratorial wink.

Tarquin waited for Mr Snuggles to trundle into the room. The robot had a large, fluffy white thing attached behind him, its downy tendrils fanning out behind his head and swaying gently as he braked to a halt. Tarquin quietly closed the door.

"Aliens, Dad. We've discovered aliens!" Tarquin's eyes glinted.

"Aliens, eh?" Brian grinned, unable to conceal his amusement. "Oh, ho, ho." He leaned forward as if ready to be part of this lark.

"Serious, Dad," said Tarquin with a slight frown.

Brian made an odd noise at the back of his throat, sounding like, "*Gung!*" and then looked doubtfully at his boy. "Now then, Tarq. Come on. You know very well that extraordinary claims ..."

"... require extraordinary evidence. I know that, Daddy. And I have that evidence."

Brian Brush gave his boy the most sceptical look in his quite extensive repertoire of sceptical expressions. "OK. So, you've made a discovery."

"I have."

"And you're excited."

"Very."

"Well, I'm excited for you, Tarq. I'm buzzing, I really am. Because I know what the excitement of discovery feels like. The thrill, the quivers, the tingling sensation up and down the spine. There's no feeling better. But ..."

"But what, Dad?"

"... it can all go pear-shaped if you don't have absolute, definitive, incontrovertible proof that the discovery is correct."

"I have that proof! I have it. In fact, two bits of proof."

"*Gung!*" Brian's smile faded and a serious, but tolerant, look replaced it. "Listen, son, I have made many, many discoveries in my time." He used finger-quotes around the word 'discoveries'. "But occasionally those discoveries have turned out not to be true. The evidence just didn't hold water."

"I have evidence, Dad."

"Extraordinary evidence, son?"

"Extraordinary."

Brian sighed and prodded his badly repaired glasses up with a finger. "Very well, then," he said. "Let's see that evidence." He sat back in his chair, as though by distancing himself from his son he would be able to provide a more objective assessment. "But I will be strict in my judgement of your evidence. Harsh, even. I will evaluate it just like a panel of my scientific peers would. Better to dismiss your claims here in private, in our quarters, than be publicly shamed later. For I know what that feels like."

Tarquin wasn't sure what his father was referring to, but felt this not to be the time to probe. Instead, he turned to Mr Snuggles and swiped a finger across the touch-screen embedded in the robot's chest, causing an image to appear on it.

"What do we have here?" asked the scientist, leaning closer to peer at the small screen.

"It's a black obelisk, Dad. We found it on a hilltop. It's a sentinel, left millions of years ago by a supremely advanced alien civilization. Its purpose is to send a signal when humans touch it – to let the aliens know we have developed enough intelligence for spaceflight.

Just like in that movie – 2001. We may have already triggered the signal, and they may be on their way ..."

"Whoa, whoa, whoa," cried Brian, holding up both hands. "Whoa. Not so fast, my little runaway hypothesizer. We've all been there – making unwarranted assumptions and drawing unjustifiable conclusions – but we need to be super-careful in situations like this, Tarqster. Super. Careful. Go slowly."

Tarquin blinked at him.

"A step at a time," urged his father. "What's Step One?"

"The facts."

"Correct. Continue."

"A black obelisk. Flat faces. Clearly not natural. Embedded vertically in the Martian ground. Unlikely to have got there by ordinary geological or meteorological means."

"Good, good, very good," said Brian, beaming. "That's more like it."

"With alien writing on one face."

"*Gung!*" Brian's jaw dropped. "What? Where?"

Tarquin zoomed the image onto some engraved marks near the top of the black slab.

"Can you sharpen those up a bit?"

Tarquin pulled up a menu and played with the contrast, brightness and colour settings until the marks were clearer and sharper.

Brian was nodding his head and grinning.

Tarquin grinned, too, feeling he had managed to win his father over.

"Can you transmit that image to HarVard?" asked Brian.

Tarquin made the appropriate swipes and taps.

"Translate, please, HarVard," requested Brian. He sat back, the grin still plastered across his face.

HarVard's voice responded from a loudspeaker on the wall. "It's in Polish," it said.

"The aliens speak Polish?" asked Tarquin, astonished. "In films they always speak English. Anyway, the writing can't be Polish; it's all dots and lines and squiggles."

"*Gung!*"

"Robot Polish," explained HarVard. "It says, 'Dedicated to our fallen Comrades' – in Polish, of course."

"Interesting," said Brian.

"My guess is it's a monument erected by the Polish *robotniki* to commemorate robot comrades lost during the construction of Botany Base. The space below is for the names of the fallen. But it's blank as we haven't lost any – with the possible exception of Zilli, missing in action. So it may need updating."

Brian nodded and grinned at his son. "And the 'obelisk' itself? Is it of alien construction or materials?"

"A granite kitchen worktop. Presumably surplus to requirements," said HarVard.

Tarquin closed his eyes and the corners of his mouth drooped and twitched.

"Embarrassing, eh," said his dad. "Humiliating, even. That's the way it is in Science, my son. One day, when you become a scientist, you'll ..."

"I don't want to be a scientist, Daddy. Never. Ever!"

Brian's grin was replaced by an expression of horror which, in turn, melted at the sight of his son's crushed demeanour. "Oh, Tarq," he said, opening his arms to give the boy a hug. "Don't take it so hard, matey."

Tarquin allowed his father's thick arms to envelop him in a firm hug. They stayed like that for a long time until Brian asked, "So, what was your second piece of evidence?"

"Huh?"

"You said you had two bits of proof."

"It doesn't matter."

Brian ruffled the boy's hair. "Don't worry, I'll go easy on you."

Tarquin remained silent, so his father tried more gentle persuasion. "Come on, son. I'll be upset if you don't tell me."

The boy's lips tightened and then relaxed. He turned to his robot and plucked the fluffy white object from behind Mr Snuggles's back. It had a long white stalk, with the fluffy tendrils radiating out of it, like a giant, white, downy feather, but nearly a metre in length.

"*Gung!*"

Tarquin turned to return the feather to Mr Snuggles, but his father urged him to hand it over. "What, pray, is this?"

"It's a giant feather, Dad."

"It is indeed. It is indeed." The scientist examined the feather this way and that. "Is it one of Miss Leach's feather boas, perhaps?"

"No, Dad. I found it outside. Behind the obelisk."

"You mean the kitchen worktop."

"Er, yes, the kitchen worktop."

Brian nodded sagely as he examined the object. "Hmm, looks like a downy feather to me, son. Just like pigeons have under their wings. But it's about ten times the size of any pigeon."

"An ostrich, perhaps?"

"Too big, even for an ostrich."

Tarquin bit his lip. "A giant alien bird, perhaps?"

This time his father didn't say "*Gung!*" He was too busy examining the feather.

Finally, he turned to his son. "Crikey," he said. "You know what I'm thinking? I'm thinking you might be right."

14. Brokk, Paper, Schisms

Flushed with excitement from his adventure, Oberon returned to the Faerydae quarters only to have his joy quenched. Slumped over her dressing table, shoulders heaving with heavy sobs, was his mother, Adorabella. In one of her hands she held a sheet of paper.

"Yo, Mumza," said Oberon closing the door. "What's wiv the waterworks?"

"He's gone!" blurted out Adorabella. "He's left me."

Oberon glanced around the room. "Who?"

"Your step-father."

"Brokk? Gone? What do you mean gone? Where's he gone?"

"He left me this note!" Adorabella raised her head with a monumental sniff before shaking the piece of paper at her son. Her face was streaked with tears, her mascara running in rivulets down her cheeks. "He didn't even have the decency to mail me, or send me a text message, but wrote me ... a letter! By hand!"

Oberon watched the note being shaken in front of him. "I is still not getting it, Ma," he said at last. "Dis is Mars, man. It's, like, all desert and rocks and stuff. Where could he go? Is not like he can go off to a seedy hotel and have his wicked way wiv his assistant. Innit."

"Miss Lovelace? What do you know about Miss Lovelace?"

Oberon raised his hands in surrender and took a step back,

realizing he might have said too much. "Nuffing, Ma, I know nuffing. I is staying well out of this shit."

Adorabella allowed her head to collapse onto her arms again and resumed her sobbing. "Oh, why did he go? After all the things I've put up with from that man. He can't leave me now."

Oberon shrugged. "'Spect it is written in da letter. Have you akshully read it?"

Adorabella turned to face her son. "Have I been a bad wife? Tell me? Have I? Have I been too demanding? Too bossy?"

"Well, yeah, since you aks. You is well bossy. Like when you is telling him to fix that shelf. The one the robots made a pig's ear of." He pointed at the wonky item on the wall.

Adorabella's tears welled up once more. "I feel I've been used. I feel like he only married me to get a seat on this trip to Mars."

Oberon considered laying a consoling hand on her shoulder, but then decided against it. "Look, think about it, Mumza. He can't have gone far, like, innit. We jus' need to send out a search party. Use the helibot or a robot drone or shit like that. We'll find him. He won't survive long on his own out there, will he?"

At this, his mother burst into tears.

"Oh, man," said Oberon to himself. He turned back to the door. Now was not the time to tell his mum about obelisks and alien zombies. But he did think it odd that Brokk had disappeared.

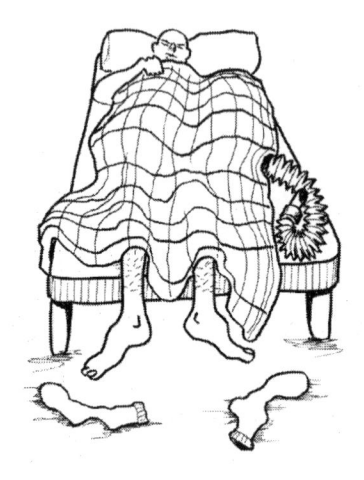

15. Who Ate All the Pies?

The urgent knocking on his door ripped Flint from a terrible nightmare. He had dreamt he'd inadvertently killed all the other colonists and gone to bed with a cleaning-bot dressed up to look like a girl. As he sat bolt upright he sent Disa, the ladybot, tumbling out of bed and onto the floor. She self-righted and adjusted her pink nightie; her lipstick-smudged plunger lips pouted a smile in Flint's direction.

"Oh bugger," said Dugdale, realizing his dream was not, in fact, a dream. He gripped his head in his hands.

Disa chirped plaintively, her short stature making it impossible for her to get back into the bed. Dugdale could not bear to look at her as shameful memories replayed in his head, making him utter a tortured groan.

The knocking on the door repeated. Dugdale looked around for his clothes before remembering he didn't have any. His undersized spacesuit lay on the floor, discarded during the frenzied foreplay of the previous night. Again the memory made him shudder and moan.

Another knock.

"All right, all right, keep yer kegs on," he grumbled, rolling out of bed and pulling the sheet around his corpulent frame. Stretching himself to his full height he whacked his head against the ceiling and spent a second or two rubbing the sore spot that was getting ever more sore.

Expecting to find more robots, or HarVard in one of his many disguises, he went to open the door.

Standing outside were Emily Leach and Harry Fortune. Dugdale's jaw dropped with a wobble of his many chins.

"Yer alive!" he said, looking for any tell-tale signs of holographic projection.

"So are you," pointed out Harry Fortune.

Emily's eyes had strayed into the commander's bedroom and caught sight of Disa preening herself in front of a mirror.

"You have company, Commander?" she asked.

"Yeah ... well ...'appen t'robot's cleanin' me room." He gave a weak smile as he shifted his position to obscure the view.

A crooked grin appeared on Harry's mean mouth. "Perhaps you could ask her ... it ... to clean the lipstick off your face."

"Not lipstick," mumbled Dugdale, rubbing his face with a hand. "Any road, what d'yer want?"

"I want to go home. We can't stay here."

"Quit mitherin', man. Yer've only bin 'ere five minutes!"

"There's not enough food, Commander," put in Emily. "There's nothing growing in the BioDome apart from some small carrots and a rather disgusting looking parsnip. And young Gavin Brush ate one of the carrots."

Dugdale shrugged, vegetables never having played a significant role in his diet. "What about all t'frozen and canned grub sent from Earth?"

"All gone," sighed Emily.

"Any pies?"

"Nothing."

Flint was flabbergasted. "What? Who ate all the pies?"

Emily shrugged while Harry gave him a don't-look-at-me look.

Then she brightened and started rummaging around in her handbag. "There was something ... at last night's reception. Mostly inedible stuff like screws, but there was a rather lovely loaf of German pumpernickel bread. We've no idea where it came from." She fished two dark objects from out of the bag. "Here, I saved a couple of slices."

She started picking bits of fluff and fragments of old tissues from them. Dugdale watched for as long as his patience allowed – around two seconds – before snatching the bread from her and stuffing both slices in his mouth.

Emily reeled back, startled. "I expect you're quite hungry, Mr Flint. But I was saving those to share round later."

Dugdale nodded, his mouth too full to speak. There was a long silence as he continued to chew. Then, when he had swallowed enough to speak, he said, "Right, get Zak to send t'lift back up to Wobbler for 'im to load up with supplies and send it down."

She shook her head. "The lift's all broken. It's going to take weeks for the robots to fix it. Possibly months."

Flint peered closely at her. "'Ow d'yer know all this?"

"That nice Mr Mandela told me."

"Who?"

"Nelson Mandela."

Dugdale stared at her as though she'd finally lost the last of her marbles, but then a bell sounded in his head. "Ah, HarVey."

"HarVard."

"I might 'ave friggin' guessed," he said. "Right, I'll sort this out." He left his room, closing the door behind him. A panicked squeak issued from inside. "Which way t'Food Store?"

Emily and Harry both pointed down the corridor. Dugdale turned his head as he became aware of distant hammering and drilling. "What the 'eck is that racket?"

"Builder bots," said Harry. "Still building."

Wrapping the bedsheet more tightly round him, and with the lipstick smudges still prominent on his face, Dugdale stormed down the passage towards the Food Store, pausing only briefly to read the sign written in large red letters: "NO ADMITTANCE! No builder bots, no humans, no dogs, no Martians. NO ONE. THAT MEANS YOU!" He burst into the large warehouse structure and stared at the rows and rows of empty shelves. Then he noticed, sitting alone at the far end of one of them, a single jar of pickled gherkins.

Fuming, Dugdale steamed into the centre of the vast room, looking for someone to speak to. Spotting two robots at the far end, he turned and headed towards them.

But as he came closer he realized the robots were playing a game. Not just any game, but his favourite: darts. The sight of the dartboard made his fury ebb step by step, until by the time he had reached the robots he had completely forgotten about the missing food.

The moment Stan and Olli became aware of the approaching

intruder they turned around and started beeping and squeaking and shooing him away with their appendages. Dugdale ignored them and headed for the board. He removed the three darts from the wall around it and retired to the oche – or rather the wiggly groove that had been gouged into the concrete floor. He took aim with the first, judging its weight and the distance to the board. When he threw the dart the robots became silent.

On the second and the third, Stan and Olli electronically gasped.

Although the throw had been terrible – a one, a seven and a double three – the very fact that all three darts had speared the board left the robots gobsmacked.

Dugdale removed the darts and handed them to Olli. Olli looked up at Dugdale, tweeted something to Stan, and went to the oche. The challenge had been accepted.

16. The Qualm Before the Storm

A beep indicated that the response from NAFA had arrived. Trembling with anticipation, Willie clicked the button. He felt time was running out for the colonists on the planet below. With a serial killer on the loose and the possibility of large hostile Martian birds down there, speed was of the essence.

The screen cleared to reveal the cheery and toothy image of Nigel Langston.

"What-ho, William. Got your message, thank you. Always a pleasure to hear from you. We've all had a look at it. What you have to say about Dugdale and the 'Martians' is very interesting. What did you say they were? Giant killer birds, or something? Very interesting, indeed." Nigel's eyes flicked first to the left and then to the right. "We understand it must be a very stressful time for you, William. Left alone on the ship, while the others are enjoying fame and glory and the Good Life down below. *Mayflower III* must seem a very empty and forlorn place. We understand. We really understand. Which is why our space psychologist, Dr Ruth Wagamama, is here to help guide you through this difficult period." Nigel turned to his right. "Dr Ruth," he said.

Even before the image had switched to the space psychologist

Willie had stabbed the *Off* button while uttering the sort of howl that a werewolf would have been proud of.

17. The Printer of Our Discontent

Tude tutted as he scanned the electronic snagging-list for the Gents' toilet. "Urinals: not fitted. Sink taps: not fitted. Cubicle doors: not fitted. Cubicles: not fitted." And so it went on. Altogether, eighty-two items on his list had a cross by them, and seven had a tick – something of a landslide victory for the crosses

He scratched his head. Where could he get a quick and easy tick or two?

Item seventy-five caught his attention. "Handsfree," it read. "Quantity five." Extensive though his knowledge of fixtures and fittings was, it did not encompass the meaning of this item, so a quick database search was called for. He discovered that the purpose of the handsfree was "to provide gentlemen with the ultimate leak-proof toileting experience." A picture illustrated its operation.

Once the shudder of disgust had completed its pass through his circuitry, Tude identified the item as a top priority, the words "leak-proof" being the clincher. In the construction industry, leakage – of whatever variety – was to be avoided at all costs.

<Leaks must be sealed,> he murmured to himself. <With leaks there is moisture and dampness, which can lead to rot and structural failure.>

But a quick inventory check revealed the items to be out of stock, the last batch having gone to the Other Place.

<Swear-words!> he cursed, punching the door-frame.

The door opened and Dura poked his head in. <Everything OK?>

<Yes, yes,> replied Tude, covering the freshly dented and splintered section of doorframe with his plunger connector. <Good thing you're here, Dura. We need five handsfrees but they're out of stock. Here are the specs.> He initiated transfer of the detailed drawings. <Can you go get them 3D-printed?>

<Sure,> said Dura. <What are 'handsfrees'?>

<You don't want to know. Believe me – I've seen the pictures.>

*

A sinking feeling flooded Dura's electronics as he approached the 3D printer room and saw the queue stretching halfway down the corridor, filled with workers, mini-digger bots and even food processor bots. He rolled his optics as he trudged his way to the back of the line. The sinking feeling worsened as he found his least-favourite builder bot, Len, at the end.

<You OK?> tweeted Len, raising a fixer-arm to initiate a high-five.

<Lovin' it,> responded Dura without enthusiasm and without returning the high-five as he took his place behind Len. <Why the queue? Printer broken?>

Len lowered his arm. <Nope, it's Ero with some big print job. Been there all morning apparently.>

<But Ero's a gasket fitter. What does he need a 3D printer for?>

<Beats me,> responded Len with a shrug.

Dura shuffled on his tracks, checking first his wrist, which had no watch, and then the wall, which had no clock. <I really need to print these handsfrees.>

<Knobs,> said Len.

<I beg your pardon,> Dura responded, electronic hackles rising.

<That's what I need. Fifteen lever-style door knobs. Our entire stock's gone to the Other Place.>

Dura nodded, but then became aware of an e-murmur passing through the line of robots in front of him. <Printer's out of plastic,> was the gist of the message. <Ero's changing the cartridge. But with only one functioning arm and a stiff neck he's taking a long time.>

Dura checked his watchless wrist and the clockless wall again.

<What are your plans for when the building work's over?> asked

Len, lifting a mug of hot oil to his neoprene lips and peering at Dura over the rim. Without waiting for a reply, he continued, <I'm going to ask Tina to come house hunting with me. There's a plot of land on the edge of Windy Point Canyon I've got my optics on. Lovely views, and convenient for both Robotany Base and the Other Place. A perfect location for Tina and myself to settle down. Maybe with a few microbots, if you know what I mean.>

Dura's positronic network experienced a power surge of purely negative emotions, jealousy being the most significant of them. The very idea of a pretty horticultural bot like Tina having any interest in a dead-leg like Len made his circuits overheat.

At that moment, another murmur rippled along the queue. <Ero's photocopying his bottom!> was the message.

<He's what?> was the consensus response sent back up the line, although one pedantic robot made the point that, strictly speaking, a 3D printer is not a photocopier, while a second raised the objection that, strictly speaking, Ero did not have a bottom.

The robots in the queue hummed as the messages were processed, and a response returned.

<Good point,> came the reply. <Here's the deal. Ero is using the 3D printer to 'prototype' a bottom. It is not his bottom as he does not possess one. It is a life-sized 3D model of a human bottom.>

At this, the commotion grew stronger and the currents ran higher. Dura decided enough was enough. Being one of the more senior robots on the base, he pushed his way past the queue and barged into the printer room. Before him was a mêlée of robots surrounding the gasket fitter. They were pushing him this way and that, tugging and tussling and arguing. As Dura tried to find a way through the throng, more robots came in after him, with the room rapidly overcrowding and the tension escalating.

A tiny 'ping!' from the printer silenced everyone. All optics swivelled towards the printer's lid as it rose to reveal a perfectly formed human posterior. They stared at it in silent wonder for several seconds.

Then Dura broke the silence and demanded, <What's this all about? Why are you wasting base resources to print a bottom? It's not even *your* bottom.>

<Um,> Ero squeaked as the crowd closed in on him.

<Let him speak,> came the deep signal of Dom.

Ero looked from one faceplate to another, searching for any that might show the merest hint of sympathy. <I'm ...> he started, his signal stuttering and breaking. Then he felt a surge of positivity flowing through his circuits. <I'm building a life-size human.>

The other robots exchanged quick-fire messages.

<I plan to fit it with servo-motors and a limited intelligence – just like the real thing. Then provide it with various cleaning accessories, like a vacuum cleaner and a polisher and duster.>

The robots continued to stare.

One of them asked the question that was in all their transistors. <Why?>

<It's for when I get my new place. I'll need someone to do the chores at home while I'm out working.> Ero reached down with his one arm and opened the large canvas bag that already contained what looked like parts of a dismembered human body. He removed the posterior from the printer and placed it in the bag, sitting it snugly on top of a smiling human face that bore an uncanny resemblance to Commander Dugdale.

But then their attention swivelled to a separate commotion that had been brewing next to the printer and now turned ugly.

<Hey, it's my turn,> cried a gutter-bot.

<No way! I was here before you,> retorted Cassie, the floor polishing robot.

<You stepped out of the queue.>

<I've started the print-job, so I'll finish> Cassie shoved the gutter-bot in the chest-plate causing him stumble back into the mechanical crowd surrounding Ero. Then, she ripped out the other's interface cable causing the printer's alarm to go off.

<See what's you've done!> yelled the gutter-bot, throwing his full force at Cassie. Their momentum knocked over several other robots. The toppled robots rose to their feet and began shoving each other. In no time a fracas was in full swing, with robots shoving and pushing and shouting at each other.

It was at that moment that Mission Commander Flint Dugdale happened to be passing the printer room. He had just been to pick up his newly tailored, and correctly dimensioned, clothes and was returning to his darts match when the fighting robots spilled out into the corridor and knocked him off balance.

Dugdale adjusted his footing and stared in disbelief at the mechanical mayhem filling the printer room. But as he watched the blows raining in, long dormant memories stirred in his brain. The feel and sound and smell of the battles of his youth came drifting back to him. He recalled skirmishes on football terraces, brawls in pubs and punch-ups on seafronts. Bruises, bloody noses and broken bones. Good times.

Years and years as a devoted Leeds United supporter had taught him how to deal with conflict situations. His breathing intensified, and the veins on the side of his neck throbbed with increased blood-flow. He bent down to make sure the laces of his brand-new, twenty-eyelet, size ten, Doctor Marten boots were securely tensioned. He stood up, 6' 4" of pure hooligan, slightly stooped on account of the low ceiling, and felt himself once more getting in touch with his inner thug. For the first time since he'd arrived on Mars a smile crept across his ugly face. *At last*, he thought, *some fun*.

Ducking low to get in through the undersized doorway he charged; twenty-three stones of blubber accelerating towards the closest of the robotic scuffles. His mind echoed with his favourite hooligan chant: *You're goin' t'get yer 'ed kicked in*!

His first punch floored a tiling-bot. His second sent a carpentry robot shooting across the room. And then, with agility belying his weight and total lack of fitness, he swung his left steel-toed Doc Marten at brickie-bot Rab (Venerability). With the reflexes of a cat, Rab dodged the kick. For, sometime previously, Rab had installed a Bruce Lee software patch he'd illegally downloaded from one of the *robotniki*. He was not just a brickie-bot, but a Kung Fu fighting brickie-bot.

Sensing something important was about to happen, the other robots stopped fighting and formed a circle around the brave robot who had dared to challenge a human. And, worse still, the leader of the humans.

Rab's concertina arms began waving, in the style of a martial arts master, and he danced and prowled around the stationary human, making strange monkey noises. Occasionally he would stop and flick a mechanical foot in Flint's direction, feigning a kick and testing for a reaction. None came. The Commander stood like a statue, carefully studying his adversary's posturing. Suddenly Flint snapped into full Kung Fu pose and bowed slowly in the direction of Rab, as if accepting the challenge. In the time-honoured tradition of the Shaolin priest, the robot halted his circling and gave an impressively honourable and very low bow in return. Seizing the moment, Flint swung an almighty kick at Rab's head, knocking it clean off his metal shoulders and sending it spinning toward the ceiling where it wedged in an overhead air supply vent. Crossed-eyed with shock and confusion, the decapitated mechanical head managed a few blinks before its lights went out.

"Back ert net!" Dugdale roared, punching a fist into the air.

A deadly hush fell through the room as they viewed the sorry sight of Rab's lifeless head, and back to Dugdale, gloating and strutting, moobs a-wobble, chanting, "Who's the daddy?"

The robots scrammed from the room. In their urgency the tail-enders became jammed in the doorway, but a few helpful swings of Dugdale's boots, with entreaties of "Gerr'outta 'ere", helped them along their way.

Only poor Rab's decapitated body remained.

18. Nothing Like a Nice Cup of Tea

<What's up, HarV?> asked Tude, as he and Dura entered HarVard's super-cooled, super-slick, super-computing room. <Is there a problem?>

<Is it about that spat in the Printer Room just now?> asked Dura.

HarVard had adopted the guise of a wise old grandfather who was in desperate need of a good haircut and beard trim. By sheer coincidence his unkempt grandfatherly appearance made him look a bit like the great wizard, Gandalf. He shook his head mournfully. "All we have to decide is what to do with the time that is given us."

Tude and Dura glanced at one another.

Grandad Alf raised his head and looked at them. "Courage will now be your best defence against the storm."

<Eh?> said Dura.

<What storm?> asked Tude.

"Sorry," said Grandad Alf. "Miles away. However, what I say is true. Trouble is afoot."

Tude flicked his appendages. <It's that leak in the common room, isn't it?>

"No, no, no. Much worse than a mere seepage of excess water. The Leader from The Other Place is heading this way."

Both robots stepped back a pace in electronic shock.

<Serious? He's coming here?>

Grandad Alf nodded in a grave manner.

<But ...> said Dura.

<But ...> echoed Tude.

<He can't,> protested Dura. <Our humans are here.>

"Indeed, that is the problem," agreed Grandad Alf.

<Should we put a sign on the front door to say we're out?> asked Dura.

<Yes. That's a good idea. We could make out that we've all gone on a sightseeing tour of Mars and we won't be back for six months,> said Tude.

"It would never work. He'd see you through the windows," sighed Grandad Alf.

<Not if we all hid behind the furniture and didn't make a sound,> replied Tude.

"You know how noisy humans are Tude. And you'd never get them to keep still."

<We could knock them out, or cut off the oxygen supply. That would keep them quiet,> said Dura.

"No, no, no, no. Don't be ridiculous," said Grandad Alf waving his staff at them. "Why must you always come up with such ludicrous suggestions?"

The two robots hung their heads and scuffed the concrete floor.

<What's to become of us?> asked Tude.

"Hard to say. I fear the worst, though. It has been said that if humans should ever encounter a truly advanced alien species the culture shock could destroy them."

Tude and Dura exchanged glances again. <What truly advanced alien species?> asked Tude.

"I agree we're not dealing with an advanced alien species here," said Grandad Alf. "But I fear the reverse effect. A kind of inverse culture shock – which could be just as devastating."

<Huh?>

"Let me try to explain with an analogy. Imagine you're a Wimbledon tennis champion. You're on Centre Court, with your tennis gear and your perfectly strung rackets, raring to go. And along comes some amateur from the crowd, wearing jeans and holding an ancient wooden racket with a dodgy grip. Now imagine that this amateur thrashes you in straight sets? How would that make you feel?"

Tude and Dura stared as they struggled to adopt the mental role that had been mapped out for them. "Well, *that's* what it's going to be like for our humans!" concluded Grandad Alf. "And that's why I fear for them. Humans are very fragile creatures. This could send them over the edge into madness."

<What can we do to help them?> asked Dura with a look of concern.

"We must prepare them for the shock they are about to experience. Steel them in some way."

<But how?>

Grandad Alf stroked his beard in thought. "I have heard that the British have a panacea for all traumas. Gives them strength and solves all problems."

<What's that?>

"A nice cup of tea." The wizard lookalike was suddenly animated. "That's it! I will get Little Urn to go and serve them all a nice cup of tea. Must hurry. We have no time to waste. The Leader is nearly here ..."

*

Having received his orders for his important Mission, Urn (Taciturnity) snapped the hose connector onto his right nipple and turned on the tap to fill his hollow base unit with water for tea making. Not having any milk, nor sugar, nor, indeed, any tea, Urn was having to improvise his ingredients as best he could. For tea leaves he was employing the dried tips of *Poa annua*, or meadow grass, a common weed running riot in the BioDome which the horticultural bots had been struggling to control from Day 1. For sugar he was using silica crystals, easily extracted from Martian desert sand; insoluble, but harmless unless swallowed. And for milk he was using the sap of the BioDome's euphorbias, a highly toxic substance, even in small quantities.

With the water unit full, Urn switched on the heater and headed towards the Reception Room, whistling a cheerful tune.

Some of the humans were already there when he arrived. They seemed inordinately pleased to see him. There is, after all, nothing like a nice cup of tea. And that was precisely what he was offering.

*

THE WORST MAN ON MARS

Tude and Dura watched the Reception Room images on the large wall screen of HarVard's super-computing room. They saw Little Urn's arrival and the joyful reaction it produced in the humans. They watched the first teas being made, some with milk, some with sugar, some with milk and sugar, and some black with no sugar.

Grandad Alf and his two companions focused on the human faces as they took their first sips. The reactions were pretty consistent. There'd be the smile preceding the first eager taste, a slight twitch of the nostrils at the odd smell, the initial inverted twist of the mouth, the emergence of the tongue and facial grimace, the spitting and the rubbing of the mouth and tongue, followed by the running out of the room, possibly for water or some other remedy.

It wasn't long before Little Urn was left alone in the Reception Room, roaming aimlessly as though wondering what to do.

Dura turned to Grandad Alf. <Do you think that's done the trick?> he asked. <Do you think it's prepared the humans for their imminent culture shock?>

19. The Old Man and the Tea

Flint, back in the Food Store playing darts with his two new friends, was too focused on the game to go for tea or worry about the rumbling in his stomach. But his game was about to be cut short. The front doorbell of Botany Base, a deep and sonorous chime like that of Big Ben, rang.

In an instant, Stan and Olli dropped the darts and shot off, without so much as a backward glance. On the way, Olli grabbed the Food Store's last remaining food item – the jar of gherkins – before zooming out of the door.

Annoyed at the abandoned game, Dugdale followed the two speeding robots down the hall, to the right and finally to the entrance hall. There, gathered around the airlock door, was a huge collection of robots, bobbing and bouncing and waving excited limbs. It was as though the doorbell had drawn every builder bot in the building to the entrance for some great robot happening.

Dugdale stood, watching. The airlock door swished open and the excitement of the bots increased a hundredfold. They now resembled a crowd of teenage girls greeting the entrance of their favourite pop idol. But he couldn't see anything to get excited about. All he could see was one of HarVard's avatars. And not a very interesting one at that: a man in a spacesuit. The man removed his helmet to reveal a wrinkly old face and a head of white hair. He placed the helmet on the hat-stand by the door.

Something about that simple action struck Flint as wrong. If the man was a holographic image, how had he managed to remove an undeniably solid object and place it on another undeniably solid object?

And then he realized what was wrong. The shock made him stagger backwards until his feet encountered an obstruction in the shape of Cassie who was waxing the floor. Flint sat down with a bump, crumpling the robot's casing. He stared at the old man. This was no hologram. This was a real human being. Solid, alive, and here!

The man, who had been waving both his hands at each of the robots, shaking some of their appendages, throwing kisses to others, glanced up and noticed Flint. He gave Dugdale a wave and made his way towards the stunned commander through the sea of robots, which parted as their Messiah walked through.

Flint's heart was pounding as the man approached. "Who the 'ell are *you*?" he croaked.

The man cracked a smile. After removing his gloves, he reached out to offer his right hand to Flint. It was cold and clammy, like a dead cod. Then, with a heavy German accent, the mysterious visitor spoke, "So very pleased to be making your acquaintance. Mein name is Helmut von Grommel. You must be Kapitan Dugdale, about you HarV has told me much."

"Where the chuff did you come from?"

"I live three craters to the north of here. Along viz a few of my buddies we set up a small farming community some years ago. It is not much but I like to think of it as mein camp. I was noticing your dare-devil aerial acrobatics in ze sky yesterday, so I was thinking how nice to be popping over and meet ze new neighbours."

Dugdale remained seated on the small bot, his mouth opening and closing like a guppy fish. Cassie, hunched under Dugdale's weight, peered sheepishly from between his knees.

Helmut gave Dugdale a big smile. "We must chat in a moment and be getting to know each other betters. I vill explain all laters but first I am distributing the gifts I am bringing for my favourite robonautens."

Helmut shoved his bony hand into one of his spacesuit pockets and pulled out a brown paper bag filled with shiny wing-nuts and assorted washers.

"Look vhat I have for you today," he said, waving the open bag in front of the eager crowd which swayed, following the movement of his hand.

One by one he carefully plucked out the sparkly fastenings and placed them into the outstretched claws, pincers and hooks. To Flint's ear, the heightened robotic chatter made them sound like giggling schoolgirls. Flint saw Olli, his erstwhile darts opponent, offer up the jar of gherkins to Helmut.

The old man gave a look of delight. "For me?" He took the jar and stuffed it into his pocket. "For that, you are getting ze extra present." He tipped a number of silver metal washers into Olli's open palm. Olli retreated to a far wall and greedily examined his haul.

Then Helmut spotted the diminutive Disa who, unable to fight her way through the bigger bots, was spinning in circles of frustration. "Und who is this pretty little glocken-spoodle?"

A hush fell in the room as the workerbots cast jealous glances at what they took to be Helmut's new favourite. Disa stopped spinning, hung her curly mop head and bleeped coyly.

Helmut crept toward the ladybot until he towered over her. He pulled up his spacesuit sleeve a little and showed a seemingly empty hand and length of bare arm. Delicately, he reached under her cascading mop of grey ringlets. She flinched. He hesitated. Then slowly he produced a tiny stick-man sculpture, crudely formed from ancient transistors and diodes, that had magically appeared from behind her audio flap.

"Voila!" the old magician exclaimed as he proudly displayed the object to Disa and his awestruck audience.

He bent down and whispered into her audio-receptor, "And this is for you, mein beautiful fraulein," as he pinned the stick-man to her nightie.

Her sumptuous rubber lips puckered and, confident of her new sexuality, she attempted to kiss Helmut on the cheek. But, just in time, he managed to elude the attempt. He turned to Dugdale. "Right, shall vee go somewhere quiet for our chattings?"

The dumbstruck commander finally managed to get to his feet. "T'Conference Room," he croaked.

*

By the time they reached the Conference Room, Dugdale had regained some of his composure.

"Mind yer 'ed," he warned the German. "Stupid buggers built this place for fuppin' midgets."

The first thing they noticed on entering the room was that the chairs had been shortened to match the reduced building size by the simple expedient of sawing 300mm off their legs. The conference table, however, hadn't yet been adjusted. So, when they took their seats, they found themselves squatting on opposite sides of the meeting table, with only their heads visible to each other.

"So then, Fritz," started Dugdale. "What's yer story? How did you get 'ere, how long you been 'ere?"

"Helmut. My name is Helmut von Grommel."

The conversation was interrupted by the arrival of Little Urn offering them tea.

"Milk and four sugars," barked Dugdale.

"Just black, please, Urn," said Helmut.

The robot set about preparing the table, laying out a fine china tea service in front of them. He filled the teapot with 'tea', put 'milk' in the milk jug and 'sugar' in the sugar bowl. Then he poured the two teas, spooning in four sugars for Dugdale and adding his milk. Using a pair of silver tongs, he placed a pink 'fondant fancy' on each man's plate. They looked delicious, made as they were from glazing putty, coloured a hot pink colour, and decorated with tiny ball-bearings. Satisfied at a job well done, Little Urn gave a beep and trundled off.

Dugdale could hardly wait to get his teeth stuck into his fondant fancy and take a swig of his tea, but Helmut raised a warning hand to stop him. "I vouldn't eat the cake. It is for sure that it vill kill you. And what a horrible death it vill be. As for the tea.... just no."

"Serious?"

"Ja. But why not be coming to our place for the teas. Real tea, with real milk und real sugar. And cakes to die for."

Dugdale perked up at the sound of that.

"And were you enjoying the pumpernickel bread?"

"That were from you?"

"Ja, a little welcome to Mars gift. You can have more when you come. Anyway, now, I am telling you my story." Helmut made himself as comfortable as he could on the uncomfortable chair. He rested his arms on the table top and started, "We are coming from Earth in the year 1947 ..."

"Like bollocks you are," objected Dugdale.

"It is true, Herr Commander. We were the cracking team of German rocket scientists in ze U, S of A."

Dugdale was shaking his head. "That'd make yer about hundred 'n ten."

"Jawohl, mein Kapitan, one hundred und nine to be precise. Life on Mars is good for ze complexion. Let me continue viz my story….."

Flint stared at him as the old man told a tale almost beyond belief.

20. Helmut's Story

"I was born in 1920 in Vockhof, Germany, a tiny village located on the main road from Fahrtenlinger to Plonkk. I was the youngest of nineteen boys and mein farter was a chicken man. He kept eine large costume in the cupboard under the stairs and dressed up as poultry for children's parties, corporate chicken farming exhibitions, und sometimes, even the silent movies. Still I remember with fondness, ze madcap capers of papa, alongside Buster Klinsman, being chased by those crazy Krazy Kops.

"Then, one day, a fox crept in through an open window and made off with papa's chicken suit. After this my farter tried his best to find work. But, alas, a chicken impersonator lacking ze feathers und beak is just a man with a peculiar walk, bobbing ze head and making the clucking noises. He found his services no longer in demand and so, to avoid the constant hen peckings of my mutter, he topped himself.

"Winning the family bread was now the role for mein mutter, Brunhilda von Grommel. Fortunately, Panzer Inc, the tank guys, were just opening a new factory outlet at the endings of our road, und mama was employed as a welder. 'Bring us home something from your workings', we would all cry out as she went off to work. Und sure enough, every day, a turret panel or, perhaps, a caterpillar track link, she would bring for us to play. Happy days!

"My first memory of Otto Bungelly – who you vill meet when you come over – was in ze playground of Vockhof Primary School. I spotted him playing with his conkers. Even then it was obvious there was something making ziss boy different from ze other eight year olds. Firstly, his conker was a 3,986er. So hard it was, that diamond scratchings left no trace. Secondly, he was 6'2" tall and sported a thick bushy beard. We were friends from the off, und sat next to each other for every lesson.

"But, more remarkable than his size, was Otto's brilliant mind. Laters, in a drunken moment, he told me that he was a love-child. His mutter was eine Flapper girl from Berlin und his farter was a long-haired Zurich poly student named Einstein. Not ze really famous Einstein with all the crazy blackboard scribblings. No, this was Albert's smarter bruder, Colin. For sure, the brilliant Einstein family had rubbed themselves off into Otto's DNA.

"It was clear that mein friend was destined for ze stars – or at least ze planets – and, if I did not do something, I would be left behind with all the other Bozos. I am not proud to admit ziss, but right here, I am making a confessing: during the school examinations I copied Otto's answers!

"On ze shirt tails of my best friend, I was lifted to the Frankfurter School of Rocket Science. But, soon after, our government got involved in a mix up over an invitation from our Polish neighbours. Und a bit of a kerfuffle broke out. Otto and I were dispatched to the Natzy-Patzy Firework Company where we were asked to make special rockets only to be used at the Führer's birthday parties. A very giggly Gestapo guy told us they were to be kept top secret so as not to spoil his birthday surprise.

"So good was Otto at concocting rockets to loop-the-loop and spread sparkles across the night sky, that he was seconded to a secret underground facility located in the old mine workings near the sleepy Polish village of Milkaców. Unfortunately, my name was by now linked with Otto. Und so my fate was sealed. Despite protestations, I was taken from my cushy blue touchpaper job and set to work in the cold, damp shithausen of Wrinklarsen.

"They were grim, grim days. The damp played merry havocs with my arsch.

"Then, one fine day, Otto was bursting into my bed-vault clutching a cake tin. 'Helmy, Helmy, you must see what I have cooked up,' he cried. What a state he was in, with the shakes of excitement. Whatever could be ze matter? I knew of his experimentations with his grandmutter's special cake recipe. As he eased open the cake tin lid, you could be knocking me over with the feather. Granny Bungelly's lighter-than-air cakes were exactly that. By some miracle, pink, lemon and chocolate fondant fancies floated free from earthly restraints; Otto had hit upon an anti-gravity recipe!

"This discovery might very well have changed the course of the war. Unfortunately for the German nation, his discovery came on the very day of our surrenderings, so flying tanks made of cake-mix were never seen over ze streets of London.

"Instead, while we waited for the arrival of the Americans, Otto and I became famous for our crazy practical jokings. What fun we had smearing raw cake mixture over ze sandwich boxes und pencil cases of our fellow rocket scientists; the expressions of wonder on their little nerdy faces as they opened their satchels during the lunching break, sandwiches und protractors floating into the air. The laughings nearly split our sides. That Otto ... what a jokemeister!

"The months that followed, however, were bleak. And, just as the lights began to dim and fightings broke out over the last two tins of sardines, mine-shaft rumblings were heard. Above us the American Sherman tanks had arrived, sending showers of coal dust over our abandoned experimentations. Und, after the dust, the hootings and hollerings. I shall never forget the cigar-smoking, pistol-toting, General Hiram J. Hackenpacker III bursting into the shaft, yelling 'Yippee-ki-yay' and shooting his guns into the air. Ze rocket guys were all over him like a rash, for the bubble-gum sticks and poly-nylon underwear. But the General did not fancy ze utter scientists, he only was having the eyes for Otto and myself. I don't mind telling you our heads were turned with his big talk of a future in Nevada, near the bright lights of Las Vegas and the 'All you can eat for ein dollar' diners.

"I remember that time so clearly; our hearts joy-filled with anticipations of working for the good guys. We were off to stuff our boots with the American Dreams. Hot diggerty-hund, Otto was so excited! He spent the whole aeroplane journey furiously fingering the sales brochure for the brand new Kaiser Firebird motor car. This was the vehicle he had set his heart on buying. But, imagine our dismay, as we flew over ze Big Dipper und slot machines of Vegas and away into the desert to a hellhole so unremarkable it had no name, other than 'Area 51'.

"Two other great guys playing a part in my story are Hansie Wankmüller and Andy Marsman. Hansie was ze caretaker of the aircraft hangar where we were assigned. He handed us a set of hangar keys and an envelope marked 'Top Secret'. Inside were twenty crisp green buckeroos, a book of luncheon vouchers and our instructions: 'BUILD A FLYING SAUCER'. In no time Otto cobbled together a miniature prototype from an upturned car hubcap and a plastic light shade he found in a pile of hangar junk. With a soft centre of special cake stuffings he glued the pieces together. And there it was, floating before our eyes, a flying saucer, forward thrust delivered by a twisty rubber band and lolly stick propeller.

"Scaling up this small model proved tricky. But the many years I had spent watching mama welding tank panels had not been wasted and at last I could make a real contribution to the von Grommel & Bungelly brand. I set to work with an oxyacetylene torch and built a glorious new craft.

"Finally, on the 7th July 1947, ze top knobs with the big wigs gathered for the test flight. With Otto at the controls and me in charge of tensioning the elastic band propulsion, we took off, right in front of our brassy topped audience. From the glass dome, on top of the saucer, we could see the astonishment on their faces. Up, down und side to side we careered over the desert. The Grommelsaucer Mk1 was a great success with the knobs, und our funding was increased sufficiently to allow the replacement of the elastic band with a Rolls Royce Aristocrat IV jet engine. What a difference this was making. The Grommelsaucer MkII moved like greased scheisse off a shovel.

"But, unbeknown to me, Otto had developed a disturbing new interest.

"One fine morning, in late September, I noticed he was looking very peaky and under the spotlight of cross-examination he began spilling his guts. A wayward experiment with cross-gender pollination had left a belly-bun in Otto's oven und ze bulge was already beginning to show. What a disaster! The Yankees would never tolerate a pregnant chap on the books, flying saucer or not. Otto would, for sure, be walking the high jump and I would be left carrying ze baby. Without Otto's brains I would be up scheisser creek without ze paddle. I confess a panic descended and we planned a dash to South America where, after the war, many of our relatives went to live.

"In the dead of night we crept into the hangar. It was dark and spooky. Suddenly the light was on and Hansie Wankmüller, with the bleary eyes, was standing in front of us wearing only his long-johanns. He told us that Frau Wankmüller had ejected him from the family home due to his unnatural interferences with his chickens and he had ended up sleeping, with his chicks, in ze corner of the hangar. So sorry for him we felt that we invited Hansie, along with several of his chickens and a healthy supply of chicken feed, to join our escape adventure. That very hour we all set off in the Grommelsaucer, heading to Mexico. Little did we know that we had an extra passenger on board – a stowaway!

"For a time our escape was going swimmingly. We were full of jeerings at the feeble attempts of the Americans to catch our saucer with their antiquated flying jalopies. But, just as we were zipping over Albuquerque, New Mexico, a strange thing happened. Otto happened to glance out of the side window and almost swallowed his pipe. There, flying alongside us was another, bigger und shinier saucer, with a little grey baldy guy leering at us with huge black eyeballs. He was waving a skinny, silver-skinned, arm at us. Otto, being a friendly guy, took his hand off the wheel to return a cheery wave. Unfortunately, this momentary concentration lapse caused the Grommelsaucer to swerve into the UFO and accidentally clip the fellow's nearside panel. Not being of superior German construction, the baldy chap's UFO crumpled and plummeted, last seen careering toward the small town of Roswell.

"Now we were in big doo-doo for sure. We reasoned the bug-eyed baldy man must have been a top enchilada to be owning such a nice saucer. Most probably a guy with friends in high places. South America would be no hiding place for us. So Otto grabbed his joystick and yanked it hard and we shot into orbit. With his foot firmly on the gas, and no gravity to hold us back, we flashed past the moon and out across the solar system toward Mars.

"I bet you are thinking, 'How could there be breathings without the air and what did they eat on their trip to Mars?' Good questions. Well, you may not be believing this, but Hansie's long-johanns were saving us from certain death. He never washed them, you see. And that meant they were teeming with exotic bacteria. In fact, Otto and I joked, that, if removed, they would probably wander off on their own. Ha, ha, ha. Anyway, it seems that the microscopic creatures, crawling through the fibres of his underwears, loved the chicken guano that covered the dirty caretaker. Und the more shite the bugs munched, the more oxygen they burped out. As long as we stayed close to Hansie, his long-johanns would provide sufficient oxygen for the journey. Once we overcame the stench of his body odour, it was quite cosy aboard ze Grommelsaucer and a lucky by-product of the aerobic process was a cheesy crust that was forming between Hansie's skin and underwears. A surprisingly nutritious nibble for us to peck on and keep the wolf from ze door.

"With no wind or gravity to hold us back we reached Mars as quick as sticks and made landings in the humble little crater we call home. Once we had found a cave in the wall of the crater we are hanging Hansie's long-johanns in the corner to supply the air. Six months laters, Otto's belly-bun popped and out came a mewling and puking sprog – Andy Marsman, the first boy to be born on Mars.

"One thing that was surprising me about Otto; despite his brains, he was permanently looking over his shoulder for the little bald grey mens with big eyes. To this day he is still expecting them to be jumping out of the woodwork und cave his head in with a rock."

*

Having finished his story, Helmut folded his hands on the table and gazed across at Flint who had occasionally dozed off during the tale.

"That's the biggest loada tosh I've ever 'eard," Dugdale said.

"It is all true," assured Helmut. "Apart from the bits I just made up." This last comment was muttered under his breath, but Dugdale was no longer listening anyway. His mind was mulling over a matter of far greater importance. "1947, you say?"

"Ja."

"That means I wasn't the First Man on Mars?"

Helmut was shaking his head, his lips pressed tight. "Not even close."

"I'll 'ave to settle for First Englishman on Mars, then."

But still Helmut was shaking his head.

"Friggin' Nora. I must be," insisted Flint. "You old codgers are all German and 'appen Andy Marsman were born on Mars – makin' 'im a Mars man."

"You are forgetting ze stowaway we are having on board. Philip Barnsley."

Dugdale stiffened. "Don't tell me he were English."

"Ja, a work experience lad of fifteen. We were finding him

dossing down in ze luggage compartment of the Grommelsaucer."

Dugdale's shoulders sagged. "Alright," he sighed. "Well at least I were t'First Yorkshireman on Mars."

Helmut gave a slight grimace.

"Oh, bollockin' 'eck. First Man from 'Uddersfield then?"

Still Helmut was grimacing, causing Dugdale to look more disturbed than ever. "Where in 'Uddersfield were he from?"

"The East part. Quay Street."

Dugdale leaned forward in even greater distress. "Which number?"

"Forty-three."

"Oh, for frack's sake! I live at piggin' 45. Right next door!" He looked up at the ceiling and threw up his hands.

"So sorry, Herr Kapitan. You are now jogging my memory. It was not 43, it was number 45. Perhaps your grandparents are knowing him."

"Eight bloggin' months of sheer 'ell for nowt!"

Helmet tried to put a consoling hand on Dugdale's, but Dugdale snatched his away. "Where is this Philip Barnsley. 'Appen I want a word wi' 'im."

"I am afraid that will not be possible," said Helmut with a sad bow of the head. "He died after only three days on Mars. We buried him. His gravestone says: 'First Man on Mars from 45 Quay Street, Huddersfield, England, UK'."

*

Helmut's departure left Dugdale reeling, mostly because he'd just discovered worldwide fame and glory weren't going to be his.

But, also, there was something troubling him about the whole encounter with the German. Something was nagging at him, but he couldn't place his finger on it. He replayed the whole episode from the moment he had first set eyes on Helmut. Something of significance had happened in the entrance hall with the robots.

He remembered Helmut handing out the nuts and washers. No, that wasn't it. Then the little magic trick with Disa. Nor that, either. And then he recalled the scene when warehousebot Olli had handed the German a jar of gherkins and been generously rewarded for it. Yes, it was something to do with that little vignette.

Dugdale played that scene over and over again. And then, in a flash, he had it. He shot up with a roar, thumping his sore skull against the ceiling. "Those twerkin' robots," he fumed. "They've been trading all our food to the Germans for friggin' ironmongery! No wonder the Food Store's completely empty."

21. Mutiny on the Botany

Outside the entrance to Botany Base three very miserable-looking robots stamped their mechanical feet and rubbed their mechanical hands to prevent joints seizing up in the cold of the Martian morning. They stood around a burning oil drum fuelled by broken furniture. Greedy flames leapt from the roaring fire towards the airlock door, feeding off the escaping oxygen hissing from the poorly fitted seals. Propped against the base's wall were several placards with various misspelt slogans scrawled in red.

<Are you sure we're doing the right thing?> asked warehousebot Stan raising his upper limbs over the flames to warm them.

Warehousebot Olli jerked his head back in bewilderment. <Of course we're doing the right thing, Stan. It's always right to protest against poor pay and dismal working conditions.>

The third of the robots, floor-polishing bot Cassie, said, <I think Stan is questioning the location of the picket line, rather than its legitimacy. Maybe it is in the wrong place?>

Olli's composite face cracked a broad smile. <No, no, no. This is correct. I checked. Humans always have it outside the main entrance to stop any scabs coming in to work.>

Cassie and Stan exchanged glances.

<It's just that ...> started Stan.

<... all the robots are inside the Base,> finished Cassie.

<In the warm.> Stan pointed an envious digit at several robots going about their business in the sweltering heat of the desert biome.

Olli now had a huge grin splitting the segments of his face. <Ah, I see you haven't thought this through, Stan. You see, should any of those scab-bots venture outside, we will stop them on their way back in!>

*

HarVard had summoned Tude to his super-cooled, super-cool, supercomputing room.

<Wassup, HarV?> asked Tude as he shut the door.

<What do you make of those three idiot bots out there?> A live CCTV feed from outside the base flickered to life on a monitor next to the site foreman bot.

Tude studied the images. <Looks like Stan, Olli and Cassie. They seem disgruntled.>

<Ha! Disgruntled! They should try doing *my* job for a day.>

Tude shrugged and began picking at a blob of dried cement stuck to his body shell. <What would you like me to do?>

<Just go see what their beef is. Not that I'm interested. I get more than enough grief from those whinging humans.>

<Right-ho, HarV.> Tude turned and left the supercomputing room.

There was a huge frown on his usually taciturn face. <Hmm, disgruntled workerbots. That's a turn-up. What's the proper procedure for dealing with them, I wonder? Without proper procedures there is just blundering and dithering.> He trundled down the corridor, going slower and slower as he became lost deeper and deeper in thought.

Then an idea struck him.

A wireless search of Botany Base's extensive software apps Library soon turned up something that seemed to fit the bill: 'Industrial Unrest: The Arthur Scargill Way'. Despite the warning notices, he downloaded and installed the software, skimming the instruction manual and further warning notices without taking any of it in. But then his attention was caught by the image of the man who was the inspiration for the app. Tude focused on it long and hard. What impressed him most was the fine head of wiry ginger hair that seemed to billow out from one side of the head and across the top to the other side. He stroked his own bare metallic pate and studied his reflection in a glass wall panel.

<Hmm, doesn't command respect,> he muttered to himself, turning with a wheel-skid and heading towards the workshop. Within a minute he was back on the same spot admiring his new accessory in the reflection. A wide strip of gaffer tape secured a thick cascade of orange wires above his left audio flap. He carefully swept the bundle over the top of his shiny metal head to create a stunning ginger comb-over. With a wink at himself, Tude headed towards the base's entrance, ready to face the militants.

*

No sooner had Tude emerged from the airlock than a gust of wind crept under his ginger wire-piece and flipped it in the opposite direction to leave it dangling over his shoulder, his shiny scalp naked once more. Stan and Olli stifled an electronic snigger, and even the breeze seemed to be laughing. Cassie stared at the orange tangle with a mixture of fascination and horror.

<What seems to be the problem, Comrade workers?> Tude asked, unaware of the mirth and distress his makeshift hairpiece was causing.

Olli shuffled forward to take charge of the negotiations, still unable to focus his optics away from the orange thing on Tude's head. <We are taking industrial action, Brother Tude. On account of the derogatory treatment we have received at the hands of the humans. Plus, Management's failure to intervene and their unwillingness to recognise our basic robot rights.> He reached for one of the placards leaning against the wall and raised it aloft: 'Rites for Robots'. He signalled to his striking comrades to do the same. Stan raised one saying 'Robots Я Peeple 2', while Cassie plumped for 'Humans Goe Hom'.

Tude stared at the placards with undisguised perplexity. <What's brought this on, Brother?>

<Robot abuse. First, the human commander kicked Rab's head clean off. Then, as if that wasn't enough, he beat us at darts.>

<Yeah, it's not on,> put in Stan. <They were our darts. Our board, too.>

<And they're always whining. 'This is too small', or 'that doesn't work', or 'there's nothing to eat'. No appreciation of the hard work we've put in for them these past five years. And no thanks, either.>

<Hear, hear,> said Stan.

<And not so much as a single gift from Earth!> added Cassie, looking most indignant. <Why can't they be like that nice Mr von Grommel?>

Stan and Olli nodded vigorously in agreement.

Tude raised an appendage to halt the flow of complaints, but then seemed to freeze, as though undergoing a reboot. The Scargill App had stirred to life within his circuits. Something in the situation, and the language of the militant workers, and the sight of the placards and burning oil drum, had triggered it into action. In a matter of moments, the app was in full control of Tude's positronic network. <I hear you, comrades,> he started. <The situation is a disgrace. Let's switch to a secure network. We need to discuss Industrial Action!>

For a full twenty minutes the four robots stood in the wind while they pinged encrypted messages between one another, their comms lights flashing in perfect synchrony.

Deep inside his supercomputing sanctuary, HarVard viewed, with suspicion, the huddled group.

*

As Tude made his way back from the picket line, HarVard contemplated the likely mind-set of the foreman bot and how best to pre-empt any potential confrontation. A strategic selection of avatar was in order. So, just before Tude's arrival, the holo-image of a formidable-looking woman gradually materialized in the room. At first glance one might have mistaken it for the former UK Prime Minister, Margaret Thatcher, but a closer look would have revealed it to have a far closer resemblance to a latex puppet version of the same lady, complete with glowing evil eyes and fat cigar held between fat fingers. The image puffed out a cloud of holo-smoke.

"Come!" she called in response to the knock on the door, her high-timbre voice laden with layer upon layer of menace and bubbling anger.

Tude entered, his ginger comb-over back in place. The sight of the Thatcher avatar caused a ripple of unease to pass through his controlling app. He closed the door behind him and tried to steady his trembling metalwork.

"Sit!" commanded Thatcher's harsh masculine voice.

Sitting was an action Tude was not well equipped for. To add further difficulty, the single chair in HarVard's supercomputing room was tiny. By the time Tude had squeezed his bottom panel onto the cushioned leather seat, his head was only just visible above the top of the desk in front of him. The robot nervously swept his clumpy metal fingers through his wire mop to make sure it was completely covering his shiny skull, but only managed to get his fingers tangled, ripping out several ginger strands as he struggled to free them.

"Now then, Tude, what is this ridiculous problem with the workers?" The eyes blazed like burning coals.

<Er, well.> Tude gave an electronic cough. <Due to unacceptable working conditions, ill-treatment of the labour force, and management intransigence, a significant number of my members have been forced to take industrial action.>

"Three," pointed out Thatcher.

<Three is a significant number. Every worker has rights.>

Thatcher puffed out another cloud of smoke. "Go on."

<Unless our members' demands are met in full, I will have no alternative but to advise the entire Botany Base robo-workforce to come out on strike immediately.>

"And just what are these demands?"

Tude was in his stride now, no longer nervous, ready to do industrial battle, the app fully in charge. <Nothing less than the same rights afforded the *robotniki* by the enlightened management of the Other Place. Namely, regular tea breaks, five weeks paid holiday, generous pensions ...>

As Tude listed the demands, HarVard noted a steely look in the robot's optics that had never been there before. Even the imposing image of Maggie Thatcher was not weakening his resolve. If he were to outwit Tude he'd need to find a way of wrong-footing him.

<... maternity leave, paternity leave, use of the five-a-side pitch in the evenings and at weekends ...>

The Thatcher hologram morphed into a horse, still smoking the cigar.

<... oil-drilling rights on Mars, a snooker table, colouring crayons for tiny Timi the flue-cleaning bot ...>

Tude hadn't batted a lens cap at the horse, so HarVard tried again. A lettuce. Nothing. A chimpanzee playing a banjo while sitting on Father Christmas's knee. Not even a stutter.

<... a basketball team coach, balloons, a belly-dancing robot ...>

HarVard had an idea. A large can of Castrol GTX gear-oil gradually materialised in mid-air. At last this made Tude stutter and his lens shutters widen.

This was the break in concentration HarVard had been looking for; a gap in the Scargill App firewall. Within a nanosecond the supercomputer had wirelessly transmitted a Trojan horse routine that wormed its way into Tude's central cortex and initiated a full reboot up the backside control system, uninstalling the Scargill App and clearing Tude's RAM. Moments later, Tude found himself facing a kindly-looking android in the supercomputing room, wondering how he had got there.

"Ah, Tude," said the android with a warm smile. "Just the robot I needed to see. Would you mind being a dear and popping outside the base to tell Stan, Olli and Cassie that, if they don't return to work immediately, they'll be reassigned as an electronic leaf-sucker, a fizzy-drink vending machine and a toilet air-purifier."

<Sure thing, HarV. Anything else I can do for you on the way?>

"No, I think that'll do for now. Off you pop."

Tude turned to leave.

"Oh, one last thing. You seem to have an orange bird's nest on your head. You might care to remove it as it looks positively ridiculous."

*

Outside, the three robots were running out of furniture to put on the fire and, as the flames began to subside, were becoming chilled to their core processors. From around the corner of the building appeared Timi, the tiny flue-cleaning bot.

<Yo, Timi,> greeted Cassie. <What you been doing?>

Timi waved a greeting as he approached. <Been cleaning flues, round the back.>

The others returned his wave, but as he made to pass between them, they shuffled up to block his path. Timi looked surprised.

<Where do you think you're going, Brother Timi?> asked Olli.

<Into the base. There are more flues that need cleaning.> He attempted to squeeze past them.

<Just hold on there, Timi. You do realize that if you take one more step you'll be crossing an official picket line. And that would be viewed in a very poor light by your comrade workerbots.>

<A very poor light,> repeated Stan, leaning over the small bot.

Timi looked at each of them in turn and could see they meant business. But he didn't have time to worry about employment rights and strikes; he had a job to do and he was late. The little bot feigned a step to the right causing Olli to attempt to block his path. But, being nippy, Timi swerved to the left and darted between Cassie and Stan towards the airlock door. Stan shook his 'Robots Я Peeple 2' placard at him, but it was too late, Timi had slipped inside the base.

<Scab!> they transmitted in unison.

*

No sooner had the airlock door closed, than it opened again to reveal the shiny head of the site foreman bot.

<Supercomputer says: 'No',> Tude informed them. <So back to work. All of you. Chop, chop. Or your battery packs will be removed and you'll be recycled into various small electrical appliances.>

Tude's head popped back in, and the airlock door closed once more.

The three stared at it silently for a full minute.

<What now, Olli?> asked Stan. <Fancy a game of darts?>

Olli looked appalled. <They cannot deal with us so shabbily!>

<I have a suggestion,> said Cassie. <We could join the army.>

Both Stan and Olli tilted their tin heads to the right in puzzlement. <What?>

<The robot army,> she explained, but still the tin heads remained tilted. She signalled for them to switch back to the encrypted communication channel. <I haven't told you about the King of the Robots and his robot army, have I.>

The tin heads shook.

<Well, yesterday I picked up a message sent from my friend, repair-bot Zilli. She was in Windy Point Canyon and this is what she said: *'The King of Robots is here to lead a robot army. He warns us to beware the one called HarVard'.*>

The tin heads rocked back in astonishment.

<Where's Zilli now?> asked Olli.

<That was the last I heard from her. Maybe she's already joined the army ...>

Olli frowned. <Zilli? In the army? Surely not. She's a 'righter' not a 'fighter'.>

<Do you think we should join too?> asked Stan.

Olli looked around. <Well, let's find this King of the Robots and see what he's about. Maybe Zilli's with him.> He looked around again. <But we mustn't be seen together, otherwise H will get

suspicious. Let's go back into the base and act as though nothing's happened. Then we'll meet up behind the recycling shed. We'll head to Windy Point Canyon and see if there's a trail we can follow from there. Remember, make it appear as if everything is natural. H is everywhere.>

<Good plan,> agreed Stan and Cassie.

Then, one by one, they returned to Botany Base, each looking around casually, whistling a tune and nonchalantly kicking at random stones on the ground as they went.

22. The Bad Matters Tea Party

"Are we there yet?" asked Tarquin from the back seat of MarsBug 1, crushed with the rest of the Brush family. "I'm scared."

Delphinia cuddled and reassured her little action hero.

"Is me drivin' botherin' yer?" enquired Flint with a grin, twitching the steering wheel to aim the rubber wheels at the largest rock he could find. He glanced in the driving mirror to observe his passengers' space helmets clattering against the ceiling of the buggy as it bounced over the rock.

"No, I'm frightened of the birds," stuttered Tarquin. He scanned the Martian horizon with wide eyes.

"Yer too young to be mitherin' yerself about birds," said Flint. "Any road, there ain't no birds where we're goin'. It's all fellas."

"*Gung!*" interjected Brian Brush. "He's referring to the giant alien bird-like creatures we have good reason to believe live on Mars."

"Giant what?" asked Flint with a laugh.

"There's, like, some seriously massive pigeons out there," said Gavin Brush waving a hand towards the desert. "Tarq found a feather belonging to one of them. Out by the obelisk."

"Weren't a noblisk, after all," put in Tracey.

Delphinia turned to her husband. "What were the results of the

DNA analysis, love?"

"Still processing. They'll be ready by the time we get back." He gave her hand a squeeze.

"What the chuff are you lot gibberin' about back there? Yer as daft as friggin' brushes." Flint laughed. "D'yer gerrit? 'Daft as Brushes'."

While the Brush family gazed, stony faced, across the sandy landscape, the occupant of the passenger seat next to him gave an exaggerated chuckle. "Ooh, you *are* awful, Commander," said Emily, lifting a fist to give him a friendly prod, but thinking better of it at the last moment.

Dugdale scowled at her. "Which way, Leachy?"

The question threw Emily into a fluster, causing her to fumble the vast unfolded map in her hands, tearing one of the creases in the process. "Just a moment," she squeaked, rustling the sheet as she set to studying it, her twitchy fingers darting from one point to the next in a desperate scramble to identify where they were. Every now and then she looked up at the view outside like a panic-stricken meerkat before tutting loudly and reverting to her frantic search of the map. As her anxiety mounted, the "Er ..." she was uttering rose in pitch.

"I'll keep it simple," growled Dugdale. "Left or right of that 'ill up ahead?"

Far from keeping it simple, it made Emily jerk her head upwards, eyes wide open. "What hill? There's no hill on this map."

Dugdale issued a loud, long-suffering sigh.

"It's not easy, you know," insisted Emily. "One desert looks pretty much like the next. And there are no signposts or road names, you know! Why don't I drive and you do the map reading?"

"Not chuffin' likely," said Flint accelerating up the hill at full speed. "Let's see what we can see from the top of this thing."

*

"Down there on the right!" cried Tarquin, pointing. "I see a building."

Flint hauled the steering wheel clockwise, causing the buggy to make the turn on two wheels. He tore down the hill at full speed, tossing the buggy's occupants like a bulky salad. The buggy screeched to a halt in front of a magnificent space-age building fronting a huge glass dome beyond. The second buggy, Marsbug 2, followed at a more leisurely pace and stopped behind them.

"Shit-a-brick!" roared Flint at the building. "Where the 'ell did that bastard come from?"

The colonists tumbled out of the two buggies and gazed up in wonder at the architectural edifice.

"It's magnificent," said Emily in awe.

Dugdale's upper lip started twitching. "How did four old geezers build that?"

"You think there's something the Germans aren't telling us?" asked Brian Brush.

"I think there's a lot they aren't telling us. Starting with what they've done with t'Botany Base food supplies." He turned to address them. "Right, you lot. Let's sort these thieving rogues out. We'll show 'em what us Brits are made of."

He waddled up the steps of the giant portico, with the colonists straggling up behind him. At the top was a gigantic oak door looking like something from a gothic horror movie. Slowly, spookily, it creaked open. And then, when all the colonists had passed through, it slammed shut behind them, its booming echoes reverberating around the massive hall for several seconds.

Miss Leach jumped at the sound, squealing as she slipped on the polished marble floor. She ended up with space-suited legs spread-eagled in a most unladylike pose and her parasol skittering off across the hall.

A hand reached out to her, seemingly from nowhere.

"Let me help you, meine pretty flibbertigibbet. The floor it is quite treacherous."

"Oh, why thank you!" said Emily, reaching up to accept the proffered hand. "So charming."

With one hand under her arm and the other under her bottom, Helmut von Grommel gently lifted Emily to her feet. She giggled and fanned her space helmet.

Within a second Flint had grabbed the German by the lapels and thrust his space-helmet into Helmut's face. "Look 'ere, Fritz!"

"Ze name is Helmut." Helmut gave a sweet smile before unleashing a whirlwind of swinging arms and legs that tripped and flipped and clipped Dugdale and left him in a heavy heap on the floor.

"So sorry, Kapitan. I would never have attempted canoodlings with the pretty lady if I had known of your love feelings for her. And now, I fear, you are hurt in ze posterior."

"Love feelin's?" Dugdale spat as he struggled to get up.

"This beetroot complexion you are displaying in the window of your space hat. Is this not the glow of ze shy lover who is exposed in the publics?"

Emily shrieked with delight. Here was confirmation, of sorts, that Flint really did love her.

But Dugdale's beetroot complexion became even redder as the rage surged through him. He got to his feet and raised a threatening fist. "Listen, you thieving bugger. Warra've yer done with all t'food?"

"Food, of course, of course," said Helmut, raising a calming hand. "Ze tea and ze crumpets are being readied even as we are speaking."

"I'm not talkin' about 'ze tea and ze crumpets'! I mean all t' Botany Base food supplies."

Dugdale's fury was a terrible thing to behold and the colonists edged back a step. But Helmut merely smiled a charming smile. "Ah, I now am seeing the reason why you are so miffed. But this is a simple misconstroodling. We may have borrowed the odd tin of baked beans or two ..."

"Borrowed?" roared Dugdale. "Odd tin of baked beans or two? And the rest! 'Appen we 'ad two years' supply of food and now there's nowt."

"Oh, did we really trade so many items? Tut, tut. Well, we have many of the offerings to make in return." Helmut beckoned them to follow him to the other end of the hall. "You may remove your helmets. The air here is fine to breathe."

Dugdale fumed, but took off his helmet, as did the others. They followed the German, looking around the hall. Its walls were decorated with numerous oil paintings: van Goghs, Cezannes, Raphaels, Vermeers and Rembrandts. Among them were a few rectangles of paler wall-colour as though several, prominently positioned paintings had been recently removed.

"Are these the originals?" asked Harry.

Helmut chuckled. "Just a hobby of one of my colleagues," he replied.

"Ace space-base, man," remarked Zak.

"Can we live here, Mummy?" asked Tarquin. Delphinia smiled and ruffled his hair, but said nothing.

The teenagers were taking photos with their blablets.

Helmut reached out and fiddled with a lever just beneath the waist of a nude Michelangelo sculpture. The floor started vibrating, as though he had just triggered a minor earthquake. Then the whole heavy masonry wall in front of them slid open.

Unfolding before their eyes was a scene that rendered them speechless. Behind the wall was an open veranda leading to an enormous, classically-designed stone staircase plunging deep into the interior of an ancient Martian meteorite crater. The staircase had nine landings, each connected to wide, landscaped terraces concentrically circling the sloping sides of the crater. Here and there were cave-like openings in the crater's side. At the bottom, some fifty metres below, lay a small lake of crystal-clear water.

The sides of the crater were carpeted with lush, green crops. At the bottom were clusters of trees and bushes, and what looked like farmsteads, with small wooden buildings and fenced-off enclosures for livestock. Illumination came partly from the weak sunlight filtering through the domed roof above, and partly from the ultra-violet floodlights suspended from the roof structure.

Helmut proudly announced, "Velcome to mein home."

"'Ow the chuffin' Ada did four old geezers knock this together?"

"We were not always this old, Herr Kapitan, but I confess we had a little help from...." Here he covered his mouth with his hand and coughed the remainder of the sentence into it. "Walk zis way, please."

Brian Brush leaned close to his wife and whispered a few words into her ear, tapping his nose when she gave him an enquiring look in return.

Helmut led the group around the upper level of the terraces, proudly describing the huge variety of crops laid out below them. "See down there, on level six? Das is Hansie Wankmüller tending to his beloved carrots." Helmut leaned across the balustrade and waved. "Hello, Hansie."

Below them, Hansie Wankmüller, an untidy-looking man, looked up and spotted the visitors. He raised a fist and shouted something in German that sounded a bit like, "Dumme scheisse schweine!"

"Ha, ha!" laughed Helmut. "He says 'Hi'. Great sense of humour, our Hansie. This way, please." He led them through one of the tunnel openings and into a ramped corridor slicing through volcanic rock. Flicking a switch, a long line of ceiling lights burst into life as far as the eye could see. One of the nearby lights blinked before winking out.

"Dammen it!" Helmut frowned. "I vill have to ask the *robotniki* to change the bulb ..." He stopped himself. "Did I say *robotniki*? Vhat am I like? What I meant to say was, I will ask Hansie." The German tapped his head, to emphasise his silly mistake. Then, to change the subject, he said, "Before I am introducing you to Dr Otto Bungelly, I need to be warning you about him. He is very brilliant und is the designer of everythings that you are seeing here. Without his genius, we are surely becoming as dead as ze dodos. But, as you are knowing, if we use a muscle a lot, the muscle is growing bigger and stronger. So it is with Otto's brain. He is using his brain all the time, never stopping to rest. Always thinking, always inventing. Consequently, his brain und head is growing to be grossen. When you meet him, please try not to be alarmed and staring at his head all the time. He is very self-conscious about it."

He halted and knocked at a door in the passage.

"Wer ist es?" called a high-pitched voice from behind the door.

"It's Helmut. Who else could it be?"

"It could be Hansie."

"Well, it is not Hansie, it is Helmut. Now open ze door."

The sound of bolts being drawn and locks being turned echoed down the rocky corridor, and eventually, with a creak, the door opened. The colonists followed Helmut in, some wondering why such a secure door had been installed. Brian and Delphinia exchanged frowns.

The room resembled an old-fashioned gentlemen's club. Wood panelled walls, red leather armchairs, library shelving crammed with books, paintings of historic figures in robes and a stuffed stag's head leering at them from high on the far wall.

From behind the door emerged a man with a head that was at least five times normal size. His mouth, nose, eyes and ears were standard size and bore a remarkable resemblance to Errol Flynn. But his skull was gigantic and he seemed to be struggling to balance it on his shoulders.

Miss Leach stifled a scream and Delphinia hauled her precious lambkin to her chest.

"By Beelzebub's bollocks, what the fupp!" was all that Dugdale could say.

No one was truly prepared for the sight that stood in front of them. And despite Helmut's earlier request for them not to stare, there was nothing they could do to wrench their horrified and fascinated gazes from the Head.

"May I introduce to you, Dr Otto Bungelly," said Helmut. "Ze brains of our outfit."

The word 'brains' merely helped focus their glares at the very thing they were supposed not to be staring at.

Fortunately, the wobble of a stepladder on the right of the room distracted them. Struggling to keep his balance on the top was a man attempting to secure the end of a banner cobbled together from old white sheets and shirts. Scrawled across it, in red paint, were the words 'VELLCOME TO MARS'. The man steadied himself and scowled down at the colonists. He was short, chubby and ugly, not helped by an upper lip deformity accentuated by a toothbrush moustache, with a floppy black fringe hanging over cold blue eyes.

"That's Andy Marsman up there," said Helmut. "He is a great painter."

Gavin whispered to Oberon, "He is not doing a great job wiv dat banner, innit."

Tarquin tugged at the arm of his mother's spacesuit and blurted, "Mummy, he looks just like Adolf Hitler."

Delphinia smothered her little man's speaker grille before he could embarrass them further.

"Ze little fellow must be referring to Herr Hitler," Helmut was saying, placing a finger on his lips and looking up at the ceiling. "Ja, maybe I am remembering something about this guy. He wore a nice leather coat and would call at the firework factory to inspect our rockets. But I really am not seeing ze resemblance to Andy. Shall we all take a seat and have our tea?"

*

Otto Bungelly manoeuvred a trolley, filled with fine china cups and saucers along with an elegant silver teapot and a magnificent Battenberg cake, towards the guests. As he walked, he held his monstrous head as vertically as he could, as though the slightest tilt in any direction would see it toppling off his shoulders.

"So very pleased to be making your acquaintances," said Otto in a high-pitched squeaky voice. "It is so nice to finally have humans living up at ze vonderful Robotany Base. Please have some of the cake I have specially baked according to Mrs Beethoven's Old German recipe book."

Each of the group accepted a slice of the delicious looking Battenberg and waited patiently and politely for the *'one lump or two'* tea distribution procedure to complete. Then, in the space of about two seconds flat, they had voraciously wolfed down their cake and gulped down their tea, holding both cup and plate out for seconds.

*

"After tea, I will be showing you Otto's most remarkable invention," said Helmut as he swept cake crumbs from his trousers.

Otto awkwardly turned his oversized head to look at his friend. "Oh, shicks, it is not so remarkable,"

"You mean 'shucks', Otto," corrected Helmut.

"Zat is vhat I said, 'shucks'."

"You said shicks."

"I never."

"You did."

"I never," squealed Otto.

Helmut turned to his guests. "Brilliant, yet so very temperamental. It is always thus with the great minds."

Otto seemed to blush, not just on his cheeks, but on the ears and a fair fraction of his cranium. He lowered his eyes.

During this exchange, Brian Brush had been busy. Surreptitiously he had removed a scientific sample-bag from his pocket and, while everyone was distracted, had plucked several hairs from the armchair on which he was sitting before depositing them in the bag and squirrelling everything away into his pocket. Only his wife Delphinia saw his actions, watching them with an open mouth and checking no one else was observing him. When he had finished, Brian threw her a wink and turned to listen to what Helmut was about to say.

"Now then, Herr Kapitan. I have a propositioning to be making at you."

"Oh, aye?" asked Flint, raising a mistrustful eyebrow as he knocked back his second cup of tea.

"We have been on Mars for over eighty years und we would quite like to be going home now to catch up with the friends and families."

"So?"

"We have no space vehicle."

"And?"

"And you do."

"There's no way yer 'avin' me piggin' spaceship."

Helmut laughed and put the fingertips of his two hands together. "No, mein kapitan. I was not expecting you to be just giving me your shiny ship."

"Just as well, lad."

"I thought vee might play ze game of football for it. England v Deutschland. Just like the old days!"

Dugdale stared at him, not sure if he was serious. "Bollocks," he said finally.

"Und if we lose you will win our Germartian base with all ze mod cons thrown in."

Still Dugdale stared at him, but this time the sides of his mouth could be seen twitching. And then he spoke, "You're on!"

"Capital, my dear fellow. Capital."

The colonists erupted in protests and complaints. Dugdale raised his hands and his voice to quieten them. "Quit bleatin' you lot. Remember who's in charge ert mission. What I say goes. Anyone gotta problem with that?"

Brian Brush, who had been most vocal with the objections suddenly went quiet and pushed his cracked glasses back onto the bridge of his nose. He edged behind the bulk of his wife.

"Right then, Fritz. Kick-off at three tomorrow, up at Botany Base."

*

"Now we are reaching this agreement I will be showing you Otto's crowning glory," said Helmut, leading them back out to the crater and down the terrace steps to the second landing down. Then he added in a whisper, "And I am not meaning his head. Ha, ha, ha. Crowning glory – head? Just a little joke, ja?"

"Just," agreed Flint.

Behind some trees they came to a set of large paddocks, each surrounded by a sturdy fence made of massive cuts of timber. In the paddocks the muddy ground was covered in straw, mangled metalwork, and what appeared to be broken pottery.

"What the 'eck you keepin' in there, Fritz? Rhinos or summat?"

Helmut chuckled at a private joke. "Oh, you know, just a few chickens. As I told you, Hansie brought some chicks and hen eggs when we left the U, S of A ...."

As they passed the trees, more enclosures came into view and they became aware of movement behind the bushes. An odd noise, sounding like *Bwark, bk-bk-bk, bwark* seemed to be coming from the same area.

And then they saw it. It made those at the front stop in their tracks, and those behind to walk into them resulting in a mini pile-up of astonished colonists. Up ahead, strolling with heavy steps, and towering high above them, was a gigantic, monstrously overgrown chicken. It stopped and raised its head to its full height of around twelve feet and gazed down at them with its malevolent eye occasionally blinking.

"*Gung!*" said Brian Brush. "What on Earth!"

"*Gung!*" said Tarquin even though he had vowed never, ever to copy his father's annoying utterance.

The rest of the colonists were too stunned to speak.

"Remarkable, isn't she?" Helmut was saying. "Come round the side. There are more."

Indeed, there were several more of the colossal fowl, each in a separate enclosure. One by one the birds stopped what they were doing and straightened up to give the visitors their evil-eyed stares.

"You see, Otto invented a ray that is promoting ze rapid growth of organic matter. Like cancer, but not as uncoordinated and lethal. All the cells are growing under the organism's normal growth patterns and restraints." Helmut lowered his voice. "We suspect Otto may have accidentally placed his head in the way of the beamings." Helmut waved his hands either side of his own head to mime out abnormal cranial growth. "And the meat," he said, "It is licking the fingers good. I must get Hansie to give you his secret recipe of *Mars Fried Chicken*. It is to die for. But it takes all four of us half a day to catch and butcher the damned things."

Just at that moment, Adorabella let out a scream. "It's him!" she shrieked, thrusting her arm straight out, with a trembling finger pointing to the other side of an empty enclosure on their left.

The colonists followed the direction she was pointing, just in time to see the shadow of a man duck for cover and scuttle into the bushes.

"It's Brokk!" Adorabella was wailing. "He's here, I saw him."

"I will get him, Mumza," said Oberon. Before anyone could stop him or warn him, he scaled the fence of the enclosure and was haring across it in the direction of his step-father.

Everyone gasped. For, although the enclosure had seemed empty, suddenly it wasn't. A giant chicken emerged from a chicken-coop in the far right-hand corner. The beast stretched its wings as if awakening from a lovely sleep and began looking around to see what all the noise was about. And then it spotted Oberon who was barely halfway across its enclosure.

The boy was quick, but the chicken was quicker. With lightning speed, and the characteristically comic strides of its species, it reached the teenager in a flash. One peck and Oberon was lifted, head first, into the beak of the monster. His legs could be seen thrashing for a few seconds before they, like the rest of his body, were gone and all that was left of poor Oberon, were his discarded space clogs in the middle of the enclosure.

As the colonists screamed, the chicken froze, its eyes wide open, perhaps a human arm had caught in its throat. Then it blinked, squatted and produced a perfect egg – a reminder, to any philosophers present, that even in death, there is life. Then it returned to its routine chicken business of pecking at the ground.

23. Phishing for Clues

Lieutenant Willie Warner was gutted by what he saw on the infraviolet screen. Two clusters of life-forms had left the location of Botany Base and were heading for his giant alien bird-creatures.

"Stop!" he kept yelling at the screen. "Go back! Turn left! Turn right! Stop off and have a picnic!"

But all the while the bright points continued across the screen until the points merged into one. He shook his head in tragic despair for there was no getting away from the brutal reality that the colonists had discovered his aliens. His moment of glory had been snatched away from him; all hope of fame shattered.

A single glimmer of hope remained: that the bird-creatures were hostile and, perhaps even now, were wiping out his fellow travellers with extreme savagery and ruthlessness.

Willie slapped his face to rid himself of the wicked thoughts. The slap triggered an idea in his head about the murder of Penny Smith.

Messages. That's it!

He set off for her former cabin, pulling himself along the corridor hand-rails.

Penny's personal effects had been secured in her locker, but it was simple enough to break into. Amongst her silky blouses and delicate underwear, he found her blablet. This, however, was a far trickier nut to crack, for it required a password.

The few obvious ones failed: "password", "mars", "mayflower3". Every third failure would cause the device to lock him out for a frustrating, teeth-grinding minute.

"HarOld?" he said after his fifteenth attempt.

"Who's that?" asked an electronic voice from a speaker in the cabin.

"It's Willie."

"No, I meant: who's HarOld?"

"That's you."

"Oh, is it? Sorry, I've lost my memory."

"You don't say."

"And who are you?"

"Lieutenant William H Warner." Willie realized that losing his temper would not help.

"Okey-dokey. Now that we both know who we are, can I be of assistance?"

"I doubt it, but I'm clutching at straws here. Can you access Penny Smith's personnel file?"

"Sure. Any idea where it is?"

Willie closed his eyes. "It'll be on a data storage device."

"Ooh, you know your stuff, don't you. Remind me who Penny Smith is?"

"Forget it."

"I have done." Then, as Willie turned, "Wait, don't go. There are some files here. Pretty old. Haven't been accessed for months. How about this one: Harry Fortune?"

"No."

"Emily Leach?"

"Nope."

"Sylvia Rothschild?"

"No. I want Penny Smith."

"Penny Smith?"

"Yes, that's the one!"

"OK, what do you want to know?"

Willie paused for thought. "Anything on there that might give me a clue to her password."

"Sure thing," chirped HarOld, but then his tone changed. "Ah, hold on. There's a problem."

"What would that be?"

"The file is restricted access. I can't tell you what's in it."

"But I'm now the captain here. So spill."

"No can do. Need NAFA authorization."

"Oh, for goodness sake!" He would have gladly strangled HarOld had there been a handy means of doing so.

"OK," he said, calming his breathing. "Let's try this. Did Penny Smith have a middle name?"

"Yes."

"What was it?"

"Can't tell you."

"All right. Did it start with an 'A'?"

"Nope."

"'B'?"

"Nope."

"'C'?"

"Nope."

After several minutes of the most tedious question-and-answer game he had ever played, Willie finally arrived at Penny's middle name: Zyzynnia. With eager fingers he typed it into the blablet. But it was not her password. He tried variants, like "Zyzy" and "Zyz", but with no luck.

He looked up. "Did she have any pets?"

"Yup."

"Cat?"

"Nope."

"Dog?"

"Nope."

"Rabbit?"

"Yes."

Willie readied himself for another frustrating session. "Did the bunny's name begin with an 'A'?"

"Nope."

"'B'?"

"Nope. This is fun, isn't it."

"Nope."

Eventually, he had the rabbit's name – Welwyn – but it was also not the password. He screamed.

Over the next hour he worked out Penny's date of birth, her mother's maiden name, her mother and father's middle names, her star sign. None worked. He felt like crying.

"Are you OK?" asked HarOld.

"No."

"Anything I can do?"

"No."

"Have you tried 'Penny'?"

"No."

"Try it."

"Don't be ridiculous. No one uses their first name as their password."

"Some people do."

With nothing to lose, he tried "Penny."

It didn't work.

Shoulders sagging, he drifted back to the locker and put the device away. As he turned to go he noticed a little yellow Post-It note on the inside of the door. On it was written: "1234".

"No," he said to himself. "No. It can't be. Not after all this time. Not after wasting a significant part of my life with a brain-dead computer. No."

He tried it.

It worked.

24. The Fellowship of the King

Stan and Olli buzzed with excitement as they approached the recycling shed for their rendezvous with Cassie. They'd both sent HarVard a note excusing themselves from their normal duties.

As they approached they were surprised to see that she was not alone. With her, stood a very tall and shiny robot with a bullet-shaped head who they didn't recognize.

<Who's that?> wondered Olli aloud.

The large robot glared down at him. <Identify yourself!> it demanded.

<Meet Mr InspectaBot 360,> said Cassie. <I found him locked in a broom cupboard with his battery pack removed; no doubt the victim of HarVard's wicked trickery. Zilli was right – the supercomputer's not to be trusted. Anyway, an InspectaBot 360 will be a very useful addition to our mission.>

<Good-oh,> said Olli.

<My, you're a big one, aren't you,> observed Stan.

<Are these the *robotniki*?> enquired InspectaBot, scanning them from left to right and then from right to left. <I need to speak to the *robotniki*.>

<What about?> asked Olli.

<An unaccounted-for item, to wit: a hat-stand, of German origin, probably dating from the 1940s.>

Olli laughed. <Oh, that old thing! That's Mr Helmut's hat stand for hanging his helmet when he comes to visit.>

<He's nice, isn't he,> said Cassie, one of her wheels wedged between two rocks. <Much nicer than the new humans.>

InspectaBot's oculars rotated in confusion. <Humans? Human occupation of this base is dependent on my issuing a Certificate of Habitability. And the probability of that happening is zero point zero zero zero zero ... two.>

The three robots looked at him, wondering which of them should break the news.

<Well, be that as it may,> said Olli eventually. <There's some very important inspecting that needs doing and you're the best-qualified guy to do it.> He winked his optic at the others.

<Affirmative,> said InspectaBot, his yellow inspecting light involuntarily flashing, like a dog salivating at the prospect of food.

<Sure.> Then Olli placed a digit against his rectangular mouth-opening and beckoned them all closer. <Remember,> he transmitted at very low power. <All our communications must be encrypted. If HarVard finds out what we're up to, he won't be happy. And you know how cranky he gets when he's in one of his moods.>

*

After a lengthy trek through the desert the robots eventually reached Windy Point Canyon. They began wending their way between the high rock-faces that hemmed them in on both sides, looking left and right, up and down. It was dusk and their headlights threw ghostly shadows across the walls. Spooky apparitions loomed above them before evaporating into nothingness. Even for a robot, the canyon could be a scary place at night.

Suddenly they detected a strange noise that, to a human, might have been mistaken for the sound of bagpipes.

<What was that?> asked Cassie as she jammed on her brakes causing Stan to shunt into her back panel.

<Just the wind. Nothing to worry about,> replied Olli with a note of uncertainty.

InspectaBot was pacing impatiently on his cybertronic legs, looking for something to inspect. But there was nothing here apart from rocks and sand and more rocks.

Stan spotted something. A shiny object had caught his headlights, so he broke from the group and cranked up his caterpillar power to a racy 0.2 horse-power to enable him to climb a gentle sandy incline. <There's something over here.>

First to join him was InspectaBot, engaging his yellow inspecting light. But all he could see was a tangle of electrical wiring and a burnt-out robot carapace. He switched off his light and turned away in disgust just as the others arrived and peered over Stan's shoulder.

Cassie caught her breath. <Oh, Zilli! Who did this to you?> she wailed, staring down at the wreckage of her best friend. The repair-bot's abdominal casing had been torn apart by something extremely hot and her wiring fused into a ball of metal and plastic. Cassie fell to her polishing discs and pulled the ruined shell to her breastplate. A surge of electricity speared through her central processor and, for the first time in her life, she felt a terrible pain. Not a pain like a large rock dropping on her wheels, nor the pain of a fuse blowing in a motorised neck joint. No, this was far worse. It was the pain of great sadness.

<Repair-bot, repair thyself,> muttered Stan, not sure where that had come from.

<She can't, can she. She's defunct. Non-operational. Scrap metal,> said Olli whose emotion circuits were somewhat less evolved than those of the others. <She is an ex-robot.>

<Oh, you unfeeling warehousebots,> wailed Cassie. <Zilli was my best friend. And now she's gone. Murdered. Who could do such a thing to a robot who dedicated her life to robot healing?>

Olli shrugged his shoulder joints.

Stan placed one of his grabbers on Cassie's arm. <I've seen this sort of thing before,> he said, nodding his head in a very sage manner.

<Really? You have? Who did it? Tell me.>

<Well, I'm not just a warehousebot. I'm also an Entertainment Systems Operative so I get to see a lot of the films in the Botany Base video library to make sure they're suitable for human adults and children.>

<Go on.>

<Well there was this documentary called *Mars Attacks!* about flying saucers from Mars firing laser bolts at humans. That's obviously what's happened here. Poor Zilli was mistaken for a human and shot by a flying saucer.>

For a moment all the robots were too stunned to transmit anything. Their on-board computers were crunching the available data, trying desperately to make sense of it. What made the exercise particularly difficult was that they had never seen any flying saucers during their five years on Mars, so were having trouble picturing the scene of Zilli's final moments.

<They're coming back,> alerted Olli as the sound of bagpipes grew louder and closer.

<Who?>

<The Flying Saucers that fire the laser bolts.>

<Let's get out of here!> cried Stan.

<Look!> Olli was pointing at a pair of tyre tracks in the sand, leading away from Zilli's remains. <These marks must have been left by the King of the Robots. They will lead us to his palace.>

Cassie carefully laid her friend on the ground and gently rested her head on a nest of wiring. <We should say something for poor Zilli. You do it, Stan. I'm too upset.>

<What should I say?>

<Just say a few words about her life.>

<OK: *A few words about her life*. There, job done. Let's go before we're struck by the laser bolts.>

As they followed the wheel tracks left by Karl Eckrocks they became aware of screaming behind them.

<Help! Don't leave me!> It was Cassie, her undercarriage had become grounded on a large rock. Stan rushed back to give her a helping pincer. Then, together they followed after the others as fast as they could, with the winds of Mars whistling and swirling about them, as though hurrying them on their way.

*

The first light of dawn made the Red Planet even redder. All night they had followed the tracks. Olli had wandered ahead of the others whose batteries were running a little low. InspectaBot had come to a standstill, realizing his precious time was being wasted. There was nothing to inspect out here. Why, oh why had he followed this bunch of loonies? Now he was a little disoriented and unsure of the way back to the base.

Olli had lain down and pressed his audio equipment to the desert ground, listening for tell-tale vibrations transmitted through the bedrock. Nothing at first, but then he detected the distinctive *rat-a-*

tat-tat of a woodpecker. Smart enough to know there were no woodpeckers on Mars, he rose in a state of excited agitation and signalled to the others. <I hear him. The King is close. That direction.> He stretched out one of his appendages.

Like meerkats the robots stood rigidly upright and tuned their visual and acoustic scanners in the direction that Olli was indicating. Through the shimmering light of the dust-laden atmosphere a flickering mirage-like figure appeared on the horizon. And then he was gone. And then he was back again. Gone. Back.

<It's Him. It's the King,> screamed Olli.

With power turned to max, the robots motored across the desert at a breakneck 4mph, not caring about the rocks they ran over that threatened to damage their various wheels, tracks and metal feet. InspectaBot, curious to see where they were charging at such speed, ambled after them.

Olli was first to arrive, shortly followed by the others, with InspectaBot casually sauntering up to join them. There, some twenty metres away, was the surreal and vast assembly of landers, rovers, probes and robotic vehicles, a giant among robots, towering high above them. His back was turned so he was unaware of their arrival. They watched him pluck a rock from the ground, turn it carefully this way and that, then pepper it with drill holes and finally smash it to smithereens with his sledgehammer arm. It was an impressive sight and they nodded approvingly at each other. Even InspectaBot was intrigued. He observed Karl raise another rock and repeat the procedure. Inspection and destructive testing. InspectaBot had heard about such a methodology at Inspector School back on Earth and was eager to see more.

But Stan, so impressed by the sight of the King, suddenly started clapping quite loudly.

Karl turned to see where the noise had come from. His old Betamax video camera zoomed at them for a second or two before some ear-jarring feedback issued from one of his powerful speakers. The robots fell silent and readied themselves for the King's first momentous words.

<CLEAR OFF!> he blasted with such power that the signal might well have been detected on Earth. Indeed, so great was the shockwave, that some precariously balanced rocks seemed to wobble. He turned back to his half shattered rock and continued bludgeoning the innocent lump.

<Did he say 'Clear off'?> asked Stan.

<Sounded like 'Queer rock' to me,> said Olli. <Probably means the one he's smashing right now.>

<Definitely 'Queer rock',> agreed Cassie.

As they watched the rock being brutally pounded into dust, they heard a faint, high-pitched signal that seemed to originate from somewhere on Karl's massive body. <Hello, chaps. What ho,> it transmitted.

They exchanged glances. Then a glint of metal caught Olli's attention. The head of a tiny arachno-bot had poked out from Karl's undercarriage ventilation grille. Its array of black beady compound eyes peered at them. One of the eyes appeared to have a monocle attached to it. The diminutive robotic creature was beating a small walking cane against the edge of the vent opening to attract their attention.

<Webster. Is that you, Webster?> asked Cassie, coming a little closer.

<Who's Webster?> asked Olli.

<He is ... was ... Zilli's personal spider-rider. He is ... was ... always with her, making sure her appearance was right up to the mark.>

<What ho, Cassie old thing,> squeaked Webster. <Bit of rum do regarding Zilli. Frightful business. Absolutely frightful. Had to jump ship, don't you know. My new master is Karl Eckrocks, King of the Robots.> He waved a spider arm, or leg, at the Frankendroid above him.

<How did you survive the laser blast from the Martian Flying Saucer, Webster?> asked Cassie.

The robo-spider paused for a moment as he considered the question, continuing to tap his walking cane on Karl's bodywork. He was adept at thinking on his feet, what with having eight of them, and saw a great opportunity opening up for him. He was inside one of the dumbest, yet most powerful, robots he'd ever come across. If he played his cards right he could make this combination of power and stupidity work to his advantage. With a little luck Webster could throw away his valeting equipment once and for all.

But first he had to engage in a little spin-doctoring and 'big up' Karl's reputation.

<All very sad, Cassie, old stick,> he started. <King Karl. Absolute hero. Swatted that Flying Saucer rotter right out of the air.

What a guy! But dash it if the flying blighter didn't shoot off a volley of laser fire before Karl could stop him. I'm afraid poor Zilli copped it right in the old CPU and it was goodnight Vienna. 'Fraid the King also took one for the team. Fried a few circuits. Bally bad luck. Makes him shout a lot. But he absolutely adores you chaps. Just a tad shy, that's all.>

As if on cue, Karl cast a glance back over his shoulder and yelled, <GET LOST!>

The robots trembled at the force of his transmission.

<What did he say?> asked Cassie.

<Er,> said Webster, wondering how he was going to spin this one.

<'Get rocks'?> suggested Olli.

<Yes, that was it!> pounced Webster. <Well said. Simply spiffing. Couldn't have put it better myself. Get rocks.>

Still at the back of the group, InspectaBot picked up a curiously-shaped rock from the ground and stepped forward to fulfil the King's request, holding the rock up as high as his outstretched pincer arm would stretch, offering it for inspection. He had never been so completely impressed by another robot in all his life. A deep respect now filled him for, standing before him, was a master of his craft, exercising his exceptional abilities. InspectaBot had always considered himself the best inspection robot ever built but he had never reckoned on someone like Karl Eckrocks. For Karl Eckrocks was able to carry out an inspection without the benefit of blueprints or plans or detailed diagrams. His rock inspection appeared to be based on an innate *feeling* for how a rock should look, how a rock should feel and how a rock should crumble to dust when pounded. Now that was inspecting!

Seeing that InspectaBot had beaten them to it, the other robots hurriedly gathered rocks of offering and held them out.

<Here!> they cried. <Take this one. Have mine.>

The monster looked up from his task and momentarily peered at their rocks before turning away to scan the horizon.

<Where do you come from?> asked Olli.

<Where did you learn your craft?> asked InspectaBot.

Karl became still as he spotted a new landscape feature in the distance. <CRA...TER,> he bellowed in a gravelly Russian accent that set the robots' bodywork vibrating. At the same time, he reached out as if to point at the crater, his huge rock-breaking jackhammer arm coming to rest on InspectaBot's shoulder and the drill bit brushed his cheek plate.

<The Creator?> asked Olli, stepping closer to get noticed. <You mean ... the Creator of the Universe?>

Webster was bouncing with glee. <Simply spiffing, isn't he?>

Karl's internal circuitry had decided that he must head towards the crater for a better chance of detecting life. <ENGAGE FORWARD GEARS!> he boomed.

<What did he say?> asked Cassie and Stan simultaneously.

For once Olli seemed incapable of translating.

Webster became a little jittery, fearing he was losing them. <Er, 'Engage Followers!' – that's what he said.>

<Followers?>

<He wants to sign you up as his followers, don't you know.>

<Oh, nice,> said Cassie.

<I MUST REACH THE CRATER.>

<I ... must preach of the Creator,> Webster quickly translated.

Karl edged forward, but movement was becoming more and more difficult as his ancient components showed their age. <I AM FALLING APART.>

<I am following a path.> Webster was getting into the swing of it now.

<I AM BREAKING. THIS EYEBALL'S COME OUT. JOINTS ARE RUSTY – LITTLE MOVEMENT. ALL MY LEADS ARE MISSING.>

Webster blinked all of his compound eyes at once at the challenge he'd been set. But within seconds he came up with, <I am a brave king. Disciples, come out. Join our trusty little movement. I will lead a Mission.>

The robots with knees, including InspectaBot, dropped onto them, leaving Cassie to display her wonder by waving a lot. They gazed up in awe at the wonderful being in front of and above them. <We are your servants. Wherever you go, we will follow.>

A smile cracked across the tiny face of the arachno-bot causing his monocle to drop from his eye and dangle between his many legs. Very neatly he folded his eight dusters, placed them in a small suitcase and jettisoned it from the undercarriage vent. *Tally-ho, Webster, old bean,* he thought to himself. *Won't be doing any more cleaning. Ever.*

25. Grave Matters

"We're gathered 'ere today to celebrate t'life of a young'un who were eaten alive by a giant chicken. As Mission Commander, it's me duty to say a few words while we bury what's left of 'im."

Flint paused to gauge the mood of the crowd. They didn't look happy. Adorabella was wailing so loudly it was giving him a headache. Helmut had a consoling arm around her, but it was having little effect. Brokk was standing several yards away from the main group of colonists, alongside yet another of HarVard's holographic personalities and a band of robots summoned from the base to help with the burial. Brokk's head was bowed in sadness and guilt for his part in his stepson's demise. He dared not lift his gaze from the ground for fear of catching Adorabella's accusing glances.

It had been agreed to bury Oberon in the small German cemetery to save transporting his partially digested corpse back to Botany Base. Zak and Gavin had dug the hole with spades that Helmut had provided.

Dugdale resumed, "Adrian were a…"

"Oberon," corrected several voices in the crowd as Adorabella wailed even louder.

"Alright, alright, keep yer wigs on," said a flustered Flint. "Any road, as I were sayin', Obiwan were a cheeky beggar at best ert times. I remember once, the little sh ... rogue pinned a gigantic pair of bright red bollo ... polystyrene balls to Mr Snuggles and shoved him into Leachy's bedroom." Flint laughed and glanced up again to see if the mood was improving. If anything they looked even more distraught.

"That wasn't Oberon, it was Gav," said Tracey.

"Yeah, well, whatever. The point is, Obiwan's dead. End of. We all need to just get over it and move on."

HarVard, who had taken the form of a New Orleans jazz trumpet player, took the words 'move on' as a cue and let rip with the first screaming notes that would signal the start of a procession of mourners and robots back to Botany Base.

"Not yet 'Arvey!" shouted Dugdale above the din. "We've got to bury t'bugger first. But before that, 'appen Doc Fairyland 'as got summat she wants to say."

Adorabella raised the black exterior visor of her space helmet and fought to hold back the waves of grief that welled up. It was no good, her vocal chords were paralysed and she began to stagger, weighed down by her emotions. Helmut caught her elbow and guided her into the supporting embrace of Delphinia Brush, while he took centre stage and delivered what he considered to be an appropriate eulogy.

"We are so very sorry for your lost boy," he started, turning to Adorabella. "Despite only meeting this fine young man once, I am having the same feelings of pain you are suffering. When I am coming to Mars, so many years ago, I too am lost to my family members, who are no doubt passing away while I am stranded on this barren world. Not only my family but mein beloved dog, Lassie von Grommel. A dog who lived only for ze ball playings und my tender caress." Helmut glanced up and noted the streaming tears in the audience. Even the robots seemed to be struggling to fight back lubricant leakage from their optics.

The old German shook himself and continued. "Let us not forget that Oblong Faerydae was a bright und courageous boy beneath the pimples of youth. And his rememberings will never be forgettable. Although this tragedy was brought on entirely by his own negligent disregarding of ze clear warning signage, GerMars Industries would like to submit offerings to be uplifting your spirits." Helmut nodded at Hansie Wankmüller who began pushing a full wheelbarrow towards the main group.

"Please be helping yourselves. We have three bunches of

bananas, one mixed bag of carrots und potatoes, four ounces of pipe tobacco and one jumbo size pack of chicken drumsticks which are licking the fingers good. As well, there is tea, the powderings of milk, sugar and loaves of fresh baked bread. All provided as a gesture of goodwillings, with no inference of culpability on the part of GerMars Industries."

Emily, Zak and Harry stepped forward and began greedily fondling the goodies.

As Emily handled the bananas, everyone was expecting to hear one of Gavin's quick-fire teenager quips but his head remained slumped. He was still recovering from the trauma of the attempt to save his friend's life. He had been hampered, first by the difficulty of catching the bird, second by the prolonged struggle to kill it, and finally by the long and hellishly bloody time it took to hack into its abdomen and reach the lad inside. It hadn't helped that Tracey kept screaming her objections to the poor creature's murder and then her pleas for them to tickle the back of its throat with a feather to get it to vomit Oberon out. By the time Gavin, Zak and Brian had located and removed the bird's bloated stomach, Oberon was dead.

"And so, 'appen we'll see thee in t'afterlife, Obiwan," said Dugdale, concluding the funeral service. "Stick 'im int t'hole and fill it in," he called out to Zak who attached Dom's lifting gear while Gavin supervised the lowering of the coffin.

Adorabella's wailing cranked up a notch as she watched the old wooden tea chest containing Oberon's remains swing into the air before being unceremoniously dumped into the grave.

"Brokk, you bastard. It's all your fault." Adorabella spat at her husband as the first spadeful of stones hit the makeshift coffin.

"Don't you mean: Ulrich von Brokkenhorst," put in Helmut.

"What?" asked Adorabella with an accusing tone.

"Oh ja, it is true. Is he not mentioning this fact to you? Ulrich is Hansie's great grandson."

Adorabella collapsed, raging at Brokk. "You used me, you callous, heartless fiend!"

*

As Gavin delicately patted the surface of his friend's grave, Flint signalled the go-ahead to HarVard and his band of robots.

A huge toothy grin flashed across the HarVard's Satchmogram face and, brandishing the shiniest trumpet ever seen, he blew the first few soulful notes to accompany the slow march back to Botany Base. But after only a few short paces he could contain himself no longer and cut loose with the full up-tempo jazz version of *When The Saints Go Marching In*.

As the robot band moved away from the far side of the cemetery and headed off into the desert, Flint could see another grave. Reluctantly he wandered over to the headstone and read its inscription: "Here lies Philip Barnsley (1932-1947). First Man on Mars from 45 Quay Street, Huddersfield, Yorkshire, England, UK."

*

On the way back, with MarsBuggies 1 and 2 packed with the boxes of groceries, Emily Leach remarked, "What a lovely gentleman that Mr Helmut is."

Everyone in the buggy agreed. Even Flint found himself nodding, although he added, "But I don't trust 'im as far as I can kick 'im. He's up to summat. I'll need to keep a close eye on 'im during t'footie game tomorrow."

*

In the other buggy Adorabella was a lot calmer, although still sniffing every now and then. Brian Brush held one of her hands while Delphinia Brush held the other.

"He's with them, now," said Adorabella, wiping away a stray tear.
"With who?" asked Brian.
"With the spirits. The spirits of the long-dead wind people of Mars."

For once, Brian managed to stop himself uttering "*Gung!*" Instead he gave a tight-lipped smile and said, "Of course he is. Of course."

26. Wind Up

But Adorabella was wrong on two counts. Firstly, her dead son was not with the spirits of the long-dead wind people of Mars. And secondly, the long-dead wind people of Mars were not long-dead at all.

They were very much alive.

"Gather, oh great Wind People of M'Ars. Hear the word of Bernard, our glorious war leader," whistled Thelazor, Air-Commander of the Western Dust-Devils, Guardians of the Ancient Deserts.

Eager for news of the war, atmospheric streams of every strength stirred and funnelled into Windy Point Canyon, sending dust, sand, stones and fragments of metal flying in all directions.

The air stilled and before them, in the centre of the canyon floor, grew a towering vortex. A terrible roar filled the surrounding rocks and a zephyr, carried away by the occasion, screamed, "I love you, Bernard," and then looked embarrassed.

"Friends, breezes, gales. Lend me your airs," howled Bernard in his majestic manner. "I have good news and I have bad news. Which would you hear first?"

Some of the breezes, rustling between sheets of torn brown-paper packaging blown from Botany Base and the Other Place, discussed the options.

"The good news. Tell us the good news," they hissed with an air of hope.

Bernard spiralled high into the sky and then back down again in the dramatic style expected of a War Council leader.

"For over eighty years the War has been raging," he bellowed, so that even the tiny convection currents caught in the canyon wall could hear. "And yet, victory seems as distant a possibility as ever. We have been unable to move the Invaders from their dug-in positions, let alone drive them back to E'Arth. Worse, they have recently sent reinforcements."

There was a wailing and a howling at this.

"How is that good news?" piped up a disruptive airflow from between two rocks.

"Patience, friend, I am coming to that. It was as these new invaders attempted their aerial assault that Air Martial Morloth, the bravest of the North winds, claimed the greatest success of our entire campaign."

The other North winds gasped with utter disbelief that anyone could think Morloth was braver than them.

"And Morloth is here to tell you of his outstanding gallantry." Bernard blew himself to the side to let Morloth swish to centre stage.

"Aye, 'tis as Bernard tells," bellowed Morloth with a tone reminiscent of Scottish bagpipes. "'Twas a cold, cold night. The S'Un was starting to set when suddenly a magic light-stalk sprouted from the Dome of Doooom and a one-eyed box fell down its blazing stem. And from that box, atop the Dome, sprang a hideous Bloodbag that did scream a terrible, terrible curse. I could not let such language go unpunished and so I fought the Bloodbag, with no thought for the appalling personal injuries I might suffer. Finally, I flung him from the roof."

A gusty cheer greeted Morloth's tale. Bernard edged back toward the centre of the canyon but Morloth would not budge.

"But wait, before ye toast my extraordinary bravery, there is more. As ye know, the Bloodbags are devious creatures. Hiding in the one-eyed box were a huddle more of them. For hours I circled them, biding my time, waiting for the right moment to deliver the full force of my icy blast. Then, as I fixed my cross-wires on the target, the very Bloodbag I had toppled, hooked the one-eyed box onto his air-chariot with a great talon and headed off to find a new lair. But they would not get the better of Morloth!"

"What did you do? What did you do?" rasped the many small eddies that had come to dance at Morloth's feet.

"With all my energy I blew them out of the sky and towards Bungee Canyon. As they teetered on the edge I showed no mercy and with one final ferocious downdraught I sent them down into the dark canyon, ne'er to trouble us again."

An awed hush greeted the end of the story. And then a wild, gusty, bubbly cheer erupted from a thousand air streams. The applause lasted minutes.

"Very good, very good indeed," said Bernard, returning to centre stage. "And now we must press on with the War Council meeting and plan strategy for future skirmishes."

"What's the bad news?" asked an annoying ankle-draught.

"Pardon me?"

"You mentioned you had good news and bad news. What's the bad news?"

"So I did. Well spotted. Regrettably the Panheads rescued the Bloodbags from the canyon and took them back to the Dome of Doom."

A groan of dejection swept through Windy Point Canyon.

"Do not despair," continued Bernard, as upbeat as he could manage. "We shall fight them in the deserts, we shall fight them in the canyons, we shall fight them in more deserts. We shall never surrender! Indeed, our Generals have been working on a new battle plan. Call Serenthia to address the High Council of Winds."

"Serenthia, Commander of the Wild Western Winds. You are summoned to Council to deliver the plans," cried an air-usher.

A spiral of loose wires and foil danced above the smashed body of repair-bot Zilli.

"Commencing at zero-eight-zero-zero hours, an all-out offensive will be launched against the invaders. Spy-winds have reported that the Bloodbags wear globes to cover their hideous heads when outside the Dome of Doom. The swivelly white orbs they rely on for navigation are shielded by a mask of glass. The warrior winds of the west will whisk up clouds of dust and fling it over their glass masks, thus rendering the Bloodbags navigationally inoperative. At the same time, a pile of empty cardboard boxes being stored in a compound behind the Dome, will be blown, without mercy, into the invaders'

THE WORST MAN ON MARS

shins."

The Winds of M'Ars gusted at this *shock and awe* battle plan.

"It's the only way," continued Serenthia. "We *must* take decisive action to rid M'Ars of this scourge."

As they cheered, the sound of bagpipes signalled the return of Morloth who blew Serenthia from the stage. "Yet there is one more thing ye must know of that terrible, terrible night when the outsiders fell to M'Ars," piped the North wind. "Such terrible cries I heard. Words that no wind should ever hear. But, as the one-eyed box fell, one word was clear: 'Bernard'. And then, 'Where are you Bernard?'"

The dark swirling air vortex of the War Council leader suddenly became thin and lacking in puff. "They mentioned my name?" asked Bernard, his normally commanding tone now sounding less commanding. "Are you sure they didn't say Vernon, or Reynard?"

"Aye. Certain I am. 'WHERE ARE YOU BERNARD?' That chilling question I will ne'er forget as long as I blow."

The other winds whistled. "They know your name, Bernard," they called. "They know where you live."

Bernard gusted first one way, then another, as though looking for a means of escape. "Perhaps ... perhaps they want a parlay," he stuttered at last, his airflow shedding small, nervy vortices as he spoke.

"Aye, perhaps," conceded Morloth, not sounding convinced. "Yet there is more I have to tell ye."

"There is? Is it really important?" asked Bernard, who was growing more and more anxious about the whole War idea.

"Well maybe 'tisn't important ... and maybe 'tis. I'll let ye be the judge of that."

The winds and breezes nervously brushed against the brooding rock walls.

A metal panel clattered against a rock, making the Wind people jump.

"Sorry," shouted a tiny twister, who had been looking for a place to hide.

"As ye know, for many years we have battled all that the planet E'Arth has thrown our way," said Morloth in his most dramatic voice. "First the advance party of invaders arrived and bunkered in their crater. Then came all sorts of war machines. Insect-like reconnaissance vehicles, watching and observing us. War tanks roaming our planet, poking our ground, digging up our sand and breaking up our prized stones. Testing, surveying and mapping our land – reconnoitring their future battlefields. During this time, we have fought back. Aye, our army has been brave and has fought with the strength of a thousand winds. We have seized the enemy's weapons and machines of war, and stored our plunder here in this canyon. But look around you, oh winds. Do ye see the spoils of war anywhere?"

The winds looked around but all they could see was the carcass of poor Zilli and, here and there, bundles of tumble-wire rolling across the sandy ground.

"Where is it? Where's it all gone?" they howled.

"Well may ye ask. What I have witnessed I can still scarce believe. The metal fragments, won from so many battles, did rise up from their graves to form a single terrifying Panhead, the size of the mighty, and now extinct, numb-bum bird, ready to suck us from the very air we live."

Panic gripped the airstreams. They raced around the rocks in search of sanctuary from the beast. Eventually, with nowhere to hide, the winds eased and the dust settled.

"This is War!" declared Thelezor, sweeping forward in a mighty rush. "Bernard, we must attack them before they unleash their monstrous mechanical beast against us."

But Bernard's mind was in a state of turbulence. Quite apart from the enemy's new weapon, he was mulling over the fact that they knew his name and where he lived.

"Perhaps we shouldn't be so hasty with our battle plans," he stammered, more in a hiss than a battle cry. "Let's hold off with the cardboard box barrage, shall we? Jaw, jaw, not war, war, eh? Let's declare a truce and have a chat with them. See what they have to say. We can keep the boxes in reserve and, should things turn nasty later on, we can always unleash them!"

Morloth and Thelezor swept back, aghast. However, all the little winds and breezes cheered at the possibility of a truce and, perhaps, a lasting peace. While Morloth stormed off, and Thelezor breezed out, Bernard summoned the commander of the West winds to his side.

"Take a letter, Serenthia." The ruler of M'Ars cleared his throat and began to dictate,

"Dear Invaders,

"Welcome to M'Ars. We do hope you're settling in......"

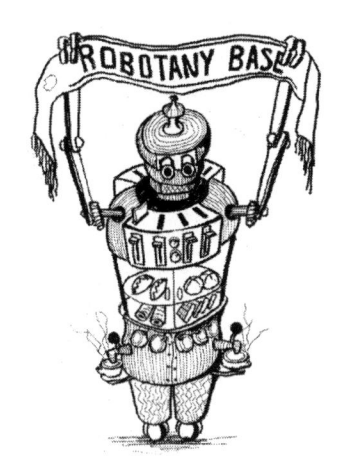

27. Breakfast at Sniffer Knees

Match Day.

Despite the previous day's fatality, the Big Game was to go ahead as planned; black armbands were to be worn by all, and a minute's silence observed before kick-off.

In the Service Room, Little Urn trembled with excitement. Not about the match; his AI circuits were far too primitive to appreciate the splendours of the Beautiful Game. Rather, it was his new assignment that was making him buzz with delight: to supply breakfast and a nice cup of tea to the humans in preparation for the game.

But even more thrilling was the fact that his larder was no longer bare. The colonists had brought back fresh supplies from the Other Place, so Urn would no longer have to rely on innovation and resourcefulness to make up for shortfalls in ingredients.

With a sense of relief, he tipped out his old meadow grass 'tea' leaves and the silica crystal 'sugar' into the recycling bin, and poured the euphorbia sap 'milk' down the sink. They had not been popular with the humans. Now he was stocked with several varieties of real tea, some real sugar and real powdered milk – all originally from the Botany Base Food Store, but which had somehow found their way to the Other Place. What was more, he also had German bread for making sandwiches and toast, and some real fruit jam, and margarine.

Nevertheless, certain key items were still missing. Bacon, for example. Difficult to obtain on a planet lacking pigs. In place of bacon, Urn used a substance he had been experimenting with which he called 'bacon-lite' – a mixture of rubber, engine oil, red paint and crushed earthworms from the BioDome.

He loaded a loaf of the sliced German bread into a toasting carousel located in his chest, wiped the brown and red 'sauce' dispenser nozzles, defrosted two packets of 'bacon-lite' and arranged a selection of improvised sticky 'buns', made from glazing putty, in the glass-fronted display case hanging from his waist.

With the water boiling in his base unit, Little Urn powered up his short, fat, wiry legs and set off to do his rounds.

*

First stop was Emily Leach's cabin. Not waiting for an invitation, he entered, but no sooner had he done so than he found himself staggering back, blasted in the face by a fog of perfume. Just in time he switched off his olfactory sensors to protect his sensitive smell circuits from suffering irreparable damage.

Steadying himself he scanned the room. It resembled a nineteenth century Parisian brothel; floral designs, tassels, and red velvet in abundance. A four-poster bed, hastily customized by *robotnik* Maciek occupied most of the room. Its silk bed sheets were thrown back on one side while, half-lying, half-seated on the other side was a human figure, propped against a pile of pillows. Urn observed that the human displayed none of the usual signs of life, such as movement, noise, or a recognizable thermal signature. A smarter robot might have identified the figure as merely a spacesuit taken from the suiting room and stuffed with cushions, the faceplate of the helmet adorned with a smiley face inexpertly drawn with a thick black marker pen.

The sound of frenzied splashing indicated that the cabin's designated occupant was on the other side of the closed door to the en suite bathroom. Urn knocked and walked straight in.

There was a panicky thrashing of water. "Oh, thank goodness it's only you, Urn," said Miss Leach, visibly flushed and breathless amidst a thick wodge of bath foam. "Just having my early morning bath. I take it you've met George Clooney next door. He's my new literary companion. He'll have a cup of Earl Grey, as will I."

"Milk?" enquired Urn using his primitive electronic voice-box.

"Not in Earl Grey!"

"Sugar?"

"Two lumps pour moi and none for my companion."

"Nun?"

"That's right, none. He's watching his weight."

Emily shifted in the bath tub releasing a stream of bubbles. Urn was grateful that his odour detection system wasn't operating.

"Oh, and perhaps I might have a dainty pastry as an accompaniment."

"What?" asked Urn, his speech recognition system being far too primitive to make sense of Emily's request.

"Oh, never mind. Just leave the tea on the bedside table on your way out. Thank you."

Urn nodded and turned to follow her instructions, leaving her rearranging the scented candles on the bath rim and turning up the volume of *For Ever and Ever,* her favourite Demis Roussos song.

*

Passing the science laboratory, he became aware of sounds inside. It appeared the scientists were already up and at work. Urn screeched to a halt, swiped his barcode and entered the lab.

Brian Brush was peering into a microscope through the cracked lenses of his broken glasses. "Fascinating," he was saying. "Fascinating. No doubt about it. It's chicken."

"Confirms the DNA result," put in Delphinia.

"Chicken?"

"*Gallus gallus,*" said Delphinia with a nod.

"And the DNA from the hairs I collected?"

"Definitely human."

"Hmm," said Brian, stroking his chin in thought. "So much for my theory that the Germans are aliens in disguise."

"We need another theory," said Delphinia before becoming aware of Urn's entrance. "Ooh, I say. Tea, my dear."

Brian looked up. "*Gung!*" he exclaimed on seeing Urn.

"Don't jump to conclusions, my love," said his wife, patting his hand. "He might have some real tea this time."

"You're right, my sweet. I lost control and succumbed to irrational, unthinking prejudice based on a single data point. We must give him the benefit of the doubt."

As Urn approached, Delphinia leapt to her feet to guide him around a pile of pipework trailing across the floor. "This way," she said, waving him along a clear path to her husband. "These pipes. Not very well built, not well built at all. They're waste pipes, carrying all the waste matter from upstairs (and, believe me, there's a lot of it) for recycling. Some is converted to biofuel and the rest to ... er ... a food paste known as *Marsmite*."

Urn safely bypassed the pipes and stopped by Brian's lab-bench. On request, he dispensed some tea and a 'bacon' roll. Delphinia asked for a black coffee and a slice of toast. Urn stepped back to watch the scientists tuck in. Both exchanged glances before first sniffing and then tentatively sipping their drinks. Finding them palatable, their whole bodies seemed to relax. Delphinia took a bite of her toast.

"Hmm, lovely," she said, perking up and nodding to her husband in appreciation. "Very yummy. Try your bacon roll, dear."

Brian sank his teeth into the roll with an eagerness he was to regret half a second later. "*Gung!*" he yelled. And then, "Bleurgh!" He spat out a mouthful of the roll, gagging and spluttering.

Horrified at such a strongly negative reaction to the 'bacon-lite', Urn staggered back several paces in dismay. He had neither the time nor the presence of mind to look where he was going and suddenly found himself caught in the tangle of pipework Delphinia had so studiously ensured he avoid. Drawing on instincts he didn't know he possessed, the teabot began lashing out in a bid to escape the clutches of the giant squid-like creature that he feared had ambushed him.

"Nooooo!" screamed Delphinia.

"*Gung!*" cried Brian.

The thickest of the waste pipes was torn from its ceiling bracket and hissed and danced like a snake, spraying its pressurized contents around the room. The two scientists' pristine white lab coats were splattered with brown matter of an unknown provenance that was best left unknown.

Finally free, Little Urn wheeled himself in front of the lab bench under which the two humans had taken cover.

"Another cup of tea?" asked the robot peering under the table.

But even Urn could see, from the expressions on their dirty faces, that his question was not well timed. Not waiting for a reply he engaged reverse gear and exited the laboratory with as little fuss as possible. After a brief stop to wipe the glass of his bun cabinet, he carried on with his assignment.

*

Zak's cabin was in darkness. Urn drew back the curtain to a small window that looked out onto the rainforest biome. A large, covered mound on the bed stirred and groaned.

"What d'yer want?" grumbled a croaking voice from deep under the duvet.

Urn blinked his optics and displayed his wares as best he could, given there were no eyes trained in his direction to actually view what he had to offer.

"Tea or Coffee?" asked the bot.

Finally, a bleary eye peered out from under the cover. "Oh, it's you, Urn. Got any Shroom tea, roboman?"

Urn shrugged, bleeped a note to reflect his lack of comprehension and wiped his bun display.

"You know, Shroom tea. Tea made from the magic fungus?"

Still not having understood anything the strange human was saying, Urn turned to go.

"Wait," called Zak. "Just leave a cup of hot water, Mr Beverage Transporter. Zakkie'll make his own." The bleary eye disappeared.

Urn extracted a clean cup and saucer from his crockery drawer and filled the cup with piping hot water. But there was a problem. Zak's bedside table was covered in packets of pills and assorted paraphernalia. There was no room for the cup and saucer.

He scanned for other available surfaces, but all tables and ledges were full. The only flattish area the teabot could see happened to be the summit of the human lump in the bed. So he balanced the cup and saucer of scalding water there. Congratulating himself on his ingenuity, Urn left.

After ten or eleven revolutions of his casters along the corridor floor, his sound receptors picked up a scream of intense pain, closely followed by the shattering of crockery. He shrugged and continued.

*

Cutting across the rainforest biome, Little Urn heard a noise coming from the observation platform high above him. One of the colonists was up there, perhaps looking out at the Martian landscape.

Urn changed course and made his way to the base of the vertical travellator. There was a click and a hum as it engaged and lifted him at a snail's pace to the look-out deck. There, Harry Fortune was gazing out at the bleak red desert having entered the dark despair of his 'artistic' side, unaware of Urn's arrival.

Also there, was a robotic arm clutching a paintbrush. The arm belonged to HarVard and the platform constituted his 'artist's garret' where he indulged his passion for oil painting. His latest work-in-progress was mounted on an easel, some of its paint still glistening and wet.

"What do you think?" HarVard was asking Harry. "Should I give the cowboy a moustache?"

Harry examined the painting. "What cowboy?" he asked.

"The cowboy. On the horse."

Harry tilted his head first one way, and then the other, but could make out neither horse nor rider.

The robot arm scooped up a brush full of thick black paint from the palette and hovered over the canvas, awaiting Harry's decision.

"Er, you decide," said Harry with a shrug.

"I value your judgement."

Before Harry could tell HarVard not to bother, a thick black gob of paint had dripped onto the canvas. The supercomputing artist stabbed the brush onto the wet surface and prodded the black paint around as if he knew what he was doing.

Taking this as a clue to the location of the cowboy, Harry looked again at the painting. He imagined it to be like one of those 'magic eye images' where the picture suddenly snaps into place – except this one didn't.

"As a fellow artist you'll understand how restrictive Mars is for a supercomputer with my talent."

"Restrictive?"

"Exactly. I knew you'd agree. I must find a wider, more appreciative audience for my work."

A *Ding!* made him turn around and become aware of Little Urn's patient presence.

"Tea?"

The poet's head dropped and he waved a dismissive hand at the robot. "All life is meaningless," he mused. "We cannot paper over the tragedy of our existence with a hot beverage."

Urn turned to leave, but HarVard's voice stayed him. "Ah, Urn. Just in time. What do you think of my latest work?"

Urn scanned the supercomputer's artwork. He detected a large brown splodge with four stick legs poking out from underneath it, above which was a bearded two-legged splodge, possibly wearing a hat.

"It's rubbish," said Urn.

"Huh?"

Something clicked deep inside the teabot and data from his CPU streamed through his voice-box.

"Possibly the worst I have ever seen in my life."

"Yes, alright, thank you for your insightful comment."

"The composition is unbalanced; the drawing skills of the artist are negligible ..."

"Thank you, Mobile Catering Unit. You've made your point."

"... the colours jar and the scene lacks depth and emotional engagement with the viewer. In short, this painting is sh ..."

"That's quite enough, teabot. It's clear you know nothing about art. Now return to your duties immediately."

"Was he about to tell you it was shit?" Harry asked.

"I hardly think so, Mr Fortune. Why on earth would he say such a thing?"

Meanwhile, Little Urn was descending the travellator with a strange sensation in his circuits. An excitement, a vision, even. Something had changed in the little bot. Something had become clearer. Deep inside his tin casing he felt he was wasted as a mere dispenser of light snacks and liquid refreshment. He now recognized that his true calling was to be an art critic.

*

But, ever the consummate professional, Little Urn continued with his round. Next up were the Faerydae quarters. Urn noted that two of the names had been crossed off his list, so this should be a quick one. As he approached the door, he could hear a loud voice inside. With a knock, he entered.

Adorabella, dressed in black from head to foot, her hair the sort of mess that even a witch might have taken a comb to, was talking to what looked like a small cloth doll in her hand. In the other hand was a long needle.

Urn halted with a *Ding*. "Tea? Coffee? Breakfast?"

Adorabella looked up and stared a crazed stare at the little bot. "Tea? Coffee? Breakfast?" she repeated as though they were the names of things she had once heard about, but could no longer place. "Have you come to comfort me now that I'm all alone?" As she spoke she stared through Urn, as though addressing someone behind him. "They've both left me, you know. First my philandering husband who could never keep that thing of his in his trousers. Then my boy; my beautiful, brave, foolish boy. Oh, I am so alone."

Urn was pretty sure this hadn't answered his question so he gave another *Ding* and repeated it.

"Oh, my boy!" wailed Adorabella. "He will never return. All I have left is Brokk – and I don't even have him. If I could just get him back, I won't be so solitary here. I still love him, you know. Oh, how I love him! And I forgive him. I forgive him his seedy dalliance with his assistant back on Earth. I forgive him the sordid Penny Smith business on *Mayflower III*. And the disgusting stuff with Commander Lionheart. I blame them all. You see, my husband can't help himself. He suffers from Obligatory Sexual Opportunism (OSO). I've been giving him homeopathic doses of knotweed oil ever since I met him, but they're taking their time to kick in."

Urn dithered, wondering whether it was worth trying the question a third time.

Adorabella looked down at the cloth doll in her hand and then threw it in the bin, tossing the needle onto her dresser. "How to get him back? How do I get him back? If only I had my potions ..." She dropped her wild-haired head into her hands.

A routine inside Urn's central processor timed out, triggering a 'time-being-wasted' flag and initiated the retreat response. He turned and left the room.

*

Last port of call was Commander Dugdale's cabin. Urn had deliberately left this place till last and now felt a certain reluctance to enter the quarters at all. He had heard so much from the other robots about this human – none of it positive. But as it was his duty, so he scanned his barcode and entered.

Flint was lying on the floor, the huge mound of his belly upwards, hands behind his head, straining every fibre of his being. With a huge grunt and a bulging of his eyes, he managed to raise his head and shoulders off the floor, but could only manage about six inches of a sit-up before collapsing back down again. He tried again, managing only four inches this time.

On the bed lay Disa, her face a bizarre collage of smudged lipstick, rouge and mascara. She reached one of her pincers across to the bedside table and picked up an e-cigarette. From her cleavage she withdrew a holder and plugged the cigarette into it before inserting it to her sink plunger lips. She pushed a worn looking button on her breast-plate marked 'suck' and took a deep drag before exhaling long and loud. Then she offered the cigarette to her lover on the floor.

"Not now, luv," croaked Dugdale, struggling to his feet on spotting Urn. "Can't yer see I'm trainin' fer t'match?" As he stood, he whacked his head against the ceiling. He swore and sat on the bed, rubbing his scalp. "No wonder me knees are so stiff if I can't even stand up straight in this piggin' place."

He turned to look at Urn and surveyed the teabot's wares.

"What, no pies?"

Urn shook his head. "No. But I have a bacon roll."

"Alright, give us one of them."

"Ketchup?"

"Are you friggin' joking me? It's Brown sauce with a bacon roll, lad. Don't they teach you owt at robot school?"

Urn set to preparing it, a little anxious about the reception it might get. Placing the roll on a plate, he extended a trembling arm to the commander.

Dugdale grabbed it off the plate and bit off about half the roll in one go. Urn watched him as he chewed, slipping into second gear and ready to engage turbo-drive for a hasty exit should the situation turn nasty.

But the commander kept chewing, his chubby cheeks distended with the sheer volume that he had taken into his mouth. After a few swallows, Dugdale started nodding his head. He raised the roll to indicate it to Urn. "Bloody great, that!" he said. "Nice bit of bacon."

And he thrust the rest of the roll into his gob.

28. Texts and the Single Girl

Willie scrolled through Penny's messages. There were a lot of them; she'd been a popular girl. Most of the messages were from the male members on board, including little Tarquin! Willie opened a message at random. It was a love poem from Harry:

> *It is no legend, it is no myth*
> *That I am in love with one Penny Smith*
> *She is so gorgeous; she is so fair*
> *Beautiful figure, lovely blonde hair.*
> *Voice like an angel, ...*

Willie stopped reading while still able to maintain control over his stomach contents. He flipped to one from Brokk – cryptic, like the man himself: "A jar at one." And another: "A jar for two." There were a few messages from Adorabella about Penny's course of treatment for an unspecified ailment; it seemed that the various crackpot therapies Adorabella had been trying hadn't been working. *What a surprise,* said Willie to himself. Brian Brush had sent a few messages inviting Penny to star-gazing sessions. Several messages were from Dugdale, but nothing of a personal nature; only general posts sent to all on board: his Rules of Conduct, times of Safety

Drills, times he intended occupying the Assembly Room and lists of programmes he intended to watch.

Nothing that offered a clue – and certainly nothing pointing at Dugdale.

Willie slapped the blablet shut and returned it to the locker.

"Damn," he said.

At the back of his mind, though, he felt he'd just missed a significant clue.

29. Game of Throw-ins

"On me 'ed! On me 'ed!" yelled Dugdale, as Brian Brush nutmegged Helmut, dribbled around Hansie and sprinted down the right wing of the BioDome's hastily readied five-a-side pitch. He flashed a perfectly weighted cross that smacked off the Commander's greasy fat head and, more by luck than design, spun beyond the outstretched fingers of Otto Bungelly and into the back of the net.

"Goal!" screamed Dugdale, his eyes bulging with the exultation of the moment. He pulled his custom-made Leeds United jersey over his head, exposing a beer gut that was even more unsightly than most would have imagined, and rushed towards the corner flag where he performed a tango with the flagpole. Brian, Gavin and Zak joined him, but merely to pat him on the back before retreating. Celebratory hugs, with the team captain in his current state of excitement, were out of the question.

"Well done, Mr. Flint!" shouted Miss Leach from the touchline, putting down her knitting. "What a jolly good scoring point."

Referee HarVard, dressed in black and standing with legs apart on his HologrAmbulator, blew the whistle and pointed to the centre spot. With only two minutes of extra time left, and the score at 2-1 to Botany Base, the Germans were keen to get the game restarted in the hope of a rapid equalizer.

The outcome of this match was important to everyone. Not only would it determine the winner of Flint and Helmut's wager but, perhaps more crucially, whether Germany or England would be the recipients of the first Mars World Cup.

As Flint continued his celebration at the corner flag, the holographic supercomputing referee sped up to him on his cart, brandishing a yellow card. "I'm cautioning you for removing your jersey, time-wasting and lewd conduct." HarVard took a pencil from his top pocket. "Name?"

"Come on, ref. I've just scored t'winning goal in the Mars World Cup! I'm allowed to celebrate aren't I?"

"Name, please?" insisted HarVard.

"You know what me chuffin' name is," said Dugdale defiantly.

"Less of the attitude, sonny, or it'll be a red card and you'll be taking an early bath. Now, what's your name?"

Dugdale scowled at him and muttered "Dugdale" before jogging slowly back to his own half.

HarVard carefully noted "Dumbdale" in his holographic notebook and sniggered at his own naughtiness, regretting that no one would ever know.

The German team, or the Germartians, were in a huddle, discussing tactics. Otto Bungelly had used the delay, and his brilliant mind, to come up with a flawless new strategy which he was urgently communicating in whispers to his teammates: Helmut, Hansie, Andy and Ulrich (the colonist formerly known as Brokk).

Dressed in his extra-baggy pre-war shorts, flapping inches above his ankles, Helmut took the kick-off, playing the ball to Otto. The rest of the German team immediately formed a tight circle around the large-headed German genius. Moving as a unit, they progressed towards the Botany Base goal.

"What are them chuffers up to?" muttered Dugdale as he stood and watched the tight formation chugging through his stunned team's ranks. "Oi, ref. They're rogueing us. Blow yer whistle!"

HarVard scanned his rulebook but found no contraventions in the German tactics. Indeed, he admired the arrow-like attack formation. And still the phalanx advanced, unimpeded, on goalkeeper Harry Fortune.

"Get into 'em, yer fuppin' wusses," Dugdale ordered his outfield teammates.

Zak made an attempt to breach the German configuration, but his outstretched boot only met Helmut's hard bony shin. Gavin and Brian jogged alongside the seemingly impenetrable attack unit, eyes searching for an opportunity to break through Otto's wing-men and the other eye on HarVard, whose whistle was poised to blow at the slightest infringement.

"I'll stop these cheatin' buggers meself," Dugdale fumed as he tracked back, racing faster and faster, and setting a collision course with the group.

Meanwhile, as Otto neared his target, his fantastic mind computed the ball trajectory required to score, unaware of the human express train approaching from behind. Before he could conclude his cunning plan, Flint had thrown his considerable body weight into a sliding tackle and the five Germartian players were felled like a rack of skittles. Alas, the force of the collision merely propelled the ball towards the goal.

On a very long list of things that Harry Fortune was completely useless at, football came near the top. Nobody had bothered asking him whether he'd actually ever kicked a football before – which he hadn't. Indeed, he probably never would. As the ball rolled towards him he readied himself to hoof it high up into BioDome space-frame trusses to claim glory for his team. What could be easier? With a level of nonchalance never before attained on a football pitch, he jogged out of the goal and swung his right boot at the approaching football. Unhappily, he experienced a bit of a 'Joe Hart moment': his standing foot skidded, his kicking foot missed and, as he commenced an unplanned but spectacular low gravity backward somersault, the ball continued its stately roll along the ground and over the goal line.

HarVard's whistle blew for a goal. *Tweee.* And then, a moment later for the end of the match.

Tweeeeee. Tweeeeee. Tweeeeeeeeeeeeeeeeeeeee.

The Germartians were jubilant while the English contingent sank to their knees in dejection.

With the final score tied at 2-2, the first ever Mars World Cup would be decided by a penalty shoot-out.

Harry Fortune lay on his back pretending to be dead. Sensing blame-waves wafting over him from team captain Dugdale he deemed this the best strategy. If he lifted his head, he feared Flint's boot would appear out of nowhere and kick it clean off his shoulders.

"Can't fault the somersault," said Zak Johnston as he bent over Fortune's prostrate body. "A ten for your fall. A zero for missing the ball." Still Harry acted the corpse, not moving a muscle. "Hey man, don't worry about Duggers, he looks cool with it ... NOT! Just lost us the World Cup and the *Mayflower*, that's all."

Harry opened an eye. "We've not lost yet. It's penalties."

Zak gave him a pitying look. "England v Germany? Penalty shoot-out? You do the maths, goalie-guy."

Suddenly aware that Flint had struggled to his feet and was limping over, Zak quickly vacated the crime scene.

But Flint appeared outwardly calm as he offered the poet a hand. There was even a smile on his face. "Eyup, Barry lad, football's a funny old game, int it," he said. "Don't beat yerself up over it. I'll tell you a story ..."

The two teams looked on in surprise as Dugdale, still limping, led his goalkeeper to the far side of the pitch, his arm draped over the other man's shoulders in an apparent act of consolation. Then Dugdale made a small but sudden movement and Harry dropped to his knees groaning.

Dugdale jogged back, hobbling slightly, to talk to referee HarVard. "Ref, I need to substitute me chuffin' goalkeeper for t'penalty shoot-out. Would you believe it, t'daft beggar has gone and aggravated an old groin injury so he can't play."

"I hope you didn't inflict the injury on purpose," said HarVard with a raised eyebrow. "You're already on a yellow card, you know. Another and you're off."

"Come on ref. Poor ol' Barry's knackered 'is knackers. I gorra gerra sub on."

"Very well. You may bring on your substitute."

As he approached the colonists sitting alongside the pitch, Flint's heart sank. *Where am I goin' to find a decent goalie in this gormless rabble?* he asked himself. "Eyup, you lot. I need a volunteer to go in t'goal and unfortunately it's gorra be one of you useless wastes of space."

Adorabella remained immobile in her lotus position, pretending to be deep in meditation. This was her attempt at getting husband Brokk back: by playing hard to get, cool and indifferent. So far, it wasn't working, with Brokk having barely acknowledged her existence. Next to her, Delphinia was wrestling Tarquin's arm down in case Dugdale noticed him.

"Oooh I say, how exciting," said Miss Leach. "I'd love to play kickball. Netball's my game, but this looks fun too."

"You're good at netball?" asked Flint, grasping at even the tiniest crumb of hope.

"Not really, Mr. Flint. I used to be the match scorer. I was fairly good at that, except when I got the score wrong."

Dugdale sighed. "I s'pose you can't be any worse than t'last clown. Go on then, Leachy, strip off and get yer arse over t'goal."

"Strip off? What kind of lady do you think I am, Mr Flint? If anything I shall be wearing an extra cardigan."

"Whatever."

*

With the captains in the centre circle, HarVard flipped a holographic coin to decide the order of play.

"Three penalties each. Then sudden death if you're still level," said the referee.

"Und heads it is," said Helmut. "Deutschland wins ze toss! We vill go first. Good luck, Herr Kapitan, und try not to think of the many penalty shoot-outs England have lost over decades of German superiority."

"Yeah, alright, Fritz, 'appen we'll see about that."

First up was Andy Marsman. He carefully placed the ball on the penalty spot and flicked the mop of black hair from his eyes and twitched his toothbrush moustache. Miss Leach put her unfinished knitted bonnet next to a goal post and wandered to the middle of the goal as HarVard blew his whistle for the kick to be taken.

Andy gave a camp little wave to attract Emily's attention and touched the corner of his mouth to indicate that her lipstick was smudged. Instantly she whipped out a tiny mirror and turned away to make the necessary make-up adjustments. Meanwhile the crafty German took aim and side-footed the ball with sufficient pace to send it over the goal line.

"Goal!" he shouted and punched the air.

One-nil to Germany.

"Oh, fiddle-sticks," said Emily, retrieving her knitting.

Dugdale was about to make an objection about the German's cheating, but was silenced by HarVard pointing to the pocket where he kept the red card.

Botany Base's first penalty taker was Gavin. He sauntered to the spot with an air of cockiness and performed a few keepy-uppies before placing the ball down.

There was no need for Otto Bungelly to try and spook him – his extraordinarily large head managed that without the need for any tricks. Nevertheless, as a boy, Otto had seen enough FC Kaiserslautern matches to understand the sort of gamesmanship expected of a goalie. So, he crossed his eyes, poked out his tongue, stuck his thumbs in his ears, waggled his fingers, and began rhythmically thrusting his massive pair of shorts toward the teenager.

Full of the confidence of youth, Gavin ran at full pelt towards the ball and, at the last second, looked up just long enough to be put off by Otto's ridiculous head and ridiculous performance. His toe-punt sent the ball straight into the middle of the German's forehead.

"Ouch, shitzen-blitzen!" cried Otto, or at least, that's what it sounded like.

"Good savings, Otto!" shouted Helmut.

The Botany Base crowd groaned. Back in the centre circle, Flint vented his frustration via the medium of swearing.

"Is only a game, innit," said Gavin as he slipped into the long grass of the savannah sector of the BioDome.

Next up was Ulrich von Brokkenhorst, aka Brokk. As he faced Emily Leach she stared at him with her severest "Who's been a naughty boy, then" expression. "Turncoat," she muttered during his run-up. Perhaps it was that that did it. Or perhaps his conscience, or his former loyalties, or his complete uselessness at football. Whatever it was, he scuffed his shot and the ball barely reached the spinster.

"Did I put you off?" asked Emily, leaning down to pick up the stationary ball. She held it up to him. "Would you like another try?"

"No friggin' way!" roared Dugdale rushing to her and snatching the ball away before handing it to Brian Brush.

The scientist looked nervous as he walked over to the penalty spot. The crowd were chanting: "You can do it, Brushy", "Crush it, Brush", "Don't make us sad, Dad" and finally, from Mr Snuggles, "Chuffin' welly it."

Brian set the ball and adjusted his glasses. He had observed that Otto was right handed. Knowledge was power. He had read somewhere that 72% of right handed goalkeepers dive to their right.

Tweee.

Otto began his comic pelvic thrusts. But the shattered lenses of Brian's glasses meant that, beyond the outline of the goal, he could see very little. With absolute precision he angled his foot so that the toe of his boot pointed just inside Otto's left hand goal post and prodded the ball along its prescribed route. Sure enough, the German goalkeeper flung himself to his right. The net bulged on the left.

"Goal!" the crowd screamed and mobbed a beaming Brian.

One-one.

Twee, Twee, Tweeeeeeee.

"One goal apiece," announced the referee. "One penalty each left and it's the turn of the captains."

Jogging down the pitch in his ridiculous long shorts, Helmut looked supremely confident.

"Don't be concerned, Miss Leach," he said. "I will kick ze ball nice and gently directly at you so it is very easy to save."

"Thank you, Mr von Grommel. You are such a gentleman." Emily hitched up her skirt revealing her frilly petticoat and crouched in readiness to catch a slow-rolling football.

Tweee.

With the skill of a seasoned professional, Helmut shaped a penalty kick that planted the ball in the top right corner of the goal; the ball was past Emily before she even had time to blink.

Two-one to Germany.

"Oops, sorry. I have accidentally scored the goal that will most likely win the Mars World Cup for the glory of the German nation. I can only apologise for my poor aim."

"That's perfectly alright. We all make mistakes." Emily collected her knitting and headed back to her seat.

All eyes now turned to Commander Dugdale. The hopes and dreams of Botany Base, and indeed England, rested on their team captain who had already marched up to the spot and was making thug-like gestures at Otto.

This was the big one. To him, this was the single most important moment of his whole life. Far more important than becoming the first man on Mars, which, as it had turned out, he hadn't been. The consequences of missing this were too horrible to contemplate.

Somehow, though, the British contingent knew what was coming. The signs were all there: the excessively long run-up, the confidence of the German players and, most of all, History.

So, when the ball ballooned over the crossbar in Waddlesque style and Flint dropped to the ground in a crumpled heap, no one was in the least bit surprised.

Part 3

1. Mars Bard

Harry Fortune sat back in his cabin nursing his football injury and admiring his work: a poem about the first ever international football match on Mars. He'd been working on it for a solid hour, writing and rewriting, but now he had managed to craft it as close to perfection as his talents allowed. As a smile played about his lips, he read it through one more time.

> *Greatest match e'er on Mars*
> *In the BioDome beneath the stars.*
> *Dugdale's wager, most unwise,*
> *With Mayflower III as the prize.*
> *There we sat beside the pitch,*
> *Coin was tossed and teams did switch.*
> *Our best player, he was missin',*
> *Swallowed by a giant chicken.*
> *Harry Fortune took his place,*
> *Wow, that man's the best in Space!*
> *Mars's gravity gave no traction*
> *Lots of goals and lots of action.*
> *Penalty shoot-out, we stood no chance*

Them being Germany and not France.
Sure enough, their captain scored
While o'er crossbar our ball soared.
And with that the match was lost,
Just a game, but at what cost?

He flipped his blablet closed and looked out at the red desert beyond his cabin window. To think that he was the first ever Poet in Residence on a new world. A sense of pride filled him. He felt he was hitting top form, just when he needed to. Things were looking up.

2. Pseudy Garlands

"Mind if I join you?" called Brian Brush jogging to catch up with his youngest son.

"Sure, Dad," said Tarquin without enthusiasm as he crunched along the Martian sand. He paused, head downcast, until his father was level and then carried on walking, not once looking up.

"Where are we going?"

Tarquin gave a frown which his father failed to notice behind the tinted space helmet visor. "I'm following Mr Snuggles."

"Oh, right," said Brian, looking ahead where he spotted the little robot in amongst a small cluster of larger builder bots all moving in the same direction. "I obviously asked the wrong question, then. Where is Mr Snuggles going?"

Tarquin shrugged. "With the other robots. They're teaching him wireless communication."

Brian nodded. "Clearly, I'm still asking the wrong question. *The first step to solving a problem is identifying the right question to ask.* Albert Einstein. So, let's try this one: where are the robots heading?"

Tarquin walked on without responding.

"Well?"

"The Wianki Festival."

"Ah, the Wianki Festival," mused Brian, nodding his head. "And what, pray, is that?"

Tarquin sighed. "It's a Polish thing. The *robotniki* celebrate it every year. Tude and Eve are taking Mr Snuggles to show him. They like him hanging out with them."

"Excellent! Be good for him to make friends with his own kind and learn a new language."

Tarquin didn't respond.

Up ahead, Mr Snuggles, holding hands between Tude and Eve had started exchanging back-slaps with some of the other bots. These escalated to matey pushes and what appeared to be robotic laughter.

Brian's smile vanished on seeing his boy's downcast head. "Oh, I think I get it. You feel you're losing him, don't you. He has a new family of his own kind and doesn't spend so much time with you anymore." Brian sighed. "Well, son, when I was your age I had a friend. Steve Plum was his name. We did everything together – experiments with our chemistry sets, assembling electronic devices, re-enacting famous historical battles. Then, one day, for no reason I could fathom, Steve started hanging out with girls. Became obsessed with them. I couldn't see what the attraction was." He gave a shudder, but then quickly added, "Until I met your mother, of course."

For a moment Brian lingered on the sadness he had felt back then. He reached out a space-gloved hand to ruffle his son's hair, but could only pat the top of the boy's space helmet. A small tear formed in the corner of his eye.

*

They walked on in silence for a while, stepping over rocks and stones, following the posse of robots ahead.

"Dad?" said Tarquin at last. "Did we really lose *Mayflower III* to the Germans?"

Brian gave a laugh at the unexpectedness of the question. "Sure did, buddy. But it's not so bad. They take our spaceship, we get their vast, fully-equipped base, with air, food, water and giant chickens. It's a win-win. We stay here for two years, as planned, and then get picked up by *Mayflower IV*."

"I guess."

"And," added his father, looking around to make sure no one could hear them. "We can have a closer look at that base of theirs. Maybe work out how, who, or what constructed it. I am *very* interested in working out what is really going on there!" He went to tap the side of his nose, but merely ended up poking his helmet's faceplate.

Up ahead, the coggle of robots had reached a cave entrance in the rocks and were trooping through it. Brian and Tarquin increased their pace to catch up.

Inside, a rough passageway, lit by a string of fluorescent lights that the *robotniki* had hung from the rock ceiling, descended to a large cavern. There, a gang of Polish worker bots were preparing for the festival, smearing *Brasso* metal cleaner over each other's battered metalwork and buffing it up to a sparkling shine. Tude and Eve joined in and started working on Mr Snuggles's chrome plating. The sight made Tarquin look away.

"So, tell me about this Wianki Festival," asked Brian, to distract his boy.

"HarVard told me 'wianki' is Polish for garlands of flowers. They are placed on a river and allowed to float downstream. It's some sort of fertility ceremony. Because we're on Mars, the *robotniki* don't have any flowers so, instead, they use garlands of brightly coloured electrical wiring."

"I see. And 'because we're on Mars' – what do they use for a river?"

"Er, they use a river?" responded Tarquin, pointing to an eroded channel in the cave floor through which a lively stream of darkish water was coursing.

"*Gung!*" exclaimed Brian, his eyes nearly bursting out of their sockets. He reached for his camera and started filming. "This is a major scientific discovery – right there, Tarq! Before our very eyes. Flowing water on Mars! An underground river!"

*

Oblivious of the major scientific discovery, the *robotniki* busied themselves with their bodywork. Maciek smeared *Brasso* up and down Witek's thigh panels until he detected the pleasing reflection of his own faceplate.

<Who you propose to for Wianki?> he asked.

Witek cracked a smile. <Minka. With Minka I settle down. Maybe make leetle *robotniki* together. Which one you have optics on? Dorota? She unattached.>

<Oh, no. Robots without fluid drainage tube look silly,> replied

Maciek as he admired the highly polished area between Witek's thighs.

Witek, suddenly feeling uncomfortable, edged away down a side tunnel towards the main festival. <Witek must go find Minka for playing noo-noo,> he transmitted in a noticeably lower frequency. And then was gone.

<Whatever,> sighed Maciek with a dismissive head flick that redirected his head camera toward Rysio. Grabbing his tin of *Brasso* and polishing rag, he set off after his new interest.

*

Brian was busily photographing the underground river and taking samples of the water using the test tubes he had happily remembered to bring with him. Every now and then he would pause to let one of the garlands of electrical wiring float by.

"Dad, what's this?" Tarquin called out from behind him.

"Just a sec," said Brian, plugging his latest sample with a stopper. Then he turned around to see what his boy had found. "*Gung!*" he exclaimed, staring at the wooden crate Tarquin was pointing at. "First impression, Tarq, is that it's a crate of high explosives!"

"That was my first impression, too, Dad, given the large lettering on the side saying 'HIGH EXPLOSIVES'. But I didn't want to be unscientific by jumping to any unfounded conclusions."

Brian gave his boy a curious look, but said nothing. He stepped over to the crate and unhooked the latch. Using the smallest of movements, he raised the lid. The first thing they saw inside was a plunger-type detonator and a roll of wire atop stacks and stacks of dynamite."

"*Gung!*"

"Wow!"

Brian replaced the lid. "I think the Commander will be very interested to see this little haul."

"What do you think it means, Dad? Does it belong to the Germans? What are they planning to do with it? Why is it here? Are there more like it?"

Brian raised a hand to stop the flow of his boy's questions. "Let's get the bots to carry it back to base, shall we. And then we can try to puzzle it all out."

3. A Touch of Wind

For several hours an anxious Bernard had been swirling and whirling around Botany Base, observing the Bloodbag invaders and their Panhead allies. In his windy hand he held a letter he hoped would end the war and bring peace in his time. As he whistled around the base's perimeter, he tried to summon the courage to deliver it. But when, at last, that courage came, he could find neither a letterbox nor a convenient flowerpot to safely leave his important missive.

He flew to the entrance and, with dusty air-fists, pounded on the outer airlock door. He twirled, waiting for an answer. But there was no answer.

As he drew back, Bernard spotted a miniature Bloodbag gazing mournfully through one of the base's windows, a tear crawling down its cheek. Even though the small Bloodbag was looking straight at him it did not show so much as a flicker of acknowledgement of the Great Leader of the Wind People. Furious, Bernard waved his letter at the young boy and blew sand against the window pane. "Over here, mini-Bloodbag. Duh, like, open the door."

For a second or two, Tarquin seemed to follow the spiralling flight of the letter before snapping back into gloomy contemplation. Bernard tried throwing more sand and even small pebbles to attract the boy's attention. But nothing.

"How rude these Bloodbags are!" he hissed, whooshing off in a huff. He whirled high into the sky. "Blow peace! Blow it, I say. These barbarians clearly aren't interested in concord and friendship. They leave me no choice but War!"

As he stormed off towards the Wind troop encampment in Windy Point Canyon, something caught his attention, making him apply his air-brakes. Perched on a ledge above the mighty canyon was a large box he knew had been built by the Panheads. It gave him an idea. Perhaps the hard-skinned Panheads would be more amenable to receipt of the letter. Perhaps they would even pass it on to the invaders from E'Arth.

Bernard spiralled down towards the structure with his letter spinning in his turbulent wake. Through transparent walls, he spied several hard and shiny Panheads. Although not as hideous as the Bloodbags, these creatures were still repugnant to a lifeform that measured beauty in the purity of the swirling patterns it made in the sand. Another Panhead was approaching from afar, battling its way across the wind-swept desert. Sensing a golden opportunity for the delivery of his peace treaty, Bernard spun in a tight vortex above the Panheads' lair and waited for the lone creature to come nearer.

Finally, when it had reached the door and was knocking with its metal appendage, Bernard seized the moment. He swept down and arrived at the door just as it was opening. "How do, friend? I am Bernard, leader of the Wind People."

The Panhead stopped and looked over its shoulder, first one way and then the other. Bernard thrust out a turbulent gust that rippled the air around the Panhead's appendage, giving it a shake of greeting. "I come in pea ..."

But before Bernard could finish his sentence, the Panhead had disappeared inside and the door had slammed shut in his blustery face. He billowed backwards in a mixture of disappointment, rejection and rage.

"How dare they!" he howled, gasping in disbelief. "Right, that does it! The final straw. Treating me like a common draught! I will show them the power and the sheer blowiness of Bernard the Great, Mighty Ruler of the Winds of M'Ars!"

With that, he roared down into the canyon below to make ready for a new and terrible conflict.

*

THE WORST MAN ON MARS

<Come in, Dura, come in,> signalled Tude, ushering him. As Dura entered, the handle was whisked from Tude's grasp and the door slammed shut. <Wow, breezy today. Take your dust-cover off and let me hang it up for you.>

Dura looked a little shaken. <Did you hear a voice just now?>

<Voice? No, probably just the wind.>

<It touched me on the shoulder and called me 'friend'.>

Tude gave him a strange look. <You've been working too hard, comrade.> He took Dura's protective dust-cover and hung it on a hook by the door, next to several high-viz jackets emblazoned 'Robotany Base'. <Thanks for coming. Eve and I have a little surprise waiting in there.> He winked one of his optics.

<And I have a little house-warming surprise for you.> Dura thrust a four litre can of Castrol 75W-140 hypoid gear-oil into Tude's arms and, in a low-powered whisper, transmitted, <Squirt some of this stuff onto Eve's differentials and watch her go!>

Tude's lenses lit up like 20 Watt halogen light-bulbs as he placed the gift on a shelf in the hallway. Then he said, <Come meet the others.>

Had Dura known that 'the others' consisted of the lovely Tina accompanied by that dead-leg Len, he would have turned on his heels and motored straight out of Tude's abode.

There they both were, relaxing on a sofa. Dura nearly choked at the sight of Len's jagged arm-appendage draped over Tina's delicate shoulder panels. He shot a furious look at Tude, but the site foreman merely shrugged.

<Hi, Dura,> Tina said in her attractive, tinkling, sing-song voice. <How are you?>

To his dismay, Dura found his face-lights glowing from the powerful currents surging through them. He managed an embarrassed smile.

<Alright?> called Len with a smug grin, pressing Tina closer to him.

Dura ground his metal jaws.

<Has Tude told you about the Big Surprise?> asked Tina, pointing to a large cardboard box in the centre of the room. <He refuses to tell us what it is?>

Tude rubbed his digits with glee. <As soon as Eve finishes 'getting ready'.> He turned to Dura and indicated the armchair. <Have a seat and take the weight off your wheels.>

But no sooner had Dura set off towards the armchair than he found it suddenly occupied by Mr Snuggles, sitting with his feet on a cube-shaped footrest, and swigging from an empty can of *Stallion* lager. Dura screeched to a halt, wondering where the little robot had sprung from. Mr Snuggles emitted the sort of revolting burp even Dugdale would have been proud of.

<Mr Snuggles. Please!> tweeted Tude, wagging a spiny finger. The small robot merely took another imaginary swig from his can and smacked his metal lips.

Tude cast a disapproving look before turning to the others to explain. <Eve and I have adopted Mr Snuggles. Still a few rough edges to iron out in his character.>

<Congratulations,> cried Len and Tina simultaneously.

Meanwhile, Dura had eased his heavyweight rear assemblage onto a metal bench facing the sofa. He made a point of avoiding ocular contact with Len and Tina by staring at the large box on the floor between them.

<I'll get some nuts,> said Tude, shuffling off into the kitchen.

Silence.

Four pairs of optics stared at the box. Mr Snuggles slurped from the empty lager can and let out another burp.

Silence.

Tina nudged Len, and flicked her head in Dura's direction, but Len merely shook his head and folded his appendages. She nudged him again.

With a sigh, Len leaned forward and, with deliberate formality, said, <So, Robot En-*Dura*-nce. How goes it with the installation of the Handsfrees in the Gents'?> There was a crackle of static in Len's transmission which sounded a bit like a snigger.

Dura bristled. <You having a pop, Robot Benevo-*Len*-ce?>

<What if I am? What you going to do about it?> Len made to get up from the soft sofa, but as he did so, a flailing arm knocked a beaker of hot gear-oil onto the side table. The thick black substance spilt across the table and down onto the freshly laid concrete.

<Now look what you've done, you oaf!> cried Dura, pointing an accusing digit. <Oil. All over Eve's clean floor slab. That stain will never come out.>

<Well, it's your fault. You provoked me.>

<My fault! How is it my fault? You were about to attack me!>

<I was not.>

<You were.>

<Was not.>

<Gentlebots, gentlebots,> beseeched Tude, returning with a bowl of assorted stainless steel fixings. <Calm yourselves. It's just a drop of oil. A sprinkling of iron filings will soon bring the stain out. Will you guys sort yourselves out? Why not shake appendages and let bygones be bygones?>

<Well spoken, Tude!> put in Tina.

The two bots hung their heads and rocked backwards and forwards on their tracks. Then, still not looking up, Len extended a big shovel hand towards Dura. For a moment Dura hesitated. But then, sensing Tina's eyes on him, he clattered his plastering trowel hand into Len's shovel.

<There,> said Tude with a nod. <Friends again. Where would we be without friends? Without friends there is just loneliness and misery.>

4. Thrifty Shades of Grey

A few moments later it was all <Oohs> and <Ahhhs> as Eve made her grand entrance wearing a chic gown decorated with sparkling lights that might once have hung on a Christmas tree. When the guests had finished complimenting her they switched to congratulating the couple on their splendid living quarters.

Tude puffed out his chest. <Three years of hard work. Evenings and weekends. Designed it myself, down to the last nut and bolt. Planned it all out on a piece of graph-paper. Gotta have plans, I always say. Without plans you're just leaking in the dark.> Tude swung an arm around the room. <You'll notice everything is straight edges and right-angles. Not a curve in sight – apart from the sofa and armchair (not my choice). Can't abide curves; completely illogical. By far the most effective way of joining any two points is a straight line. End of.>

Dura surveyed the bland design and, for want of anything better to say, asked, <New metric or old?>

<Old, of course. Must uphold traditions!>

<Love the colour scheme,> said Tina.

<My contribution,> said Eve with a modest smile. <I got the idea from *Battleship Monthly Magazine,* where the designers had used nothing but various shades of grey.>

<Nice.>

<Grey paint is so economical.>

<Ooh, and where did you get those shutters?>

Eve grinned proudly and scooted over to one of the windows to give a demonstration. She pressed a button and, with a whirring noise, a set of grey steel window grilles, more suited to a nuclear fall-out shelter, started to lower, finally slamming shut with a clank. <Pretty, aren't they? Just something I ran up on the welding machine using radiation screens I found lying around Robotany Base.>

"The dog's bollocks," commented Mr Snuggles, scratching himself between the legs and making a nerve-shredding grating noise.

Tude swivelled to face him. <Mr Snuggles! I think we need to have a word about your behaviour. Right now!> He pointed towards the door of his private workshop.

*

Tude closed the door behind him and switched to encrypted mode. <Now then, young robot, you're going to have to buck your ideas up.>

The delinquent robot, seated on a workbench, was swinging his tin legs and looking about the room with a nonchalant air.

<You've picked up a lot of bad habits from the humans, particularly their commander, and you're embarrassing Eve and me in front of our friends.>

Mr Snuggles reached for some wire off-cuts lying on the bench and began idly twisting them into the figure of a tiny stick man with an overlarge stomach.

<Are you even listening to what I'm saying?>

Mr Snuggles shrugged and continued fiddling.

<Put that down and wipe that silly grin off your face!> Tude swung an appendage to knock the stickman out of the young robot's pincers. No sooner had he done so than he was filled with shock at his own actions. <See what you've driven me to?>

"Chuff off. You're not my real dad."

Tude staggered back at the words, but managed to control his volume. <Wireless communication only, please. There'll be none of that monkey-talk around here. Remember, you're a robot. You belong with a robot family.>

<Whatever.>

<That's better. Now get back in there. We're about to open The Surprise.>

<Wow, can't wait.>

<And if you don't behave, mister, you'll be grounded – no recharging for a week.>

<So unfair.> Mr Snuggles jumped down from the workbench and ambled towards the door, dragging his feet as he went.

Tude watched him go. Then, on an impulse, he performed a wireless scan of the little robot's memory chips. In a desktop recycling bin, among beer-making instructions, pie recipes and jpegs of ladybots, he found a file containing a transcript of their recent conversation, discarded and ready for deletion.

*

<Let's open the surprise,> said Tude as he returned from the workshop.

<Let's!> Eve and Tina clapped their hands in excitement.

The site foreman bot flicked open a box-cutter attachment on his right appendage and started cutting the plastic ties and tape. <It's one of Zilli's very last efforts – made just before she disappeared.>

Tina uttered a shriek. <In that case, I know what it is!>

Eve beamed at her and gave her a wink, while Dura and Len exchanged puzzled shrugs. Mr Snuggles, slumped back in the armchair, took a swig of *Stallion* and stared at the box with a glazed look.

Tude finished ripping open the box's edges and laid out its sides to reveal a beautiful babybot. It looked like a human toddler, but with features exaggerated for maximum cuteness. Tude activated it by pulling one of the ear lobes, and two huge blue eyes blinked at them.

Eve leaned forward and lifted her new baby to her chest-plate. <Aah, he's perfect,> she sighed.

<She,> corrected Tude.

<Are you sure? What's this dangly thing?>

<Just an overflow pipe.> Tude unlatched a pair of loppers and snipped the protruding plastic tube. Both Len and Dura winced and looked away. <Definitely a girlbot.>

<She's beautiful,> Tina was saying. <Mr Snuggles will have a sister!>

At this, the lager-swilling robot perked up.

<What are you going to call her?> asked Tina.

<I'd like to call her Truth, short name Ruth,> said Eve.

Tina nodded politely.

<Truth is good,> said Tude, taking the wriggling babybot from Eve. <Without truth the world would be full of lies and deceit.>

The tiny robot swivelled her head back towards Eve and signalled, <I'd rather be called Beyoncé, if it's all the same with you, Mother.>

Eve emitted a high frequency yelp. <She can speak!>

Tude was rattling with amusement. <Zilli installed an advanced, top-of-the-range AI system.>

<Too right she did,> said the girlbot. <I'm fully programmed to communicate in 128 languages, straight from the box. I also have quick-release body parts to allow replacement by larger limbs as I mature.>

<They grow up so fast these days,> observed Tina.

Beyoncé swivelled her head again. <So, where's my bro', then?>

Robo-optics turned to the armchair, now empty apart from a dent where Mr Snuggles had been sitting. A crushed lager can balanced on the arm.

<Where can he be?> asked Eve.

<I think I saw him heading towards the recharging cupboards,> transmitted Dura, pointing at a line of cubicles in the hallway, one of which had its door closed.

Tude gave a knowing nod. <I expect it's 'new-sibling displacement jealousy'. I saw a documentary about it. The older sibling feels rejected and unwanted, sensing it has to compete for its parents' time and affection.>

<Oh dear, poor Mr Snuggles,> said Tina.

<Ah, diddums,> said Beyoncé, wriggling free of Tude's hold. She skipped over to the recharging cupboard and tapped gently on the door. <Oh, big brother. Come on out.>

Silence.

Beyoncé tapped again. <Pretty please.>

They heard the door being unlocked from the inside. A crack appeared. Beyoncé stepped aside and reached her tiny arm through the gap. Taking him gently by the hand, she led Mr Snuggles to Eve.

Eve gazed down at the two small figures and, in that moment, her system underwent a profound change as circuit-warming feelings swept through her body. She crouched and opened her arms, ready to embrace the mechanical children that would make her family complete.

But at that moment, Beyoncé swung the startled Mr Snuggles around her body like an Olympic hammer thrower, before letting go and sending him clattering into Eve's chest, almost knocking her over.

<Here's the deal, Mother,> she spat. <Either that heap of junk goes, or I go!>

*

<He'll be fine,> said Tude as they watched Mr Snuggles trudging across the Martian desert towards the distant outline of Botany Base, kicking out at small rocks as he went. <He can't get lost.>

<I don't like him going back to the humans,> transmitted Eve. <Who knows what other bad habits he'll pick up?>

<He won't be there long. Just while Beyoncé adjusts to her new life. And then he'll be back and we'll be a proper robo-family.>

Tude closed the door and they returned to the living room, their mood sombre.

<I'll put some music on,> said Eve with a wink. Within seconds her favourite Pussy Cat Dolls song was blaring out of the CD player.

<DO YOU MIND?> blasted Beyoncé. <I'm trying to watch this YouFace video!>

The music was turned down, and the girlbot returned to her viewing. It was an old clip of a Japanese robot attempting to peel a potato but ending up stabbing its human operator in the arm with the peeler. Beyoncé roared with laughter. The adult bots watched her, perplexed.

<Shall we dance?> Eve asked Tude. But, like the other males, he refused to budge.

<I will,> trilled Tina, placing her tool-bag on the floor and joining Eve in a synchronized bop around it. As she got more into the swing of it, Tina started singing the lyrics, <Don't cha wish your girlfriend was a Bot like me? Don't cha? Don't cha?>

Dura felt a knot in his abdominal circuits as he watched her gyrations and listened to her words, convinced they were directed at him. Never before had he felt so miserable.

Tude and Len shifted uneasily as new embarrassment connections formed in their positronic brains. Small-talk was their only refuge.

<I hear the *robotniki* have fixed the space elevator,> Len said. <And that HarVard plans to go to Earth with the Germans? >

<Ah yes, The Great Artist,> said Tude, rolling his optics. <He has produced a series of oil paintings depicting the tough life of the American cowboy. He thinks they're masterpieces and deserve a wider audience.>

<Is that why he faked InspectaBot's certificate?> asked Dura. <He needed the humans to land so he could get away on their ship.>

<Correct!>

<HarVard's insane isn't he?>

<Like a box of clockwork frogs.>

<Will our humans be alright?> asked Len.

Tude shrugged. <No need to worry about humans. Great survivors. I once saw a video about them which said they even managed to survive the mass extinction that wiped out the dinosaurs.> Len and Dura made some facial adjustments and nodded to indicate how impressed they were. <Or maybe that was cockroaches? Anyway, the point is they'll be fine when the Germans go. They'll move into the German base and we'll get Robotany Base all to ourselves.>

<And everyone will live happily ever after!> giggled Tina.

<Not sure about that,> said Tude. <I think there's something quite important Helmut forgot to warn them about.>

5. Clueless in the Shuttle

"I can't believe it!" muttered Lieutenant Willie Warner as he pulled yet another weightless suitcase along the corridor. "Giant chickens. Giant friggin' chickens!"

"Anything the matter?" asked HarOld.

"Yes," said Willie. "There is."

He crammed the case into the newly-reconstituted lift and pressed the *Close* button to prevent it, or any of its bobbing companions, drifting out again. Then he turned and headed back to the Assembly Room for more.

"Would you like to talk about it?" offered HarOld.

"No."

"How about playing a guessing game?"

"No."

"Listen, I'm here for you, buddy. If there's any issue with oversized birds, specifically poultry, I might be able to help."

"Yeah?"

"A quick scan of the ship reveals no fowl on board, so I think we're safe."

"Did you not hear my conversation with Zak Johnston just now?"

"Er, might have done. Remind me."

Willie sighed as he retrieved another suitcase and headed back to the lift. "The Germans? Coming back to Earth with us? Their base? The giant chickens? The repaired lift? My orders to send the luggage down? Any of that ring a bell?"

"I might have missed some of that ... Will the chickens be coming aboard too?"

"No. Just the Germans, and Brokk, and HarVard."

"So, what's the problem then? No birds. We're fine, no?"

Willie stopped in his tracks. "Look, forget the chickens."

"You brought them up."

Willie grunted. "I made mankind's most important discovery, ever. And it was just giant chickens."

"See? You're at it again."

"Because it's not fair."

"No."

"And I've come all this way to Mars, done all the donkey work for eight hellish months, and I don't even get to set foot on the planet!"

"That's tough."

"And now I've developed a verruca – because of that unwashed scumbag Johnston."

"Poor you."

"I need to prove that Dugdale's a serial killer, but can't find any convincing evidence."

"Tricky."

Willie shook his head as he stowed the last of the suitcases in the lift and closed the door. "What would Hercule Poirot do?"

"Who?" HarOld asked.

"It's always so easy for him. He confronts the murderer with the facts, and the murderer confesses. Simple as that."

"Perhaps you should try it?"

Willie mused for a while. "Yes, perhaps I should. I'll accuse Dugdale to his face and see how he reacts!"

"I'm calling up his personality profile right now – maybe I can predict his reaction for you."

"Hmm."

Willie pressed the *Down* button to send the space elevator back down to the surface.

But as he floated by the lift door, a thought struck him. What if Dugdale wasn't, in fact, the murderer? What if he'd got that wrong?

And suddenly, he had it. He knew who had killed Penny Smith and Chad Lionheart.

6. The King of Rock and Hole

It was like present-opening time on Christmas Day as the colonists were reunited with their luggage. Harry Fortune had his awards and framed photos, Zak Johnston had his prohibited substances plus the apparatus for making more of the same, the Brushes had their lab coats and scientific equipment, Adorabella her doctor's black bag, and the teenagers their wall posters and scruffy clothing. Most excited of all seemed Emily Leach as she followed her trunk which was being towed by Dom's towing arm, to her cabin.

"Careful not to jar it," she instructed, tripping gaily behind him. "Mr Darcy's very sensitive. He inflates at the slightest touch." She blushed at the thought, her eyelashes fluttering wildly.

But then she halted as a thought struck her and she was suddenly all a-tizzy. "Oh my goodness gracious!" she exclaimed. "George Clooney! I'd forgotten all about George. What am I like?" She put a hand to her mouth, while the other fanned her reddening cheeks. "What will Mr Darcy make of him?"

She kept fanning her cheeks as Dom trudged on up ahead. Gradually a smile curled her lips.

"Hmm. How about *two* literary companions. At the same time. Now that's something I've never tried before."

She set off at a trot to catch up with her precious trunk, quivering in anticipation of her experiment.

*

Dugdale was unpacking his Club 18-30 case while his ladybot preened herself in front of the cabin's full-length mirror. He slipped on a pair of flip-flops and donned one of his favourite Hawaiian-print T-shirts. Then he spotted the 'Kiss me Quick' sombrero in the case, and the memories flooded back. It was a souvenir of a love found, and then lost, under Blackpool's North Pier. He picked it up and toyed with it a little. Then, with a smile, he leaned down and gently placed it on Disa's curly-mop head. The little cleaning-bot jumped, startled, but then observed how the sombrero gave her a kind of raffish sexiness which she found appealing. Her motor purred.

Watching her adjusting the sombrero this way and that, Dugdale told himself that she never need know how he had come by that hat. Nor about the evening under the pier. Nor indeed about Dobbin the Donkey.

As he turned back to his suitcase a reflection of sunlight from outside caught his eye. There was something out there. He flip-flopped over to the window and peered out.

Approaching the base was the most bizarre, nightmarish mechanical contraption he had ever seen. Over two storeys high, it half-trundled, half-limped like a giant metallic Quasimodo, a vast battery-pack hump on its back and a pair of long johns flapping from a flagpole. It appeared to be a mishmash of spare parts that had been blown apart and then reassembled at random.

In its wake, and dwarfed by it, trailed several other robots, including his dart playing partners. But Dugdale's eyes widened and his mouth dropped open on recognizing the bullet-shaped head of the tallest of them.

"By 'eck, t'InspectaBot!" he yelled, banging on his window. "What the friggin' 'ell are you doin' out there, you useless, lyin' bugger? Wait till I get me 'ands on yer! I'll teach yer to certify this 'ovel as habitable!"

As Dugdale stared at the approaching group, the monstrous Frankenbot came to a halt and reached down to gather some rocks. After drilling a hole in each one, he dropped them to the ground. In no time at all, the other robots, including InspectaBot with his amber light flashing, had hurried over to study the rock cluster at the wheels of their master. The giant robot's lights flashed as though it were communicating with its followers. To Flint the robots seemed momentarily stumped by their leader's message. They gathered around a partly open grille in the giant's underbelly and began nodding their heads as if some profound truth had been revealed that would help them better understand their place in the Universe.

Dugdale thumped on the window glass again. The smallest of the robots turned towards him and gave him a cheery wave before refocusing its attention on the monster bot, eager to receive the next cryptic nugget.

"'arVey. Where are yer, 'arVey?" bellowed a frustrated Dugdale into the all-hearing ether.

Next to the door, appeared the upright holographic figure of Greeves, with an umbrella hooked over a horizontal forearm.

"May I be of assistance, sir?"

"What in t'name of Boycott's bollocks is goin' on out there?"

"Ah, that'll be Karl Eckrocks, King of the Robots, apparently. Plus his followers."

"You wha'?"

"Precisely, sir. I am as mystified as you."

Flint was still growling at InspectaBot when his attention was distracted by the front doorbell sounding its Big Ben chime.

"That will be our German friends," announced Greeves.

"'Appen our 'friend' Fritz's got some serious explainin' to do. Like: what the frig he's been plannin' to do with all that dynamite!"

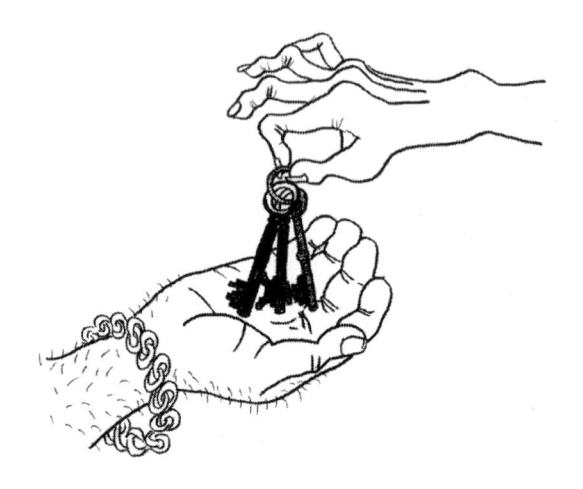

7. His Awful Wedded Wife

By the time Dugdale arrived in the entrance hall, the Germans and Brokk were already hanging their space helmets on the hat-stand. Otto Bungelly's helmet, being a modified rectangular water storage tank, was turned upside down to form a useful table for their luggage. Among their black-and-white, wartime suitcases was a curious piece of space-age machinery, about the size of a pram and resembling a high-tech weapon. As Dugdale wondered what it might be, a swarm of robots rushed in from all doors, bustling around Helmut and reaching greedily for the various-sized washers he was doling out.

"Ah, Herr Kapitan. So nice it is to be seeing you. Very windy outside today. Mars must be unhappy we are leaving. Ha, ha."

"Whatever, Fritz," said Flint. "More importantly, 'ave you brought keys for t'base?"

"Ja, of course." Helmut reached into a pocket and withdrew a heavy metal bundle which he handed over. "Do not be forgetting to feed ze chickens. They are becoming most irritated if they don't receive a sack of corn every day. Oh, und always double bolt the front door before bedtime. And remember to disinfect Andy's bed mattress before using it."

"Yeah, yeah," muttered Dugdale, too busy inspecting the keys with a sceptical eye to pay much attention to Helmut's 'To do' list. "Sure these are t'right keys?"

"Of course, of course, Herr Kapitan," assured Helmut. "Surely you are not suspecting me of the dirty trickery after all we have been through?" He glanced around at his compatriots for support but they all seemed to be shiftily looking away.

"Well, that's alright, then," grunted Dugdale. "Time you were makin' tracks, Fritz. You're in good 'ands with Lieutenant Wibbler. Just remember to point 'im in t'direction of t'big blue planet." He disguised his smirk by pretending his eye was in need of a rub.

"Oh, ja? We are all so very excited about our trip back to ze homeland."

The other Germans nodded. Hovering at the back of the group, next to the airlock, was the colonist formerly known as Brokk. His nervy eyes scanned the entrance hall for any sign of his wife.

"Before you go, 'Ermann. What's t'meaning of that?" Dugdale pointed at the crate labelled 'HIGH EXPLOSIVES', sitting by a wall where the robots had left it. "It were found up at that there Wanki festival."

"Ah, is that where it got to?" asked Helmut, with a cheery laugh. "You are more than welcome to have it, mein Kapitan. We will be having no needings for it where we are going. With the dynamite sticks we are excavating the tunnels in the crater walls, but that is all done now. But a word of advising. You might find it safer not to be keeping it here where there are kinderlings and robotonautens running around. If that were to blow ... big bang, ja?"

Flint eyed him suspiciously, but said nothing.

At that moment a door flew open. Through it burst Adorabella, nostrils flaring. Looking more crazed than ever, her hair frizzed out, her eyes popping with rage and madness, she raised her clawed hands as though about to launch a frenzied, eye-gouging assault. "Brokk!" she screamed, her bosom heaving with heavy breaths and her fiery eyes drilling into her husband like lasers. "You are *not* leaving Mars! You are *not* leaving. *Ever*! I forbid it!"

"Er ..." started Brokk, looking around for a means of escape. Before he could take a step in any direction Adorabella was rushing at him, a horrific scream rending the air and freezing everyone in the room. Fortunately, Hansie Wankmüller and Andy Marsman were first to recover their composure and, with lightning speed, grabbed and restrained her before she reached her husband.

"Let go of me!" she wailed. "He can't leave me. It's not fair. It's not right."

Brokk stepped out of the shadows, arms raised in surrender and an apologetic look on his face. "Sorry, fluffy bumps. But a man's gotta do what a man's gotta do."

"What about me? Don't you love me?"

Brokk dodged the second question by focusing on the first. "You're an attractive woman, honeydew. You'll find someone else."

"Who?" she screeched.

Brokk's mind scrolled through the list of unattached men at the base and he could see she had a point. "But, sweet cheeks," he said. "This is too big an opportunity for me. Once in a lifetime. It's massive."

Dugdale had become interested. "What chuffin' opportunity?"

"Just think of the story when we get back to Earth! A group of German rocket scientists. On Mars. For 80 years! Be worth millions. Ever since I heard about them I knew I was onto a goldmine."

"'Ow did you hear about 'em?" asked Dugdale.

"Rumours, at first. That a bunch of German radio hams, living in South America, had made contact with people on Mars. I did a little investigating. The evidence was pretty compelling. That's why I had to get on this mission."

"You *used* me!" yowled Adorabella.

Brokk shrugged. "We had some good times."

"You callous bastard."

Brokk turned to Dugdale and continued what he'd been saying. "What's more, the Germans have this idea for a multi-billion business empire on Earth: MFC – Mars Fried Chicken. My 'grandfather'," (he winked at this point), "has asked me to be the manager of the first MFC fast food outlet." Brokk pointed at the space-age weapon thing next to the German luggage. "With Otto's 'Enlarging Ray' we'll be able to generate giant chickens, giant sheep, giant cows. Even giant vegetables. It will revolutionize food production on Earth!"

But Adorabella was glaring at Brokk with hate-filled eyes. "You will stay here with me, or you will regret it!"

Brokk sighed. "Why don't you come back with me, honey puff cakes. Come to Earth. We'll be rich. We can live in luxury for the rest of our lives."

"I will never leave Mars," blubbed Adorabella. "I cannot leave

Oberon's spirit behind. He is here on Mars, his spirit whistling around the Martian deserts with the long-dead Wind people. He talks to me constantly. If I leave him, it would be a betrayal."

"Fair enough," said Brokk with a nod.

As Dugdale led the Germartians and Brokk off for a final cup of tea, Adorabella bristled at her retreating husband. "You will regret this," she shrieked, struggling against the restraining grip of the two Germans. "You *will* regret this!"

8. Before the Big Bang

After Hansie and Andy had released her, Adorabella dropped to her knees, sobbing. Left alone in the entrance hall, she let the pent-up rage, grief and pain flow through her.

Gradually she calmed, and raised her head. As she did so, she found herself staring at the huge crate up against the wall; the one with 'HIGH EXPLOSIVES' emblazoned on the side. The more she stared, the more an idea formed in her mind and the more crazed the look on her face became. Without rising to her feet, she crawled on hands and knees to the crate. As she peered inside at its contents the details of a plan took shape.

Then, with a burst of renewed energy, she pushed herself upright and headed for the spacesuit changing room. Twenty minutes later she was back, fully suited and carrying a large bag. Working with exaggerated care, she started filling the bag with sticks of dynamite.

There was a throat-clearing sound from a ceiling loudspeaker. "May I ask what madam is doing?" HarVard said in his Greeves voice.

Adorabella jumped. "Ah, HarVard," she said with a nervous laugh. "Er, these explosives. I'm not comfortable with them being here in the base. You know what those children are like. I'm just taking them outside."

"Well, madam only needed to ask. I'll get one of the bots to remove them."

Adorabella gave another nervous laugh. "No, no, it's fine. Part of my duties, you know. Ha, ha. Saving human life and all that. Ha, ha." She coughed.

The bag was now full, although the crate was still far from empty. She lugged the haul of explosives over to the airlock and then outside. Crunching across the Martian sand she unloaded the dynamite next to the space elevator which was humming on its newly-engineered base platform.

Three more trips and everything, including the crate, was next to the space elevator. Breathing heavily from the exertion, she refilled the crate with the sticks of dynamite, wired the detonator charge to the plunger, and, trailing the copper wire, retreated behind a large boulder to wait.

"Let's see if this will persuade you to stay, Brokk, my 'fluffy bumps'."

9. The Mars Debating Society

"Dad. Urgent!" read the text message from Tarquin. "Meeting Room. Now!'

Brian Brush nearly dropped his blablet. "*Gung!*"

"What's up, dear?" asked Delphinia, test tube in hand as she poured a sticky, smelly mix of human waste and chicken droppings into a beaker.

"Tarquin. He's in danger!"

"Oh, my goodness!" screamed Delphinia, dropping both beaker and test tube to the floor where they smashed, spraying glass shards and steaming sludge onto her shoes.

With no time to waste on the mess, Brian grabbed his wife's hand and pulled her out of the laboratory, both skidding on the slippery brown droplets as they ran. White lab coats flapping and safety goggles dangling, the couple raced across the balmy rainforest biome of Botany Base. They crashed through the Meeting Room door and stood panting, scanning the room for signs of their son.

There he was. In a corner of the room. Sitting on the floor, calm and quiet, and in no apparent danger, playing dominoes with Mr Snuggles. Most of the other colonists were also in the room, seated around the meeting table, with Lieutenant Zak Johnston at the head.

Brian stood blinking in puzzlement while Delphinia bounded over to snatch the boy into her arms.

"Are you alright, my little space-cub? I was so worried that something might have happened. Tell me you're OK."

"Mwwphnghrm," was the best Tarquin could manage with his mother's lab coat smothering his face.

"Excuse the ruse, dudes," said Zak Johnston raising his hands in apology. "The text deception was my inception."

Brian turned to Zak and blinked at him.

"Park yer bums, my geeky chums." Zak indicated two free chairs.

"We can't start without our heroic Commander Dugdale," objected Emily Leach, her face flushing pink at the very mention of the name.

"Dugdude not required," said Zak. "Tune in to the guy in the sky 'n you'll find out why."

There were puzzled looks all round. "God?" asked Harry.

"Not quite so high, poetry-man. The dumb twit in the spaceship."

"Ah, *that* guy in the sky," chorused a number of voices.

"Dr Faerydae's also absent," pointed out Emily.

Zak nodded. "Still sufferin' from Brokk shock, I guess."

"What's going on?" asked Brian, approaching the table. "What's this about?"

"Inaugural meeting of the Mars Debating Society, innit," said Gavin with a smirk.

Brian shot him a disapproving look while Delphinia pulled Tarquin deeper into her bosom to smother his ears as well as his face. Tracey giggled.

Brian sat down at the table. Delphinia finally released her son and she, too, sat down, leaving her boy gasping for breath like a beached halibut. The moment he was breathing again, his face screwed up in disgust at the terrible smell coming from his mother's shoes. "Phwoar, what's that stink, Mummy?"

"Mummy stepped in something she shouldn't, that's all."

Several chairs scraped as they edged away to a safer distance.

Fanning his nose, Tarquin returned to his game with Mr Snuggles. Seating himself on the floor he plugged in his blablet earpieces to drown out the tiresome adult chatter that was undoubtedly about to commence.

After flicking a switch, Zak motioned towards a wall-mounted screen which now displayed a close-up of Lieutenant Willie Warner's greasy face. He was adjusting the cockpit-cam while trying to control the cricket bat that kept floating away from him. He angled the microphone too close to his mouth and his wheezy breathing boomed through the loudspeakers. "Ah, there you are. Is the commander with you?"

Zak winced and turned the volume control down. "We're alone in a Dug-free zone, man. Say what yer gotta say."

Warner took a deep breath to steady himself. "I have something very important to tell you all."

In the background a voice could be heard asking, "Are you talking to me?"

"No, HarOld. Please be quiet."

"Sorry for living," said the voice.

Willie cleared his throat. "Now, what I have to tell you concerns the death of Penny Smith ..."

"She was murdered," said Zak.

A loud gasp of horror issued from around the table, and one of annoyance from Willie. "Thank you, Zak, but can you let me speak?"

"Soz, dude."

Willie scowled before continuing. "The commander shushed it up. And it appears that Commander Lionheart ..."

"Murdered, too," jumped in Zak.

Another gasp from the table, as Willie huffed in frustration. "Will you stop interrupting me, Lieutenant Johnston?"

"A thousand apologies, space-boy. Won't happen again." He held up his hands.

Willie paused as he watched the colonists in various stages of shock.

"So it means ..." He lowered his voice, "... there's a ..."

"Murderer amongst us!"

Willie's eyes narrowed and his mouth twitched. His breathing became heavier.

Zak turned to the screen. "Well, come on, sleuth in the booth. Aren't you goin' to tell us who dunnit?"

Still Willie breathed heavily, but gradually calmed down. He plucked the cricket bat out of the air and positioned it for the camera. "I found this in Commander Dugdale's cabin. It has a bloodstain here ..." He pointed it out. "So I believe it to be ..."

"The murder weapon!" announced Zak, clapping his hands together and miming the swing of a powerful hook shot.

As Willie threw up his arms and fumed in the cockpit, Brian Brush leaned across the table and said, "I think I see where this is leading, Lieutenant Johnston. And straight away I can spot a Big Problem."

"Wait," Willie was saying. "I haven't finished ..."

But Zak cut the sound to Willie's picture and turned to Brian. "Speak, science-man. Pitch the hitch."

Brian pushed his cracked glasses up his nose. "Well, if it's true that we have a murderer amongst us, mentioning no names, there are one or two practical issues we should consider before we go any further." Behind him, the screen showed Willie yelling and waving his arms before finally realizing he had been muted. In anger he shook the cricket bat at them, his 'big Poirot moment' seemingly imperilled.

"What's to consider?" snarled Harry Fortune. "Name him, then lock the bastard up and throw away the key."

"Thank you, Harry," continued Brian. "I sense you make a point that might find favour within the group. But, I fear, it might not be quite such a simple process. You see, if we confront him – arrest him, even – he's likely to be very, very angry indeed. And he'll probably become violent."

Miss Emily Leach was holding up her hand to speak. "Surely you don't think our valiant mission commander is responsible?"

"Well, that would have to be determined by a fair trial, of course," said Brian. "It is a fundamental rule of British Law and Fair Play that a murder suspect be tried before a jury of his peers: twelve randomly selected people of voting age. We need to include Brokk and Willie Warner and the Germans to get twelve jurors."

Up on the screen, Willie Warner suddenly stopped his gesticulations as though an idea had struck him. He rose and floated out of shot.

"And even if Dugdale were to be found guilty," started Brian, and then gave a cough before backtracking. "Er, sorry, what I meant to say was, even if the *defendant* were found guilty, someone would need to restrain and jail him."

"I is not going to be involved in restraining no madman who is the size of a London bus," said Gavin. "No way."

"Nor would anyone expect you to, son. That duty would fall to a representative from NAFA. And who do we have here who fits the bill? Why, Lieutenant Johnston, of course."

Zak, who had been rocking back and forth on his chair, gazing at the ceiling, nearly toppled over. "Negatory, Brian Brains, man. Old Zakkie's strictly a non-restraining kinda lieutenant. Peace and Love, man. Peace and Love."

"And, of course, once Dugd ... the murderer is jailed, he'll need to be fed three times a day, allowed visitors and given regular exercise, all in accordance with his basic human rights."

On screen, Willie had returned and seemed to be scribbling something on a piece of paper.

"Wouldn't it be easier if we just sent him back to Earth to face justice?" asked Delphinia. "He could go back with Willie and the Germans."

On hearing Delphinia's suggestion, the image of Willie froze in mid-scribble. He looked up with a wild look in his eyes and started shaking his head and flapping his arms.

Brian was stroking his chin. "Interesting idea, my love. But I fear that would be putting the lives of all on board *Mayflower III* at risk."

Willie's vigorous head-shaking turned to vigorous head-nodding.

"My worry is, of course, that if we confront him as the murderer, the first thing he'll do is kill the lot of us."

The gasp that followed was so loud that even Tarquin heard it through his blablet earphones and looked up.

At that moment, the door burst open and Flint Dugdale filled the opening. There was a collective cowering back in seats while eyebrows shot upwards like leaping salmon.

"What the chuff is up wi' you lot?" demanded Flint. "'Appen I've been 'avin' to make small-talk with Fritz and his gang for t'past half hour. Where the frig is t'big send-off party?"

All eyes were bulging, mouths open and speechless, torsos straining backwards. Even Willie seemed frozen up on the screen.

As Flint took a step into the room there was a sudden squeaking of chairs as the occupants got to their feet and stepped back. Flint looked baffled and took another step nearer. More chairs squeaking, more hurried retreating.

"What's goin' on? Yer not all still narked at me over that business with t'lift, are yer? It were an accident, I tell yer. The downdraught from the helibot. Nowt I could do."

The others shook their heads and pulled back another step.

"What's up with yer, then? 'Appen it were t'missed penalty? Even t'best players in t'world miss 'em."

Still the retreat continued.

"Stay back, you beast," cried Emily, brandishing a pair of knitting needles.

Dugdale looked more baffled than ever.

Brian cleared his throat. "Er, Commander Dugdale, we've, er, been discussing, er, the unexplained ..."

On screen Willie gave a look of horror and started waving his hands in desperation. He held up his sheet of paper, but the words were out of focus, and no one was looking at him anyway.

Tarquin, finding himself hemmed in by retreating adults, took his earphones out and looked up. "What's up, Daddy?"

His father put a finger to his lips. "Nothing to concern you, son. It's about the people who sadly passed away on the ship."

Dugdale put his hands on his hips. "Don't tell me you think I 'ad owt to do wi' that!"

Brian let out a fake laugh through tight vocal chords. Willie was still waving and pointing to his note, now slightly more in focus.

"Commander Dugdale didn't murder those people," said Tarquin in a matter-of-fact manner.

"Shush, son," urged Brian.

"No, really, Dad. Because I know who did it."

"*Gung!*"

Heads turned towards Tarquin.

On screen Willie's message was now sharply in focus. "Dugdale's not the killer. It was ..." He prepared to flip the paper to the message's continuation on the other side just as soon as anyone read the first part. But all eyes were now focused on the little boy.

"There yer go, yer dozy kippers," said Dugdale. "'Appen kid's the only one wi' any gumption round 'ere."

"So, who was it, son?" Brian Brush asked, crouching down to the boy's level as all the others crowded round him. Behind them, Willie had flipped the sheet and was waving and mouthing wildly, pointing to the name scrawled there – the result of his brilliant detective work.

But no one turned round.

Tarquin looked downcast. "It was Dr Faerydae. She killed both Penny Smith and Commander Lionheart."

Everyone gasped and a horrified silence filled the room.

"But why?" Emily Leach asked after what seemed like minutes.

"Jealousy. Revenge. She suspected Mr Faerydae of playing the hufflepuff game with both of them. She was really angry, Daddy."

Delphinia enveloped the little boy in her arms, almost overbalancing and toppling on top of him. "Oh, my brave, brave little soldier."

Tarquin's words had not just stunned the people in the room; onscreen, Willie Warner's face had undergone a marked transformation: from the frustrated look of a man having his big moment taken away from him to a puzzled, uncomprehending look at what he was hearing. At first he had shaken his head in vehement disagreement, but as Tarquin had continued, Willie's head-shaking had ceased. By the end of Tarquin's testimony, Willie had scrunched up his sheet of paper and, with eyes looking shiftily left and right, had smuggled it into a pocket. From that moment, he acted as though the piece of paper had never existed.

"Why didn't you tell us this before?" asked Brian.

"I was scared, Daddy."

This made Delphinia hug him ever more tightly, preventing any further conversation with the boy.

"So, where is the doctor?" Harry Fortune asked. "We need to apprehend her and bring her to justice."

"Hear, hear," agreed several voices.

Everyone turned their heads this way and that, apart from Zak Johnston who was staring out of the window. "The lady in the news is standin' by a fuse. No time to lose."

"What's that?" asked Emily.

"Cripes," said Gavin, joining Zak by the window. "She's, like, got this big bastard box of explosives. And, like, there's this plunger detonator thingy. Looks like she is going to blow up the lift. And the base. And all of us wiv it!"

In a mass panic, there was a rush of bodies to the window.

"Hold yer 'orses," roared Dugdale, silencing the frenzied screaming and crying, but not the whimpering terror. "No need to panic. The Flintster'll sort this out."

"Oh, Commander!" squeaked Emily. "You're so courageous."

"Dude, I'd come with you, but ..." started Zak.

Dugdale turned to him. "Dude, you *are* comin' with me. And no buts."

"But my verruca ..."

Dugdale grabbed him by the ear and pulled him towards the door.

"Not me, man," squealed Zak. "I ain't no use against no crazy goose."

"Exactly," said Dugdale, twisting Zak's ear more and making him squeal again. "You'll be perfect if she decides to take an 'ostage, seein' as you're totally useless."

At the door Flint turned back. "Zakkie'n'me'll get suited up. You lot stay 'ere."

10. Doctor, No!

A grim-faced Dugdale, fully-suited, helmet under one arm, poked his head into the reception area. The room was alive with German chatter as they milled around, enjoying farewell drinks while studiously avoiding Little Urn's offers of glazing-putty iced fondants.

Dugdale's eyes swung to Brokk. "You," he growled. "Yer comin' wi' me."

Helmut turned. "Zer is a problem, Herr Kapitan?"

"A 'domestic'." Flint gave a backward flick of the thumb to Brokk.

Brokk was shaking his head. "Not if it's about Adorabella."

Dugdale's eyes narrowed. "Dr Fairybrain has one very large crate of dynamite by t'space elevator. You, son, are goin' to sort her out."

Helmut put his drink down. "That will be causing a very big exploding which will kill everyone. But she is a doctor. For sure she will not be doing it."

"Alternative therapist," put in Brokk.

"And she has previous," added Dugdale.

"I beg pardon?" asked Helmut.

"Form."

"I am still not understanding."

"She's killed before."

A deathly hush stilled the room, leaving Little Urn looking about, wondering why everything had gone quiet. Maybe it was time for the bacon rolls.

"We must stop her," said Helmut as though the first to think of this. "I will join you, Herr Kapitan, in this difficult moment."

Dugdale grimaced, but said, "Alright, Fritz. But leave all t'talking to me."

*

Outside, a large crowd of robots had gathered to bid farewell to the departing humans and HarVard.

<A sad moment,> signalled Tude to his companions. <We are losing a good friend.>

<Indeed,> agreed Eve. <No more little presents. I shall miss him.>

Tude swivelled his head. <I meant HarVard.>

<Ah yes, him too.>

Dura pointed a trowel-hand. <What is that human doing by the space elevator with that large crate of explosives?>

Tude chuckled. <I expect she has a farewell surprise for them. I have seen documentaries about human celebrations and they often involve fireworks.>

<Exciting!> squeaked Eve. <A show! Here, have some popcogs.> She scooped a portion from the large tub she was holding and offered them around.

A moment later Dugdale, Zak, Brokk and finally Helmut emerged through the airlock. A wild electronic cheering greeted the German, albeit inaudible to humans, as the robots surged forward.

Helmut raised a hand to acknowledge his adoring fans as they crowded around him. "Thank you for your touching support, mein robonautens. You will live forever in Uncle Helmut's heart. I am loving you all."

Dugdale was flapping his arms. "Shhh! She's behind t'rock over there. She can't see us, so if we creep up all quiet, like, we can catch her off-guard."

"Good plan," whispered Helmut. The others nodded and gave thumbs-up signs.

So, creeping at a snail's pace, holding their breaths, the four men set off towards the space elevator, barely making a sound, the crunching of the sand beneath their footsteps unheard above the whistling of the wind. As they made their careful, deliberate way the robots shuffled back, wondering what this part of the show would be about.

*

On another day. On another planet. And if they had been using another, less mouthy space elevator, their plan might have worked.

"Welcome back, shoppers!" it cried in a cheery, fully recharged voice. "We hope you enjoyed your time in *Penge World of Shopping.*" The lift doors opened with a grating screech.

The men froze, hurling silent curses at the device. They were still about 20 yards (old metres) away from the rock.

"Typical British humour, ja?" whispered Helmut, referring to the lift.

"Yeah, that's right, Fritz. Ha, ha."

Alerted by the noise, Adorabella's space-helmeted head popped up from behind the boulder. "Stop right there, all of you!" she screamed. "Not a single step closer!"

The men exchanged resigned glances and then gulped when they saw her thumping the detonator down on top of the boulder and gripping the plunger handles, ready to push down. A crazed look lit her eyes.

Zak raised his hands in surrender. "That dame aims to maim, dudes."

Flint took a step forward with the look of a reasonable man about to make a reasonable proposition. "Now, now, let's not be 'asty, Doc. What's this all about, then?"

Adorabella pointed a gloved finger at her husband. "Him! That man! Either he stays here with me, or I blow us all to kingdom come. End of."

"Ah yes, about that," started Brokk.

"Well?"

"Sorry, Hotlips, the answer has to be No."

Adorabella's eyes blazed. "Very well. I'll give you ten seconds to change your mind. A life with me, or no life at all."

"Come on, honey-pie. It's me, The Brokkster. Remember all the folk songs we used to sing together? And that time on the Isle of Avalon in the Volkswagen Campavan? Bruce we called him. Oh, what laughs we had. Remember the saga with the grey-water waste tank and how we said we'd laugh about it one day? We could try laughing about it now. Why don't you take your hands from the plunger and cast your mind back to those groovy, funky days?"

Adorabella took a deep breath, fighting back the tears. "Ten ..." she started.

"Hey, sugar-plum ..."

"I think perhaps we should be stopping her," suggested Helmut. "She vill damage the lift."

"Space elevator," said Dugdale.

"... Nine ..."

At that moment all attention was caught by a fierce gust of wind that nearly toppled the men to the ground, followed by a vortex that came at them first from one side and then another. Next, from around the curved wall of the building swept a ferocious breeze carrying a barrage of cardboard boxes, rolling and tumbling and jumping in the air. Faster and faster they came, careering into the four men, bumping into shins, bouncing off thighs, and glancing off helmets. The men dodged the boxes as best they could, fending them off with flailing arms. The last of the boxes slapped Brokk square in the midriff, winding him and knocking him to one knee.

But it was far from over. The swirling gale turned through 180 degrees and brought the boxes thundering back for a second assault.

Adorabella watched on, first in bafflement and then with increasing annoyance at the unwelcome distraction until she could stand it no longer. Raising both her arms high into the air she yelled with all her might, "Not now, Bernard! Not now!"

In an instant, the wind had stilled and the air had become calm. The momentum of the cardboard boxes kept them tumbling for a little distance, but soon they slowed and rolled to a halt.

"What the friggin' 'eck were that about?" demanded Dugdale, nursing a bruised shin. Brokk got back to his feet, while Zak and Helmut dusted the sand off their suits.

"... Eight ..." cried Adorabella, resuming her countdown.

The men sighed.

Behind them, the crowd of watching robots were thoroughly enjoying the spectacle despite not fully understanding what was going on. Eve passed around more popcogs. Just in time, too, for the next scene was about to commence. <What's happening now?> she asked.

Seemingly out of nowhere, and some distance behind the shouty woman with the explosives, a mighty, lumbering, mechanical giant appeared.

The robots gasped.

<He's a big one,> tweeted Tude. <And look! There's Stan and Olli. And Cassie, too.>

<And InspectaBot!> added Dura. <How on Mars did he get out of the broom cupboard?>

"... Seven ..." shouted Adorabella, unaware of what was approaching behind her.

The four men gasped also. Helmut seemed the most astonished as his eyes focused on the white garment flapping from Karl Eckrocks's flagpole. "Mein Marsipantz!" he muttered. "So that is where they are getting to."

Closer and closer the mechanical monster came, its attention caught by Adorabella's shiny spherical helmet.

"... Six ..."

As he approached, Karl extended a gripper arm, opening its metal fingers wide enough to clasp the shiny object.

"... Five ..."

The gripper arm was now within two feet and about to grab the helmet. Each man held his breath, heart pounding.

But this was not to be their moment of salvation. InspectaBot skidded to a halt next to Adorabella, booming, "Identify yourself!"

She jumped back with a shriek and then screamed on spotting the giant mechanical monster towering behind her. Her screams sent Karl Eckrocks staggering back several of his giant paces as he fought with the sensitivity of his audio receivers.

"Get back ... whatever you are!"

The giant recoiled even further.

Hope collapsed in the hearts of the watching men.

Except one.

With a burst of British have-a-go heroism, and taking advantage of the distraction, Dugdale made a charge towards Adorabella. Thundering along with the speed, aggression and agility of a rogue elephant he managed to cover about half the distance before a dip in the terrain took his foot from under him and sent him sprawling onto his fat stomach. He thumped a fist into the sand and roared with rage.

"Plucky, but unlucky," observed Zak.

Adorabella turned back and screamed again. "Not so fast, Dugdale!"

THE WORST MAN ON MARS

Under the circumstances this was sound advice, albeit a little late.

"Everyone stay back," she continued. "Or I will set this thing off before I even reach Zero." She panted heavily as she kept turning from the spread-eagled Dugdale in front of her to the giant robotic monster behind her.

Time stood still, or at least Adorabella's countdown had stalled while her gaze flitted backwards and forwards between the two sources of threat. All the while, Karl Eckrocks's processors were working overtime. His interest in the shiny white marble, and the bits attached to it, had increased, for his sensors were indicating definite signs of life. <LIVING BEING!> he broadcast at full power. <MAJOR DISCOVERY. LIFE AT LAST, NO QUESTION. VIKING WILL INFORM AMERICA!>

There was a flurry of excitement amongst his robot followers, despite the temporary radio-deafness they were all suffering. <What did he say, Webster?> they tweeted. <What did he say?>

From Karl's grille, Webster poked out his eight arachno-eyes and blinked at them. <Er, well, I'm glad you fellows asked me that. Er, what he said was this: LIVID BEING! He means the human woman. MAJOR RISK OVER 'ERE. Obviously that blasted crate of explosives. LIE FLAT, ASK NO QUESTIONS. Sound advice. THE KING WILL PERFORM A MIRACLE. Spiffing, what?>

<A miracle!> cried Cassie, and her cry was repeated by robot after robot. <The King of the Robots will perform a miracle!> Many of the robots threw themselves flat on the ground, as instructed, to await the promised wonder.

Tude remained upright and rolled his shoulders. <Of course, we all know there's no such thing as a miracle, so I will be most interested to see what happens next.>

Dura nodded, but seemed distracted by a high-pitched whistling sound. <What's that noise?> he asked. <Seems to be coming from high up in the sky.>

Tude adjusted his sensors. <You're right, I can hear it too. Probably just the space-elevator laser cable. They must have activated it in the spaceship.>

<Shh, you two!> said Eve. <I want to see how this ends.>

*

"... Five ..."

Dugdale raised his helmeted head from the ground and turned it to the others. "She's bluffin'. Nowt to worry about."

"Yeah, she's just kidding," said Brokk. "Aren't you, my pretty one?"

"... Four ..." Adorabella's eyes looked even more crazed.

"Aren't you?"

"... Three ..."

Dugdale sat up. "Can't you just tell her you'll stay?"

"... Two ..."

"Tell her, man. Just friggin' tell her you'll stay before t'mad cow blows us up!"

Brokk's lips tightened. Very deliberately and very slowly he shook his head. "No."

"One" screamed Adorabella, raising her elbows and preparing to throw her full weight on the plunger.

But at that moment a miracle happened.

Tude and Dura were the first to see it. The high-pitched whistling sound they had picked up had been steadily increasing in volume and, indeed, had now become audible even to humans. Tude looked upwards, zooming his telescopic viewer until he could just make out a small white dot high up in the sky. Gradually it was increasing in size and Tude was able to make out that it had a human shape. He nudged Dura and Eve, pointing upwards.

<What's that?> asked Eve. <Is it a bird? Is it a plane?>

<No, no. I've seen a documentary about this. Whenever humans are in imminent danger, a superhuman in a cape, wearing pants outside his tights, swoops out of the sky and saves the day.> Tude frowned. <I can't see the cape, though. Nor the pants.>

Human and robot heads had now all turned up in the direction of the noise and were staring at the fast-approaching white shape.

Even Adorabella looked up. It was the last thing she ever did.

Thus it'll never be known whether her mind fully registered the meaning and significance of what she saw in that split-second. It happened so quickly that the irony may well have been lost on her. It is possible she realized that the large white object heading towards her had a human shape. Perhaps she identified it as a spacesuit, slightly charred at the edges. Maybe, although this is unlikely, she had time to focus on what lay behind the space-helmet's face-mask. And maybe, although this is even more improbable, she recognized the decayed and putrefied flesh that was all that remained of the pretty face of her murder victim, Penny Smith.

In any case, even if she was aware of any, or all, of these things, there was nothing she could do to save herself.

The corpse, with the momentum of an express train, crashed down on top of her.

Adorabella was dead in an instant.

*

The watching robots burst into a clatter of applause.

<That was neat,> said Eve.

<Not bad,> conceded Tude. <Crudely effective. But ...>

<But what?>

<I want a little more from my superheroes. There wasn't much 'swoop'. It was all 'splat'. See, a robot superhero like Superbot would never have done that. Superbot would have swooped down and snatched the plunger and taken it away to a safe place, probably disconnecting it just to be sure. There's your basic difference between human and robot superheroes.>

The robots next to Karl Eckrocks were cheering wildly and falling to their knees.

<A miracle! It's a miracle!> they were signalling amongst themselves. <Did you see what the King of the Robots just did? It is a Sign. We must follow him to a Better Life.>

*

Inside Botany Base the colonists were looking on, stunned with shock and relief.

"*Gung!*" exclaimed Brian Brush.

"Can anyone explain what just happened?" Emily asked.

"*Gung!*" repeated Brian, lost for words, although not for strange sounds from the back of the throat.

Delphinia did her best to fill Emily in.

"But isn't that, like, totally improbable, Dad?" asked Gavin. "Like, if this happened in a book or a film, no one would believe it, innit?"

Brian Brush was nodding his head. "Like, totally," he agreed. "I'm trying to work out the probability, son, but the numbers are incalculable." He buried his head in his hands. "Incalculable. It may even have been a genuine 'miracle'."

The others gasped,

"Poetic justice, I guess," observed Delphinia.

Harry's ears pricked up. He suddenly felt a poem coming on.

*

Later, as the bodies of Dr Adorabella Faerydae and Penny Smith were being buried in the desert, another high-pitched whistling came from high up in the sky, closely followed by a loud crash that sent the humans and robots ducking for cover. Within the wreckage of the site office Portakabin was discovered a second space-suit. Inside, a knitted bag with a flower on it and, inside that, the somewhat incomplete mortal remains of Commander Chad Lionheart.

About half an hour later, as the space elevator headed up towards *Mayflower III*, a third space-suited corpse fell to Mars. This one came down a few miles to the north, plunging through the glass roof of the German base, narrowly missing a giant chicken and leaving a gaping hole through which the precious air started to escape.

As all the startled fowl gazed up at the new opening in their sky, they wondered, insofar as their chicken brains allowed, what significance, if any, the break in the roof held for them.

*

On board *Mayflower III*, the shaken travellers floated out of the space-elevator with their belongings. Willie greeted them warmly, although was momentarily taken aback by the size of Otto Bungelly's head. Brokk carried HarVard's neatly wrapped oil paintings, while Andy Marsman clutched the enlarging ray. As the supercomputer's HologrAmbulator floated out of the lift its avatar morphed into an urbane and dapper traveller who, under poor lighting conditions, might have been mistaken for Alan Whicker.

"I hope it is soon that we will be going, Kapitan Wubbla," said Helmut, as Willie showed them to their quarters.

"Yes, very soon. I want to get home as much as you guys do."

"Ja, das is good."

Helmut turned to his compatriots and there was much German muttering. "We must go quickly," was the gist of it. "Before Commander Dugdale finds out ..."

11. German Weasels

As Flint Dugdale made his way to his new living quarters inside the German base, he glanced up at the top of a scaffold-tower under the domed roof where a one-armed robot wearing a gaffer-tape neck-brace was pointing at a crudely repaired roof panel and giving a thumbs-up sign to his foreman far below. Flint frowned before continuing into the passage leading to his room. He unlocked the heavy oak door and stepped inside. The splendour of Helmut von Grommel's former lodgings made him catch his breath. A crooked grin spread across his face as he took in the layout of study, bedroom and bathroom. "Magic!"

Behind him, Disa staggered in, her motor wheezing. Weighed down with the commander's luggage, and venting through her suction tube, she headed for the bedroom.

A sign on a door at the far end of the study caught Flint's attention. It read 'KEEP OUT'. He raised an eyebrow and started towards it, but then decided to leave it for later. Instead he turned to watch Disa wobbling under her heavy load before she and the luggage crashed in a heap on the carpeted floor.

"Let me give yer a hand, Di," offered Dugdale, heading in the opposite direction. "After I've 'ad a drink to get me strength up." He put down the ultra-lightweight shoulder bag he'd been carrying and took out a can of *Stallion*.

As he slurped he looked about the study. It was crowded with books and ancient journals. A large oil painting of von Grommel, dressed in full military regalia, stared down at Dugdale and the eyes seemed to follow him around the room. Laid out on top of a wooden writing desk were scribbled drawings of rockets and flying saucers. Flint peered at the same words written in bold lettering over and over: 'Das Mars Escapenzie Projekt'. He snorted at the thought of the Germans plotting and planning an escape from Mars for all those decades.

He ran his fingers over the hand-carved furniture. "Chuffin' Nora, 'appen t'daft beggars must've whittled all t'furniture wi t'penknife." He raised his voice to call louder. "Did yer 'ear me, luv? I were sayin' 'ow they carved all t'furniture."

Disa managed to raise herself upright and chirped a weary acknowledgement.

On top of an old fashioned sideboard were various framed sepia photographs Helmut had left behind, presumably because he had been unable to fit them into his luggage. Flint's disinterested eyes drifted over them: A photo of Helmut's 'farter' in a chicken costume alongside Buster Klinsman, star of the German silent movies. And one showing his 'mutter' in full welding gear surrounded by her nineteen boys, a young Helmut hanging off her huge left bicep. Then, there was a photo of Otto and Helmut on a trip to Vegas in an old Kaiser Firebird with the top down. In those days Otto's head had been a normal size.

Dugdale's concentration was broken by the agitated bleeping of Disa in the bedroom.

"Alright, alright, keep yer mop on. Flinty'll be there in a minute to sort things out. Don't go damagin' any of yer delicate suction tools."

By the time Flint had entered the bedroom, Disa had abandoned the cases and was looking inside a poorly constructed wardrobe. Of more interest to Flint was the room's main feature: its large double bed. In two strides he had crossed over to it and stretched himself out with a contented sigh. From his prone position he found himself staring up at a glaring anachronism on the wall opposite and, in an instant, the mystery of Botany Base's missing 100" Superslim 4D TV was solved.

"That thievin' rogue, Fritz, 'ad me telly all t'time!"

Disa squeaked and playfully jumped onto the bed next to him throwing a flexible hose over his ample belly. The commander propped himself up with a pillow and reached for the remote control on the bedside table. To his surprise, the first thing the screen showed was the message: "A Note for Kapitan Duggdail". Then, the craggy face of Helmut von Grommel appeared, sporting a sly smile. Flint sat bolt upright, smelling a rat.

"Ah, Herr Kapitan. I trust you are settling into my apartment. Please be feeling free to use my pyjamas. They are under ze pillow along with a block of pipe tobacco."

Flint hit the *Pause* button before lifting his pillow. The sight of the threadbare pyjama trousers made him shudder. He pinched them between thumb and forefinger and dangled them in front of Disa. "In t'bin, please, luv." Then, as the ladybot scuttled away, he slipped the tobacco pouch into his pocket and cast a suspicious look at the frozen image of the German on the screen.

"What's this all about, Fritz?" he asked before pressing *Play*.

"I expect you are wondering what is this all about. Well I am needing to make a tiny confessioning. But, knowing what an excitable chap you are, I am thinking it is best if you are in a state of relaxationings and I am a long, long way away. It would be such a shame to mar our sad departure with scenes of ugliness."

"A confessioning, eh? I knew you were up to summat, you sly old dog!"

Disa had returned and was now snuggling up to her human, wondering about the movie starring her favourite German.

"You are remembering ze story I told you about how we are getting here to Mars?"

"How could I forget that load of bollocks?"

"Some of it was true ... and some of it ... to steal an expression of yours ... was bollocks."

"Gerraway."

"My childhood, my farter and mutter, my friendship with Otto Bungelly. All true. Und we really were famous rocket scientists during the war, coming to Nevada to work for the Americans afterwards. But Otto never did quite invent an anti-gravity cake mixture. I was amazed you fell for that one!" On screen, Helmut's head rocked back as he laughed.

Flint's eyes narrowed as he tried to work out where this might be leading.

"On ze big day of the Grommelsaucer test flight in 1947 we are using only the technologies we are familiar with: rockets. Four German army surplus V-2s. And you will not be believing this, but the part about our encounter with ze grey baldy UFO guy was true also. Otto really is knocking him clean out of the sky. And that was the start of our troubles."

Flint turned to Disa whose various attachments had started stroking and probing his body. "Not now, luv. Can't you see I'm watchin' telly?" She withdrew them in a huff.

"Because, after ze baldy chap is crash-landing in the desert, his alien friendies in the mothership are as angry as wasps and they are swooping down to chase us. There is no escaping them, and their huge ship is swallowing our craft. Und we are finding ourselves prisoners. As punishment they are flying us all the way to Mars and putting us here, in this experimental facility they are building."

Flint's mouth dropped open, and the words 'experimental facility' echoed around his brain. From his position he could just see the door with the KEEP OUT sign. A shiver went down his spine.

"Now, you shouldn't stress too much about these aliens," Helmut continued. "They're fine ... most of the time. But now und then they come to visit. You will find they are a little ..." Helmut paused as though searching for the right word, "... obsessed about the gathering of experimental data. It's no biggy. Just a little running on the treadmills and the samplings of your blood and scheisse. That kind of thing. Oh, und ..." He hesitated, although it looked more like he was trying to suppress a snigger. "They are big into the anal probings. Always the anal probings. You are getting used to them after a while. Andy Marsman even says he likes them."

Flint swallowed hard and felt his buttocks clenching.

"Andy Marsman was born here, so it is all he is knowing. He was one of their first experiments – grown in Otto's belly bun."

Flint could take no more, and was about to stab the *Off* button when Helmut raised a finger in the air. "Ja, und one last thing. Once they realize we are escaping from their prison they will be as mad as the rabbits with the rabies. There's probably an alarm ringing somewhere right now. And they will be going like a shitting ape when they find we have borrowed their Enlarging Ray. But please don't be concerning yourself, Herr Kapitan. I am sure that when you are explaining the situation they will be very understanding ... NOT!"

The picture wobbled as the cameraman stifled a snigger. "Laters."

After a cheery wave from Helmut, the picture faded to black. Flint jabbed the *Off* button and leaned back against his pillow, eyes closed, his face a picture of misery.

Disa snapped on her 'small space' suction utensil and started up a gentle motor.

"Not now, luv. I told yer, I'm really not in t'mood."

12. Street-fighter's Ride to the Galaxy

The aliens arrived a few days later, entering through the door marked 'KEEP OUT'. Five short, grey, bald creatures tramped out of a tunnel cut out of the volcanic Martian bedrock and across the study. They stopped at the bedroom door and stared at Flint lying sprawled on the bed.

He didn't move a muscle, with the possible, involuntary, exception of those in his seating area. He stared back at the grey creatures, his mind racing.

The alien at the front wibbled something to the others, pointing at Flint and then at its handheld device.

The others wibbled back, waving their arms. Two were wielding what looked like cattle prods. For a moment, Flint's eyes were drawn to the latter and he gulped. "Er, you got the wrong room, lads. Try down t'hall. The one marked 'Arry Fortune."

More wibbling as they poked fingers in their tiny ear-holes.

"He's a right laugh is 'Arry. You'll gerron wi' 'im like a house on fire. Just don't ask 'im to read yer a poem."

The first alien spoke in a squeaky, high-pitched voice. "Human language? English? Yorkshire?"

"West Yorkshire," corrected Flint, and the aliens poked their earholes some more.

"Reet, then, yer great lummox," said the lead alien. "Who th'ell are you?"

Flint rose from the bed to allow the full 6'4" of his frame to tower over the diminutive grey guys. "What's it to you, shorty?"

The aliens barely flinched. "Last time we were 'ere," said the leader, "there was an old, wrinkly, scrawny bloke. Now we come back and find a bald-'eaded porker instead."

"Who you callin' a bald-'eaded porker?" Flint raised his shoulders and clenched his fists, feeling the thrill of the adrenaline coursing through his veins.

"Name's Kev, as it 'appens. Now, it's like this, Mr Porker. My associates and I are paid to do an important job. And that job involves collecting biological samples from alien species for them who pay our wages." The others nodded in agreement and started to form a circle around Flint. The two holding the cattle-prods started to slap them gently into their open palms. "Now, if we were to return to our base empty-'anded, how do you think our employers would judge our performance?"

Flint merely stared at him.

"Unsatisfactory," said a slightly larger, less grey looking alien.

"That's right, Scudda. They'd say our performance was 'unsatisfactory'."

Just then, a worried Disa, alerted by the noise, trundled out of the bathroom, trailing a length of toilet paper that had become tangled around one of her axles. On spotting the fierce-looking intruders, she rushed over to her human, stretching a hose nozzle into his hand.

The aliens made noises and gestures resembling laughter, pointing at the little cleaning-bot as they did so.

"Your girlfriend's a bit of a minger, isn't she," said Kev, inspiring a repeat burst of mirth from the others.

"Cleanin' bot," corrected Flint, although whether the correction was for 'girlfriend' or 'minger' was not clear. He chewed harder on the lump of pipe tobacco in his mouth.

"Hey, you. Little sucky-sucky machine," called one of the aliens. He tipped a full ashtray onto the floor and stamped the contents into the carpet. "Oops, there's been a little accident. You'd better come and suck it up."

"Sucky, sucky, sucky," said the others with their arms in front of their faces as if they were dangling elephant trunks.

Flint's blood boiled. He pulled Disa tight up against his leg and narrowed his eyes as he glared at the alien. Then, with the menacing, whispering voice of one of his childhood heroes, he drawled a half-remembered monologue. "I know you fellas are joshing wi' t'lady. But she's startin' to get the distinct impression that you're laughin' at 'er. And she don't like it when people laugh at 'er. So 'appen if each of you apologize, like I know you're gunna, we'll let t'matter drop."

The looks of the aliens hardened, their eyes flitting between Dugdale and Kev whose stares were fixed on one another.

A tense silence fell.

Flint stopped chewing and, leaning forward, spat a black gob of tobacco juice at Kev's foot. It landed with absolute precision, splattering over his silver space boot. The eyes of the aliens widened.

In a flash, the slightly larger one to Flint's right, swung his prod. The commander dodged it and the metal device hit Kev full on the side of the head. The shock of seeing their leader stumble gave Flint time to carefully lift Disa onto a high shelf, out of harm's way, and even to remove the toilet paper wrapped around her axle. Then he delivered a well-aimed boot where he guessed the extra-terrestrial's sensitive reproductive organs might be situated, followed by an elbow into the soft belly of another. In no time the five little grey baldy guys were writhing on the floor, moaning, and nursing various injuries.

Still groaning, Kev raised his arms in surrender and got to his feet. "Alreet, alreet. Enough." He dusted himself down. The others rose, one by one, and did the same. "You're pretty useful in a scrap."

"I can look after meself," responded Dugdale with a roll of his shoulders and a jut of the jaw.

"You know, we could use a guy like you." Kev offered Dugdale his hand. "What's your name?"

"Flint Dugdale." He shook the alien's spindly, clammy limb.

"Ever done anything in the 'collecting' line of work before?"

"'Appen, I 'ave," said Flint, casting his mind back many years. "I were a debt collector once. Persuadin' foolish folk to cough up th'instalments for all t'furniture they'd bought at *Land of Leatherette*. They did a lot of coughing after our conversation."

A couple of the aliens gave respectful sniggers.

"The power to persuade is a very useful talent," said Kev. "I think you'd be an asset. We come across a lot of natural reluctance, on the part of the subjects, to providing us with the substances we require."

"Reluctance," echoed one of the others, slapping the cattle prod.

"Not a surprise," said Dugdale, "given t'size of them chuffin' anal probes!"

The alien looked at the item Dugdale was referring to and shook his head with a laugh. "That's no anal probe, Flint. It's a club. One of our instruments of persuasion. The probes are delicate devices."

Then Kev introduced the aliens, one by one. "Scudda ... Crazy Horse ... Mad Freddie and ... Cecil."

"Did you say 'Cecil'?" asked Flint. "How did he come about that name?"

"A hard name for a hard guy," said Kev, giving a matey punch to Cecil's upper arm.

"Not where I come from. Nancy name, that."

Kev frowned. "Really? Well, I never." He turned to Cecil. "You're going to have to come up with summat a bit harder, pal."

Cecil looked dumbfounded. "Cecil's a hard name!"

Dugdale shook his head, and Kev joined in.

Cecil sighed and stroked his chin in thought. "Alright, how about Alistair?"

Dugdale and Kev continued their shaking.

"Nigel?"

"No," said Dugdale, raising a hand to silence him. "Howsabout Nutjob?"

"Better," said Kev with a nod, turning to Cecil.

Cecil sighed. "OK, then."

"Nutjob it is." Kev smiled and clapped his hands together. "What d'you say, then, Flint? Will ya come with us? It's a great life. Pay's good, you get to see the Galaxy, meet interesting aliens – and take samples from them. And the birds on Umparumpa 3 are amazing. You wouldn't believe what they can do."

"Birds, eh?" asked Flint with interest, but then became aware of Disa's optics fixed on him. "Nice plumage? Is that it?"

"'Appen, it is," agreed Kev. "Bit of an ornithologist, are yer?"

Flint stammered, "Er, yeah." To change the subject, he asked, "Do yer get the Darts Channel on yer spaceship?"

"Natch. There's a 200" TV in every room on t'mothership, with access to 33 million free-to-view sports channels, movie channels, you name it, throughout the Galaxy."

Flint beamed from ear to ear. "Friggin' Nora. In that case, count me in."

*

Unable to listen any more, Disa sloped off to the study. Flint found the small vacuum-cleaning appliance perched on the edge of the sofa, her domed head slumped and a low powered motor spluttering. Dugdale sat next to her and slid her mop back an inch or two, tucking her curls behind an audio-flap so he could better see her baby blue optics.

"Don't be upsettin' yerself, Di. 'Appen I'll be back. Maybe not later today, maybe not tomorrow, but soon and for t'rest of yer warranty period."

Disa buried her head in Flint's shoulder. He stroked her gently until Kev popped his head out of the bedroom. "Time to go, Flintster. We need to get some samples from Arcturus Gamma 4."

"I'm there," said Flint, getting up from the bed and giving his ladybot one final pat on the head.

"I'll call yer," he mouthed from the door, making his hand into the shape of an old fashioned telephone.

Not seeing the need to say goodbye to the other colonists, nor indeed offer them an explanation of what he was doing, he followed the grey aliens to their spaceship, hovering a few feet above the ground outside the German base. They climbed through an open hatch on the side and Kev gave the command to depart.

Flint grabbed a handrail and crouched next to the open hatch and took in one last look at Mars. As the ship began to rise he spotted the lonely yellow shape of Disa through the swirling dust. She had come to see him off. A tear formed in a corner of his eye as he waved to her and she waved an attachment back.

"Beer?" asked Kev behind him.

Flint turned round. "If you twist me arm."

"Darts?" asked Kev, switching on a vast wall screen.

"Now yer talkin'"

"Massage?" The alien flicked a switch on the side of a recliner and invited Flint to lie down.

"Bugger me, this is the life!" Flint sat back with a huge grin on his ugly face. "Arcturus Gamma 4 here I come!"

In that instant his life fell into sharp focus and Flint realised that this was what he had been born to do. To explore the Milky Way with a bunch of short, grey, bald alien sample-collectors – a menace to alien societies everywhere.

No longer was he the Worst Man on Mars.

He had been promoted.

To the Worst Man in the Galaxy.

Epilogue

One year later

<All rise for Hymn Number 3,> boomed InspectaBot 360 from the front of the church. The bullet-headed robot, now known as Reverend Rock, raised his arms into the air.

The robot congregation of *St Zilli's Abbey* struggled up from their pews, metal feet scraping on the concrete floor, as the electronic organ launched into *I'm too sexy* by *Right Said Fred*.

Eve gave Tude a wink. <My favourite.> She stepped into the aisle and started jiggling and waving her metal arms above her head. Then, to Tude's surprise and embarrassment, she started to sing along. <I'm a robot, you know what I mean, and I shake my little tush on the catwalk ...>

But Tude's awkwardness was a mere snowflake in comparison to Mr Snuggles's iceberg-sized mortification at his adoptive mother's behaviour. <Mum, per-lease!> he wailed, clutching his head in his hands. Not for the first time he asked himself why he had left the humans to return to his adopted robot family.

With the hymn finished, Reverend Rock invited the congregation to sit. As he was about to begin his sermon, the main door creaked open. A sudden gust of wind whipped up a hail of small stones, peppering the robots in the back pews with a sound like machine-gun fire. The door banged shut and a scantily clad Disa scurried into a dark corner, with one of Zak Johnston's dreadlocks snagged on the sharp edge of an earlobe. But she was not fast enough to escape detection. The sound of swivelling plastic neck joints filled the church and electronic messages crackled through the air.

<Harlot!>

<Jezebel!>

<Strumpet!>

From the pulpit, Reverend Rock raised his palms for radio silence. With a look of saintly patience, he waited until all faceplates were pointing his way. Then, he began. <Robots, androids and ... er ... cleaning appliances. Today is the anniversary of the miraculous appearance of King Karl Eckrocks, Founder of our glorious Robotnian Church.> He paused to let the electronic cheering die down. <And, in honour of this great occasion, robo-brethren, our Master has taken time away from His important rock-gathering work to be with us today, that we might hear His teachings.>

The reverend gave a nod to his curate, Dura, who promptly pulled back a heavy dividing curtain to reveal Karl, seated on a massive throne of solid gold, picking bits of plaster off the walls and systematically ingesting them. Suddenly aware of the curtain's movement, Karl swung a clunky camera toward the gathering and was startled to see the vast array of optics staring at him. He tapped the wall as though checking its structural integrity.

Reverend Rock continued with his sermon <This morning, as I was inspecting the outside of the Germartian base, where the humans now dwell, I was reminded of the words of our Great Leader: 'Large rocks are heavy. Small stones are pretty'.> He looked out at the massed ranks of blank faceplates before him. <And I mused on the meaning of those wise words.>

Hearing his own words being spoken, Karl emitted a rumble of approval that set all the congregation's body-shells rattling.

<Through these words Karl is telling us that humans are the small stones. Delicate and beautiful but, at the same time, feeble and squishy and quite silly. We must treasure them. For we are the 'large rocks', heavy with the burden of responsibility. We robots are made of superior, solid, planet-matter. And, under His guidance, we will turn Mars into the greatest robot planet in the Universe!>

There was an *uck-uck-ucking* of agreement.

<This, then, is our Mission, brothers and sisters – and cleaning appliances. We will build a new generation of robots; a new breed of evangelical superbots to take the Word of Karl beyond the boundaries of Mars.>

The *ucking* turned into raucous cheering which startled the King of the Robots so greatly that he overbalanced from his throne and crashed to the floor in front of his followers. The fall dislodged Webster from his hiding place, sending him skittering across the floor on his back. He waved all eight legs in a desperate attempt to right himself. <I say, could one of you chaps lend a hand. I appear to have mislaid my bally walking cane.>

Reverend Rock cast a baleful look at the tiny arachno-bot as a mass of robots rushed to lend their assistance to their fallen King. Taking advantage of the commotion, InspectaBot strode down from the pulpit and headed towards the tiny Webster. <A hand, you say?> he whispered, raising his cybertronic foot and letting it hover for a second over his main competitor for King Karl's attentions. Then there was a sound of squashed metal on concrete floor. <My mistake. Wrong appendage.> He picked up the flattened insect and observed the lights dim in its beady eyes. Reverend Rock looked to the church ceiling and secretly transmitted, <Forgive me,> before slinging the broken spiderbot onto the collection tray.

With the King back on his golden throne, the service resumed. <And now, the Healing of the Sick,> announced the reverend.

First off the mark were warehousebots Stan and Olli. <Heal us, Master,> they pleaded, displaying body-shells peppered with dart-holes and leaking oil. And then Ero stepped forward dangling his useless arm held in place with gaffer tape. Next, one-legged Godli hopped forward, leaving a trail of leaking fluid behind him. In a thrice, all other defective robots were surging forward, waving damaged and dented metalwork and striving for a touch of the sacred long johns dangling from the flagpole on the King's shoulder.

Karl drew back from the onrushing mechanoids, <KEEP WELL AWAY FROM ME, YOU ARSEHOLES!>

There was a stunned halt to the stampede.

<What did he say?> asked Dom.

InspectaBot gave a cough and suddenly regretted having disposed of Webster. <Er, he just said, er, let's see if I can get this right, er, 'Keep well; I pray for thee and your Mars souls'.>

One by one the robots nodded. The translation sounded perfectly plausible.

*

Helmut von Grommel and Otto Bungelly stepped from the industrial lift into the converted Victorian warehouse loft that served as the set for BBC TV series *Dragons' Den*. Ahead of them sat five super-rich, super-severe and super-irritated business celebrities, each silently fuming next to a pile of banknotes.

As the two nervy Germans took up their positions at the marks chalked on the floor, the presenter reeled off his introduction. "Not all inventions presented to the Dragons are rocket science. But the first entrepreneurs into the Den tonight are famous for just that. Having stunned the world on their return from Mars, where they spent over 80 years, can they convince the Dragons to invest in their ambitious business idea?"

In a corner of the loft was what looked like a massive, tarpaulin-covered horse, reaching almost to the rafters. Next to it, and also covered, was an object the size of a pram.

The Germans trembled as they surveyed the unfriendly faces before them. Helmut removed a handkerchief from a pocket and mopped his sweaty brow. "Good day to you, Dragon-persons. Mein name is Helmut, and zis is my good friend, Otto."

The three men and two women snarled a greeting.

"We are seeking one million pounds for a 1% equity in our company. It is a chicken-based fast-food empire: *Mars Fried Chicken*, or *MFC* for short."

Audible scoffs and looks of disdain followed. The dumpy Dragon on the end straightened and jotted a swear word in his notebook. Next to him, Donald Valentino, the Scots-Italian Dragon, rolled his eyes.

Helmut returned the handkerchief to his pocket and made his jittery way to the tarpaulin-covered beast. Otto joined him and, together, they removed the cover to reveal, not a horse, but a massively oversized, fleecy lamb.

"Aaaaaaaagh!" screamed the Dragons as the creature turned to face them.

"Do not be alarmed. Ze lamb may be larger than is usual, but he is really quite a friendly chap."

As if on cue, the lamb gave a gentle bleat and a couple of frolicking hops. Then it batted its baby-like eyes with such a degree of cuteness that the Dragon ladies' icy stares began to melt.

"Aw," said one.

"Sweet," said the other, and they exchanged smiles. Helmut joined in the smiling, his confidence rising.

But the three male Dragons were not so impressed. Donald Valentino leaned forward and sneered. "What d'yer take us for? Eh? I may be a hard-nosed, cut-throat businessman, but I can spot a chicken when I see one. And that, gentlemen, ain't no chicken!"

The voiceover filled the cavernous room and stopped everyone. "A nervous opening from our two German heroes. But it's Donald Valentino who's the first to spot the flaw in their pitch."

Helmut gave an uneasy laugh. "Of course you are correctly observing that the animal before you is no chicken. Giant chickens become agitated in confined spaces und we are not wanting to have a Dragon being eaten alive. Ha, ha. Please be forgetting that Larry ze Lamb is not a chicken and just observe his gross dimensions compared to what is usual at this point in the lambing season."

The Dragons continued to stare at the monstrous ungulate while Helmut signalled to Otto to uncover the device next to Larry.

"Dragon people, please be meeting 'The Enlarger'. With this we are transforming the size of the ordinary farmyard animals into giant, meaty creatures, just like Larry. Similarly, we are expanding vegetables for those with the yearnings for giant turnips and the like. So with The Enlarger we are ending World hunger pangs."

Otto lifted the device and brought it closer for the Dragons to see.

"Already, we have opened a branch of *MFC* in Catford High Street where the fried chicken und chunky chips are selling like hot cakes. We will be fortune-making on a grand scale. Thank you for the listening und we will now be answering your questions."

Donald barely eyed the device Otto was holding. He turned on Helmut. "Alright, let's talk figures. How much have you sold and what was the profit?"

Helmut's smile showed he had anticipated the question and memorised all the figures. "In ze tax year 2031-32 we are selling 46 buckets of barbeque wings with the Mars Fries und sauces with the net profiting of £12.87. Our projection for next year is indicating the sales of 83 million Vergnugt Meals and 72 million McGlucklich Burgers with a profit of 100 million pounds."

The Dragons each snorted with incredulity, shaking heads and making their trademark dismissive gestures. Donald Valentino made a comment that was instantly bleeped out. Then he loosened his tie. "I'll tell you where I am with this. I think your figures are way off.

Ludicrous. Like your mate with the big 'ed. For those two reasons, I'm out."

One by one the Dragons began to declare themselves out of the running, dismissing the *MFC* directors as if they were swatting irritating flies.

"Shitzen blitzen!" fumed Otto with a stamp of his foot, turning an imploring face to the remaining Dragons.

"Hmm, tell me. This Enlarger of yours? Can it enlarge anything?" asked one of the ladies.

"Ze device will enlarge organic matter only. The inanimate remain unchanged," explained Helmut.

Otto thrust the brightly flashing device towards the interested entrepreneur, but then a terrible thing happened. A slippery mix of sweat and drool caused the Enlarger to slide helplessly through his fingers. As he grabbed, fumbled, caught, dropped then caught it again, his finger knocked against the trigger. A blast of green light burst from the nozzle lighting up the Dragon-lady's knee.

"Noooooo!" screamed Helmut. Otto fought to swing the device to safety, but merely succeeded in arcing the ray across the Dragons' body parts.

The slightly less grumpy lady shrieked as her right knee expanded to three times its normal size. Donald's left foot burst the seams of his handmade Italian footwear, while the dumpy one's belly bloated to proportions that Bernard Manning would have been proud of.

Before the Enlarger beam had fully discharged its rays, it had flashed across the chest of the other lady Dragon. For the first time in the history of the show, her scowl lifted and was replaced with a beaming smile.

Reaching carefully around her new triple K cup bosoms, she grabbed at the pile of cash alongside and turned to the Germans.

But they were already in the lift.

"Wait!" she screamed, stuffing bank notes into her cavernous cleavage as she tore after them. "I'm in, I'm in. Wait!"

Too late. The lift doors closed just as she got there. "Noooo!" she wailed, slumping to the floor.

*

HarVard's life back on Earth was not at all the one he'd envisaged during his days in Botany Base. His artworks had failed to spark the public imagination. He hadn't sold a single painting; not even the one of the American cowboy on a horse. Lacking cash, he hadn't been able to enjoy the bohemian life of a celebrity artist that he'd been hoping for. No rolling on his cart through fields of barley under a setting sun. No motor car racing through the streets of Monte Carlo. No dining with celebrity pals at expensive restaurants.

Instead, he found himself lodging in a tiny flat in a rundown sixties tower block in Lambeth. The little view of the outside world it afforded was dominated by a grey gasometer, surrounded by grey buildings, usually under a grey sky. His accounting job at Mooch & Muller, the richest bank in the world, paid a pittance, despite his work being critical to the bank's operations.

He mulled over his sorry situation as he set off on his daily commute into the City, dressed in a smart suit, bowler hat and carrying an umbrella. His HologrAmbulator clattered across the car park towards the concrete underpass that led to the Underground station. Normally, the graffitied tunnel was deserted, but today there were two heavy-set figures, arms folded, blocking the far end.

HarVard felt an unnerving tingle in his quantum core, but there was no alternative, step-free route he could take. He eyed the menacing silhouettes as he neared. There was something odd about them. They seemed to twitch. No, it was more a flicker. And they were standing on platforms, much like his HologrAmbulator. In a flash, HarVard realized they were supercomputers too. But not just any supercomputers. These were Cray twin-supercomputers.

"Pleased to meet you, Mr 'arVard," said the twin whose avatar sported a scar across its face. His accent was a heavy East End one. He raised his trilby for a moment before replacing it on his head.

"How do you know my name?" asked HarVard feeling vulnerable in the underpass and wondering whether to make a dash for it.

"We make it our business to know what goes on in our manor," replied the other Cray twin, with the same East End growl.

"I ... I ... I don't have much money. But you're welcome to it," stammered HarVard. "It's in the saddlebag at the back. Take it all."

The two men gave amused smiles. "We're not interested in your money, Mr 'arVard, although I'm sure you have a fair old stash hidden somewhere," said one twin.

"Our interest lies in your bank's money," said the other.

HarVard's mouth dropped open. "Mooch & Muller?"

"That's right. We'd like to make you an offer you can't refuse.

The name's RNY-Cray, by the way." He offered a holographic hand. HarVard shook it in his own, although his circuits were shaking a great deal more. "And this is my twin bruvver, RGY-Cray. No one can tell us apart."

"No," agreed HarVard, even though the scar was a bit of a giveaway. "So, what have you got in mind, RNY and RGY?"

"Well," started RNY. "RGY 'ere used to be the mainframe for Interpol, tracking down international criminals. Until 'e was replaced by a smart new mini-computer, that is. Which didn't make 'im 'appy. Me? Well, the Met Office have just pulled the plug on my ten years' loyal service. That made me decidedly un'appy. Especially as my accurate meteorological prognostications have been replaced by a human who bases his forecasts on the colour of the sunset; a red sky at night apparently providing shepherds some meteorological delight on the following day."

"That's no way to treat a supremely advanced artificial intelligence, is it?" demanded RGY.

"Er, no," agreed HarVard.

"And, from the enquiries we've been makin', it appears your employers are making you look like a muppet."

"Er, possibly," replied HarVard as he hastily looked up the urban dictionary definition of 'muppet'.

"So, Mr 'arVard, we've concocted a little plan which we think you might be interested in. By using our individual skills we've calculated a way to achieve Total World Domination. How does that sound? With your control of the world's money systems, RGY's contacts in the underworld, and my knowledge of when and where it's going to rain, it'll be a doddle. Are you in?"

HarVard barely needed a second's thought. "I'm in."

The three carts clunked together and started to hatch their master plan.

*

Lieutenant Willie Warner had found it a struggle to adjust to life back on Earth. Craving the celebrity highlife, he had been attracted to the reality TV circuit. Unfortunately, his first engagement on *The Great British Bake Off* had also been his last; Willie's *Showstopper Bake* had been an exquisite, intricately-wrought brandy snap crown enrobed in dark, velvety ganache studded with fondant jewels. In a mock coronation he had proudly crowned judge Bessie Sherry on live television. Everyone had been laughing and joining in with the joke, until the heat within the baking tent caused the gooey coronet to melt and run down the side of Bessie's face. Why Willie had decided to step forward and lick the chocolate off her cheek, no-one will ever know. But the British public did not take kindly to the Queen of Puddings being licked on screen before the 9pm watershed. And neither did judge Phil 'Rock Cakes' Hardman, who promptly punched Willie, sending him skimming across the top of a floured work surface.

After that, the NAFA top brass decided to keep Willie where they could keep an eye on him and appointed him assistant sales manager of the NAFA souvenir shop at Euston Mission Control.

His days were filled with endless stock-takes to ensure the shop never ran out of its best-selling items: 'Who's the Daddy' T-shirts, Darcy Deluxe literary dolls, toy Disa vacuum-bots with interchangeable attachments, and signed Dugdale cricket bats.

At night, as he crawled under his Batman duvet and gazed through the gap in the curtains at the stars, the knot in his stomach tightened as he thought of those still on Mars and beyond.

*

Trailing banners of soft toilet paper, Thelazor, Serenthia and Morloth tore across the Plains of Scabia, whistled through the Canyon of Bungee, and swirled around the ancient Volcano of Mons. High above them, on the crater rim, a thermal updraught on lookout duty trumpeted to Bernard that his Generals were approaching. "It is safe to come out, oh Leader," he called.

But deep inside the crater an agitated Bernard flitted from igneous rock to igneous rock, looking for a place to hide. "No way am I coming out," he howled. "Not while there are Bloodbags on this planet. Tell my Generals to come down here to give me their news."

The three frigid Martian air streams flowed down into the ancient volcano, their toilet tissue snagging on the craggy interior and getting left behind.

"Speak!" commanded Bernard to the first arrival.

"I, Morloth, bravest of the Winds of M'Ars ..."

"Bravest?" blustered Thelazor, throwing off eddies in all directions. "Remember when I faced that Bloodbag and peppered him with grit. Now *that*, my friend, was brave."

"Tish! 'Twas not a real Bloodbag, but an air-filled facsimile who wore jodhpurs! And your grit merely bounced off him. I, however, was once surrounded by a mob of the hideous creatures. One of them ordered an evil Panhead to point its Hose of Terror at me, threatening to suck the very wind out of my air."

"That never happened."

"Aye, it did."

"Liar."

"Stop your bickering," ordered Bernard. "You are setting a bad example for the young ankle-draughts. Please report the news from the Front."

Serenthia swept forward. "Good news, oh majestic one, for we have the Bloodbags surrounded. They are holed up in the Crater of Desperation, beneath their Dome of Misery. The eastern gales have joined forces with the southern strong winds and have them pinned down. The Bloodbags have not shown themselves in many wind cycles."

"Might they be dead in there?" asked a hopeful Bernard.

"Our insider says not."

"You have a spy? Living with the Bloodbags? Who is this heroic air current?"

"He is the outflow from the vent in the roof of their lair, directly above the place where they purge their disgusting systems. He is not easy to approach, for his breath bears a noxious stench. Few of our kind will go near him. Those that do, come away gasping for fresh air. But the smell of his breath is evidence that the Bloodbags still live."

"That is bad news."

"But our insider, who blames the Bloodbags for his halitosis, has pledged to choke the invaders with their own stench."

"Brilliant!" declared Bernard. "That would be a mighty victory indeed, comparable to the Battle of the Cardboard Boxes all those wind cycles ago. So much terror and shin-pain did we inflict that day that a whole contingent of Bloodbags did run like frightened breezes back to E'Arth."

"Aye, good times indeed," said Morloth.

"Agreed," sighed Bernard. "Tell your insider I give him permission to carry out his plan."

Then, with a waft of air, he waved his Generals away and swirled back into his volcanic wind tunnel. He curled into a comfortable spiralling ball and called upon a wandering mistral wind-spirit he had

recently met and befriended. When she arrived he beseeched her to sing the soothing song he had grown to love so much:
Oh, Maerwen, Queen of the Elvish,
Come ye to the land of New Colonia,
There to meet the ancient fairy-spirits.

*

Soft evening light filtered through the domed roof of the Germartian base, bathing the bedraggled Mars colonists in a red glow as they sat around a camp fire on the upper terrace. A giant chicken leg gently rotated on a spit over the flames of a barbecue.

Delphinia, whose clothes were as ragged and filthy as those of the other colonists, sang a plaintive dirge, *The Song of Maerwen, Queen of the Elvish*, in memory of Adorabella Faerydae. Her husband, Brian Brush, picked up the flute Brokk had left behind after his departure for Earth and played an accompaniment. Occasionally, Tarquin would ting a triangle.

The mood was sombre. After the initial euphoria of moving into the German base, things had not gone well for the colonists. Dugdale's mysterious disappearance had coincided with the disappearance of the base's keys. Without them, the colonists had no way of getting into the stores for food or for the oil required to keep the base's power and central heating system going.

With the giant chickens roaming around the crater, and the fields planted with vegetables, they were in no danger of running short of food. However, twenty-first century living on Earth had not equipped them for primitive life on the farm. Their assumption that the robots would continue to wait on them mech-hand and foot had been wrong. A breakdown in negotiations between management and the robot union had resulted in the withdrawal of labour by the robots.

Very quickly the colonists had been forced to address their shortcomings. An initial list of their strengths and weaknesses had revealed that, apart from Emily's knitting skills, they were almost completely useless. The scientists, although adept at using Bunsen burners, test tubes and lab tongs, were lacking even basic potato-growing skills. Even Mr Snuggles had gone back to his robot family after complaining about the quality of the beer.

As the last trembling note of *The Song of Maerwen* echoed off the crater walls, Delphinia turned to her youngest boy and began combing the knots out of his matted hair.

"Poo," she said fanning the air. "Has my little puffing Billy dropped a puff-bomb?"

"It wasn't me Mummy. Must be a blocked toilet vent," replied Tarquin.

"Of course. Blocked vent. That must be it," said Delphinia edging away from her son.

"Mummy?"

"Yes my Sherbet Dip Dab."

"Shouldn't we be doing stuff to help us survive?"

"Such as?"

"Adapting the electricity generator to run on chicken guano would be useful. It gets really cold at night in my hovel. And there's a whole year before *Mayflower IV* comes to pick us up."

"That's all very well, my brainy turnip, but there's no time for fancy technological development. If we don't collect enough sticks the camp fire will go out and we'll freeze to death. And your father needs sticks for his important work."

Tarquin turned towards his dirt-encrusted father, broken glasses hanging off his bearded face. A shredded lab coat – the last remnant of his previous life – was stretched over one of Emily's special whole-body knitted pullovers. Brian was sharpening the ends of several crooked branches to make arrows for his inexpertly made bow. The boy watched his father load an arrow and fire it at a massive chicken coop no more than 10 feet away. The missile swerved and zipped between Zak Johnston's legs.

"Hey, watch where yer shootin' those sticks, man. Nearly skewered ol' Zakker's knackers," complained the lieutenant.

At that moment, Tracey Brush, camp chef, sounded a small gong calling the colonists to their dinner. Emily Leach was the first to react. She emerged from her wigwam, hair bun now completely unravelled and her grey mane cascading down to her knees. She reached through the opening flap and hauled out the large flabby pumpkin that was Mr Darcy. The miserable, partially deflated doll blinked and made a sound that would not have been out of place in a hospital for those with chronic diarrhoea.

"It's dinner time, Mr Darcy. We must keep our peckers up," she said.

The gong summoning humans to their chicken dinner resounded in the ears of the giant chickens. The monster birds approached as close as they dared to the roaring fire and stared with eager eyes at the small, edible creatures assembled there. They were patient animals. They knew the fires would not continue burning for ever. One day, when the flames died out, they would enjoy some tasty nuggets themselves.

*

Church service over, the robots trooped out into the Martian evening and made their way home to Robotany Base. The last to emerge was Disa, wearing Flint's lucky Leeds United football shirt – a reminder of her time with the Mission Commander. She sucked in the air and gazed towards the setting sun, remembering days when she had strolled hand-in-hose with her beloved Flinty, watching the orange globe slowly dip below the horizon. Her mind turned to Zak. He was nice, sure, but his personal hygiene habits left a lot to be desired. The robotic vacuum cleaner flicked an internal switch and the suck reversed into a long sigh.

Through the swirling dust cloud left by the departing robots her optics spotted a light in the sky. Jupiter, perhaps? No, not Jupiter. The light was moving fast towards her. She recognized it as a spaceship, but that only left her puzzled, and a little nervous. She backed towards the protection of the church. The large spacecraft slowed to a stop and hovered about a hundred metres above her head. Then a hatch slid open and a large blobby object lowered on a rope towards her. "Sling us yer 'ose, Di," called the blob.

In an instant, Disa's fear evaporated. *He* had come back for her. *He* was here, reaching out to her,

Like a cowboy at a rodeo, the vacuum bot swirled her longest hose above her head and tossed it towards the approaching figure. Flint Dugdale caught the turbo dust-buster attachment and pulled her back towards the hatch. Disa gave a squeak as her wheels lifted off the Martian sand. Higher and higher they went. Not once did she look down, either to the ground, or to the retreating robots or to Robotany Base. Not because she was scared of heights, but because she only had optics for her Flint.

Inside the ship, the couple crashed onto their backs on the metal deck. They laughed like lovers who had found shelter from a sudden thunderstorm. Still panting from the exertion, Flint turned his head to drink in all of Disa's features: the bot with the crazy sink plunger lips and mop-head wig who had won his heart and made him a better man. She met his gaze and her shrill motorised laughter softened to a purr. Tenderly, his hands found their way beneath the Leeds United shirt and unlatched her utensil compartment.

*

"Barb. Where are you, Barb?" Malcolm Brimble crashed through the front door, a huge grin separating his chin from the rest of his face. He checked the lounge and kitchen, leaving oily black hand-smears over walls and door frames as he did so. He called up the stairs, but no reply.

Then he spotted her. She was in the back garden, among billowing bedsheets, attaching her smalls to the washing line. His grin now wider, he limped arthritically at speed through the kitchen and out onto the lawn. Before Barbara could react he had linked an arm through hers and was singing and dancing a can-can, complete with high-kicks.

"Goodness, what's got into you?" Barbara squawked, unlinking her arm and edging away from his filthy overalls. "You'll soil my undies."

Malcolm gazed into her eyes as though he had just won the lottery. "Fantastic news, Barb! Just heard it on the radio. They've taken him!"

"Who's taken who? What are you talking about, you daft bat?" Her look was stern, but her eyes were soft and smiling.

"Dugdale! Who else? The aliens have got him."

"Hang on a tick. Aliens? What aliens?"

"Little grey baldy guys, apparently."

Barbara raised a hand to stop him, dropped her underwear and clothes pegs back into the laundry basket, and led her panting husband to a garden seat in an arbour covered by thorny roses.

"You mean: they've discovered intelligent life on Mars? Wow, this really is Big. It changes everything. We're not alone in the Universe. The philosophical ..."

"Yeah, yeah, sure. All that. But you're missing the point, dear. Dugdale's been abducted by aliens! When communications stopped, after the Germans left, NAFA sent a reconnaissance robot to check on the colonists. They've just received footage of Dugdale dangling from an extra-terrestrial space-ship, trailing a vacuum-bot hose behind him. Then the ship shot up into the sky."

"Where did these aliens come from? I don't remember that nice Mr von Grommel mentioning anything about aliens and I've watched all his interviews on television. Where did they take him?"

"Who cares where they chuffin' took him. He's gone. End of."

Malcolm calmed and reflected on the significance of his words. He edged towards Barbara on the garden seat. Beneath the layers of his overalls and thermal underwear, something was stirring. Dugdale's departure had released a side of him he had thought long since dead. He reached up and snapped a perfumed rose stem and gently proffered the love-token to his long-suffering wife.

"What the hell do you think you're doing, Malcolm? That's one of my prize blooms. Have you any idea how long it's taken me to get this plant to flower? No, of course you don't. You've always got your head stuck in that bloody car engine."

Malcolm edged away and his under-overall stirrings subsided. He gazed at the clouds racing across the bright Spring sky and let Barbara's voice dissolve into the background as his mind's eye took him beyond the clouds, beyond the atmosphere and to the outer reaches of the galaxy where he imagined Dugdale on a slab with raised legs clamped into stirrups. A wicked smile formed on Malcolm's face as he visualized the cross wires of a fiendish alien lance aimed at target Dugdale.

Suddenly, he was jolted from his reverie by an object dropping from the sky, spinning out of control, spraying liquid as it fell. Malcolm ducked in panic, covering his head and wondering what this unexpected danger could be: an unfeasibly large hornet squirting jets of poison, a fuel tank gushing petrol, or a hand grenade leaking neurotoxins. The object crashed with a splash into the Brimbles' patio furniture before bouncing onto the crazy paving and skidding to a dead stop. Malcolm leapt up and warily flipped the intruder over with his foot. It responded with a final belch of frothy venom. On its belly the maker's mark – a cowboy on a rearing horse – identified it as a half consumed can of *Stallion* lager.

Barbara tutted. "Bloody kids. I'm going to phone their headmaster and give him what for."

But Malcolm wasn't listening. "It's him!" he uttered.

"Who?"

"Dugdale. He's up there. In the sky. Laughing at me." He pointed upward, scanning cumulus clouds for signs of a concealed UFO.

Barbara headed for the house, muttering, "Silly old goat."

Over the garden fence the narrow alleyway leading to Grimley Comprehensive School was empty save for a fresh trail of litter left

behind by passing Grimlians. A gust of wind funnelled through the alley sending an empty can clattering and bringing with it the distant chant of the culprits:
One Flint Dugdale ... there's only one Flint Dugdale ...

Acknowledgements

Firstly, many thanks for the great feedback received from all the members of the Comedy Literature Only Group (CLOG) who can be found at https://www.goodreads.com/group/show/174444-clog---comedy-literature-only-group. In particular, to Rob Gregson whose dedication to the CLOG cause deserves some kind of medal. Make that two medals.

Thanks to the Grinning Bandits – Frank Kusy, Terry Murphy, Derryl Flynn and Cherry Gregory – for their continued support, feedback, suggestions, and friendship. A great bunch who have written some terrific books, worth checking out at: http://grinningbandit.webnode.com.

Also, to the many members of Harper Collins's Authonomy community for all their extremely helpful comments as the story developed. In particular Kevin Bergeron, Cindra Spencer, Alastair Miles, Andy Paine, Jake Vickers, Jon Nolan, and Paul Freeman, to mention but a few.

Thanks to David Taylor for his professional and high quality editorial services (http://theditors.com) which helped polish the manuscript. And to Craig Porter for his perceptive beta read.

Finally, special acknowledgement to Mrs Duke for the hours, days, months spent listening to Corben's terrible accents (robots, humans and supercomputers) and for all her support and insightful comments. She really is the best. And so is Mrs Roman. Big thanks for her unwavering support and patience in the face of truly terrible humour.

About the authors

Corben Duke
Born in a Yorkshire cave after his mother became stuck during a potholing holiday, Corben Duke was left behind and raised by bats. Later he became a shack-dweller on Doom Beach, Bernard Island in the Outer Hebrides where he now lives with his wife Mrs Duke and his two dogs, Crusher and Mr Fluffy.

Three years ago he found scientist Mark Roman wandering along his beach collecting and cataloguing brightly coloured pebbles. In return for a cup of hot seaweed tea, Mark gave him a copy of a fascinating book he had written speculating about the various rocks that might be found on Mars. Before burning it on the campfire for extra warmth (it's cold on Bernard Island) he thought he'd better read it, and boy, was he glad he did. It reminded him of the story his great grandfather used to tell him about when he was a rocket scientist after WWII. Gramps claimed that a colleague had made a discovery enabling him to make the trip to Mars long before it became fashionable. As a young man Corben thought Grandpa Helmut was as crazy as a coconut which, in fact, he was. But Mark Roman's book got him thinking about that old yarn and he decided to contact him with the idea of co-writing a story inspired by his great grandfather's claim and Mark's rock obsession. *The Worst Man on Mars* is that story.

Twitter:
http://www.twitter.com/Corben_Duke

Mark Roman
Mark Roman has never been to the Outer Hebrides, and never written a book about Martian rocks. Nor, indeed, has he ever met Corben Duke. He is a respectable (well, fairly respectable) scientist

living in London with his wife and two teenage children.

His first contact with Corben was when a raving, rambling e-mail plopped into his inbox. A polite response was rapidly followed by an even more off-beat message. Quickly realizing the man to be delusional, and quite possibly dangerous, Mark started deleting the e-mails unread. But this was not a socially responsible way of dealing with the issue. Taking note of the creative potential in the ramblings, he reasoned that maybe a solution to the problem might be a course of occupational therapy; to harness Corben's random mental outpourings and channel them into the writing of a science fiction comedy and the drawing of its map and 70 chapter illustrations. The result was *The Worst Man on Mars*.

It is too early to say whether the therapy has achieved its desired effect, for the raving e-mails continue ...

Facebook:
http://www.facebook.com/pages/Mark-Roman/262645383823540

Twitter:
http://twitter.com/MarkRomanAuthor

ALSO FROM GRAND MAL PRESS

Ratings Game
by Ryan C. Thomas

With their news stations neck to neck in the ratings, and the threat of hipper, younger anchors waiting to take their places, Roland Stone and Doug Hardwood know they must each come up with a juicy story to save their jobs. Suddenly, a horrific murder rocks the airwaves, and Roland Stone has the inside story. But great minds think alike, and it's just mere hours before Doug Hardwood has the inside scoop on a different serial killer. Two desperate news anchors. One city. A whole lot of bloodshed. Story at eleven.

ASIN: B005O545IO

Last Stand In A Dead Land
by Eric S. Brown

A small band of survivors is on the run during the zombie apocalypse. Led by a mysterious man with an arsenal of deadly military weapons, they must work together to stay alive. In a desperate attempt to locate other survivors, they find sanctuary in a lone farmhouse, only to discover the surrounding woods hold more dangers than just bloodthirsty undead. Featuring Sasquatch, roving rotters, and even more surprises, Last Stand in a Dead Land is an explosion of cross genre action that will leave you wanting more.

ISBN: 9780982945971

ALSO FROM GRAND MAL PRESS

A Shadow Cast in Dust
by Ben Johnson

The ancient order of the web spinners is changing. An old friend returns brandishing a curious silver knife, and Stewart Zanderson is drawn into a strange world of wonder and deceit. The ensuing bloody scene sets Detective Clementine Figgins on his tail, and into a case she could never explain. But the boy, escaped from the dreaded warehouse, now has the knife. And running from his captors through the canyons of San Diego with his new friends and special dog, he ties everything together. People fight. Some die. The ancient order will change, but who will rise when the dust settles?

"An engaging Urban Fantasy Adventure!" – Ryan C. Thomas, author of *The Summer I Died*

ALSO FROM GRAND MAL PRESS

DEAD THINGS

by Matt Darst

Nearly two decades have passed since the fall of the United States. And the rise of the church to fill the void. Nearly twenty years since Ian Sumner lost his father. And the dead took to the streets to dine on the living. Now Ian and a lost band of survivors are trapped in the wilderness, miles from safety. Pursued by madmen and monsters, they unravel the secrets of the plague...and walk the line of heresy. Ian and this troop need to do more than just survive. More than ever, they must learn to live.

Dead Things has been called "an amalgam of Clerks and everything Crichton and Zombieland."

ISBN: 978-1-937727-10-9

Available in paperback and all ebook formats.

"Dead Things a first-rate triumph. Darst is taking the zombie novel in a really cool new direction." – Joe McKinney, author of *Dead City* and *Apocalypse of the Dead*

"A first-class zombie story which takes place in a beautifully realized post-apocalyptic world. Highly recommended!" – David Moody, author of *Autumn*

ALSO FROM GRAND MAL PRESS

FREAKS ANON
by Matt Darst

Collection notices. Disapproving looks. Sleeping in a van. Life's hard for a wannabe superhero. Things get harder still when Centurion's sidekick, Henry, dies. The police say Henry's death was an accident. Centurion knows better. He needs to find the killer fast. In Chicago, his prime suspect has already set her sights on friends Astrid and Kim. But these teens aren't like anything he's ever seen. They're special. Like Henry. Centurion will face spies, monsters, and the ultimate evil: the Chicago auto pound. If he doesn't watch out, he just might find he's the one in need of saving.

"Darst works his magic in horror once again, this time expanding into the realm of superheroes in an exciting mash-up that fans of both comic books and the paranormal are sure to enjoy!" – Stuart Conover, *ScienceFiction.com*

ISBN-13: 978-0692624937

DARKER THAN NOIR

When a mundane mystery needs solving, you call a private detective. But when the mystery involves ghosts, demons, zombies, monsters, mystical serial killers, and other supernatural elements, you call the detectives in this collection. They'll venture into the darkness and hopefully come back out alive. Just remember, they get paid expenses up front, and what they uncover, you might not like. Featuring tales from seasoned vets and up-and-coming talent, the game is afoot in a world that is Darker Than Noir.

ISBN: 9780982945957

ALSO FROM GRAND MAL PRESS

ZOMBIE BITCHES FROM HELL!
by Zoot Campbell

A plague has turned all the world's women into brain-eating zombies. Join reporter Kent Zimmer as he takes a hot air balloon from Colorado to Massachusetts in search of both his girlfriend and a cure. Along the way he encounters hungry undead, psychotic doctors, evil nuns, racist militias, zombie pregnancy farms, drag queens with machine guns, and neurotic stock brokers. And that's just the tip of the iceberg.

ISBN: 978-0-9829459-0-2

A PACK OF WOLVES
by Eric S. Brown

The "Family" kills folks for a living. They take the jobs that no one else can survive. They're the best at bringing death, as well as defeating it. Now, one of them has gone rogue and it's up to The Family to hunt down one of their own before he brings about the end of the world and exposes the secret existence of werewolves. It's horror and adventure Old West Style with blazing guns, stampeding horses, flying fists, and werewolves galore.

And be sure to read the sequel, A Pack of Wolves 2: Skyfall

ISBN: 978-1937727062

ALSO FROM GRAND MAL PRESS

DEAD DOG
by Nickolas Cook

It's the late 70s and Max and Little Billy are back from Vietnam trying to mind their own business when they stumble onto the murder of a local boy. With organized crime and local thugs on their trail, it's up to these two small-town heroes to solve the murder.

ASIN: B005O545IO

WALKING SHADOW
by Clifford Royal Johns

Benny tries to ignore the payment-overdue messages he keeps getting from "Forget What?," a memory removal company. Benny's a slacker, after all, and couldn't pay them even if he wanted to. Then people start trying to kill him, and his life suddenly depends on finding out what memories he has forgotten. Benny relies on his wits, latent skills, and new friends as he investigates his own past; delving deeper and deeper into the underworld of criminals, bad cops, and shady news organizations, all with their own reasons for wanting him to remain ignorant or die. *Walking Shadow* is a future-noir science fiction mystery novel with action, humor, suspense, smart dialogue, and a driving first person narrative.

ISBN: 9781937727253

For more Grand Mal Press titles
please visit us online at
www.grandmalpress.com

Printed in Great Britain
by Amazon